BIOHACKERS

by Leah Kaminski

INTRODUCTION

Many transhumanists believe biohacking is one step toward creating the perfect human.

4   STEM BODY

A teenager walks to her classroom. She opens the door with a wave of her hand. Her eyes zoom in on the lesson plan on the whiteboard. She hears her friend walking into the building, rooms away. They plan to change their eye colors for a party this weekend.

What if this could be true? An average human ear can only hear a small part of all the sounds around it. Human eyes can see only a small portion of all light. **Transhumanists** want to improve these abilities, and more. They want to **evolve** the human race using technology.

Biohacking is one way this might happen. Biohacking is the practice of changing the body. Most biohackers change themselves without the help of doctors. They add technology to their bodies, change their DNA, or supercharge their lifestyle. The goal is to improve the performance of the body or brain.

transhumanist: someone who believes that humans, using science and technology, can go beyond their current physical and mental capabilities

evolve: to develop gradually and become more complex

BIOHACKERS 5

Implants

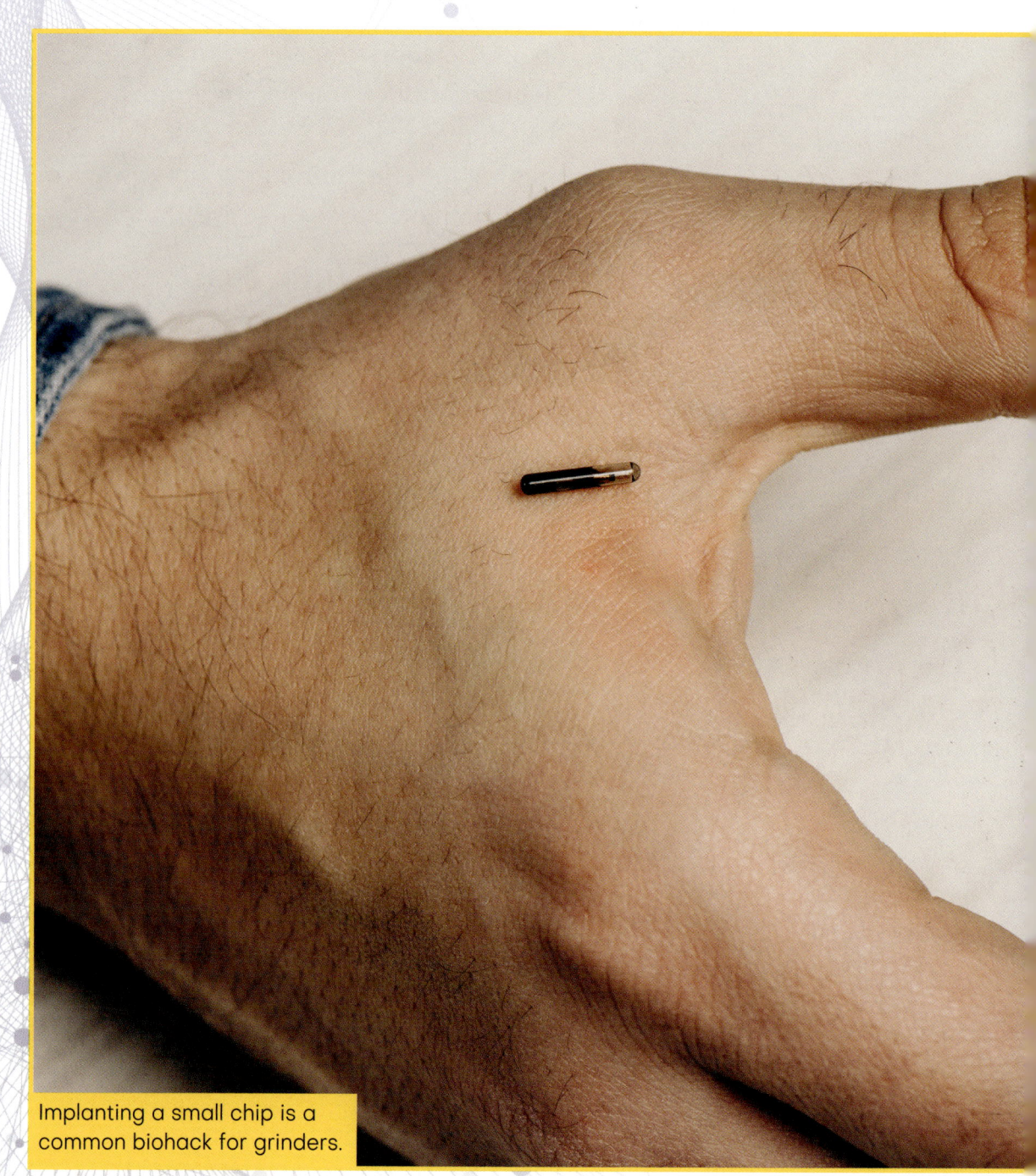

Implanting a small chip is a common biohack for grinders.

Some biohackers have surgery. Technology is **implanted** into their bodies. These people call themselves grinders or cyborgs. There may be up to 100,000 of them in the world.

Biohacking implants are made by small companies, or by grinders themselves. They can be anything from electronic tattoos on the skin to computer chips under the skin. Some implants improve existing abilities, such as hearing. Some give new ones, such as **echolocation**.

Grinders get implants for many different reasons. They might want help with a disability. If they cannot easily use their hands, a chip can unlock doors for them. They might want to make life more convenient. They can just wave at a payment machine to pay for coffee. Or they might just think it's cool.

implant: to place something new inside the body, usually with a medical procedure

echolocation: being able to locate objects by reflected sound; bats use echolocation to locate their prey

BIOHACKERS 7

DNA MANIPULATION

Genes determine physical features, such as hair color on a human and wing color on a butterfly.

12 STEM BODY

Biohackers may soon be able to change themselves from within. Some are trying to edit their own **genes**. They could use a new technology called CRISPR. It makes changing genes easy. Scientists knew that some bacteria cut viral DNA into pieces when defending themselves. The scientists used this ability to cut DNA on purpose. CRISPR became widespread very quickly. Scientists are already using it to make medicines and cure diseases.

People can even buy CRISPR kits online. The kits let users change bacterial DNA at home. A California company called Odin sells them. **Amateur** scientists have worked with CRISPR kits to switch butterfly wing color. Soon it may be possible for people to change their own DNA. But selling kits for this purpose is not allowed by the government.

---

gene: the part of a cell that influences the appearance or growth of a living being

amateur: someone who does something for fun instead of professionally

BIOHACKERS 13

Josiah Zayner (red shirt) works with others to make personal DNA information and biohacking techniques more accessible to the average person.

    A former NASA biochemist started Odin. His name is Josiah Zayner. Zayner is also the first person to ever try to change his own genes. In October 2017, he injected himself with DNA and other chemicals. In theory, the mixture would change one of his genes. The change would increase his muscle size. The same drug doubled the muscle size of dogs injected with it in China.

    Zayner didn't actually expect it to work. He wanted to make a point. He believes these products might cure terrible genetic diseases. People should be allowed to use them to save themselves.

Timeline of DNA

1953 James Watson and Francis Crick discover the shape of DNA.

1981 Thomas Wagner at Ohio University inserts a rabbit gene into a mouse, making the first "transgenic" animal.

Francis Crick

1993 The bacterial behavior that inspired CRISPR is discovered by Francisco Mojica in the marshes of Spain.

2003 A global community of scientists completes a project to map out human DNA. This allows genetic science to leap forward.

2012 Jennifer Doudna and Emmanuelle Charpentier learn to use CRISPR for DNA editing. The first human embryo is edited with CRISPR in 2015.

2019 The state of California passes the first CRISPR law. It requires CRISPR kits to have labels saying they are not to be used on humans.

Others disagree. The state of California passed a 2019 law. DNA biohacking kits must have clear labels. They cannot be used on humans. Zayner himself is under **investigation** in California. The government says he should not have injected himself, because he is not a doctor.

It is difficult to successfully use CRISPR at home. It's hard to get new genes into cells. Scientists now use viruses to deliver genes into cells. But there is still a lot to discover.

---

investigation: an attempt to learn about someone who might have committed a crime

BIOHACKERS 15

CRISPR

CRISPR gene editing borrows from bacteria to alter DNA. A bacterial cell can cut into foreign viruses to defend itself. STEM researchers use this technique to "cut and paste" human DNA too.

SCIENCE
The knowledge of biology and genetics necessary to discover and use CRISPR was built over decades. It started with the discovery of DNA's structure by James Watson and Francis Crick in the 1950s.

TECHNOLOGY
The technology of CRISPR is unique in that it is not a machine or device built by humans. Scientists learned to use technology already created in nature.

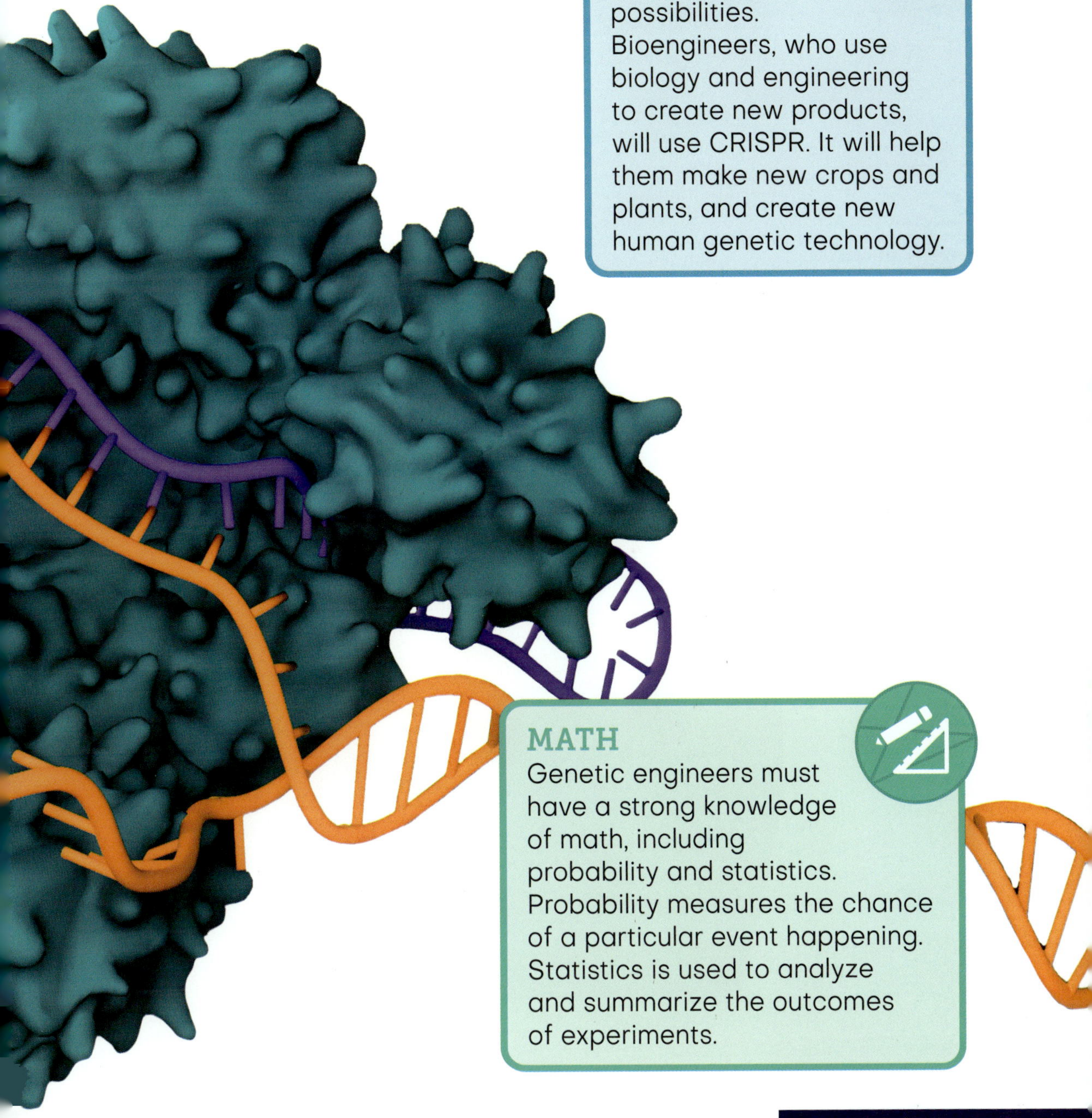

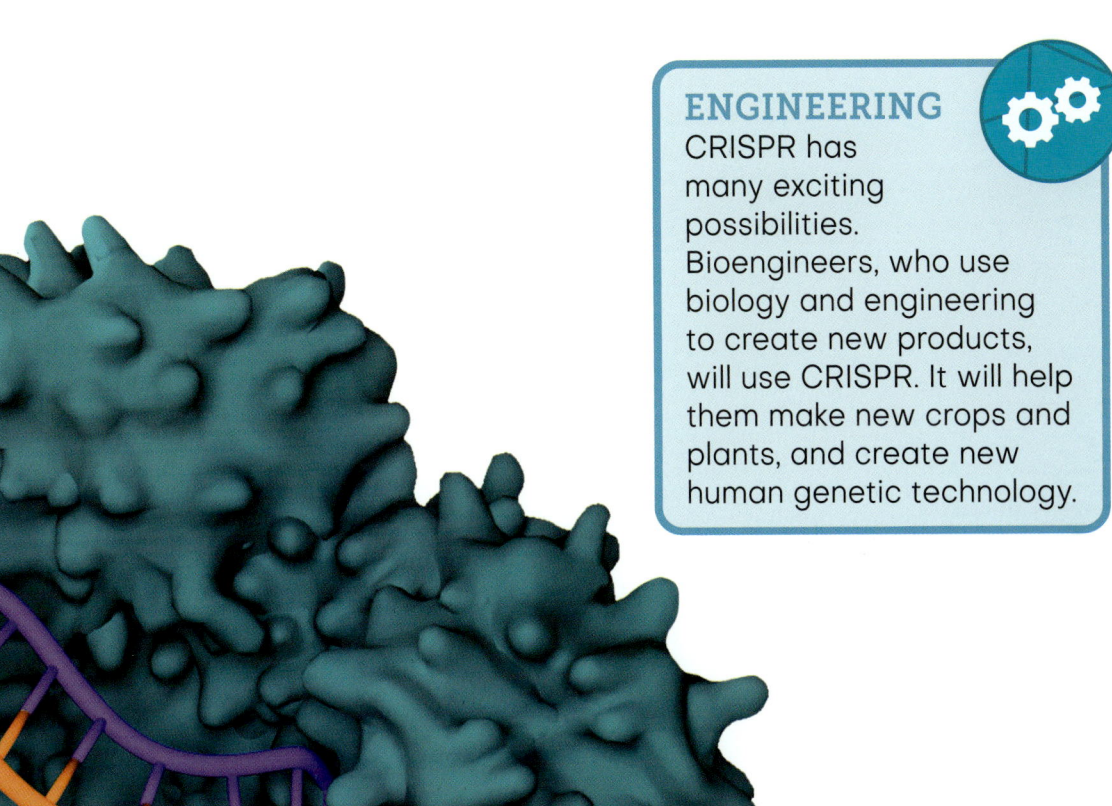

ENGINEERING

CRISPR has many exciting possibilities. Bioengineers, who use biology and engineering to create new products, will use CRISPR. It will help them make new crops and plants, and create new human genetic technology.

MATH

Genetic engineers must have a strong knowledge of math, including probability and statistics. Probability measures the chance of a particular event happening. Statistics is used to analyze and summarize the outcomes of experiments.

BIOHACKERS 17

Peak PERFORMERS

Jack Dorsey is worth an estimated $4 billion. The self-made billionaire never graduated from college.

Many Silicon Valley technology executives are known biohackers. They try to **optimize** their bodies and minds. Twitter CEO Jack Dorsey tweets about his biohacking. For example, he works under a special light. It is supposed to slow the effects of aging. This kind of biohacking can be cutting edge. But the research is not confirmed yet. Not all of it ends up being true.

A lot of biohackers try to slow aging. One doctor wants people to live to 1,000 years old. Another scientist says that it's possible. Taking **supplements** and changing genes are ways it could happen in the future. Science and research will discover how. In the meantime, tech billionaires do research on themselves.

optimize: to make something as effective as possible

supplement: something that is added in order to make something else complete, such as a vitamin supplement for complete nutrition

BIOHACKERS 19

Dave Asprey began to change his lifestyle in his 20s. He lost more than 100 pounds.

    In 2009, a geneticist found out why up to 3 percent of people don't need much sleep. They had a change in one gene. Scientists do not know how to edit that gene yet. But many people want shorter, more restful sleep. They hack their behavior to get it.

    Dave Asprey is a CEO of a company called Bulletproof. He spent $1 million on biohacking. Of that, $200,000 was on sleep. Polyphasic sleep is one strategy. It means to sleep in short chunks of time all day long. Nikola Tesla and Leonardo Da Vinci are thought to have tried this.

    Asprey also injects **stem cells** into his joints. He also bathes in special light. He wants to live till he is 180 years old. The CEO also takes many supplements. Asprey sells something called Bulletproof Coffee. It is a nootropic. Nootropics are supplements that are meant to improve mental performance. Many companies make these products.

---

stem cell: a cell that can turn into any of the 200 kinds of human cells

Extreme Measures

Intermittent fasting is when people switch between fasting and eating. It is a popular biohacking trend. People fast for mental clarity. They also do it to live longer. Another biohack is cryotherapy. People make themselves very cold. They want to increase energy. Virtual float tanks deprive people of their senses. This is supposed to relax them. Even more extreme, some biohackers do at-home **fecal transplants** to help stomach problems. This practice is known to have health benefits. Doctors do not recommend people doing this by themselves. Other methods are not backed by science. One example is biohackers paying thousands of dollars to inject the blood of young people into their veins. These biohackers hope to lengthen their lives. Many scientists doubt that this practice works.

A lot of biohacking uses technology too. Biohackers track everything from sleep to heart rate. They often use "wearables" to track their bodies. It's likely that in the future, wearables could become implants. Biohackers could track their bodies from the inside.

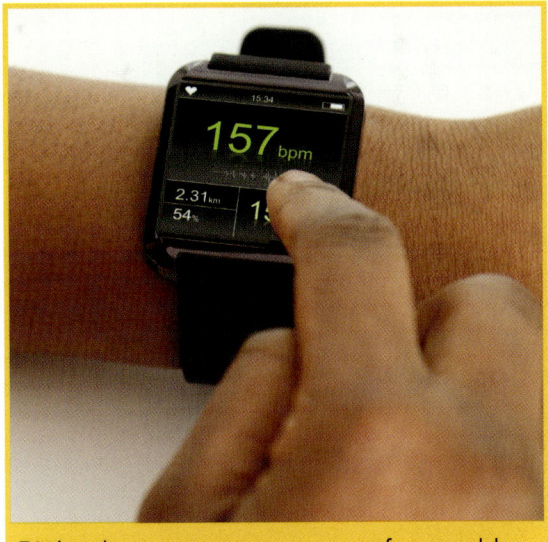

Biohackers can use an array of wearable technology. This includes rings, watches, and waist belts.

fecal transplant: moving feces from a healthy donor into another person to restore healthy bacteria in their gut

BIOHACKERS 21

NOOTROPICS

Nootropics and other supplements are very popular in biohacking circles. They are meant to improve human performance. Science, technology, engineering, and math are all necessary to make these products.

SCIENCE
Chemists help discover which nutrients might help the body work better. Someday nootropics might be more mainstream. Then pharmacists will be another type of scientist working to make them.

TECHNOLOGY
Sometimes supplements are extracted from natural sources. Other times, they are made in a lab. For example, vitamin B1 can be made from coal. Either way, sophisticated laboratory equipment and other advanced technology are used.

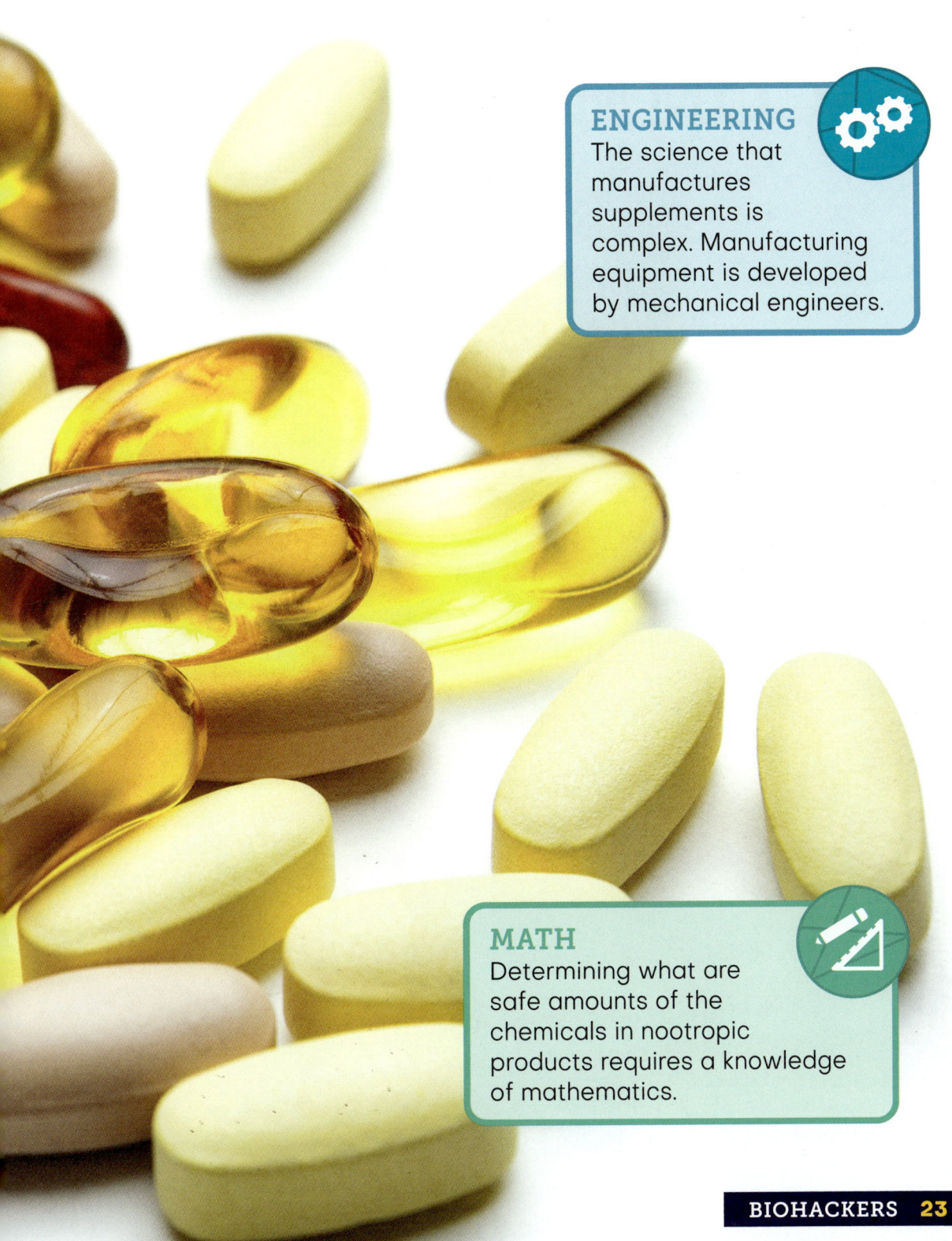

ENGINEERING
The science that manufactures supplements is complex. Manufacturing equipment is developed by mechanical engineers.

MATH
Determining what are safe amounts of the chemicals in nootropic products requires a knowledge of mathematics.

The Biohacking COMMUNITY

In middle and high school, students can learn the basics of the science behind biohacking.

Biohackers have a STEM mind-set. Biological problems like aging and poor eyesight are seen as engineering problems. They believe anything can be solved with technology. Biohackers also believe that the power to change their bodies should be in the hands of the people. They often work by themselves and in **informal** communities.

There are biohacking conferences and community labs around the United States. Many different people gather. Some are high school students, and some are professional scientists. They work on many different projects. Some are glow-in-the-dark drinks and oil-spill cleanup methods. Many of these experiments don't work. But they lay the groundwork for the next biohacker. What keeps them going are the infinite possibilities.

informal: not official

BIOHACKERS 25

BIOHACKING SCIENTISTS

STEM workers from around the world are leading the way in biohacking science.

ELON MUSK
Elon Musk is the billionaire behind Tesla and SpaceX. He believes humans have to become cyborgs if they are going to survive among **artificial intelligence**. His company Neuralink will make a device to be implanted in the brain. It might do anything from improving memory to connecting the brain to computers.

JENNIFER DOUDNA
Jennifer Doudna is a biologist at the University of California, Berkeley. She helped invent the breakthrough technology of CRISPR. She believes scientists should be careful with CRISPR until they understand its effects.

KEVIN WARWICK
Kevin Warwick is a famous cyborg. A set of wires are implanted into his arm. They read his nerve signals. He has used them to control a robotic hand from far away. His wife also has this implant. When the implants are connected via the internet, they can physically feel each other without touching. For example, Warwick's implant can receive pulses when his wife moves her hand.

DR. SATCHIN PANDA
Dr. Satchin Panda is a world expert in circadian rhythm. This is our natural sleeping and waking process. Panda discovered special light sensors in the brain. He also proved the benefits of intermittent fasting, which he calls "time-restricted eating."

artificial intelligence: computer systems that can do tasks that normally require a human

BIOHACKERS

QUIZ

1 Do most biohackers have the help of a doctor?

2 There may be up to how many grinders in the world?

3 What are two examples of medical implants?

4 What new technology are scientists already using to make medicines and cure diseases?

5 In what year did California pass the first CRISPR law?

6 What math subjects do CRISPR engineers need?

7 What are nootropics?

8 Do all biohacking projects work?

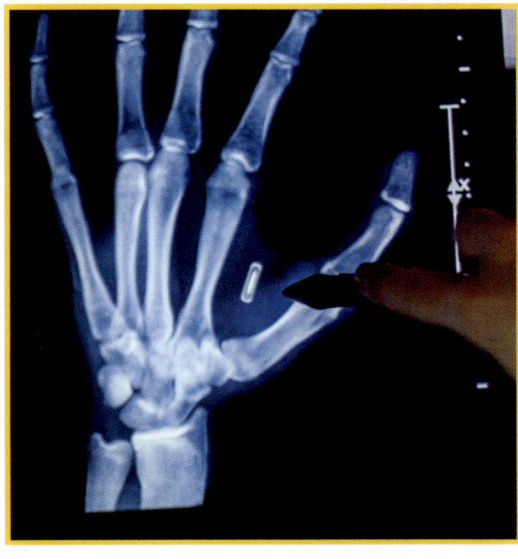

ANSWERS

1. No
2. 100,000
3. Cochlear implant and blood test implant
4. CRISPR
5. 2019
6. Probability and statistics
7. Supplements meant to improve mental performance
8. No, but they lay the groundwork for the next biohacker.

28 STEM BODY

ACTIVITY
Write a Letter to the Editor

RFID chips are the implants most likely to be used in the future by average people. This is exciting technology. But there are possible downsides. Explore the debate by writing a letter to the editor of a local newspaper.

STEPS

1. Use a search engine. Search for articles about the benefits and advantages of RFID chip implants. Then search for information about the risks and disadvantages.

2. After you read, decide which side you think is correct. What should be done about these implants? Are the risks too great to allow it? Are the benefits so wonderful that it should be supported?

3. Write a letter to the editor of your local newspaper discussing your opinions. Use facts and numbers to back up your opinion. Contact the newspaper to submit your letter to the editor.

INDEX

Asprey, Dave 20

CRISPR 13, 15, 16, 17, 26

DNA 5, 12, 13, 14, 15, 16
Dorsey, Jack 18, 19
Doudna, Jennifer 15, 26

evolution 5

genes 12, 13, 14, 15, 19

implants 7, 8, 9, 21, 27
intermittent fasting 21, 27

Musk, Elon 26

nootropics 20, 22, 23

Panda, Dr. Satchin 27

RFID chips 8, 9, 10, 11

stem cells 20

transhumanists 4, 5

Warwick, Kevin 27

Zayner, Josiah 14, 15

West's Law School Advisory Board

JESSE H. CHOPER
Professor of Law,
University of California, Berkeley

DAVID P. CURRIE
Professor of Law, University of Chicago

YALE KAMISAR
Professor of Law, University of San Diego
Professor of Law, University of Michigan

MARY KAY KANE
Chancellor, Dean and Distinguished Professor of Law,
University of California,
Hastings College of the Law

LARRY D. KRAMER
Dean and Professor of Law, Stanford Law School

WAYNE R. LaFAVE
Professor of Law, University of Illinois

JONATHAN R. MACEY
Professor of Law, Yale Law School

ARTHUR R. MILLER
Professor of Law, Harvard University

GRANT S. NELSON
Professor of Law,
University of California, Los Angeles

JAMES J. WHITE
Professor of Law, University of Michigan

2005 Supplement to Eleventh Editions

MODERN CRIMINAL PROCEDURE
Cases — Comments — Questions

BASIC CRIMINAL PROCEDURE
Cases — Comments — Questions

and

ADVANCED CRIMINAL PROCEDURE
Cases — Comments — Questions

By

Yale Kamisar
Professor of Law
University of San Diego
Clarence Darrow Distinguished University Professor Emeritus of Law,
University of Michigan

Wayne R. LaFave
David C. Baum Professor Emeritus of Law
and Center for Advanced Study Professor Emeritus,
University of Illinois

Jerold H. Israel
Ed Rood Eminent Scholar in Trial Advocacy and Procedure
University of Florida, Levin College of Law
Alene and Allan F. Smith Professor Emeritus of Law
University of Michigan

Nancy J. King
Lee S. & Charles A. Spier Professor of Law
Vanderbilt University Law School

AMERICAN CASEBOOK SERIES®

Mat #40383611

Thomson/West have created this publication to provide you with accurate and authoritative information West, a Thomson business, has created this publication to provide you with accurate and authoritative information concerning the subject matter covered. However, this publication was not necessarily prepared by persons licensed to practice law in a particular jurisdiction. Thomson/West are not engaged in rendering legal or other professional advice, and this publication is not a substitute for the advice of an attorney. If you require legal or other expert advice, you should seek the services of a competent attorney or other professional.

American Casebook Series and West Group are trademarks registered in the U.S. Patent and Trademark Office.

COPYRIGHT © WEST, a Thomson business 1999, 2002
© 2005 Thomson/West
      610 Opperman Drive
      P.O. Box 64526
      St. Paul, MN 55164–0526
      1–800–328–9352

Printed in the United States of America

ISBN 0–314–16216–X

Preface

This Supplement to the eleventh edition of MODERN CRIMINAL PROCEDURE and companion books contains all significant United States Supreme Court cases decided since publication of those eleventh editions. It also contains a goodly number of state court and lower federal court cases and substantial extracts from many law review articles. Finally, this volume contains selected provisions of the U.S. Constitution (App. A); selected federal statutory provisions (App. B) (including various USA PATRIOT Act amendments); the Federal Rules of Criminal Procedure (including recent amendments) (App. C); pending amendments to the Rules (App. D); and proposed amendments to the Rules (App. E).

YALE KAMISAR
WAYNE LAFAVE
JEROLD H. ISRAEL
NANCY J. KING

July, 2005

Acknowledgments

Excerpts from the following books and articles appear with the kind permission of the copyright holders.

Bayley, David H., Law Enforcement and the Rule of Law: Is There A Tradeoff?, 2 Criminology and Public Policy 133 (2002). Copyright © 2002 by the American Society of Criminology. Reprinted by permission.

Bogira, Steve, Courtroom 302 (2005). Copyright © 2005 by Random House, Inc. Reprinted by permission.

Godsey, Mark A., Rethinking the Involuntary Confession Rule: Toward A Workable Test for Identifying Compelled Self-Incrimination, 93 Calif. L. Rev. 465 (2005). Copyright © 2005 by the California Law Review. Reprinted by permission.

Harris, David A., Good Cops (2005). Copyright © 2005 by The New Press. Reprinted by permission.

*

Table of Contents

Preface	iii
Acknowledgments	v
Table of Cases	xi

PART ONE

INTRODUCTION

CHAPTER 2. THE NATURE AND SCOPE OF FOURTEENTH AMENDMENT DUE PROCESS; RETROACTIVITY; THE FEDERAL "SUPERVISORY POWER"; STATE RIGHTS PROTECTIONS — 1

1. *THE "ORDERED LIBERTY"—"FUNDAMENTAL FAIRNESS," "TOTAL INCORPORATION" AND "SELECTIVE INCORPORATION" THEORIES* — 1
   - Roper v. Simmons — 1
7. *ENFORCEMENT OF TREATY OBLIGATIONS* — 4
   - Medellin v. Dretke — 4

CHAPTER 3. SOME GENERAL REFLECTIONS ON LAW ENFORCEMENT OFFICIALS, THE LEGISLATURES, THE COURTS AND THE CRIMINAL PROCESS — 13
- David H. Bayley—Law Enforcement and the Rule of Law: Is there a Tradeoff? — 13
- David A. Harris—Good Cops — 16

CHAPTER 4. THE RIGHT TO COUNSEL, "BY FAR THE MOST PERVASIVE" RIGHT OF THE ACCUSED; EQUALITY AND THE ADVERSARY SYSTEM — 19

2. *THE GRIFFIN-DOUGLAS "EQUALITY" PRINCIPLE* — 19
   - Halbert v. Michigan — 19

CHAPTER 5. THE ROLE OF COUNSEL — 24
4. *THE RIGHT TO "EFFECTIVE" ASSISTANCE OF COUNSEL* — 24
   - Rompilla v. Beard — 24

PART TWO

POLICE PRACTICES

CHAPTER 6. ARREST, SEARCH AND SEIZURE — 41
1. *THE EXCLUSIONARY RULE* — 41
2. *PROTECTED AREAS AND INTERESTS* — 41

TABLE OF CONTENTS

4. *SEARCH WARRANTS* 42
   Muehler v. Mena 42
5. *WARRANTLESS ARRESTS AND SEARCHES OF THE PERSON* 43
   Town of Castle Rock v. Gonzales 44
   Donald A. Dripps, The Fourth Amendment and the Fallacy of Composition: Determinacy Versus Legitimacy in a Regime of Bright-Line Rules 45
8. *STOP AND FRISK* 46
9. *ADMINISTRATIVE INSPECTIONS AND REGULATORY SEARCHES: MORE ON BALANCING THE NEED AGAINST THE INVASION OF PRIVACY* 47
   Ronald M. Gould & Simon Stern, Catastrophic Threats and the Fourth Amendment 47
10. *CONSENT SEARCHES* 48

CHAPTER 7. WIRETAPPING, ELECTRONIC EAVESDROPPING, THE USE OF SECRET AGENTS TO OBTAIN INCRIMINATING STATEMENTS, AND THE FOURTH AMENDMENT 49

2. *BERGER, KATZ AND THE LEGISLATION THAT FOLLOWED* ... 49

CHAPTER 9. POLICE INTERROGATION AND CONFESSIONS 50

3. *THE MIRANDA "REVOLUTION"* 50
   State v. Sawyer 50
   United States v. Lewis 51
   Blake v. State 51
5. *THE PATANE AND SEIBERT CASES: IS PHYSICAL EVIDENCE OR A "SECOND CONFESSION" DERIVED FROM A FAILURE TO COMPLY WITH THE MIRANDA RULES ADMISSIBLE? THE COURT'S ANSWERS SHED LIGHT ON DICKERSON* ... 53
6. *THE "DUE PROCESS"—"VOLUNTARINESS" TEST REVISITED* 54
   State v. Swanigan 54
   Saul M. Kassin, Christian A. Meissner & Rebecca J. Norwick, "I'd Know a False Confession if I Saw One": A Comparative Study of College Students and Police Investigators 54
   State v. Harris 56
   Mark A. Godsey—Rethinking the Involuntary Confession Rule: Toward A Workable Test For Identifying Compelled Self-Incrimination 57
7. *MASSIAH REVISITED; MASSIAH AND MIRANDA COMPARED AND CONTRASTED* 60

TABLE OF CONTENTS ix

**CHAPTER 10. LINEUPS, SHOWUPS AND OTHER PRE-
TRIAL IDENTIFICATION PROCEDURES** --- 61
1. *WADE AND GILBERT: CONSTITUTIONAL CONCERN
ABOUT THE DANGERS INVOLVED IN EYEWITNESS
IDENTIFICATIONS* -- 61
Steve Bogira, Courtroom 302 ----------------------------- 61

CHAPTER 11. GRAND JURY INVESTIGATIONS --------------- 63
2. *FOURTH AMENDMENT CHALLENGES TO THE INVESTIGA-
TION* --- 63

**CHAPTER 12. THE SCOPE OF THE EXCLUSIONARY
RULES** -------------------------------------- 65
2. *THE "FRUIT OF THE POISONOUS TREE"* ----------------- 65
United States v. Pulliam ---------------------------------- 65
United States v. Fellers ------------------------------- 68

PART THREE

THE COMMENCEMENT OF FORMAL PROCEEDINGS

CHAPTER 13. PRETRIAL RELEASE -------------------------- 73
1. *THE RIGHT TO BAIL: PRETRIAL RELEASE PROCEDURES* 73

CHAPTER 14. THE DECISION WHETHER TO PROSECUTE 74
1. *THE OFFICE OF PROSECUTOR AND THE NATURE OF
THE DECISION WHETHER TO PROSECUTE* --------------- 74
Bruce A. Green & Fred C. Zacharias —*Prosecutorial Neutrality* 74
2. *SOME VIEWS ON DISCRETION IN THE CRIMINAL
PROCESS AND THE PROSECUTOR'S DISCRETION
IN PARTICULAR* -- 75

CHAPTER 16. GRAND JURY REVIEW ------------------------ 76
1. *THE ROLE OF GRAND JURY REVIEW* -------------------- 76
4. *MISCONDUCT CHALLENGES* ---------------------------- 76
United States v. Navarro–Vargas ----------------------- 76

**CHAPTER 19. THE SCOPE OF THE PROSECUTION: JOIN-
DER AND SEVERANCE OF OFFENSES AND
DEFENDANTS** ------------------------------ 91
2. *FAILURE TO JOIN RELATED OFFENSES* ----------------- 91

PART FOUR

THE ADVERSARY SYSTEM AND THE DETERMINATION OF GUILT OR INNOCENCE

**CHAPTER 22. COERCED, INDUCED, AND NEGOTIATED
GUILTY PLEAS; PROFESSIONAL RESPON-
SIBILITY** ----------------------------------- 92
1. *SOME VIEWS OF NEGOTIATED PLEAS* -------------------- 92
Steve Bogira, Courtroom 302 ----------------------------- 93

2.	*EXPECTATIONS*	93
3.	*PROFESSIONAL RESPONSIBILITY; THE ROLE OF PROSECUTOR AND DEFENSE COUNSEL*	93
4.	*RECEIVING THE DEFENDANT'S PLEA; PLEA WITHDRAWAL*	93
	Steve Bogira, Courtroom 302	94

CHAPTER 23.	**TRIAL BY JURY**	95
1.	*RIGHT TO JURY TRIAL*	95
2.	*JURY SELECTION*	95
	Miller–El v. Dretke	97
	Steve Bogira, Courtroom 302	99

CHAPTER 25.	**THE CRIMINAL TRIAL**	103
1.	*PRESENCE OF THE DEFENDANT*	103
	Deck v. Missouri	103
2.	*THE DEFENDANT'S RIGHT TO REMAIN SILENT AND TO TESTIFY*	110
4.	*SUBMITTING THE CASE TO THE JURY*	110
5.	*DELIBERATIONS AND VERDICT*	111

CHAPTER 27.	**SENTENCING**	112
2.	*ALLOCATING AND CONTROLLING SENTENCING DISCRETION*	112

PART FIVE

APPEALS, POST-CONVICTION REVIEW

CHAPTER 28.	**APPEALS**	116
1.	*THE DEFENDANT'S RIGHT TO APPEAL*	116
3.	*PROSECUTION APPEALS*	116

CHAPTER 29.	**POST–CONVICTION REVIEW: FEDERAL HABEAS CORPUS**	117
2.	*ISSUES COGNIZABLE*	117
6.	*LATE OR SUCCESSIVE PETITIONS*	117

APPENDICES

App.		
A.	Selected Provisions of the United States Constitution	118
B.	Selected Federal Statutory Provisions	121
C.	Federal Rules of Criminal Procedure for the United States District Courts	193
D.	Pending Amendments to Federal Rules of Criminal Procedure	253
E.	Proposed Amendments to Federal Rules of Criminal Procedure	256

Table of Cases

The principal cases are in bold type. Cases cited or discussed in the text are in roman type. References are to pages. Cases cited in principal cases and within other quoted materials are not included.

Arizona v. Evans, 514 U.S. 1, 115 S.Ct. 1185, 131 L.Ed.2d 34 (1995), 46
Atwater v. City of Lago Vista, 532 U.S. 318, 121 S.Ct. 1536, 149 L.Ed.2d 549 (2001), 44, 46

Batson v. Kentucky, 476 U.S. 79, 106 S.Ct. 1712, 90 L.Ed.2d 69 (1986), 96, 97, 99, 100
Bigby v. Dretke, 402 F.3d 551 (5th Cir. 2005), 102
Blake v. State, 381 Md. 218, 849 A.2d 410 (Md.2004), 50, **51,** 53
Booker, United States v., ___ U.S. ___, 125 S.Ct. 738, 160 L.Ed.2d 621 (2005), 112
Bradshaw v. Stumpf, ___ U.S. ___, 125 S.Ct. 2398 (2005), 91, 93
Brady v. United States, 397 U.S. 742, 90 S.Ct. 1463, 25 L.Ed.2d 747 (1970), 93
Breard v. Greene, 523 U.S. 371, 118 S.Ct. 1352, 140 L.Ed.2d 529 (1998), 5
Bulger, People v., 462 Mich. 495, 614 N.W.2d 103 (Mich.2000), 19

Castle Rock, Colorado, Town of v. Gonzales, ___ U.S. ___, 125 S.Ct. 2796 (2005), **44,** 75
Chidester, State v., 570 N.W.2d 78 (Iowa 1997), 95

Deck v. Missouri, ___ U.S. ___, 125 S.Ct. 2007 (2005), **103,** 110
Dodd v. United States, ___ U.S. ___, 125 S.Ct. 2478 (2005), 117
Douglas v. People of California, 372 U.S. 353, 83 S.Ct. 814, 9 L.Ed.2d 811 (1963), 116
Drayton, United States v., 536 U.S. 194, 122 S.Ct. 2105, 153 L.Ed.2d 242 (2002), 46
Durham, United States v., 287 F.3d 1297 (11th Cir.2002), 110

Estelle v. Williams, 425 U.S. 501, 96 S.Ct. 1691, 48 L.Ed.2d 126 (1976), 108

Faretta v. California, 422 U.S. 806, 95 S.Ct. 2525, 45 L.Ed.2d 562 (1975), 109
Fellers, United States v., 397 F.3d 1090 (8th Cir.2005), 54, 60, **68**
Fellers v. United States, 540 U.S. 519, 124 S.Ct. 1019, 157 L.Ed.2d 1016 (2004), 68
Florida v. Bostick, 501 U.S. 429, 111 S.Ct. 2382, 115 L.Ed.2d 389 (1991), 46
Fulton, State v., 57 Ohio St.3d 120, 566 N.E.2d 1195 (Ohio 1991), 95, 96

Germany v. United States, 2001 ICJ 104 (June 27) (*LaGrand*), 5
Glover v. United States, 531 U.S. 198, 121 S.Ct. 696, 148 L.Ed.2d 604 (2001), 40
Godwin, United States v., 272 F.3d 659 (4th Cir.2001), 111

Halbert v. Michigan, ___ U.S. ___, 125 S.Ct. 2582 (2005), **19,** 116
Harris, State v., 279 Kan. 163, 105 P.3d 1258 (Kan.2005), **56**
Harris, State v., 272 Wis.2d 80, 680 N.W.2d 737 (Wis.2004), 93
Hedgepeth v. Washington Metropolitan Area Transit Authority, 386 F.3d 1148, 363 U.S.App.D.C. 260 (D.C.Cir.2004), 44
Hensley, United States v., 469 U.S. 221, 105 S.Ct. 675, 83 L.Ed.2d 604 (1985), 46
Herrera v. Collins, 506 U.S. 390, 113 S.Ct. 853, 122 L.Ed.2d 203 (1993), 111
Holbrook v. Flynn, 475 U.S. 560, 106 S.Ct. 1340, 89 L.Ed.2d 525 (1986), 108

Illinois v. Allen, 397 U.S. 337, 90 S.Ct. 1057, 25 L.Ed.2d 353 (1970), 108, 109
Illinois v. Caballes, ___ U.S. ___, 125 S.Ct. 834, 160 L.Ed.2d 842 (2005), 42, 46
In re (see name of party)

Jackson, State v., 150 Wash.2d 251, 76 P.3d 217 (Wash.2003), 42
Jansen, In re, 444 Mass. 112, 826 N.E.2d 186 (Mass.2005), 41

TABLE OF CASES

Johnson v. California, ___ U.S. ___, 125 S.Ct. 2410, 160 L.Ed.2d 949 (2005), 96
Johnson, United States v., 380 F.3d 1013 (7th Cir.2004), 67

Knotts, United States v., 460 U.S. 276, 103 S.Ct. 1081, 75 L.Ed.2d 55 (1983), 42

Le v. State, 2005 WL 977007, ___ So.2d ___ (2005), 96
Lewis, United States v., 355 F.Supp.2d 870 (E.D.Mich.2005), **51**

McClendon v. Story County Sheriff's Office, 403 F.3d 510 (8th Cir.2005), 43
Medellin v. Dretke, ___ U.S. ___, 125 S.Ct. 2088 (2005), **4,** 117
Mexico v. United States, 2004 I.C.J. 128 (March 31) (*Avena*), 6
Miller–El v. Dretke, ___ U.S. ___, 125 S.Ct. 2317 (2005), **97,** 100
Missouri v. Seibert, 542 U.S. 600, 124 S.Ct. 2601, 159 L.Ed.2d 643 (2004), 54, 60
Morales, People v., 770 P.2d 244 (Cal.1989), 96
Mota, United States v., 982 F.2d 1384 (9th Cir.1993), 44
Muehler v. Mena, ___ U.S. ___, 125 S.Ct. 1465, 161 L.Ed.2d 299 (2005), **42, 46**

Navarro–Vargas, United States v., 408 F.3d 1184 (9th Cir.2005), 75, **76,** 95
Nettles, In re, 394 F.3d 1001 (7th Cir.2005), 102
New York v. Belton, 453 U.S. 454, 101 S.Ct. 2860, 69 L.Ed.2d 768 (1981), 46
Nix v. Williams, 467 U.S. 431, 104 S.Ct. 2501, 81 L.Ed.2d 377 (1984), 68

Oregon v. Elstad, 470 U.S. 298, 105 S.Ct. 1285, 84 L.Ed.2d 222 (1985), 68
Owens v. United States, 387 F.3d 607 (7th Cir.2004), 40

Patane, United States v., 542 U.S. 630, 124 S.Ct. 2620, 159 L.Ed.2d 667 (2004), 54, 60
People v. ___ **(see opposing party)**
Pulliam, United States v., 405 F.3d 782 (9th Cir.2005), **65,** 67

Quercia v. United States, 289 U.S. 466, 53 S.Ct. 698, 77 L.Ed. 1321 (1933), 110

Raines, State v., 383 Md. 1, 857 A.2d 19 (Md.2004), 47
Rompilla v. Beard, ___ U.S. ___, 125 S.Ct. 2456 (2005), **24,** 39
Roper v. Simmons, ___ U.S. ___, 125 S.Ct. 1183, 161 L.Ed.2d 1 (2005), **1,** 113
Ruiz, United States v., 536 U.S. 622, 122 S.Ct. 2450, 153 L.Ed.2d 586 (2002), 93
Rutledge, United States v., 900 F.2d 1127 (7th Cir.1990), 56

Sanders v. Woodford, 373 F.3d 1054 (9th Cir.2004), 96
San Jose Charter of Hells Angels Motorcycle Club v. City of San Jose, 402 F.3d 962 (9th Cir.2005), 43
Sawyer, State v., 156 S.W.3d 531 (Tenn. 2005), **50**
Stanford v. Kentucky, 492 U.S. 361, 109 S.Ct. 2969, 106 L.Ed.2d 306 (1989), 1
State v. ___ **(see opposing party)**
Swanigan, State v., 279 Kan. 18, 106 P.3d 39 (Kan.2005), **54**

Town of (see name of town)
Trop v. Dulles, 356 U.S. 86, 78 S.Ct. 590, 2 L.Ed.2d 630 (1958), 1

United States v. ___ **(see opposing party)**
United States Dept. of Justice v. Reporters Committee For Freedom of Press, 489 U.S. 749, 109 S.Ct. 1468, 103 L.Ed.2d 774 (1989), 64

Weaver v. State, 894 So.2d 178 (Fla.2004), 110
Whren v. United States, 517 U.S. 806, 116 S.Ct. 1769, 135 L.Ed.2d 89 (1996), 46
Williams v. Taylor, 529 U.S. 362, 120 S.Ct. 1495, 146 L.Ed.2d 389 (2000), 40
Wrinkles v. State, 749 N.E.2d 1179 (Ind. 2001), 110

2005 Supplement
to Eleventh Editions
MODERN CRIMINAL PROCEDURE
Cases — Comments — Questions
BASIC CRIMINAL PROCEDURE
Cases — Comments — Questions
and
ADVANCED CRIMINAL PROCEDURE
Cases — Comments — Questions

*

Part One

INTRODUCTION

Chapter 2

THE NATURE AND SCOPE OF FOURTEENTH AMENDMENT DUE PROCESS; RETROACTIVITY; THE FEDERAL "SUPERVISORY POWER"; STATE RIGHTS PROTECTIONS

SECTION 1. THE "ORDERED LIBERTY"—"FUNDAMENTAL FAIRNESS," "TOTAL INCORPORATION" AND "SELECTIVE INCORPORATION" THEORIES

11th ed., p. 28; after the extract from *Duncan v. Louisiana*, add:

Compare the comments of Justice White in *Duncan* with those of Justice KENNEDY for a 5–4 majority in ROPER v. SIMMONS, 125 S.Ct. 1183 (2005), overruling *Stanford v. Kentucky*, 492 U.S. 361 (1989), and holding that the execution of individuals who were older than 15 but younger than 18 at the time their capital crimes were committed is prohibited by the Eighth and Fourteenth Amendments. After recalling that in interpreting the Eight Amendment's prohibition against "cruel and unusual punishments," the Court had "established the propriety and affirmed the necessity of referring to 'the evolving standards of decency that mark the progress of a maturing society' to determine which punishments are so disproportionate as to be cruel and unusual, *Trop v. Dulles*, 356 U.S. 86 (1958) (plurality opinion)," the Court went on to say:

> "Our determination that the death penalty is disproportionate punishment for offenders under 18 finds confirmation in the stark reality that the United States is the only country in the world that continues to give official sanction to the juvenile death penalty. This

really does not become controlling, for the task of interpreting the Eight Amendment remains our responsibility. Yet at least from the time of the Court's decision in *Trop*, the Court has referred to the laws of other countries and to international authorities as instructive for its interpretation of the Eighth Amendment's prohibition of 'cruel and unusual punishments.'

" * * * Article 37 of the United Nations Convention on the Rights of the Child, which every country in the world has ratified save for the United States and Somalia, contains an express prohibition on capital punishment for crimes committed by juveniles under 18. * * * No ratifying country has entered a reservation to the provision prohibiting the execution of juvenile offenders. Parallel prohibitions are contained in other significant international covenants.

"[O]nly seven countries other than the United States have executed juvenile offenders since 1990: Iran, Pakistan, Saudi Arabia, Yemen, Nigeria, the Democratic Republic of Congo, and China. Since then each of these countries has either abolished capital punishment for juveniles or made public disavowal of the practice. In sum, it is fair to say that the United States now stands alone in a world that has turned its face against the juvenile death penalty.

"Though the international covenants prohibiting the juvenile death penalty are of more recent date, it is instructive to note that the United Kingdom abolished the juvenile death penalty before these covenants came into being. The United Kingdom's experience bears particular relevance here in light of the historic ties between our countries and in light of the Eighth Amendment's own origins. The Amendment was modeled on a parallel provision in the English Declaration of Rights of 1689 * * *.

"It is proper that we acknowledge the overwhelming weight of international opinion against the juvenile death penalty, resting in large part on the understanding that the instability and emotional imbalance of young people may often be a factor in the crime. The opinion of the world community, while not controlling our outcome, does provide respected and significant confirmation for our own conclusions.

" * * * It does not lessen our fidelity to the Constitution or our pride in its origins to acknowledge that the express affirmation of certain fundamental rights by other nations and peoples simply underscores the centrality of those same rights within our own heritage of freedom."[a]

---

[a] In a brief concurring opinion, Justice Stevens, joined by Ginsburg, J., observed that "[if] the meaning of [the Eighth] Amendment has been frozen when it was originally drafted, it would impose no impediment to the execution of 7-year-old children. [That] our understanding of the Constitution does change from time to time has been settled since John Marshall breathed life into its text."

Justice SCALIA, joined by Rehnquist, C.J., and Thomas, J., protested:

"[The Court] finds, on the flimsiest of grounds, that a national consensus which could not be perceived in our people's laws barely 15 years ago now solidly exists. [The Court] proclaims itself sole arbiter of our Nation's moral standards—and in the course of discharging that awesome responsibility purports to take guidance from the views of foreign courts and legislatures. Because I do not believe that the meaning of our Eighth Amendment, any more than the meaning of other provisions of our Constitution, should be determined by the subjective views of five Members of this Court and like-minded foreigners, I dissent.

"Though the views of our own citizens are essentially irrelevant to the Court's decision today, the views of other countries and the so-called international community take center stage. * * *

"[The] basic premise of the Court's argument—that American law should conform to the laws of the rest of the world—ought to be rejected out of hand. In fact the Court itself does not believe it. In many significant respects the laws of most other countries differ from our law—including not only such explicit provisions of our Constitution as the right to jury trial and grand jury indictment, but even many interpretations of the Constitution prescribed by this Court itself. The Court-pronounced exclusionary rule, for example, is distinctively American. * * * England, for example, rarely excludes evidence found during an illegal search or seizure and has only recently begun excluding evidence from illegally obtained confessions. Canada rarely excludes evidence and will only do so if admission will 'bring the administration of justice into disrepute.'

"[The] Court has been oblivious to the views of other countries when deciding how to interpret our Constitution's requirement that 'Congress shall make no law respecting an establishment of religion. . . .' [And] let us not forget the Court's abortion jurisprudence, which makes us one of only six countries that allow abortion on demand until the point of viability.

"[To] invoke alien law when it agrees with one's own thinking, and ignore it otherwise, is not reasoned decisionmaking, but sophistry. * * * [The Court's statement that] 'the express affirmation of certain fundamental rights by other nations and peoples simply underscores the centrality of those same rights within our own heritage of freedom' * * * flatly misdescribes what is going on here. Foreign sources are cited today, *not* to underscore our 'fidelity' to the Constitution [and] 'our own American heritage.' To the contrary, they are cited *to set aside* the centuries-old American practice—a practice still engaged in by a large majority of the relevant States—of letting a jury of 12 citizens decide whether, in the particular case, youth should be the basis for withholding the death penalty. What these foreign sources 'affirm,' rather than repudiate, is the Justices' own notion of how the world ought to be, and their diktat that it shall be so henceforth in America. The Court's parting attempt to downplay the significance of its extensive discussion of foreign law is unconvincing. 'Acknowledgment' of foreign approval has no place in the legal opinion of this Court *unless it is part of the basis for the Court's judgment*—which is surely what it parades as today."[b]

11th ed., p. 58; at the end of Chapter 2, add:

SECTION 7. ENFORCEMENT OF TREATY OBLIGATIONS

As to enforcement of treaty obligations within the criminal justice process, consider MEDELLIN v. DRETKE, 125 S.Ct. 2088 (2005). Defendant Medellin was charged in Texas with capital murder (the gang rape and killing of two teenage girls), convicted at trial, and sentenced to death. In a state postconviction proceeding, he raised, for the first time, an alleged violation of the Vienna Convention on Consular Relations [Vienna Convention], which was ratified by the President (with the advice and consent of the Senate) in 1969. Article 36 of the Vienna Convention provides:

Communications and contact with nationals of the sending state

1. With a view to facilitating the exercise of consular functions relating to nationals of the sending state:

(a) consular officers shall be free to communicate with nationals of the sending State and to have access to them. Nationals of the sending State shall have the same freedom with respect to communication with and access to consular officers of the sending State;

(b) if he so requests, the competent authorities of the receiving State shall, without delay, inform the consular post of the sending State if, within its consular district, a national of that State is arrested or committed to prison or to custody pending trial or is detained in any other manner. Any communication addressed to the consular post by the person arrested, in prison, custody or detention

---

b. Because she did not believe that "a genuine *national* consensus against the juvenile death penalty has yet developed" or that "the Court's moral proportionality argument justifies a categorical, age-based constitutional rule," Justice O'Connor wrote a separate dissent. Although the evidence of an international consensus did not "alter [her] determination that the Eighth Amendment does not, at this time, forbid capital punishment of 17-year-old murderers in all cases," Justice O'Connor "disagree[d] with Justice Scalia's contention that foreign and international law have no place in our Eighth Amendment jurisprudence. Over the course of nearly half a century, the Court has consistently referred to foreign and international law as relevant to its assessment of evolving standards of decency. [This] inquiry reflects the special character of the Eighth Amendment, which, as the Court has long held, draws its meaning directly from the maturing values of civilized society. Obviously, American law is distinctive in many respects, not least where the specific provisions of our Constitution and the history of its exposition so dictate. [But] this Nation's evolving understanding of human dignity certainly is neither wholly isolated from, nor inherently at odds with, the values prevailing in other countries.

shall also be forwarded by the said authorities without delay. The said authorities shall inform the person concerned without delay of his rights under this sub-paragraph;

(c) consular officers shall have the right to visit a national of the sending State who is in prison, custody or detention, to converse and correspond with him and to arrange for his legal representation. They shall also have the right to visit any national of the sending State who is in prison, custody or detention in their district in pursuance of a judgement. Nevertheless, consular officers shall refrain from taking action on behalf of a national who is in prison, custody or detention if he expressly opposes such action.

2. The rights referred to in paragraph 1 of this Article shall be exercised in conformity with the laws and regulations of the receiving State, subject to the proviso, however, that he said laws and regulations must enable full effect to be given to the purposes for which the rights accorded under this Article are intended.

Medellin alleged that he told the officers who arrested him that he was born in Laredo, Mexico, and told the Harris County Pretrial Services that he was not an American citizen, but that he was detained follow his arrest, tried, convicted, and sentenced to death without ever being informed that he could contact the Mexican consulate.

The state postconviction court rejected Medellin's claim on several grounds, including: (1) procedural default as a result of defense counsel's failure to raise the Vienna Convention claim at trial; and (2) a lack of standing to enforce the Vienna Convention, viewing that treaty as not creating judicially enforceable private rights. Medellin then raised the Vienna Convention claim in a federal district court on a federal habeas petition, relying in part on an International Court of Justice ruling, *Germany v. United States*, 2001 ICJ 104 (June 27) (*LaGrand*). The Optional Protocol to the Vienna Convention, ratified along with the Convention, provides that "disputes arising out of the interpretation or application of the Convention shall lie within the compulsory jurisdiction of the International Court of Justice," and Article 94 of the United Nations Charter (also a treaty) provides that "each member * * * undertakes to comply with the decision of the International Court of Justice in any case to which it is a party." Medellin argued that the habeas court was therefore bound by the interpretation of Article 36 advanced in the ICJ ruling. *LaGrand* ruled that the Vienna Convention's article 36 did create an individually enforceable right and that paragraph 2 of Article 36 precluded application of a procedural default rule, if that rule "prevents the detained individual * * * from challenging a conviction and sentence by claiming * * * that the competent national authorities failed to comply with their obligation to provide the requisite consular information 'without delay.'" *LaGrand* (par. 90). The federal habeas court reasoned that *LaGrand* was inconsistent with the earlier Supreme Court ruling in *Breard v. Greene*, 523 U.S. 371 (1998), and it was bound by *Breard*. The *Breard* Court held that ordinary procedural default rules could bar habeas review of a Vienna Convention claim.[a] The habeas court further reasoned that even if Medellin could surmount his procedural default, he would not gain relief because (1) his claim was barred by other aspects of federal habeas law, and (2) *Breard* had indicated that relief under a Vienna Convention claim would require a showing that the failure to notify caused "concrete, non-speculative harm" and the state habeas court had found that defendant failed to make such a showing (in light of his "effective legal representation").

Following the district court's denial of habeas relief, Medellin sought a certificate of appealability (COA), which was also denied. Medellin then sought a COA from the Fifth Circuit, relying, in part, on the intervening ICJ ruling in *Mexico v. United States*, 2004 I.C.J. 128 (March 31) (*Avena*). *Avena* considered the claim of Mexico that 51 Mexican nationals had been arrested, convicted, and sentenced to death in various state courts without being informed of their rights to consular notification and access as established in Article 36(1)(b). Relying on *LaGrand*, *Avena* determined (as subsequently described by the Supreme Court) "that the Vienna Convention guaranteed individually enforceable rights, that the United States had violated those rights, and that the United States must provide, by means of its own choosing, review and reconsideration of the convictions and sentences of the [affected] Mexican Nationals" to determine whether the violations "caused actual prejudice," without allowing "procedural default rules to bar such review." 125 S.Ct. at 2089.

The Fifth Circuit concluded that *Avena* did not require issuance of a COA in light of *Breard* and its own prior ruling that the Vienna convention did not create an individually enforceable right. The Supreme Court then granted certiorari "to consider two questions: first, whether a federal court is bound by the International Court of Justice's (ICJ) ruling that United States courts must reconsider petitioner José Medellin's claim for relief under the Vienna Convention on Consular Relations, without regard to procedural default doctrines; and second, whether a

---

a. *Breard* characterized as "plainly incorrect for two reasons" the defendant Breard's contention that "the Convention is the 'Supreme law of the land' and thus trumps the procedural default doctrine." First, "it has been recognized in international law that, absent a clear and express statement to the contrary, the procedural rules of the forum State govern the implementation of the treaty in that State. * * * This proposition is embodied in the Vienna Convention itself * * * [in] Article 36(2). * * * Second, although treaties are recognized by our Constitution as the supreme law of the land, that status is no less true of provisions of the Constitution itself, to which rules of procedural default apply. We have held 'that an Act of Congress ... is on full parity with a treaty, and that when a statute which is subsequent in time is inconsistent with a treaty, the statute to the extent of conflict renders the treaty null.' * * * The Vienna Convention—which arguably confers on an individual the right to consular assistance following arrest—has continuously been in effect since 1969. But in 1996, before Breard filed his habeas petition raising claims under the Vienna Convention, Congress enacted the Antiterrorism and Effective Death Penalty Act (AEDPA), which provides that a habeas petitioner alleging that he is held in violation of 'treaties of the United States' will, as a general rule, not be afforded an evidentiary hearing if he 'has failed to develop the factual basis of [the] claim in State court proceedings.' 28 U.S.C. § 2254(a), (e)(2). Breard's ability to obtain relief based on violations of the Vienna Convention is subject to this subsequently enacted rule, just as any claim arising under the United States Constitution would be."

federal court should give effect, as a matter of judicial comity and uniform treaty interpretation, to the ICJ's judgment."

In an *amicus curiae* brief, the Justice Department argued that various habeas corpus doctrines (including recognition of state procedural default rules) precluded granting habeas relief. It further argued that the Vienna Convention does not give a foreign national a judicially enforceable right to challenge his conviction, and that the ICJ interpretation, if contrary, was not binding, as an "ICJ decision, standing alone, establishes solely an international obligation for the United States," and "it is for the president, not the courts, to determine whether the United States should comply with the decision, and if so, how."

The government's brief also suggested that the writ of certiorari should be dismissed as improvidently granted in light of the President's recent determination to comply with the *Avena* decision. It noted: "In this case, the President, the nation's representative in foreign affairs, has determined that the United States will comply with the ICJ decision. Compliance serves to protect the interests of United States citizens abroad, promotes the effective conduct of foreign relations, and underscores the United States' commitment in the international community to the rule of law. Accordingly, in the exercise of his constitutionally based foreign affairs power, and his authority under the United Nations Charter, the President has determined that compliance should be achieved by the enforcement of the ICJ decision in state courts in accordance with principles of comity. That presidential determination, like an executive agreement, has independent legal force and effect, and contrary state rules must give way under the Supremacy Clause. * * * In accordance with the President's determination, petitioner can seek review and reconsideration of his Vienna Convention claim, without regard to state law doctrines of procedural default, by filing an appropriate action in state court for enforcement of the ICJ's decision under principles of comity. State courts will then provide the review and reconsideration that the President has determined is an appropriate means to fulfill this nation's treaty obligations."

The brief further explained that the President's determination was limited to the 51 Mexican nationals who were the subject of the *Avena* ruling, as "ICJ decisions are binding only 'between the parties' and 'in respect to the particular case.' 59 Stat.1062." Thus, the President's determination was "without prejudice to the courts' power to consider afresh in other cases the underlying treaty-interpretation and application issues subsumed in the ICJ's rulings."[b]

The Supreme Court majority, in a per curiam opinion, subsequently dismissed the petition for certiorari as improvidently granted. The majority opinion noted:

b. Indeed, the State Department subsequently announced, on March 7th, 2005, that the United States was withdrawing from the Optional Protocol to the Vienna Convention which establishes the compulsory jurisdiction of the ICJ. See 125 S.Ct. at 2101 (O'Connor, J., dissenting).

"More than two months after we granted certiorari, and a month before oral argument in this case, President Bush issued a memorandum that stated the United States would discharge its international obligations under the *Avena* judgment by 'having State courts give effect to the [ICJ] decision in accordance with general principles of comity in cases filed by the 51 Mexican nationals addressed in that decision.' George W. Bush, Memorandum for the Attorney General (Feb. 28, 2005), App. 2 to Brief for United States as *Amicus Curiae*. Relying on this memorandum and the *Avena* judgment as separate bases for relief that were not available at the time of his first state habeas corpus action, Medellin filed a successive state application for a writ of habeas corpus just four days before oral argument here. That state proceeding may provide Medellin with the review and reconsideration of his Vienna Convention claim that the ICJ required, and that Medellin now seeks in this proceeding. This new development, as well as the factors discussed below, leads us to dismiss the writ of certiorari as improvidently granted.

"There are several threshold issues that could independently preclude federal habeas relief for Medellin, and thus render advisory or academic our consideration of the questions presented. These issues are not free from doubt. * * * First, even accepting, *arguendo*, the ICJ's construction of the Vienna Convention's consular access provisions, a violation of those provisions may not be cognizable in a federal habeas proceeding. In *Reed v. Farley*, 512 U.S. 339 (1994), this Court recognized that a violation of federal statutory rights ranked among the 'nonconstitutional lapses we have held not cognizable in a postconviction proceeding' unless they meet the 'fundamental defect' test announced in our decision in *Hill v. United States*, 368 U.S. 424, 428 (1962). * * * Second, with respect to any claim the state court 'adjudicated on the merits,' habeas relief in federal court is available only if such adjudication 'was contrary to, or an unreasonable application of clearly established Federal law, as determined by the Supreme Court.' The state habeas court, which disposed of the case before the ICJ rendered its judgment in *Avena*, arguably 'adjudicated on the merits' three claims. It found that the Vienna Convention did not create individual, judicially enforceable rights and that state procedural default rules barred Medellin's consular access claim. Finally, and perhaps most importantly, the state trial court found that Medellin 'fail[ed] to show that he was harmed by any lack of notification to the Mexican consulate concerning his arrest for capital murder.' * * * Medellin would have to overcome the deferential standard with regard to all of these findings before obtaining federal habeas relief on his Vienna Convention claim. * * * Third, a habeas corpus petitioner generally cannot enforce a 'new rule' of law. *Teague v. Lane*, 489 U.S. 288 (1989). Before relief could be granted, then, we would be obliged to decide whether or how the *Avena* judgment bears on our ordinary 'new rule' jurisprudence. * * * Fourth, Medellin requires a certificate of appealability in order to pursue the merits of his claim on appeal. 28 U.S.C. § 2253(c)(1). A certificate of appealability may be granted only where there is a 'substantial showing of the denial of a *constitutional* right.' § 2253(c)(2). * * * Fifth, Medellin can seek federal habeas relief only on claims that have been exhausted in state court. See 28 U.S.C. §§ 2254(b)(1)(A), (b)(3). To gain relief based on the President's memorandum or ICJ judgments, Medellin would have to show that he exhausted all available state court remedies.

"In light of the possibility that the Texas courts will provide Medellin with the review he seeks pursuant to the *Avena* judgment and the President's memorandum, and the potential for review in this Court once the Texas courts have heard and decided Medellin's pending action, we think it would be unwise to reach and resolve the multiple hindrances to dispositive answers to the questions here presented. Accordingly, we dismiss the writ as improvidently granted."

Justice O'CONNOR, joined by Justice Stevens, Souter and Breyer dissented. The dissent noted:

"Three specific issues deserve further consideration: (1) whether the International Court of Justice's judgment in Medellin's favor, *Case concerning Avena and Other Mexican Nationals*, is binding on American courts; (2) whether Article 36(1)(b) of the Convention creates a judicially enforceable individual right; and (3) whether Article 36(2) of the Convention sometimes requires state procedural default rules to be set aside so that the treaty can be given 'full effect.' Accordingly, I would vacate the denial of a certificate of appealability and remand for resolution of these issues.

"The Court dismisses the writ (and terminates federal proceedings) on the basis of speculation: Medellin *might* obtain relief in new state court proceedings—because of the President's recent memorandum about whose constitutionality the Court remains rightfully agnostic, or he *might* be unable to secure ultimate relief in federal court—because of questions about whose resolution the Court is likewise, rightfully, undecided. These tentative predictions are not, in my view, reason enough to avoid questions that are as compelling now as they were when we granted a writ of certiorari, and that remain properly before this Court. It seems to me unsound to avoid questions of national importance when they are bound to recur. I respectfully dissent."[c]

c. In a separate dissent, Justice Souter noted that, while he joined Justice O'Connor's dissent, the "best course * * * would be to stay further action for a reasonable time as the Texas Courts decided what to do," therefore keeping the Court "in a position to address promptly the Nation's obligation under the judgment of the ICJ if that should prove necessary." Justice Breyer, in a separate dissent joined by Justice Stevens, also noted that he would have preferred a stay. In a separate, opinion, Justice Ginsburg also noted her preference for a stay, but concurred in the majority's disposition as preferable to the remand proposed by the dissenters.

The dissent noted that the three issues it had posed were of special urgency as "noncompliance with our treaty obligations is especially worrisome in capital cases. As of February 2005, 119 noncitizens from 31 nations were on state death row." It also provided a summary of the arguments that had been presented on these three issues. As to the possible binding effect of the ICJ rulings, it noted:

"Medellin argues that once the United States undertakes a substantive obligation (as it did in the Vienna Convention), and at the same time undertakes to abide by the result of a specified dispute resolution process (as it did by submitting to the ICJ's jurisdiction through the Optional Protocol), it is bound by the rules generated by that process no less than it is by the treaty that is the source of the substantive obligation. In other words, because *Avena* was decided on the back of a self-executing treaty, it must be given effect in our domestic legal system just as the treaty itself must be. Medellin asserts, at bottom, that *Avena*, like a treaty, has the status of supreme law of the land. * * * On the other hand, Texas and the United States argue that the issue turns in large part on how to interpret Article 94(1) of the United Nations Charter, which provides that '[e]ach Member of the United Nations undertakes to comply with the decision of the International Court of Justice in any case to which it is a party.' 59 Stat. 1051. They maintain that the charter imposes an international duty only on our political branches. A contrary result could deprive the Executive of necessary discretion in foreign relations, and may improperly displace this Court's responsibilities to an international body. * * * Medellin [responds] that Article 94(1) cannot answer the question of whether, under domestic law and the Supremacy clause, our courts are bound to comply with the international obligation reflected in *Avena*."

Speaking to the second and third issues, the dissent noted:

"We also granted certiorari on a second, alternative question that asks whether and what weight American courts should give to *Avena*, perhaps for sake of uniform treaty interpretation, even if they are not bound to follow the ICJ's decision. That question can only be answered by holding up the *Avena* interpretation of the treaty against the domestic court's own conclusions, and then deciding how and to what extent the two should be reconciled. Accordingly, the second question presented encompassed two other issues, both pressed and passed upon below, that are themselves debatable and thus grounds for a COA: whether the Vienna Convention creates judicially enforceable rights and whether it sometimes trumps state procedural default rules.

"This Court has remarked that Article 36 of the Vienna Convention 'arguably confers on an individual the right to consular assistance following arrest.' *Breard*. The United States maintains, on the contrary, that Article 36 does not give foreign nationals a judicially enforceable right to consular access. On that theory, a detained foreign national may never complain in court—even in the course of a trial or on direct review—about a state's failure to 'inform the person concerned without delay of his rights under' Article 36. The complainant must be the sending state, and any remedy is political, diplomatic, or between the states in international.

"When called upon to interpret a treaty in a given case or controversy, we give considerable weight to the Executive Branch's understanding of our treaty obligations. * * * But a treaty's meaning is not beyond debate once the Executive has interpreted it. * * * Article 36 of the Vienna Convention on Consular Relations is, as the United States recognizes, a self-executing treaty. * * * Because the Convention is self-executing, then, it s guarantees are susceptible to judicial enforcement just as the provisions of a statute would be. * * *

"To ascertain whether Article 36 confers a right on individuals, we first look to the treaty's text as we would with a statute's. * * * Article 36(1)(b) entails three different obligations for signatory host countries. Their competent authorities shall (1) inform the consul of its nationals' detentions, (2) forward communication from a detained national to his consulate, and (3) 'inform the person concerned without delay of his rights under this sub-paragraph.' Of these, the third exclusively concerns the detained individual, and it is the only obligation expressed in the language of rights. If Article 36(1) conferred no rights on the detained individual, its command to 'inform' the detainee of 'his rights' might be meaningless. Other provisions in the treaty appear to refer back to individual rights. See Art. 36(1)(a); Art. 36(2).

"To be sure, the questions of whether a treaty is self-executing and whether it creates private rights and remedies are analytically distinct. If Article 36(1)(b) imposed only two obligations on signatory countries—to notify the consul and forward correspondence—then Medellin could not invoke the treaty as a source of personal rights by virtue of its self-executing character. But the treaty goes further—imposing an obligation to inform the individual of his rights in the treaty. And if a statute were to provide, for example, that arresting authorities 'shall inform a detained person without delay of his right to counsel,' I question whether more would be required before a defendant could invoke that statute to complain in court if he had not been so informed.

"This Court has repeatedly enforced treaty-based rights of individual foreigners, allowing them to assert claims arising from various treaties. These treaties, often regarding reciprocity in commerce and navigation, do not share any special magic words. Their rights-conferring language is arguably no clearer than the Vienna Convention's is, and they do not specify judicial enforcement. * * * Likewise, the United

States acknowledges with approval that other provisions of the Vienna Convention, which relate to consular privileges and immunities, have been the source of judicially enforced individual rights. * * *

"There are plausible arguments for the Government's construction of Article 36. * * * The preamble to the Vienna Convention, for example, states that 'the purpose of such privileges and immunities [contained in the treaty] is not to benefit individuals but to ensure the efficient performance of functions by consular posts on behalf of their respective States.' 21 U.S.T., at 79. Moreover, State Department and congressional statements contemporaneous with the treaty's ratification say or indicate that the Convention would not require significant departures from existing practice. * * * The United States interprets such statements to mean that the political branches did not contemplate a role for the treaty in ordinary criminal proceedings. * * *

"Of course, even if the Convention does confer individual rights, there remains the question of whether such rights can be forfeited according to state procedural default rules. Article 36(2) of the treaty provides: 'The rights referred to in paragraph 1 of this Article shall be exercised in conformity with the laws and regulations of the receiving State, subject to the proviso, however, that the said laws and regulations must enable full effect to be given to the purpose for which the rights accorded under this Article are intended.' Medellin contends that this provision requires that state procedural default rules sometimes be set aside so that the treaty can be given 'full effect.' In *Breard*, in the course of denying a stay of imminent execution and accompanying petitions, we concluded that the petitioner had defaulted his Article 36 claim by failing to raise it in state court prior to seeking collateral relief in federal court. Subsequently in *Avena*, as explained above, the International Court of Justice interpreted Article 36(2) differently. In the past the Court has revisited its interpretation of a treaty when new international law has come to light. See *United States v. Percheman*, 7 Pet. 51, 89 (1833). Even if *Avena* is not itself a binding rule of decision in this case, it may at least be occasion to return to the question of Article 36(2)'s implications for procedural default."

Chapter 3

SOME GENERAL REFLECTIONS ON LAW ENFORCEMENT OFFICIALS, THE LEGISLATURES, THE COURTS AND THE CRIMINAL PROCESS

11th ed., p. 69; after the extract from Professor Stuntz, add:

DAVID H. BAYLEY—LAW ENFORCEMENT AND THE RULE OF LAW: IS THERE A TRADEOFF?
2 Criminology & Public Policy 133–35, 146–48 (2002).

The public in every society worries about the integrity of its police. Some have better reasons for this than do others. But everywhere, regardless of the objective incidence of misbehavior, people become easily concerned that the police do not abide by the law and misuse their power. At the same time, it is my experience that the police in every society believe that they must occasionally cut legal corners in order to provide effective protection to that very same public. Among police there is a nearly universal mindset that abiding by the rule-of-law and adhering to recognized standards of human rights is sometimes too restrictive, preventing victims from obtaining justice, allowing criminals to go unpunished, and placing society at unacceptable risk.

This mindset of the police and the behavior it engenders, shows up in a number of ways. Police complain almost everywhere about the uncertainties of criminal justice processing—slipshod prosecutions, inept and venal judges, unwilling witnesses, cumbersome procedures, and laws loaded in favor of suspects. Police are regularly accused, even in countries with human rights records that are good by world standards, of engaging in unjustified stops and seizures. They have been found to fabricate evidence and testify falsely in order to gain convictions. So common did these practices seem to be in New York City recently that the Mollen Commission coined a new word to describe them—"testilying" (1994). Complaints of excessive use of force ostensibly to control crime are also common around the world, whether to obtain confessions from unwilling suspects or to intimidate would-be criminals. Intimidation is especially disturbing when it is directed at whole classes of individuals, as when police say that "those people only understand force" or "people like that" have to be taught respect for the law.

Although the public is most concerned about dramatic infringements of the rule-of-law, such as brutality, planting false evidence, and lying in courts, most of the liberties taken by police are more mundane, routinized, and difficult to detect. For example, a Texas police officer told me how he had developed a challenge-proof method for stopping motorists on suspicion, without a shred of probable cause. After stopping a car, he would thump the left rear fender with his hand as he walked up to it. If the driver asked why the officer had stopped him, the officer would say that the left rear taillight was not working. If the driver checked for himself, which was unusual, the officer would say that his thump must have restored the connection and he would advise the driver, in the interest of safety, to get it checked at a service station. Thus, an illegal stop could be disguised as helpful assistance.

The usual explanation for such behavior is that the police do not understand what is right and wrong; that the values of the police need changing to emphasize more scrupulous adherence to law and to human rights. It follows, then, that the solution is to raise the normative consciousness of the police, to convince them that they have a duty both to uphold the rule-of-law and to provide public safety. I think this diagnosis is mistaken. The problem is not normative, but cognitive. The police generally know what behaviors are right and wrong. The problem is that they believe that the violation of law and of human rights is sometimes required for effective law enforcement. * * *

If my thesis is correct, police must be shown that the costs to them of violating the rule-of-law are greater than are the benefits, that doing right is not only commendable normatively, but also furthers their own collective self-interest. Moral exhortation alone is unpersuasive because it does not address the tradeoffs that police are convinced they face. This explains why, in my experience, lecturing to the police about human rights is met with palpable lack of interest—eyelids droop, note-taking stops, and faces become wooden. The police act as if they know all that, which in many cases is true. The problem is that lectures on human rights are a necessary but not sufficient corrective to the dilemma police officers face. What is needed instead is an evidence-based demonstration that rectitude is useful to the police in fulfilling their mission of preventing and controlling crime. This sort of argument will get their attention. * * *

[Professor Bayley then sets forth and discusses "seven arguments [that] can be made that violating the rule-of-law does not serve the interests of the police: (1) it produces very small, if any, gains in reducing criminality; (2) it impairs crime control by alienating the public; (3) it weakens the authority of law; (4) it "scapegoats" the police, *i.e.*, it not only causes the police not to "take responsibility for crime onto themselves," but to "deflect attention to themselves and away from the negligence of others"; (5) it jeopardizes criminal prosecutions and, because of lawsuits, wastes community resources; and (7) places police officers "at risk for the presumed sake of public safety."]

Conclusion

In democratic societies, the objective of law enforcement is to maximize both deterrent criminal effectiveness and conformity to the rule-of-law based on recognized human rights. The common assumption is that these goals are in conflict. I have given seven reasons why I believe this view is mistaken. * * *

If my assumption is correct that police often violate the rule-of-law because they believe it improves their ability to control and prevent crime, then gathering additional evidence that it does not is an important undertaking. But it is clearly not a sufficient response to the problem. The information must be used so that it changes behavior. How is this to be done?

One possibility would be to broaden the approach to the teaching of law and ethics to police recruits. In addition to instructing them in the requirements of due process and the value of the rule-of-law in democratic societies, they would be presented with the utilitarian arguments made in this paper. In effect, the tradeoff problem would be met head on with police officers at the very beginning of their careers.

At the same time, I am doubtful whether changing the cognitive understanding of police officers individually will be sufficient to offset the occupational culture within which they work. It is unrealistic to expect individual police officers, no matter how well instructed in the arguments made in this essay, to stand against the crime-control understandings and expectations of their colleagues, the public, and their senior officers. The more effective strategy, then, for changing the mindset of police officers is to convince the leaders of police agencies that violating the rule-of-law is not a sound law enforcement strategy, so that they will then be emboldened to change the moral tone, disciplinary mechanisms, management priorities, and career incentives within the organization. Research has shown time and again that organizations are the most powerful determinants of the behavior of the people within them. Cognitive instruction of the kind suggested here should be focused initially and repeatedly on senior police executives. If they can be convinced that violating the rule-of-law is not useful in achieving the goals of police organizations, they will find the means to convince the rank-and-file.

The conclusion of this essay, then, supported by current social science research, is that violating the rule-of-law in order to control crime is mistaken and that the best place to start in reorienting police practices is with the managers of police agencies.

11th ed., p. 76; end of chapter, add:

DAVID A. HARRIS—GOOD COPS
pp. 1–12 (2005).

When U.S. Attorney General John Ashcroft and his Department of Justice pushed Congress into enacting the sweeping USA PATRIOT Act just weeks after September 11, 2001, they also set in motion another set of initiatives. These changes—call them "Ashcroft policing"—were designed to alter the role of local police forces. Although they were among the least visible of the Ashcroft Justice Department's antiterror efforts, they have the potential to affect public safety and the quality of American life in important and dramatic ways—ways that could, ironically, make safety and security against terrorism even more difficult to achieve.

The gist of Ashcroft's approach involves transforming state and local police agencies into an adjunct force in the federal effort to fight the war on terror, much as the Department of Justice did in the 1980s when it recruited state and local police into the war on drugs. Two key features of Ashcroft's policing in particular—the involvement of local police in immigration control (formerly the almost exclusive province of the federal government) and the police questioning of "nonsuspects"—represent major departures from traditional policing.

Ashcroft policing shows a lack of understanding of the foundations of good police work. Worse yet, these practices come at a point in time when the whole field of policing is poised to move in a very different, potentially far more productive, direction. Ashcroft policing runs counter to this new, successful approach, which I will call "preventive policing." Preventive policing envisions police forces that make it a priority to stop crime before it occurs rather than simply to just respond to crime after the fact. Preventive policing incorporates innovative, forward-thinking methods of law enforcement that have been productively implemented in cities and towns across the country. Where Ashcroft policing shifts away from field-tested, community-based policing strategies, rendering the police less effective against both terrorism and garden-variety crime, preventive policing collects the best aspects of successful, progressive policing and combines them into a plan that presents real hope for reducing crime, preserving rights, and enhancing civil society in the twenty-first century.

Policing Immigrants

[In] the wake of the 9/11 attacks, many called for tougher border controls and a dramatic tightening of immigration regulations. Every one of the nineteen suicide hijackers responsible for the 9/11 attacks had come from foreign countries. Thus it just seemed to make sense to the Department of Justice and to many Americans that the country should ratchet up immigration enforcement.

In April 2002, word came that the U.S. Department of Justice would begin to ask local police to enforce federal immigration law for the first time. This represented a real departure from past procedure. Since the passage of the Immigration and Nationality Act in 1952, local police had only the most limited authority to enforce immigration law. * * *

Attorney General Ashcroft's Office of Legal Counsel reversed this long-standing policy in one stroke, declaring that state and local police had "inherent authority" to join the federal government in enforcing civil immigration law. The department went ahead with this significant policy shift despite the fact that laws of many states actually prohibited their police from making arrests for these very infractions. * * *

Surely opposition from community activists and the press could not have surprised top officials in the Department of Justice; they might well have regarded it as nothing more than noise from the "usual suspects." But one can easily imagine the surprise in the attorney general's office at comments that quickly began to come from an unexpected source: law enforcement agencies themselves. Scores of state and local law enforcement leaders, who might have been expected to applaud a proposal to give them greater authority to arrest and detain people in the war on terror, said they wanted no part of immigration enforcement.

[The] most compelling reason to not involve them in enforcing immigration law, local police said, was that acting as surrogates of the Immigration and Naturalization Service (INS) would destroy their ability to do the critical job of building connections with immigrant communities. If police began patrolling for immigration irregularities, immigrants would quickly come to fear them, law enforcement officials argued, ruining the trust-based relationships that have long helped police fight crime on the community level. * * *

[P]erhaps the most stinging criticism of the attorney general's local police immigration enforcement initiative came from two men with long experience fighting terrorism at the highest levels. In an appearance in Washington, D.C., in April 2003, Harry Brandon, former director of counterterrorism operations for the FBI, and Vince Cannistraro, former head of counterterrorism for the CIA, said unequivocally that most of the immigration changes made by the U.S. Department of Justice since September 11, 2001, would *not* have prevented the attacks. Further, they said, these changes had also done little to make the nation safer since the Department of Justice put them in place. Instead of working with immigrant communities as partners, Cannistraro said, "we are using immigration enforcement as a proxy for law enforcement at a time when we need the help of those communities." What might have prevented the 9/11 attacks, Cannistraro said, would have been better networks of contacts among members of law enforcement and immigrant communities, which might have resulted in the passing on of crucial information to law enforcement.

POLICING "NONSUSPECTS"

Just a few months after 9/11, Ashcroft's Department of Justice announced another new role for local police: helping federal agents to identify and questions large numbers of noncriminal immigrants. [Given] their demographic similarity to the September 11 hijackers, the department thought that the men might know something—even things they did not realize were important—that might produce leads or otherwise assist in preventing and investigating terrorism. Once again, Ashcroft policing contravened the fundamental tenets that years of law enforcement, intelligence experience, and intensive research had shown to be at the heart of effective crime prevention.

In response, local police weighed in. Officials in Portland, Oregon, and in Detroit, for example, announced that they would not participate in the interviewing process. Andrew Kirkland, then Portland's acting chief of police, said flatly that his department could not participate because state law did not allow police questioning of persons not suspected of involvement in crime. * * * Benny Napoleon, then Detroit's chief of police, viewed the Department of Justice's interviewing plans as unconstitutional.

[What] these local police were actually most concerned about was the very real danger that interviewing thousands of nonsuspects would jeopardize their hard-won relationships with immigrant communities. * * * Even harsher criticism of the roughly five thousand "nonsuspect" interviews came from eight prominent former federal law enforcement officers, including William Webster, former head of both the FBI and the CIA. Rather than hide behind anonymous comments, as many former officials in Washington might have, all eight felt strongly enough to speak out personally in the press against the Justice Department's mass questioning initiative. The FBI had run many antiterrorism investigations in the past, they said, and had successfully headed off a significant number of planned terrorist attacks. From a law enforcement point of view, the possible benefits of the interviews did not offset the massive squandering of goodwill and relationships with the community. * * *

Tactics similar to the Ashcroft antiterrorism initiatives had been abandoned by federal law enforcement in the late 1970s, the officials said, because they proved ineffective at preventing terrorism and led to abuses of civil liberties. * * * Yet despite this criticism—from those with years of law enforcement experience with both street-level anticrime work and federal antitterrorism operations—the Department of Justice proceeded with the mass questioning. And, despite little evidence of any substantive gains from the initial round of interviews, the department actually expanded the program; it began to interview *another* three thousand young Arab men in the spring of 2002. In a gross miscalculation, the Department of Justice traded state and local law enforcement's connections to the communities they served—and the potential for intelligence-gathering those ties provided—for a hostile approach to collecting information that runs contrary to everything we know about effective policing of crime or of terrorism.

Chapter 4

THE RIGHT TO COUNSEL, "BY FAR THE MOST PERVASIVE" RIGHT OF THE ACCUSED; EQUALITY AND THE ADVERSARY SYSTEM

SECTION 2. THE *GRIFFIN-DOUGLAS* "EQUALITY" PRINCIPLE

11th ed., p. 105; replace old Note 4 with the following:

4. When appointed counsel is not provided for indigent defendants seeking first-tier discretionary appellate review of guilty pleas or nolo contendere pleas, what case governs, Ross or Douglas? Consider HALBERT v. MICHIGAN, 125 S.Ct. 2582 (2005), which arose as follows:

Michigan has a two-tier appellate system. The Michigan Supreme Court hears appeals by leave only. The intermediate Court of Appeals adjudicates appeals as of right from criminal convictions, *except* that those convicted on guilty or *nolo contendere* pleas must apply for leave to appeal. In *People v. Bulger*, 614 N.W.2d 103 (2000), the Michigan Supreme Court held that neither the Equal Protection nor Due Process clauses of the Fourteenth Amendment requires that counsel be appointed for plea-convicted defendants seeking review in the Court of Appeals. *Bulger* was based on the following reasons: review of such pleas is "discretionary"; plea proceedings are simpler and more routine than trials, and, by entering a plea, a defendant "accedes to the state's fundamental interest in finality."

Petitioner Halbert pled *nolo contendere* to two counts of criminal sexual conduct. The trial court advised him of instances when it "must" or "may" appoint counsel, but failed to tell him that it would not appoint appellate counsel in his case. Petitioner asked the trial court to appoint counsel to help him prepare an application for leave to appeal to the Court of Appeals, maintaining that his sentence had been misscored and that he needed counsel to preserve the issue before undertaking an appeal. The trial court denied this motion. Petitioner then filed a *pro se* application for leave to appeal, claiming sentencing error and ineffective assistance of counsel. The Court of Appeals denied leave for "lack of merit in the grounds presented." The Michigan Supreme Court declined review.

A 6–3 majority of the Supreme Court, per GINSBURG, J., vacated the judgment of the Michigan Court of Appeals:

"In *Ross*, [in not extending the rationale of *Douglas* to a second-tier discretionary appeal, we explained that the] North Carolina Supreme Court * * * does not sit as an error-correction instance. [We also pointed out that] a defendant who had already benefitted from counsel's aid in a first-tier appeal as of right would have, 'at the very least, a transcript or other record of trial proceedings, a brief on his behalf in the Court of Appeals setting forth his claims of error, and in many cases an opinion by the Court of Appeals disposing of his case.'

"Petitioner Halbert's case is framed by two prior decisions of this Court concerning state-funded appellate counsel, *Douglas* and *Ross*. [With] which of those decisions should the instant case be aligned? We hold that *Douglas* provides the controlling instruction. Two aspects of the Michigan Court of Appeals' process following plea-based convictions lead us to that conclusion. First, in determining how to dispose of an application for leave to appeal, Michigan's intermediate appellate court looks to the merits of the claims made in the application. Second, indigent defendants pursuing first-tier review in the Court of Appeals are generally ill equipped to represent themselves.

"[Whether] formally categorized as the decision of an appeal or the disposal of a leave application, the Court of Appeals' ruling on a plea-convicted defendant's claims provides the first, and likely the only, direct review the defendant's conviction and sentence will receive. Parties like Halbert, however, are disarmed in their endeavor to gain first-tier review. As the Court in *Ross* emphasized, a defendant seeking State Supreme Court review following a first-tier appeal as of right earlier had the assistance of appellate counsel. The attorney appointed to serve at the intermediate appellate court level will have reviewed the trial court record, researched the legal issues, and prepared a brief reflecting that review and research. The defendant seeking second-tier review may also be armed with an opinion of the intermediate appellate court addressing the issues counsel raised. A first-tier review applicant, forced to act *pro se*, will face a record unreviewed by appellate counsel, and will be equipped with no attorney's brief prepared for, or reasoned opinion by, a court of review. * * *

"Persons in Halbert's situation are particularly handicapped as self-representatives. As recounted earlier this Term, '[a]pproximately 70% of indigent defendants represented by appointed counsel plead guilty, and 70% of those convicted are incarcerated.' '[Sixty-eight percent] of the state prison populatio[n] did not complete high school, and many lack the most basic literacy skills.' '[S]even out of ten inmates fall in the lowest two out of five levels of literacy—marked by an inability to do such basic tasks as write a brief letter to explain an error on a credit card bill, use a bus schedule, or state in writing an argument made in a lengthy newspaper article.' Many, Halbert among them, have learning disabilities and mental impairments. * * *

"Navigating the appellate process without a lawyer's assistance is a perilous endeavor for a layperson, and well beyond the competence of individuals, like Halbert, who have little education, learning disabilities, and mental impairments.

"[While] the State has a legitimate interest in reducing the workload of its judiciary, providing indigents with appellate counsel will yield applications easier to comprehend. Michigan's Court of Appeals would still have recourse to summary denials of leave applications in cases not warranting further review. And when a defendant's case presents no genuinely arguable issue, appointed counsel may so inform the court. See *Anders* v. *California*, [11th ed., p. 109]. * * *

"Michigan contends that, even if Halbert had a constitutionally guaranteed right to appointed counsel for first-level appellate review, he waived that right by entering a plea of *nolo contendere*. We disagree. At the time he entered his plea, Halbert, in common with other defendants convicted on their pleas, had no recognized right to appointed appellate counsel he could elect to forgo. Moreover, [the] trial court did not tell Halbert, simply and directly, that in his case, there would be no access to appointed counsel. * * *."

Justice THOMAS, joined by SCALIA, J., and REHNQUIST, C.J., except for Part III–B–3, dissented:

"[The majority] finds that all plea-convicted indigent defendants have the right to appellate counsel when seeking leave to appeal. The majority does not say where in the Constitution that right is located—the Due Process Clause, the Equal Protection Clause, or some purported confluence of the two. * * *

"Instead, the majority pins its hopes on a single case: *Douglas* v. *California*. *Douglas*, however, does not support extending the right to counsel to any form of discretionary review, as *Ross* and later cases make clear. Moreover, Michigan has not engaged in the sort of invidious discrimination against indigent defendants that *Douglas* condemns. Michigan has done no more than recognize the undeniable difference between defendants who plead guilty and those who maintain their innocence, in an attempt to divert resources from largely frivolous appeals to more meritorious ones. The majority substitutes its own policy preference for that of Michigan voters, and it does so based on an untenable reading of *Douglas*.

" * * * Like the defendant in *Douglas*, Halbert requests appointed counsel for an initial appeal before an intermediate appellate court. But like the defendant in *Ross*, Halbert requests appointed counsel for an appeal that is discretionary, not as of right. Crucially, however, *Douglas* noted that its decision extended only to initial appeals *as of right*—and later cases have repeatedly reaffirmed that understanding. This Court has never required States to appoint counsel for discretionary review. * * *

"Just as important, the rationale of *Douglas* does not support extending the right to counsel to this particular form of discretionary review. Admittedly, the precise rationale for the *Griffin/Douglas* line of cases has never been made explicit. Those cases, however, have a common theme. States may not impose financial barriers that preclude indigent defendants from securing appellate review altogether.

"[Far] from being an 'arbitrary' or 'unreasoned' distinction, Michigan's differentiation between defendants convicted at trial and defendants convicted by plea is sensible. [The] danger of wrongful convictions is less significant than in *Douglas*. In *Douglas*, California preliminarily denied counsel to all indigent defendants, regardless of whether they maintained their innocence at trial or conceded their guilt by plea. Here, Michigan preliminarily denies paid counsel only to indigent defendants who admit or do not contest their guilt.

"[The] majority does not attempt to demonstrate that Michigan's system is the sort of 'unreasoned' discrimination against indigent defendants *Douglas* prohibits. Instead, the majority says that this case is earmarked by two considerations that were also key to this Court's decision in *Douglas*: First, when a plea-convicted defendant seeks leave to appeal, the Michigan Court of Appeals adjudicates the leave application with reference to the merits. Second, the plea-convicted defendant who seeks leave to appeal is 'generally ill equipped to represent [himself].' Neither of these arguments is correct.

"[The] distinction that *Douglas* drew, however, was not between appellate systems that involve 'some evaluation of the merits of the applicant's claims' and those that do not, but instead between discretionary and mandatory review. Of course the California intermediate courts in *Douglas* evaluated cases on their merits: These courts were hearing appeals as of right.

"The Michigan Court of Appeals probably does consider 'the merits of the applicant's claims' in exercising its discretion; so do other courts of discretionary review, including this Court. For instance, this Court would be unlikely to grant a case to announce a rule that could not alter the case's disposition, or to correct an error that had not affected the proceedings below. This Court often considers whether errors are worth correcting in both plenary and summary dispositions. None of this converts discretionary, error-noticing review into mandatory, error-correcting review. * * *

"Lacking support in this Court's cases, the majority effects a not-so-subtle shift from whether the record is adequate to enable discretionary review to whether plea-convicted defendants are generally able to '[n]aviga[te] the appellate process without a lawyer's assistance.' This rationale lacks any stopping point. *Pro se* defendants may have difficulty navigating discretionary direct appeals and collateral proceedings, but this Court has never extended the right to counsel beyond first appeals as of right. The majority does not demonstrate that *pro se* defendants have any more difficulty filing leave applications before the Michigan courts than, say, filing petitions for certiorari before this Court.

III-A

"Legal rights, even constitutional ones, are presumptively waivable. *United States* v. *Mezzanatto,* [11th ed., p. 1323]. [The] presumption of waivability holds true for the right to counsel. This Court has held repeatedly that a defendant may waive that right, both at trial and at the entry of a guilty plea, so long as the waiver is knowing and intelligent. Michigan seeks a waiver no more extensive than those this Court has already sanctioned at other stages of a criminal proceeding: It asks defendants convicted by plea to waive the right to appointed counsel on appeal.

"There may be some nonwaivable rights: ones 'so fundamental to the reliability of the factfinding process that they may never be waived without irreparably discrediting the federal courts.' *Mezzanatto*. The right to appointed counsel on discretionary appeal from a guilty plea, however, is not one of them. Even assuming that the assistance of appellate counsel enhances the reliability of the factfinding process by correcting errors in that process, it cannot possibly be so fundamental to the process that its absence 'irreparably discredit[s]' the federal courts, particularly since the Constitution guarantees no right to an appeal at all. Furthermore, [the] record of a plea proceeding is fully adequate to enable discretionary review and, in turn, to permit the correction of errors in the factfinding process when necessary. [And,] finally, even if the reliability of the appellate process rather than the trial process is the relevant consideration here, the assistance of appellate counsel is not so fundamental to the appellate process that its absence deprives that process of meaning.

"Petitioner emphasizes the difficulty of the choice to which Michigan's statute puts criminal defendants: proceed to trial and guarantee the appointment of appellate counsel, or plead guilty and forgo that benefit. But this Court has repeatedly recognized that difficult choices are a necessary by-product of the criminal justice system, and of plea bargaining in particular. Michigan's waiver requires a choice no more demanding than other criminal defendants regularly face. * * *

III–B–3

"In this case, the plea colloquy shows that Halbert's waiver was knowing and intelligent, and that any deficiency in the plea colloquy was harmless. [Justice Thomas then closely examines the plea colloquy.] There can be no serious claim that Halbert would have changed his plea had the court provided further information."

Chapter 5
THE ROLE OF COUNSEL

SECTION 4. THE RIGHT TO "EFFECTIVE ASSISTANCE OF COUNSEL"

11th ed., p. 180; after *Wiggins v. Smith*, add:

9. The Court was sharply divided once again in its latest duty-to-investigate ruling.

ROMPILLA v. BEARD
___ U.S. ___, 125 S.Ct. 2456, ___ L.Ed.2d ___ (2005).

Justice SOUTER delivered the opinion of the Court.

This case calls for specific application of the standard of reasonable competence required on the part of defense counsel by the Sixth Amendment. We hold that even when a capital defendant's family members and the defendant himself have suggested that no mitigating evidence is available, his lawyer is bound to make reasonable efforts to obtain and review material that counsel knows the prosecution will probably rely on as evidence of aggravation at the sentencing phase of trial. * * *

Rompilla was indicted for murder and [other] offenses [related to the 1988 killing of James Scanlon] , and the Commonwealth gave notice of intent to ask for the death penalty. Two public defenders were assigned to the case. * * * The jury at the guilt phase of trial found Rompilla guilty on all counts, and during the ensuing penalty phase, the prosecutor * * * [established] three aggravating factors to justify a death sentence: [1] that the murder was committed in the course of another felony; [2] that the murder was committed by torture; and [3] that Rompilla had a significant history of felony convictions indicating the use or threat of violence. * * * Rompilla's evidence in mitigation consisted of relatively brief testimony: five of his family members argued in effect for residual doubt, and beseeched the jury for mercy, saying that they believed Rompilla was innocent and a good man. Rompilla's 14-year-old son testified that he loved his father and would visit him in prison. The jury acknowledged this evidence to the point of finding, as two factors in mitigation, that Rompilla's son had testified on his behalf and that rehabilitation was possible. But the jurors assigned the greater weight to the aggravating factors, and sentenced Rompilla to death. The Supreme Court of Pennsylvania affirmed both conviction and sentence.

In December 1995, with new lawyers, Rompilla filed claims under the Pennsylvania Post Conviction Relief Act, including ineffective assistance by trial counsel in failing to present significant mitigating evidence about Rompilla's childhood, mental capacity and health, and alcoholism. The postconviction court found that trial counsel had done enough to investigate the possibilities of a mitigation case, and the Supreme Court of Pennsylvania affirmed the denial of relief. * * * Rompilla then petitioned for a writ of habeas corpus under 28 U.S.C. § 2254 in Federal District Court, raising claims that included inadequate representation. The District Court found that the State Supreme Court had unreasonably applied *Strickland v. Washington,* [11th ed., p. 158] as to the penalty phase of the trial, and granted relief for ineffective assistance of counsel. * * * A divided Third Circuit panel reversed. The majority found nothing unreasonable in the state court's application of *Strickland,* given defense counsel's efforts to uncover mitigation material, which included interviewing Rompilla and certain family members, as well as consultation with three mental health experts. * * * The panel thus distinguished Rompilla's case from *Wiggins v. Smith* [11th ed., p. 176]. Whereas Wiggins's counsel failed to investigate adequately, to the point even of ignoring the leads their limited enquiry yielded, the Court of Appeals saw the Rompilla investigation as going far enough to leave counsel with reason for thinking further efforts would not be a wise use of the limited resources they had. But Judge Sloviter's dissent stressed that trial counsel's failure to obtain relevant records on Rompilla's background was owing to the lawyers' unreasonable reliance on family members and medical experts to tell them what records might be useful. The Third Circuit denied rehearing en banc by a vote of 6 to 5. * * * We granted certiorari, and now reverse.

Under 28 U.S.C. § 2254, Rompilla's entitlement to federal habeas relief turns on showing that the state court's resolution of his claim of ineffective assistance of counsel under *Strickland* "resulted in a decision that was contrary to, or involved an unreasonable application of, clearly established Federal law, as determined by the Supreme Court of the United States," § 2254(d)(1). An "unreasonable application" occurs when a state court " 'identifies the correct governing legal principle from this Court's decisions but unreasonably applies that principle to the facts' of petitioner's case." *Wiggins v. Smith.* That is, "the state court's decision must have been [not only] incorrect or erroneous [but] objectively unreasonable." Ibid

Ineffective assistance under *Strickland* is deficient performance by counsel resulting in prejudice, with performance being measured against an "objective standard of reasonableness" * * * "under prevailing professional norms." This case, like some others recently, looks to norms of adequate investigation in preparing for the sentencing phase of a capital trial, when defense counsel's job is to counter the State's evidence of aggravated culpability with evidence in mitigation. In judging the defense's investigation, as in applying *Strickland* generally, hindsight is discounted by pegging adequacy to "counsel's perspective at the time" investigative decisions are made, and by giving a "heavy measure of deference to counsel's judgments." *Strickland.*

A standard of reasonableness applied as if one stood in counsel's shoes spawns few hard-edged rules, and the merits of a number of counsel's choices in this case are subject to fair debate. This is not a case in which defense counsel simply ignored their obligation to find mitigating evidence, and their workload as busy public defenders did not keep them from making a number of efforts, including interviews with Rompilla and some members of his family, and examinations of reports by three mental health experts who gave opinions at the guilt phase. None of the sources proved particularly helpful.

Rompilla's own contributions to any mitigation case were minimal. Counsel found him uninterested in helping, as on their visit to his prison to go over a proposed mitigation strategy, when Rompilla told them he was "bored being here listening" and returned to his cell. To questions about childhood and schooling, his answers indicated they had been normal, save for quitting school in the ninth grade. There were times when Rompilla was even actively obstructive by sending counsel off on false leads.

The lawyers also spoke with five members of Rompilla's family (his former wife, two brothers, a sister-in-law, and his son), and counsel testified [in the postconviction proceedings] that they developed a good relationship with the family in the course of their representation. The state postconviction court found that counsel spoke to the relatives in a "detailed manner," attempting to unearth mitigating information, although the weight of this finding is qualified by the lawyers' concession that "the overwhelming response from the family was that they didn't really feel as though they knew him all that well since he had spent the majority of his adult years and some of his childhood years in custody." Defense counsel also said that because the family was "coming from the position that [Rompilla] was innocent ... they weren't looking for reasons for why he might have done this."

The third and final source tapped for mitigating material was the cadre of three mental health witnesses who were asked to look into Rompilla's mental state as of the time of the offense and his competency to stand trial. * * * [B]ut their reports revealed "nothing useful" to Rompilla's case, and the lawyers consequently did not go to any other historical source that might have cast light on Rompilla's mental condition.

When new counsel entered the case to raise Rompilla's postconviction claims, however, they identified a number of likely avenues the trial lawyers could fruitfully have followed in building a mitigation case. School records are one example, which trial counsel never examined in spite of the professed unfamiliarity of the several family members with

Rompilla's childhood, and despite counsel's knowledge that Rompilla left school after the ninth grade. Others examples are records of Rompilla's juvenile and adult incarcerations, which counsel did not consult, although they were aware of their client's criminal record. And while counsel knew from police reports provided in pretrial discovery that Rompilla had been drinking heavily at the time of his offense, and although one of the mental health experts reported that Rompilla's troubles with alcohol merited further investigation, counsel did not look for evidence of a history of dependence on alcohol that might have extenuating significance.

Before us, trial counsel and the Commonwealth respond to these unexplored possibilities by emphasizing this Court's recognition that the duty to investigate does not force defense lawyers to scour the globe on the off-chance something will turn up; reasonably diligent counsel may draw a line when they have good reason to think further investigation would be a waste. See *Wiggins v. Smith,* (further investigation excusable where counsel has evidence suggesting it would be fruitless); *Strickland v. Washington,* (counsel could "reasonably surmise . . . that character and psychological evidence would be of little help"); *Burger v. Kemp,* [11th ed., fn.a., p.179] (limited investigation reasonable because all witnesses brought to counsel's attention provided predominantly harmful information). The Commonwealth argues that the information trial counsel gathered from Rompilla and the other sources gave them sound reason to think it would have been pointless to spend time and money on the additional investigation espoused by postconviction counsel, and we can say that there is room for debate about trial counsel's obligation to follow at least some of those potential lines of enquiry. There is no need to say more, however, for a further point is clear and dispositive: the lawyers were deficient in failing to examine the court file on Rompilla's prior conviction.

There is an obvious reason that the failure to examine Rompilla's prior conviction file fell below the level of reasonable performance. Counsel knew that the Commonwealth intended to seek the death penalty by proving Rompilla had a significant history of felony convictions indicating the use or threat of violence, an aggravator under state law. Counsel further knew that the Commonwealth would attempt to establish this history by proving Rompilla's prior conviction for rape and assault, and would emphasize his violent character by introducing a transcript of the rape victim's testimony given in that earlier trial. There is no question that defense counsel were on notice, since they acknowledge that a "plea letter," written by one of them four days prior to trial, mentioned the prosecutor's plans. It is also undisputed that the prior conviction file was a public document, readily available for the asking at the very courthouse where Rompilla was to be tried.

It is clear, however, that defense counsel did not look at any part of that file, including the transcript, until warned by the prosecution a second time, [in] a colloquy the day before the evidentiary sentencing phase began, [that] the prosecutor * * * would present the transcript of the victim's testimony to establish the prior conviction. [In that discussion, defense counsel stated that she would need a copy of the transcript "to review" what the prosecutor intended to "read from", and clearly indicated that she had not previously seen the transcript.] * * * [C]rucially, even after obtaining the transcript of the victim's testimony on the eve of the sentencing hearing, counsel apparently examined none of the other material in the file.[3]

With every effort to view the facts as a defense lawyer would have done at the time, it is difficult to see how counsel could have failed to realize that without examining the readily available file they were seriously compromising their opportunity to respond to a case for aggravation. The prosecution was going to use the dramatic facts of a similar prior offense, and Rompilla's counsel had a duty to make all reasonable efforts to learn what they could about the offense. Reasonable efforts certainly included obtaining the Commonwealth's own readily available file on the prior conviction to learn what the Commonwealth knew about the crime, to discover any mitigating evidence the Commonwealth would downplay and to anticipate the details of the aggravating evidence the Commonwealth would emphasize.[4] Without making reasonable efforts to review the file, defense counsel could have had no hope of knowing whether the prosecution was quoting selectively from the transcript, or whether there were circumstances extenuating the behavior described by the victim. The obligation to get the file was particularly pressing here owing to the similarity of the violent prior offense to the crime charged and Rompilla's sentencing strategy stressing residual doubt. Without making efforts to learn the details and rebut the relevance of the earlier crime, a convincing argument for residual doubt was certainly beyond any hope.[5]

3. Defense counsel also stated at the postconviction hearing that she believed at some point she had looked at some files regarding that prior conviction and that she was familiar with the particulars of the case. But she could not recall what the files were or how she obtained them. In addition, counsel apparently obtained Rompilla's rap sheet, which showed that he had prior convictions, including the one for rape. At oral argument, the United States, arguing as an *amicus* in support of Pennsylvania, maintained that counsel had fulfilled their obligations to investigate the prior conviction by obtaining the rap sheet. But this cannot be so. The rap sheet would reveal only the charges and dispositions, being no reasonable substitute for the prior conviction file. The dissent nonetheless concludes on this evidence that counsel knew all they needed to know about the prior conviction. Post at [Supp. p. 35]. Given counsel's limited investigation into the prior conviction, the dissent's parsing of the record seems generous to a fault.

4. The ease with which counsel could examine the entire file makes application of this standard correspondingly easy. Suffice it to say that when the State has warehouses of records available in a particular case, review of counsel's performance will call for greater subtlety.

5. This requirement answers the dissent's and the United States's contention that defense counsel provided effective assistance with regard to the prior conviction file because it argued that it would be prejudicial to allow the introduction of the transcript. Post at [Supp. pp. 37–38]. Counsel's obligation to rebut aggravating evidence extended beyond arguing it ought to be kept out. As noted above, counsel had no way of knowing the context of the transcript and the details of the prior conviction without looking at the file as a whole. Counsel could not effectively rebut the aggravation case or build their own case in mitigation. * * *

The notion that defense counsel must obtain information that the State has and will use against the defendant is not simply a matter of common sense. As the District Court points out, the American Bar Association Standards for Criminal Justice in circulation at the time of Rompilla's trial describes the obligation in terms no one could misunderstand in the circumstances of a case like this one:

"It is the duty of the lawyer to conduct a prompt investigation of the circumstances of the case and to explore all avenues leading to facts relevant to the merits of the case and the penalty in the event of conviction. The investigation should always include efforts to secure information in the possession of the prosecution and law enforcement authorities. The duty to investigate exists regardless of the accused's admissions or statements to the lawyer of facts constituting guilt or the accused's stated desire to plead guilty." 1 *ABA Standards for Criminal Justice* 4–4.1 (2d ed. 1982 Supp.). * * *

"[W]e long have referred [to these ABA Standards] as 'guides to determining what is reasonable.'" *Wiggins v. Smith*, (quoting *Strickland v. Washington*), and the Commonwealth has come up with no reason to think the quoted standard impertinent here.

At argument the most that Pennsylvania (and the United States as *amicus*) could say was that defense counsel's efforts to find mitigating evidence by other means excused them from looking at the prior conviction file. And that, of course, is the position taken by the state postconviction courts. Without specifically discussing the prior case file, they too found that defense counsel's efforts were enough to free them from any obligation to enquire further. * * * We think this conclusion * * * fails to answer the considerations we have set out, to the point of being an objectively unreasonable conclusion. It flouts prudence to deny that a defense lawyer should try to look at a file he knows the prosecution will cull for aggravating evidence, let alone when the file is sitting in the trial courthouse, open for the asking. No reasonable lawyer would forgo examination of the file thinking he could do as well by asking the defendant or family relations whether they recalled anything helpful or damaging in the prior victim's testimony. Nor would a reasonable lawyer compare possible searches for school reports, juvenile records, and evidence of drinking habits to the opportunity to take a look at a file disclosing what the prosecutor knows and even plans to read from in his case. Questioning a few more family members and searching for old records can promise less than looking for a needle in a haystack, when a lawyer truly has reason to doubt there is any needle there. *E.g., Strickland*, at [11th ed., p.164]. But looking at a file the prosecution says it will use is a sure bet: whatever may be in that file is going to tell defense counsel something about what the prosecution can produce.

The dissent thinks this analysis creates a "rigid, *per se* "rule that requires defense counsel to do a complete review of the file on any prior conviction introduced, post at [Supp. p. 37]; but that is a mistake. Counsel fell short here because they failed to make reasonable efforts to review the prior conviction file, despite knowing that the prosecution intended to introduce Rompilla's prior conviction not merely by entering a notice of conviction into evidence but by quoting damaging testimony of the rape victim in that case. The unreasonableness of attempting no more than they did was heightened by the easy availability of the file at the trial courthouse, and the great risk that testimony about a similar violent crime would hamstring counsel's chosen defense of residual doubt. It is owing to these circumstances that the state courts were objectively unreasonable in concluding that counsel could reasonably decline to make any effort to review the file. Other situations, where a defense lawyer is not charged with knowledge that the prosecutor intends to use a prior conviction in this way, might well warrant a different assessment.

Since counsel's failure to look at the file fell below the line of reasonable practice, there is a further question about prejudice, that is, whether "there is a reasonable probability that, but for counsel's unprofessional errors, the result of the proceeding would have been different." *Strickland*. Because the state courts found the representation adequate, they never reached the issue of prejudice, and so we examine this element of the *Strickland* claim *de novo,* and agree with the dissent in the Court of Appeals. We think Rompilla has shown beyond any doubt that counsel's lapse was prejudicial; Pennsylvania, indeed, does not even contest the claim of prejudice.

If the defense lawyers had looked in the file on Rompilla's prior conviction, it is uncontested they would have found a range of mitigation leads that no other source had opened up. In the same file with the transcript of the prior trial were the records of Rompilla's imprisonment on the earlier conviction, which defense counsel testified she had never seen. The prison files pictured Rompilla's childhood and mental health very differently from anything defense counsel had seen or heard. An evaluation by a corrections counselor states that Rompilla was "reared in the slum environment of Allentown, Pa. vicinity. He early came to the attention of juvenile authorities, quit school at 16, [and] started a series of incarcerations in and out Penna. often of assaultive nature and commonly related to over-indulgence in alcoholic beverages." The same file discloses test results that the defense's mental health experts would have viewed as pointing to schizophrenia and other disorders, and test scores showing a third grade level of cognition after nine years of schooling.[8]

8. The dissent would ignore the opportunity to find this evidence on the ground that its discovery (and the consequent analysis of prejudice) "rests on serendipity," Post at [Supp. p. 37]. But once counsel had an obligation to examine the file, counsel had to make reasonable efforts to learn its contents; and once having done so, they could not reasonably have ignored mitigation evidence or red flags simply because they were unexpected. The dissent, however, assumes that counsel could reasonably decline even to read what was in the file, (if counsel had reviewed the case file for mitigating evidence, "[t]here would have been no reason for counsel to read, or even to skim, this obscure document"). While that could well have been true if counsel had been faced with a large amount of possible evidence, see fn. 4, supra, there is no indication that examining the case file in question

The accumulated entries would have destroyed the benign conception of Rompilla's upbringing and mental capacity defense counsel had formed from talking with Rompilla himself and some of his family members, and from the reports of the mental health experts. With this information, counsel would have become skeptical of the impression given by the five family members and would unquestionably have gone further to build a mitigation case. Further effort would presumably have unearthed much of the material postconviction counsel found, including testimony from several members of Rompilla's family, whom trial counsel did not interview. Judge Sloviter summarized this evidence:

> "Rompilla's parents were both severe alcoholics who drank constantly. His mother drank during her pregnancy with Rompilla, and he and his brothers eventually developed serious drinking problems. His father, who had a vicious temper, frequently beat Rompilla's mother, leaving her bruised and black-eyed, and bragged about his cheating on her. His parents fought violently, and on at least one occasion his mother stabbed his father. He was abused by his father who beat him when he was young with his hands, fists, leather straps, belts and sticks. All of the children lived in terror. There were no expressions of parental love, affection or approval. Instead, he was subjected to yelling and verbal abuse. His father locked Rompilla and his brother Richard in a small wire mesh dog pen that was filthy and excrement filled. He had an isolated background, and was not allowed to visit other children or to speak to anyone on the phone. They had no indoor plumbing in the house, he slept in the attic with no heat, and the children were not given clothes and attended school in rags." 355 F.3d, at 279.

The jury never heard any of this and neither did the mental health experts who examined Rompilla before trial. While they found "nothing helpful to [Rompilla's] case," their postconviction counterparts, alerted by information from school, medical, and prison records that trial counsel never saw, found plenty of " 'red flags' " pointing up a need to test further. (Sloviter, J., dissenting). When they tested, they found that Rompilla "suffers from organic brain damage, an extreme mental disturbance significantly impairing several of his cognitive functions." Ibid. They also said that "Rompilla's problems relate back to his childhood, and were likely caused by fetal alcohol syndrome [and that] Rompilla's capacity to appreciate the criminality of his conduct or to conform his conduct to the law was substantially impaired at the time of the offense." Id.

These findings in turn would probably have prompted a look at school and juvenile records, all of them easy to get, showing, for example, that when Rompilla was 16 his mother "was missing from home frequently for a period of one or several weeks at a time." [Lodging Reports, App. 44]. The same report noted that his mother "has been

---

here would have required significant labor. Indeed, Pennsylvania has conspicuously failed to contest Rompilla's claim that because the information was located in the prior conviction file, reasonable efforts would have led counsel to this information.

reported ... frequently under the influence of alcoholic beverages, with the result that the children have always been poorly kept and on the filthy side which was also the condition of the home at all times." School records showed Rompilla's IQ was in the mentally retarded range. Id.

This evidence adds up to a mitigation case that bears no relation to the few naked pleas for mercy actually put before the jury, and although we suppose it is possible that a jury could have heard it all and still have decided on the death penalty, that is not the test. It goes without saying that the undiscovered "mitigating evidence, taken as a whole, 'might well have influenced the jury's appraisal' of [Rompilla's] culpability," *Wiggins,* and the likelihood of a different result if the evidence had gone in is "sufficient to undermine confidence in the outcome" actually reached at sentencing, *Strickland.* * * * The judgment of the Third Circuit is reversed, and Pennsylvania must either retry the case on penalty or stipulate to a life sentence.

Justice O'CONNOR, concurring.

I write separately to put to rest one concern. The dissent worries that the Court's opinion "imposes on defense counsel a rigid requirement to review all documents in what it calls the 'case file' of any prior conviction that the prosecution might rely on at trial." Post at [Supp.p. 33]. But the Court's opinion imposes no such rule. Rather, today's decision simply applies our longstanding case-by-case approach to determining whether an attorney's performance was unconstitutionally deficient under *Strickland.* Trial counsel's performance in Rompilla's case falls short under that standard, because the attorneys' behavior was not "reasonable considering all the circumstances." *Strickland.* In particular, there were three circumstances which made the attorneys' failure to examine Rompilla's prior conviction file unreasonable.

First, Rompilla's attorneys knew that their client's prior conviction would be at the very heart of the *prosecution's* case. The prior conviction went not to a collateral matter, but rather to one of the aggravating circumstances making Rompilla eligible for the death penalty. The prosecutors intended not merely to mention the fact of prior conviction, but to read testimony about the details of the crime. That crime, besides being quite violent in its own right, was very similar to the murder for which Rompilla was on trial, and Rompilla had committed the murder at issue a mere three months after his release from prison on the earlier conviction. * * * A reasonable defense lawyer would have attached a high importance to obtaining the record of the prior trial, in order to anticipate and find ways of deflecting the prosecutor's aggravation argument.

Second, the prosecutor's planned use of the prior conviction threatened to eviscerate one of the *defense's* primary mitigation arguments. Rompilla was convicted on the basis of strong circumstantial evidence. His lawyers structured the entire mitigation argument around the hope of convincing the jury that residual doubt about Rompilla's guilt made it inappropriate to impose the death penalty. * * * [But] in the similarities between the two crimes, combined with the timing and the already strong circumstantial evidence, raised a strong likelihood that the jury would reject Rompilla's residual doubt argument. * * * Such a scenario called for further investigation, to determine whether circumstances of the prior case gave any hope of saving the residual doubt argument, or whether the best strategy instead would be to jettison that argument so as to focus on other, more promising issues. *Cf. Yarborough v. Gentry*, [11th ed., p. 173].

Third, the attorneys' decision not to obtain Rompilla's prior conviction file was not the result of an informed tactical decision about how the lawyers' time would best be spent. Although Rompilla's attorneys had ample warning that the details of Rompilla's prior conviction would be critical to their case, their failure to obtain that file would not necessarily have been deficient if it had resulted from the lawyers' careful exercise of judgment about how best to marshal their time and serve their client. But Rompilla's attorneys did not ignore the prior case file in order to spend their time on other crucial leads. They did not determine that the file was so inaccessible or so large that examining it would necessarily divert them from other trial-preparation tasks they thought more promising. They did not learn at the 11th hour about the prosecution's intent to use the prior conviction, when it was too late for them to change plans. Rather, their failure to obtain the crucial file "was the result of inattention, not reasoned strategic judgment." *Wiggins v. Smith*. * * *

Justice KENNEDY, with whom THE CHIEF JUSTICE, Justice SCALIA, and Justice THOMAS join, dissenting.

Today the Court brands two committed criminal defense attorneys as ineffective—"outside the wide range of professionally competent counsel," *Strickland v. Washington,*—because they did not look in an old case file and stumble upon something they had not set out to find. By implication the Court also labels incompetent the work done by the three mental health professionals who examined Ronald Rompilla. To reach this result, the majority imposes on defense counsel a rigid requirement to review all documents in what it calls the "case file" of any prior conviction that the prosecution might rely on at trial. The Court's holding, a mistake under any standard of review, is all the more troubling because this case arises under the Antiterrorism and Effective Death Penalty Act of 1996. In order to grant Rompilla habeas relief the Court must say, and indeed does say, that the Pennsylvania Supreme Court was objectively unreasonable in failing to anticipate today's new case file rule. * * *

Under any standard of review the investigation performed by Rompilla's counsel in preparation for sentencing was not only adequate but also conscientious. * * * Rompilla's attorneys recognized from the outset that building an effective mitigation case was crucial to helping their client avoid the death penalty. Rompilla stood accused of a brutal crime. In January 1988, James Scanlon was murdered while he was closing the

Cozy Corner Cafe, a bar he owned in Allentown, Pennsylvania. Scanlon's body was discovered later the next morning, lying in a pool of blood. Scanlon had been stabbed multiple times, including 16 wounds around the neck and head. Scanlon also had been beaten with a blunt object, and his face had been gashed, possibly with shards from broken liquor and beer bottles found at the scene of the crime. After Scanlon was stabbed to death his body had been set on fire. * * * [Also,] substantial evidence [including fingerprints and footprints] linked Rompilla to the crime. * * *

Rompilla was represented at trial by Fredrick Charles, the chief public defender for Lehigh County at the time, and Maria Dantos, an assistant public defender. Charles and Dantos were assisted by John Whispell, an investigator in the public defender's office. Rompilla's defense team sought to develop mitigating evidence from various sources. First, they questioned Rompilla extensively about his upbringing and background. To make these conversations more productive they provided Rompilla with a list of the mitigating circumstances recognized by Pennsylvania law. Cf. *Strickland*, [11th ed., at p. 161]. ("[W]hen a defendant has given counsel reason to believe that pursuing certain investigations would be fruitless or even harmful, counsel's failure to pursue those investigations may not later be challenged as unreasonable"). Second, Charles and Dantos arranged for Rompilla to be examined by three experienced mental health professionals, experts described by Charles as "the best forensic psychiatrist around here, [another] tremendous psychiatrist and a fabulous forensic psychologist." Finally, Rompilla's attorneys questioned his family extensively in search of any information that might help spare Rompilla the death penalty. Dantos, in particular, developed a "very close" relationship with Rompilla's family, which was a "constant source of information." App. p. 557. Indeed, after trial, Rompilla's wife sent Dantos a letter expressing her gratitude. * * *

The Court acknowledges the steps taken by Rompilla's attorneys in preparation for sentencing but finds fault nonetheless. "[T]he lawyers were deficient," the Court says, "in failing to examine the court file on Rompilla's prior conviction." Ante at [Supp. p. 27]. The prior conviction the Court refers to is Rompilla's 1974 conviction for rape, burglary, and theft * * * [used] to prove one of the statutory aggravating circumstances—namely, that Rompilla had a "significant history of felony convictions involving the use or threat of violence to the person." * * *

A *per se* rule requiring counsel in every case to review the records of prior convictions used by the State as aggravation evidence is a radical departure from *Strickland* and its progeny. We have warned in the past against the creation of "specific guidelines" or "checklist[s] for judicial evaluation of attorney performance." *Strickland*. * * * [As the Court noted there:] "No particular set of detailed rules for counsel's conduct can satisfactorily take account of the variety of circumstances faced by defense counsel or the range of legitimate decisions regarding how best to represent a criminal defendant. Any such set of rules would interfere with the constitutionally protected independence of counsel and restrict the wide latitude counsel must have in making tactical decisions. Indeed, the existence of detailed guidelines for representation could distract from the overriding mission of vigorous advocacy of the defendant's cause." * * * For this reason, while we have referred to the ABA Standards for Criminal Justice as a useful point of reference, we have been careful to say these standards "are only guides" and do not establish the constitutional baseline for effective assistance of counsel. Ibid. The majority, by parsing the guidelines as if they were binding statutory text, ignores this admonition.

The majority's analysis contains barely a mention of *Strickland* and makes little effort to square today's holding with our traditional reluctance to impose rigid requirements on defense counsel. While the Court disclaims any intention to create a bright-line rule, ante at [Supp. p. 29] * * *, this affords little comfort. The Court's opinion makes clear it has imposed on counsel a broad obligation to review prior conviction case files where those priors are used in aggravation—and to review every document in those files if not every single page of every document, regardless of the prosecution's proposed use for the prior conviction. Infra at Supp. pp. 38–39. One member of the majority tries to limit the Court's new rule by arguing that counsel's decision here was "not the result of an informed tactical decision," (O'Connor, J., concurring), but the record gives no support for this notion. The Court also protests that the exceptional weight Rompilla's attorneys at sentencing placed on residual doubt required them to review the prior conviction file, ante at [Supp. p. 30]. In fact, residual doubt was not central to Rompilla's mitigation case. Rompilla's family members did testify at sentencing that they thought he was innocent, but Dantos tried to draw attention away from this point and instead use the family's testimony to humanize Rompilla and ask for mercy.

The majority also disregards the sound strategic calculation supporting the decisions made by Rompilla's attorneys. Charles and Dantos were "aware of [Rompilla's] priors" and "aware of the circumstances" surrounding these convictions. At the postconviction hearing, Dantos also indicated that she had reviewed documents relating to the prior conviction. Based on this information, as well as their numerous conversations with Rompilla and his family, Charles and Dantos reasonably could conclude that reviewing the full prior conviction case file was not the best allocation of resources.

The majority concludes otherwise only by ignoring *Strickland's* command that "[j]udicial scrutiny of counsel's performance must be highly deferential." According to the Court, the Constitution required nothing less than a full review of the prior conviction case file by Rompilla's attorneys. Even with the benefit of hindsight the Court struggles to explain how the file would have proved helpful, offering only the vague speculation that Rompilla's attorneys might have discovered "circumstances that extenuated the behavior described by the [rape] victim." Ante at [Supp. p. 28]. What the Court means by "circumstances" is a mystery. If the Court is referring to details on Rompilla's mental fitness or upbringing, surely Rompilla's attorneys were more likely to discover such information through the sources they consulted: Rompilla; his family; and the three mental health experts that examined him.

Perhaps the circumstances to which the majority refers are the details of Rompilla's 1974 crimes. Charles and Dantos, however, had enough information about the prior convictions to determine that reviewing the case file was not the most effective use of their time. Rompilla had been convicted of breaking into the residence of Josephine Macrenna, who lived in an apartment above the bar she owned. After Macrenna gave him the bar's receipts for the night, Rompilla demanded that she disrobe. When she initially resisted, Rompilla slashed her left breast with a knife. Rompilla then held Macrenna at knifepoint while he raped her for over an hour. Charles and Dantos were aware of these circumstances of the prior conviction and the brutality of the crime. It did not take a review of the case file to know that quibbling with the Commonwealth's version of events was a dubious trial strategy. At sentencing Dantos fought vigorously to prevent the Commonwealth from introducing the details of the 1974 crimes, but once the transcript was admitted there was nothing that could be done. Rompilla was unlikely to endear himself to the jury by arguing that his prior conviction for burglary, theft, and rape really was not as bad as the Commonwealth was making it out to be. Recognizing this, Rompilla's attorneys instead devoted their limited time and resources to developing a mitigation case. That those efforts turned up little useful evidence does not make the *ex ante* strategic calculation of Rompilla's attorneys constitutionally deficient.

One of the primary reasons this Court has rejected a checklist approach to effective assistance of counsel is that each new requirement risks distracting attorneys from the real objective of providing vigorous advocacy as dictated by the facts and circumstances in the particular case. The Court's rigid requirement that counsel always review the case files of convictions the prosecution seeks to use at trial will be just such a distraction. Capital defendants often have a history of crime. For example, as of 2003, 64 percent of inmates on death row had prior felony convictions. U.S. Dept. of Justice, Bureau of Justice Statistics (T. Bonczar & T. Snell), *Capital Punishment,* 2003, p. 8 (Nov.2004). If the prosecution relies on these convictions as aggravators, the Court has now obligated defense attorneys to review the boxes of documents that come with them.

In imposing this new rule, the Court states that counsel in this case could review the "entire file" with "ease." Fn. 4. There is simply no support in the record for this assumption. Case files often comprise numerous boxes. The file may contain, among other things, witness statements, forensic evidence, arrest reports, grand jury transcripts, testimony and exhibits relating to any pretrial suppression hearings, trial transcripts, trial exhibits, post-trial motions and presentence reports. Full review of even a single prior conviction case file could be time consuming, and many of the documents in a file are duplicative or irrelevant. The Court, recognizing the flaw in its analysis, suggests that cases involving "warehouses of records" "will call for greater subtlety." Fn. 4. Yet for all we know, this is such a case. As to the time component, the Court tells us nothing as to the number of hours counsel had available to prepare for sentencing or why the decisions they made in allocating their time were so flawed as to constitute deficient performance under *Strickland*.

Today's decision will not increase the resources committed to capital defense. (At the time of Rompilla's trial, the Lehigh County Public Defender's Office had two investigators for 2,000 cases.) If defense attorneys dutifully comply with the Court's new rule, they will have to divert resources from other tasks. The net effect of today's holding in many cases—instances where trial counsel reasonably can conclude that reviewing old case files is not an effective use of time—will be to diminish the quality of representation. We have "consistently declined to impose mechanical rules on counsel—even when those rules might lead to better representation," *Roe v. Flores—Ortega,* 528 U.S. 470 (2000); I see no occasion to depart from this approach in order to impose a requirement that might well lead to worse representation. * * *

Today's decision is wrong under any standard, but the Court's error is compounded by the fact that this case arises on federal habeas. The Pennsylvania Supreme Court adjudicated Rompilla's ineffective-assistance-of-counsel claim on the merits, and this means 28 U.S.C. § 2254(d)'s deferential standard of review applies. Rompilla must show that the Pennsylvania Supreme Court decision was not just "incorrect or erroneous," but "objectively unreasonable." *Williams v. Taylor,* [11th ed., p.1662]. The Court pays lipservice to the *Williams* standard, but it proceeds to adopt a rigid, *per se* obligation that binds counsel in every case and finds little support in our precedents. Indeed, *Strickland,* the case the Court purports to apply, is directly to the contrary. * * * The Pennsylvania Supreme Court gave careful consideration to Rompilla's Sixth Amendment claim and concluded that "counsel reasonably relied upon their discussions with [Rompilla] and upon their experts to determine the records needed to evaluate his mental health and other potential mitigating circumstances." This decision was far from unreasonable. The Pennsylvania courts can hardly be faulted for failing to anticipate today's abrupt departure from *Strickland.* * * *

Even accepting the Court's misguided analysis of the adequacy of representation by Rompilla's trial counsel, Rompilla is still not entitled to habeas relief. *Strickland* assigns the defendant the burden of demonstrating prejudice. Rompilla cannot satisfy this standard, and only through a remarkable leap can the Court conclude otherwise.

The Court's theory of prejudice rests on serendipity. Nothing in the old case file diminishes the aggravating nature of the prior conviction. The only way Rompilla's attorneys could have minimized the aggravating force of the earlier rape conviction was through Dantos' forceful, but ultimately unsuccessful, fight to exclude the transcript at sentencing. The Court, recognizing this problem, instead finds prejudice through chance. If Rompilla's attorneys had reviewed the case file of his prior rape and burglary conviction, the Court says, they would have stumbled across "a range of mitigation leads." Ante at [Supp. p. 30]. The range of leads to which the Court refers is in fact a handful of notations within a single 10–page document. The document, an "Initial Transfer Petition," appears to have been prepared by the Pennsylvania Department of Corrections after Rompilla's conviction to facilitate his initial assignment to one of the Commonwealth's maximum-security prisons. Lodging Reports 31–40.

Rompilla cannot demonstrate prejudice because nothing in the record indicates that Rompilla's trial attorneys would have discovered the transfer petition, or the clues contained in it, if they had reviewed the old file. The majority faults Rompilla's attorneys for failing to "learn what the Commonwealth knew about the crime," "discover any mitigating evidence the Commonwealth would downplay," and "anticipate the details of the aggravating evidence the Commonwealth would emphasize." Ante at [Supp. p. 28]. Yet if Rompilla's attorneys had reviewed the case file with these purposes in mind, they almost surely would have attributed no significance to the transfer petition following only a cursory review. The petition, after all, was prepared by the Bureau of Correction after Rompilla's conviction for the purpose of determining Rompilla's initial prison assignment. It contained no details regarding the circumstances of the conviction. Reviewing the prior conviction file for information to counter the Commonwealth, counsel would have looked first at the transcript of the trial testimony, and perhaps then to probative exhibits or forensic evidence. There would have been no reason for counsel to read, or even to skim, this obscure document.

The Court claims that the transfer petition would have been discovered because it was in the "same file" with the transcript, ante at [Supp. p. 30], but this characterization is misleading and the conclusion the Court draws from it is accordingly fallacious. The record indicates only that the transfer petition was a part of the same case file, but Rompilla provides no indication of the size of the file, which for all we know originally comprised several boxes of documents. By the time of Rompilla's state postconviction hearing, moreover, the transfer petition was not stored in any "file" at all—it had been transferred to microfilm. The Court implies in a footnote that prejudice can be presumed because "Pennsylvania conspicuously failed to contest Rompilla's" inevitable-discovery argument. Fn. 8. The Commonwealth's strategy is unsurprising given that discussion of the prior conviction case file takes up only one paragraph of Rompilla's argument, Brief for Petitioner 35–36, but it is also irrelevant. It is well established that Rompilla, not the Commonwealth, has the burden of establishing prejudice.

The majority thus finds itself in a bind. If counsel's alleged deficiency lies in the failure to review the file for the purposes the majority has identified, then there is no prejudice: for there is no reasonable probability that review of the file for those purposes would have led counsel to accord the transfer petition enough attention to discover the leads the majority cites. Prejudice could only be demonstrated if the deficiency in counsel's performance were to be described not as the failure to perform a purposive review of the file, but instead as the failure to accord intense scrutiny to every single page of every single document in that file, regardless of the purpose motivating the review. At times, the Court hints that its new obligation on counsel sweeps this broadly. See ante at fn. 4 ("The ease with which counsel could examine the entire file ..."); ante at fn. 5 ("[C]ounsel had no way of knowing the context of the transcript and the details of the prior conviction without looking at the file as a whole"). Surely, however, the Court would not require defense counsel to look at every document, no matter how tangential, included in the prior conviction file on the off chance that some notation therein might provide a lead, which in turn might result in the discovery of useful information. The Constitution does not mandate that defense attorneys perform busy work. This rigid requirement would divert counsel's limited time and energy away from more important tasks. In this way, it would ultimately disserve the rationale underlying the Court's new rule, which is to ensure that defense counsel counter the State's aggravation case effectively. * * * If the Court does intend to impose on counsel a constitutional obligation to review every page of every document included in the case file of a prior conviction, then today's holding is even more misguided than I imagined.

Strickland anticipated the temptation "to second-guess counsel's assistance after conviction or adverse sentence" and cautioned that "[a] fair assessment of attorney performance requires that every effort be made to eliminate the distorting effects of hindsight, to reconstruct the circumstances of counsel's challenged conduct, and to evaluate the conduct from counsel's perspective at the time." Today, the Court succumbs to the very temptation that *Strickland* warned against. In the process, the majority imposes on defense attorneys a rigid requirement that finds no support in our cases or common sense.

Notes and Questions

1. Does the majority's opinion reflect the viewpoint attributed to Justice Ginsburg in an Associated Press report? Justice Ginsburg there is quoted as having stated in a 2001 public comment: "I have yet to see a death case among the dozens coming to the Supreme Court on eve-of-execution stay applications in which the defendant was well represented at trial.... People who are well represented at trial do not get the death penalty." See Joshua Herman, *Death Denies Due Process*, 53 DePaul L.Rev. 1777, fn. 103 (2004), citing AP, *Death Moratoriam Backed*, Hous.Chron., April 10, 2001.

2. Does *Rompilla* speak to the situation in which the defendant instructs counsel pretrial to curtail investigation into mitigating evidence and focus on defending at the trial, and the defense counsel follows the client's

directions. See Welsh S. White, *A Deadly Dilemma: Choices by Attorneys Representing "Innocent" Capital Defendants*, 102 Mich.L.Rev. 2001 (2004) (analyzing various aspects of this not-uncommon scenario). Should it be critical issue here: (1) whether the defense had an "implausible" or "strong" claim of innocence; (2) whether the defendant was strongly opposed to presenting mitigating evidence even if convicted, or simply preferred that the defense focus its limited resources on the issue of guilt; or (3) whether adhering to the defendant's pretrial request left the defense without any mitigating evidence to present at a penalty hearing or simply less evidence than counsel might have preferred to develop. As noted by Professor White, the 1989 *ABA Guidelines on Capital Representation* provide that "the investigation for preparation of the sentencing phase should be conducted regardless of any initial assertion by the client that mitigation is not to be offered," reasoning that the defendant cannot make an informed decision unless the attorney is able to present a complete picture (after a full investigation) of what evidence might be presented in mitigation. Does the ABA position necessarily rest on the assumption that the defense will have ample resources to investigate fully both mitigation and reasonable doubt?

11th ed., p.180; add to Note 2:

In *United States v. Owens*, 387 F.3d 607 (7th Cir.2004), the Seventh Circuit rejected "the narrow definition of 'prejudice' adopted in *Holman v. Page*," noting that the *Holman* ruling "stands completely alone," having been rejected in various circuits, and is "further undermined" by subsequent Supreme Court rulings in *Williams v. Taylor* and *Glover v. United States* (both discussed in 11th ed., p. 183, Note 4).

Part Two
POLICE PRACTICES
Chapter 6
ARREST, SEARCH AND SEIZURE

SECTION 1. THE EXCLUSIONARY RULE

11th ed., p. 244; at end of first paragraph of Note 4, add:

Private police have traditionally been treated as private persons, a conclusion recently questioned because today "private police participate in much of the police work that their public counterparts do," and "state action exists as a matter of degree in most cases." Elizabeth E. Joh, *The Paradox of Private Policing*, 95 Nw.U.L.Rev. 49, 51, 125 (2004).

In *In re Jansen*, 826 N.E.2d 186 (Mass.2005), the court held that the fact a judge in a criminal case entered an order requiring a third party not charged with any offense to provide a buccal swab for DNA analysis did not make the obtaining of the swab governmental where the judge's order was in response to the defendant, "acting in a private capacity [to] further[] his own ends by attempting to secure all favorable proofs in advance of trial." By footnote, the court cautioned it was not deciding "whether the buccal swab obtained by [defendant] could, at some later date, be turned over to the Commonwealth for use in a future criminal prosecution without implicating [the third party's] constitutional rights."

SECTION 2. PROTECTED AREAS AND INTERESTS

11th ed., p. 265; before *Karo* in Note 4, add:

A different form of vehicle tracking is now possible by use of a Global Positioning System device. "Law enforcement agents attach a GPS device to the underside of a vehicle, in a place where it will not be noticed. From then on the device automatically keeps a detailed time and place itinerary of everywhere the vehicle travels and when and how long it remains at various locations. Later, law enforcement agents remove the device and download the detailed itinerary of where and when the vehicle has traveled. Unlike beepers, GPS devices do not require continuous monitoring by a law enforcement agent." Dorothy J. Glancy, *Privacy on the Open Road,* 30 Ohio N.U.L.Rev. 295, 316–17 (2004). Does such activity fall within *Knotts*? Compare *People v. Jackson,* 76 P.3d 217 (Wash.2003) (a search under *state* constitution). Some vehicles come with an installed GPS device (e.g., GM's "Onstar"). If *Jackson* has it right, then what if police manage to track the vehicle owner's travels with that device? What if they use that device to locate the vehicle and its thief after the owner has reported it stolen?

11th ed., p. 277; end of Note 6, add:

More recently, a study commissioned by the American Library Association determined that "[l]aw enforcement officials have made at least 200 formal and informal inquiries to libraries for information on reading material and other internal matters since October 2001," and the House has voted 238–187 "approving a measure to restrict investigators' access to libraries," though "Bush administration officials say they are hopeful the decision will be reversed and have threatened a veto of any measure that would limit powers under the Patriot Act." N.Y. Times, June 20, 2005, p. A11 (Nat'l ed.).

SECTION 4. SEARCH WARRANTS

11th ed., p. 314, end of Note 4, add:

In MUEHLER v. MENA, 125 S.Ct. 1465 (2005), a § 1983 case involving execution of a search warrant for deadly weapons and evidence of gang membership at a home where police believed at least one member of a gang involved in a recent drive-by shooting lived, Ms. Mena and three other occupants were detained in handcuffs for the entire 2–3 hours of the search. The 5–Justice majority, per REHNQUIST, C.J., though conceding that the handcuffing made the detention "more intrusive than that which we upheld in *Summers*," concluded that such action "was reasonable because the governmental interests outweighed the marginal intrusion," for in "such inherently dangerous situations, the use of handcuffs minimizes the risk of harm to both officers and occupants" and was "all the more reasonable" because of "the need to detain multiple occupants." One of the five, KENNEDY, J., added two cautions in a separate concurrence: (1) "If the search extends to the point when the handcuffs can cause real pain or discomfort, provision must be made to alter the conditions of detention at least long enough to attend to the needs of the detainee"; and (2) the restraint should "be removed if, at any point during the search, it would be readily apparent to any objectively reasonable officer that removing the handcuffs would not compromise the officers' safety or risk interference or substantial delay in the execution of the search," not so in the instant case given that "the detainees outnumber[ed] those supervising them, and this situation could not be remedied without diverting officers from an extensive, complex, and time-consuming search." In a separate concurrence by the four other Justices (agreeing with the majority's other point, that under *Caballes,* 11th ed., p. 428, it was not objectionable that during the detention police questioned Ms. Mena on an unrelated matter, her immigration status), it was contended that the following considerations showed "that the jury could properly have found that this 5–foot–2–inch young lady posed no threat to the officers at the scene": "the cuffs kept [her] arms behind her for two to three hours" notwithstanding the fact that because they were "real uncomfortable" she had "asked the officers to remove them," "[n]o contraband was found in her room or on her person," there "were no indications * * * she was or ever had been a gang member," she "was unarmed" and "fully cooperated with the officers," she "was not suspected of any crime and was not a person targeted by the search warrant," and "lack of resources" was apparently not a problem since "there were 18 officers at the scene."

11th ed., p. 315; before Note 6, add:

5a. *Seizure of items named in the warrant.* While the police may seize discovered items named in the warrant, sometimes a question will arise as to what quantity may be seized, as when the warrant uses the term "any." Compare *McClendon v. Story County Sheriff's Office,* 403 F.3d 510 (8th Cir.2005) (warrant authorizing police to seize "any horses" on defendant's property that were "weak or malnourished" allowed them to seize entire herd when all of the horses found in that condition); with *San Jose Charter of Hells Angels v. San Jose,* 402 F.3d 962 (9th Cir.2005) (where incident to execution of warrants for Hells Angels' clubhouse and residences of persons alleged to be affiliated with Hells Angels for "any evidence" of Hells Angels affiliation, officers "seized belts, jewelry, plaques, t-shirts, hats, watches, vests, calendars, clocks, sculptures, photographs, and correspondence," among other things, and ended up with "truckloads" of evidence, court rejects police claim they justified in "reading the word 'any' in the search warrant as equivalent to 'all' ", as (1) warrants were not for purpose of finding evidence of crime, but only to obtain evidence to support a gang sentencing enhancement, significant because "the evidence on this issue would be needlessly cumulative once enough evidence was obtained to establish membership," and (2) the police had exercised no restraint whatsoever in their literal interpretation of the search warrants' commands, as "officers jackhammered and removed a piece of the sidewalk in front of the Hells Angels clubhouse because some of the members' names were written on it," and "also removed the door of the (working) clubhouse refrigerator because it had a Hells Angels decal on it").

SECTION 5. WARRANTLESS ARRESTS AND SEARCHES OF THE PERSON

11th ed., p. 324; at end of Note 6, add:

Donald A. Dripps, *The Fourth Amendment and the Fallacy of Composition: Determinacy Versus Legitimacy in a Regime of Bright–Line Rules,* 74 Miss.L.J. 341, 346 (2004), argues that "deriving specific rules from specific common-law practices detaches common-law practice from its context. Perhaps worse, identifying the rule by reference to how the common-law judges understood the police practice at issue detaches the contemporary rule announced by the Court from its context—a web of other court-made Fourth Amendment rules, each with its own arbitrary margins. To adopt an evolutionary simile, transplanting selected common-law practices into the current constitutional criminal-procedure regime is like doing a skin graft from a zebra to a horse."

11th ed., p. 339; at end of Note 2, add:

On the other hand, what is *Atwater*'s application when an arrest was made because the law *forbids* the officer from exercising any discretion in favor of the citation alternative, as in *Hedgepeth v. Washington Metropolitan Area Transit Authority*, 386 F.3d 1148 (D.C.Cir.2004), where a 12–year-old was arrested for eating a single french fry in a transit authority station, due to the combined effect of the transit authority's "zero tolerance" policy and a provision of District of Columbia law that prevented officers from issuing citations to minors? Should the minor prevail on the argument that *Atwater* "can only be understood in terms of the Court's concern to avoid interfering with the discretion of police officers called upon to decide 'on the spur (and in the heat) of the moment' * * * whether to arrest or to issue a citation"?

Are the *Mota* and *Hedgepeth* situations informed by TOWN OF CASTLE ROCK v. GONZALES, 125 S.Ct. 2796 (2005)? The court of appeals held that, in light of a state statute declaring that police "shall use every reasonable means to enforce a restraining order" and "shall arrest, or, if an arrest would be impractical under the circumstances, seek a warrant" on probable cause, Mrs. Gonzales had a cognizable procedural due process claim under 42 U.S.C.A. § 1983 because of police failure to enforce a restraining order against her husband, who then killed their three children. The Supreme Court, per SCALIA, J., disagreed:

"We do not believe that these provisions of Colorado law truly made enforcement of restraining orders *mandatory*. A well established tradition of police discretion has long coexisted with apparently mandatory arrest statutes.

> 'In each and every state there are long-standing statutes that, by their terms, seem to preclude nonenforcement by the police.... However, for a number of reasons, including their legislative history, insufficient resources, and sheer physical impossibility, it has been recognized that such statutes cannot be interpreted literally.... [T]hey clearly do not mean that a police officer may not lawfully decline to make an arrest. As to third parties in these states, the full-enforcement statutes simply have no effect, and their significance is further diminished.' 1 ABA Standards for Criminal Justice 1–4.5, commentary, pp. 1–124 to 1–125 (2d ed.1980) (footnotes omitted).

"The deep-rooted nature of law-enforcement discretion, even in the presence of seemingly mandatory legislative commands, is illustrated by *Chicago v. Morales,* 527 U.S. 41 (1999), which involved an ordinance that said a police officer 'shall order' 'persons to disperse in certain circumstances.' This Court rejected out of hand the possibility that 'the mandatory language of the ordinance ... afford[ed] the police *no* discretion.' It is, the Court proclaimed, simply 'common sense that *all* police officers must use some discretion in deciding when and where to enforce city ordinances.'"

"Against that backdrop, a true mandate of police action would require some stronger indication from the Colorado Legislature than 'shall use every reasonable means to enforce a restraining order' (or even 'shall arrest ... or ... seek a warrant'). That language is not perceptibly more mandatory than the Colorado statute which has long told municipal chiefs of police that they 'shall pursue and arrest any person fleeing from justice in any part of the state' and that they 'shall apprehend any person in the act of committing any offense ... and, forthwith and without any warrant, bring such person before a ... competent authority for examination and trial.' It is hard to imagine that a Colorado peace officer would not have some discretion to determine that—despite probable cause to believe a restraining order has been violated—the circumstances of the violation or the competing duties of that officer or his agency counsel decisively against enforcement in a particular instance."

11th ed., p. 339; at end of Note 3, add:

A report recently released by Humans Rights Watch and the ACLU charges that "the Bush administration has twisted the American system of due process 'beyond recognition' in jailing at least 70 terror suspects as 'material witnesses' since the Sept. 11 attacks, and the groups are calling on Congress to impose tougher safeguards. * * * Senator Patrick J. Leahy of Vermont, the ranking Democrat on the Judiciary Committee, said he would introduce legislation to limit the government's ability to detain a material witness indefinitely. * * *"

"Justice Department officials have defended their view of the law in interviews and Congressional testimony, saying they have sought to use it sparingly and have tried to follow legal safeguards, including allowing those who are jailed to contact lawyers and challenge their detention." Eric Lichtlau, *Two Groups Charge Abuse of Witness Law*, N.Y. Times, June 27, 2005, p. A10 (Nat'l ed.).

11th ed., p. 346; at end of Note 9, add:

10. In discussing "three important rules [that] constitute what I call the Supreme Court's Iron Triangle," DONALD A. DRIPPS, *The Fourth Amendment and the Fallacy of Composition: Determinacy Versus Legitimacy in a Regime of Bright–Line Rules*, 74 Miss.L.J. 341, 347–48, 392, 397–98 (2004), concludes that the Court is guilty of what Aristotle called "the fallacy of composition":

"To be concrete, it is not unreasonable to say [as in *Whren*] that official motive should play no role in Fourth Amendment law. It is not unreasonable to say [as in *Belton*, 11th ed, p. 389] that, incident to a lawful arrest of a motorist, the police may search the passenger compartment of the vehicle, containers included. It is not unreasonable to say [as in *Atwater*] that the police may make a custodial arrest for any criminal offense, traffic included. But to say that there shall be no inquiry into the motives of police who make custodial arrests for exceeding the speed limit by four miles per hour and then peruse every file in a laptop computer found in the backseat of the vehicle is more than a little like saying [as in Aristotle's fallacy example] that a man can sit and walk at the same time. * * *"

"The interlocking bright-line rules of the Court's Iron Triangle thus authorize police practices that no American jurisdiction regards as reasonable. Indeed, a rule simply authorizing the police to search automobiles at their whim—without articulable suspicion of any sort—would actually be less objectionable than current doctrine. At least a regime of arbitrary search would not require police to curtail the suspect's liberty as a precondition to search. What *Atwater*, *Belton* and *Whren* encourage is the practice of making unnecessary arrests in bad faith for the ulterior purpose of search, and thereby inflicting handcuffs and arrest records as well as invasions of privacy on petty offenders."

"The *Atwater* majority consoled itself with the hope that police have not exploited the overbreadth of the combined rules. It hardly seems like a point in favor of legitimacy, however, to say that the practice approved in the instant case is so outrageous that we can trust the police not to do much of it."

SECTION 8. STOP AND FRISK

11th ed., p. 413; before Note 3, add:

2a. Consider *Bostick* and *Drayton* in light of the observation in Lewis R. Katz, *Terry v. Ohio at Thirty–Five: A Revisionist View*, 74 Miss.L.J. 423, 478 (2004), that because "most persons riding interstate buses have far less influence and economic and political power than airplane passengers," the "political consequences of such behavior on an airplane would be far different," which is why it "is inconceivable that police would 'sweep the planes' for drugs."

11th ed., p. 422; before Note 6, add:

5a. Consider, in light of the observation in *Hensley* that a stop made in response to a "flyer or bulletin" will be upheld only if there is reasonable suspicion at the source, the situation as to seizures made in reliance upon the government's pervasive data aggregation/mining efforts, see Note 7, Supp. p. 63, where computer-generated patterns and relationships are relied upon to justify government action. One such use concerns airport security, but available evidence (e.g., that Senator Kennedy was placed on the "no-fly" list) has prompted the assertion that "the current airport watchlist is dysfunctional." Ronald D. Lee & Paul M. Schwartz, *Beyond the "War" on Terrorism: Towards the New Intelligence Network*, 103 Mich.L.Rev. 1446, 1469 (2005). Consider in this regard the suggestion in James X. Dempsey & Lara M. Flint, *Commercial Data and National Security*, 72 Geo.Wash.L.Rev. 1459, 1487 (2004), that "[i]f detention at an airport for more intensive scrutiny under a passenger screening program is a seizure * * *, then the use of inaccurate or unreliable data to make that detention would not be reasonable," for *Arizona v. Evans*, 11th ed., p. 245, "provides a constitutional basis for the principle that the government should not rely on databases to arrest or detain individuals unless those databases and the method of searching them are accurate."

11th ed., p. 431; end of Note 7, add:

In any event, *Caballes* was soon extended to detentions other than traffic stops or other seizures on full probable cause; see *Muehler v. Mena*, Supp. p. 42.

SECTION 9. ADMINISTRATIVE INSPECTIONS AND REGULATORY SEARCHES: MORE ON BALANCING THE NEED AGAINST THE INVASION OF PRIVACY

11th ed., p. 446; at the end of Note 8, add:

What then should be the status of a DNA testing statute (a) applicable to all those serving a sentence of imprisonment, or (b) all those thereafter convicted of a felony, or (c) all those thereafter arrested for a felony? See the various opinions in *State v. Raines*, 857 A.2d 19 (Md.2004); and Tracey Maclin, *Is Obtaining an Arrestee's DNA a Valid Special Needs Search Under the Fourth Amendment? What Should (and Will) the Supreme Court Do?*, 33 J.L.Med. & Ethics 102 (2005).

9. *A "weapons of mass destruction" special needs exception?"* RONALD M. GOULD & SIMON STERN, *Catastrophic Threats and the Fourth Amendment*, 77 S.Cal.L.Rev. 777, 779 (2004), put this hypothetical: "The government has received a credible report from a reliable source stating that an atomic bomb, no larger than a suitcase, has been smuggled into a major city. The bomb could kill tens or hundreds of thousands of residents, and the vicinity around the blast could be rendered uninhabitable for many years. The report is confirmed by sensors disclosing a track of radiation consistent with atomic weaponry within an area that includes 100 separate homes and no other structures. Unfortunately, the sensors cannot precisely identify the bomb's location, perhaps because of the limitations of the sensors, because of shielding technology, or because the bomb was moved. Besides alerting government officials to the presence of the bomb, the source of the information has warned them of a planned date and time for the bomb's detonation. The deadline does not allow time for investigation of the inhabitants of each home in the area, or of whether a bomb may have been planted in one of the homes without the inhabitants' knowledge. Nor does the deadline permit evacuation of the populace. Determined to prevent the disaster if possible, and unable to find any way to focus the search more narrowly, authorities decide to search all 100 premises within the area immediately without a warrant and without warning to residents. Within twenty hours, all the homes are searched, and the bomb is discovered, seized, and neutralized."

If you agree with their conclusion that such a case should be characterized as a variety of "special need," then what is your answer to the questions they ask, id. at 832: "If the search of 100 homes for an atomic bomb is permissible, then how about a search of 100 homes of biochemists for an anthrax terrorist? How about a search of ten homes for a shoulder-held missile capable of destroying a commercial airliner with its hundreds of passengers? How about a search for a serial killer among a likely subset of suspects?"

SECTION 10. CONSENT SEARCHES

A. The Nature of "Consent"

11th ed., p. 456; end of Note 12, add:

(c) George C. Thomas, *Terrorism, Race and a New Approach to Consent Searches*, 73 Miss.L.J. 525, 551–52 (2003), agrees, and adds another reason: "Abolishing consent searches would deprive police of their most effective racial profiling tool. As police can approach anyone on the street to ask for consent and can ask any driver who is stopped for a traffic infraction for consent, police are presently free to use race, and only race, to decide when to ask for consent in a huge number of situations. If police have to show probable cause to conduct a search, on the other hand, their discretion to use race is severely limited. Abolishing consent searches would do far more to remedy racial profiling in the real world than all the equal protection laws or statutory remedies that can be imagined."

Chapter 7

WIRETAPPING, ELECTRONIC EAVESDROPPING, THE USE OF SECRET AGENTS TO OBTAIN INCRIMINATING STATEMENTS, AND THE FOURTH AMENDMENT

SECTION 2. *BERGER, KATZ* AND THE LEGISLATION THAT FOLLOWED

11th ed., p. 479; end of Note 9, add:

For more on the Justice Department's expanded use of FISA since 9/11, see Chapter 3 of Stephen J. Schulhofer, *Rethinking the PATRIOT Act* (2005) (A Century Foundation Report).

Chapter 9
POLICE INTERROGATION AND CONFESSIONS

SECTION 3. THE *MIRANDA* "REVOLUTION"

APPLYING AND EXPLAINING *MIRANDA*

11th ed., p. 619, after Note (b), add new Note (bb).

(bb). *Is a police officer's reading of the arrest warrant or the affidavit of complaint supporting the warrant to a custodial suspect the functional equivalent of police interrogation?* Consider STATE v. SAWYER, 156 S.W.3d 531 (Sup.Ct.Tenn. 2005), which arose as follows: Following his arrest for aggravated sexual battery, defendant Sawyer was taken to the jail. Immediately upon his arrival, Sawyer was escorted to Detective Clark's office. The officers seated him facing Clark, who sat behind a desk. Detective Clark then read to Sawyer the arrest warrant and the affidavit of complaint (which set forth in detail what Sawyer had allegedly done to a 12-year-old girl). After the affidavit was read—but before Sawyer was advised of his rights—he made some incriminating statements.

Although the court, per HOLDER, J., recognized that other courts had held that the reading of the charges is not "interrogation" within the meaning of *Miranda*, it pointed out that "the facts and circumstances in this case go beyond merely reading the arrest warrant or otherwise informing the defendant of the charges."

"The officers transported Sawyer from his residence directly to Detective Clark's office. * * * Sawyer was placed in a chair in front of a desk, and Detective Clark sat directly across from Sawyer. * * * Detective Clark had not advised Sawyer of his *Miranda* rights prior to reading the affidavit. Sawyer made the [incriminating] statement only after hearing the detailed allegations contained in the affidavit.

"The detective's actions placed Sawyer in an environment in which he could reasonably believe that he was to be interrogated. [Therefore,] we conclude that under the facts and circumstances of the present case, the detective action in reading the affidavit to Sawyer was the functional equivalent of interrogation."

Consider, too, *Blake v. Maryland*, discussed at p. 51 of this Supplement. The *Blake* case also raises the questions whether the reading of the arrest warrant and statement of charges amounted to "interrogation" within the meaning of *Miranda*. In *Blake*, however, the defendant had been advised of his rights and had asserted his right to counsel *before* he was given a copy of the arrest warrant and statement of charges. Therefore, although the confession was excluded, the analysis was different. Moreover, there are also a number of special facts in the *Blake* case.

11th ed., p. 641, after *State v. Cook*, add:

Consider UNITED STATES v. LEWIS, 355 F.Supp.2d 870 (E.D.Mich.2005). Although the court, per COHN, J., did not require the police to record all interrogations, it stated that one reason it had concluded that the government had not satisfied its burden of establishing that defendants had been given, and had waived, their *Miranda* rights was that "the interviews were not memorialized by video or audio recording, notwithstanding that equipment to do so was available, and notwithstanding the fact that one of the officers had previously been involved in [an] interview situation where the failure to record was criticized."

"Affording the Court the benefits of watching or listening to a videotaped or audiotaped statement is invaluable," observed Judge Cohn; "indeed, a tape-recorded interrogation allows the Court to more accurately assess whether a statement was given knowingly, voluntarily, and intelligently. [As one] legal commentator has noted[,] Paul G. Cassell, *Miranda's Social Costs: An Empirical Reassessment*, 90 Nw. U.L.Rev. 387, 487 (1996) [:] 'Taping is [the] only means of eliminating "swearing contests" about what went on in the interrogation room.'"

As the court noted, in 2004 the American Bar Association unanimously accepted a resolution "urg[ing] legislatures and/or courts to enact laws or rules of procedure requiring videotaping of the entirety of custodial interrogations of crime suspects at police precincts, courthouses, detention centers, or other places where suspects are held for questioning, or, where videotaping is impractical, to require the audiotaping of such custodial interrogations, and to provide appropriate remedies for non-compliance."

See generally Steven A. Drizin, & Marissa J. Reich, *Heeding the Lessons of History: The Need for Mandatory Recording of Police Interrogations to Accurately Assess the Reliability and Voluntariness of Confessions*, 52 Drake L.Rev. 619 (2004).

11th ed., p. 655; after Note (ii), add new Note (iii).

(iii). ***More on "initiating further communication with the police.*** Consider BLAKE v. STATE, 849 A.2d 410 (Md.Ct. of App. 2004), cert. granted, 125 S.Ct. 1823 (2005), which arose as follows: Petitioner, a murder suspect, was arrested at his home between 4:30 and 5:00 a.m. He was wearing boxer shorts and a tank top and no shoes. He was handcuffed and taken to the police station where he was advised of his rights. When he stated that he did not wish to talk to the police without a lawyer present he was placed in a holding cell. That took place at about 5:25 a.m.

Approximately 45 minutes later, Detective Johns, accompanied by a uniformed officer (Reese), went to petitioner's cell and gave him a copy of the arrest warrant and statement of charges. (A Maryland rule provides that "the officer shall inform the defendant of the nature of the offense charged and of the fact that a warrant has been issued" and that "a copy of the warrant and charging document shall be served on the defendant promptly after the arrest.")

After giving petitioner a copy of the arrest warrant and statement of charges. Detective Johns explained the charges to petitioner and told him he needed to read the document and make sure he understood it. The statement of charges indicated that petitioner was charged with first degree murder and other crimes. The document also contained a statement that the penalty for first degree murder was—in capital letters—"DEATH." This was not so. Petitioner was 17 years old and under Maryland law a person under the age of 18 at the time of the offense could not be sentenced to death.

As the detective turned to leave the cell, after giving petitioner the charging document, Officer Reese said to petitioner in a loud voice, "I bet you want to talk now, huh!" Detective Johns testified that he was surprised by Reese's statement and that he responded in a very loud voice, so that he could be sure petitioner heard him: "No, he doesn't want to talk to us. He already asked for a lawyer. We cannot talk to him now."

The detective and the uniformed officer left. Petitioner remained in the cell, still wearing only his boxer shorts and t-shirt. About half an hour later, Detective Johns returned to the cell to give petitioner his clothing, which had been brought to the police station by another officer. Petitioner then asked the detective whether he could still talk to him. The detective replied: "Are you saying that you want to talk to me now?" Petitioner responded, "Yes." He was then taken back to the intake room, where he was re-advised of his *Miranda* rights. He then agreed to speak to the police without a lawyer present and made some incriminating statements. The court, per RAKER, J., ruled that all statements made by petitioner after he invoked his right to counsel were inadmissible:

"Merely presenting an accused with a charging document, without more, is not the functional equivalent of interrogation. [However,] in the instant case, the officers' conduct does not fall into the category of fulfilling a legal duty and merely serving a charging document upon a defendant. Instead, we have an interrogating type statement by an officer concomitant with the serving of a document containing the most egregious misstatement as to the penalty for the offense. * * *

"Although petitioner's question to Detective Johns [as to whether he could still talk to him despite his earlier assertion of his rights] might be considered an 'initiation' of contact with the officers in the 'dictionary sense' of the word as used in *Bradshaw*, it could hardly be said that, under the circumstances, petitioner initiated the contact as the term is contemplated in the legal sense. Petitioner had requested counsel; he had been given a document that told him he was subject to the death penalty, when legally he was not; he was seventeen years of age; * * * he was in a cold holding cell with little clothing; an officer had suggested in a confrontational tone that petitioner might want to talk; and the misstatement as to the potential penalty as one of "DEATH" had never been corrected. There was no break in custody or adequate lapse in time sufficient to initiate the coercive effect of the unpermissive interrogation. * * *

"We reject the State's argument that, even if Officer Reese interrogated petitioner in violation of *Miranda* and *Edwards*, Detective Johns somehow cured the violation * * *. The break in time from Officer Reese's improper interrogation to petitioner's inquiry was very short, indicating that the latter was a continuation of the former."

Notes and Questions

1. Suppose Officer Reese had never accompanied Detective Johns to petitioner's cell and thus never made any comment to petitioner about the statement of charges. Suppose further that petitioner had not been in a cold holding cell with little clothing and that he had been 27 years old rather than 17 (and thus quite eligible for the death penalty). Would (should) his incriminating statements have been admissible? Even if eligible for the death penalty, should a custodial suspect who has invoked his right to counsel (or who has not yet been advised of his rights) *ever* be given a document informing him that he has been charged with a crime that subjects him to the death penalty?

2. In *Blake*, the U.S. Supreme Court granted certiorari on the question whether, when police improperly communicate with a suspect after he has invoked his right to counsel, *Edwards* permits consideration of "curative measures" by the police, or other intervening circumstances, so that if the suspect later talks to the police, or indicates a willingness to do so, he may be said to have "initiated" communication with the police. Assuming arguendo, that the police may "cure" a failure to comply with *Edwards*, did Detective Johns do enough to "cure" the impact on Blake of (a) the misstatement of law in the charging document about Blake being subject to the death penalty and (b) Officer Reese's comment, in effect, that Blake's knowledge that he was subject to the death penalty would probably lead him to change his mind about not talking to the police? Under the circumstances, in order to effect a "cure," shouldn't Detective Johns have to tell Blake that the statement in the charging document was incorrect and that Blake was not in fact subject to the death penalty?

SECTION 5. THE *PATANE* AND *SEIBERT* CASES: IS PHYSICAL EVIDENCE OR A "SECOND CONFESSION" DERIVED FROM A FAILURE TO COMPLY WITH THE *MIRANDA* RULES ADMISSIBLE? THE COURT'S ANSWERS SHED LIGHT ON *DICKERSON*

11th ed. p. 714; add to Note 2:

Absent a deliberate law enforcement strategy to elicit incriminating statements in violation of *Massiah* and absent any police efforts to confront the suspect with the same incriminating statements he made at the earlier questioning session in violation of his Sixth Amendment right to counsel (before he was given, and waived, his *Miranda* rights), would the approach be taken in *Patane* and *Seibert* apply to *Massiah* violations as well? Would (should) the courts admit a "second confession" when (a) after a person has been indicted the police elicit incriminating statements from him in violation of his Sixth Amendment right to counsel, (b) a short time later, the suspect waives his *Miranda* rights and (c) the police then obtain a second batch of incriminating statements? See the Eighth Circuit opinion in *United States v. Fellers*, this Supplement, p. 68.

SECTION 6. THE "DUE PROCESS"–"VOLUNTARINESS" TEST REVISITED

11th ed., p. 724; after Note 4, add new Note 4(a):

4(a). *Should a distinction be drawn between: (a) a police interrogator's offer to convey the suspect's "cooperation" to the prosecutor for possible lenient treatment and (b) a police interrogator's threat to tell the prosecutor of a suspect's failure to "cooperate" so that the prosecutor might treat him more harshly?* Consider STATE v. SWANIGAN, 106 P.3d 39 (Sup.Ct.Kan.2005), holding defendant's confession to aggravated robbery involuntary under the totality of circumstances. Although the court, per NUSS, J., did not believe that, without more, it was improper for police officers to tell a suspect that his willingness to "cooperate" with them would be passed on to the prosecutor so that he might receive lenient treatment, it disapproved of the police tactic of threatening a suspect that his failure to cooperate with them would be passed on to the prosecutor so that he might be treated harshly. The court considered the latter tactic "inconsistent" with *Miranda*:

"We fail to see how law enforcement can be required by *Miranda* to advise Swanigan of his right to remain silent, and then can be allowed to warn him of punishment for his 'noncooperation' when he exercises that right." However, the court "[did] not regard this tactic as one which makes the confession involuntary *per se*, but rather as one factor to be considered in the totality of circumstances."[a]

Isn't police assurance that a suspect would be treated more leniently if he "cooperated" with the police rather than remaining silent also "inconsistent" with *Miranda*?

11th ed., p. 725; after Note 7, add new Note 7(a):

7(a). *How adept are the police at detecting false confessions?* A recent study, SAUL M. KASSIN, CHRISTIAN A. MEISSNER & REBECCA J. NORWICK, *"I'd Know a False Confession if I Saw One": A Comparative Study of College Students and Police Investigators,* 29 Law and Human Behavior 211 (April 2005), challenges the assumption that police officers can

---

a. This police tactic, in combination with other factors, such as the defendant's low intellect and susceptibility to being overcome by anxiety led the court to conclude that Swanigan's confession was involuntary.

usually detect a false confession when they see one. Indeed, the Kassin–Meissner–Norwick study indicates that experienced police officers are less proficient than laypeople at judging whether confessions are true or false.

In the first experiment, male prison inmates confessed to two crimes in taped interviews, one in which they confessed to the crimes for which they had been incarcerated, the other in which they confessed to a crime described by an experimenter that they did not commit. The confessions were evaluated by two groups: 61 male and female introductory psychology students and 57 male and female police investigators from Florida and Texas. The investigators had an average of about eleven years of law enforcement experience. Moreover, 58% had received special training in interviewing and interrogating and/or detecting deception. Before they were exposed to the taped confessions, all participants were told that they would be presented with a number of confessions, some true, some false.

The police investigators were less accurate than the students at judging whether confessions were true or false. The results are consistent with other studies finding that experience and training do not typically improve deception detection. Compared to the students, the police erred not by rejecting true confessions, but by accepting false ones. The police "bias," as the three authors of the study expressed it, "is not to see lies per se, but to presume guilt."

According to the authors, one possible explanation for why experienced police officers may be generally less accurate than college students in evaluating confessions is that law enforcement training and experience produce a systematic bias that reduces overall judgment accuracy. Moreover, many law enforcement professionals are trained to evaluate the accuracy of confessions by considering visual symptoms. For example, a leading police interrogation manual advocates the use of various visual cues, such as gaze aversion, nonfrontal posture, and slouching. Yet studies have indicated that such visual cues are not diagnostic of truth or deception.

Another possible explanation is that the investigators' judgment accuracy may have been "compromised by our use of a paradigm in which half of the stimulus confessions were false, a percentage that is likely far higher than the real world base rate for false confessions."

To test the second possible reason for the relatively poor showing by the police, a second experiment was conducted. This time, all participants were specifically told that half of the statements were true and half were false. This time, the police judged only 51.5% of the confessions to be true, compared to 49.5% by the students, an insignificant difference.

In both experiments the participants were asked to rate their confidence in their judgments on a 1–10 point scale (ranging from "not at all confident" to "very confident"). Although the students were considerably more accurate in their judgments than the police were in the first experiment, the police were significantly more confident. In the second experiment, the police performance improved, but they still were not more accurate than the students. Nevertheless, they were still overconfident in their judgments.

Another finding of the Kassin–Meissner–Norwick study is that "people are better judges of confessions when they listen to audiotapes [than] when they see complete audiovisual presentations. * * * This result is consistent with prior research indicating that people are better lie detectors when focused on content and auditory cues than on less diagnostic but distracting visual information."

11th ed., p. 732; after Note 4, add new Note 4(a).

4(a). *Does shackling a suspect to the floor of a police station "interview room" for seven hours render a confession "involuntary"?* STATE v. HARRIS, 105 P.3d 1258 (Kan.Sup.Ct. 2005) answered in the negative.

After being arrested for murder, defendant Harris was advised of his *Miranda* rights and waived them. He was then handcuffed and taken to the police station. He arrived shortly after midnight and was taken to an interview room, where the handcuffs were removed and he was shackled to the floor. Although he was allowed to take bathroom breaks as needed, Harris remained shackled for approximately seven hours. During that time, he was questioned for about two and a half hours. The remainder of the time Harris was alone in the room. A unanimous state supreme court, per GERNON, J., held that the shackling did not render a resulting confession "involuntary." In determining whether a confession is voluntary, observed the court, "the key inquiry is whether the statement is a product of the accused's free and independent will." "Because case law fails to support Harris's claim that his confession was coerced by a lengthy interrogation in which he was shackled to the floor," the court concluded that "this factor does not weigh in favor of finding Harris's confession involuntary."

Harris also argued that his confession was involuntary because, as a detective admitted, his request to use the phone to call someone regarding an alibi was denied. But the court could find no authority to support this claim. Finally, Harris contended that his confession should have been excluded because (a) a detective lied to him by misleading him into thinking that he had been identified by several people who had been witnesses to the shooting and (b) a detective did not advise him that four of the eyewitnesses had identified *another person* as the shooter. But the court rejected these arguments as well. The court recognized that the state has a duty to reveal any exculpatory evidence to the defense before trial, but could find no support for the view that "the same rule extends to police interrogation before the defendant has been charged with any crime."

In reaching its conclusion that Harris's confession was voluntary, the court took into account that "Harris was 24 years old at the time of his interrogation * * *, had numerous juvenile adjudications and felony convictions beginning in 1990, * * * responded coherently and appropriately to questions regarding his personal history, [and] does not claim any mental incapacity."

Does the *Harris* case corroborate Judge Posner's claim (see *United States v. Rutledge*, 11th ed., p. 731) that "product of a free choice" talk "leads nowhere"?

11th ed., p. 733; end of section, consider the following:

MARK A. GODSEY—RETHINKING THE INVOLUNTARY CONFESSION RULE: TOWARD A WORKABLE TEST FOR IDENTIFYING COMPELLED SELF–INCRIMINATION

93 Calif.L.Rev. 465, 473, 491–92, 501, 515–17, 539–40 (2005).

[Professor Godsey "delineates a new confession test, called the 'objective penalties test,' based on the self-incrimination clause, in which the touchstone for admissibility would be compulsion rather than voluntariness." This test would exclude confessions obtained "by imposing an objective penalty in any form" on the suspect in order to punish his silence or to provoke speech. In Part IV of his article, Professor Godsey sets forth various hypothetical interrogations and analyzes how these problems would be resolved under his newly proposed test.]

[Professor Godsey then underscores the distinction between the texts of the self-incrimination clause and the due process clause:] The self-incrimination clause says nothing about voluntary confessions—only compelled ones. If the self-incrimination clause provided "no involuntary confession shall be admitted against any defendant," then a subjective, totality of the circumstances test would be appropriate. The word "voluntary," after all, is an adjective that describes the state of mind of the suspect when he confesses. It semantically focuses the inquiry primarily on the state of mind of the suspect under interrogation, and it considers the conduct of the interrogators only in relation to the effect such conduct produces on the state of mind of the particular subject under interrogation.

In contrast, the term "compel," as used in the self-incrimination clause and in the context of its placement in the Bill of Rights, is a verb that relates primarily to the action of the government official performing the interrogation rather than the subjective mental state of the suspect.
* * *

Miranda stands as a watershed decision in the history of constitutional confession law not simply because of its notoriety, but because it finally corrected the historical and legal errors in confession jurisprudence that stem back through the due process era and all the way to *Bram* [discussed in 11th ed. at pp. 569, 58, 681, 718].

The first important accomplishment of the *Miranda* decision was that it shifted the focus of confession law from due process back to its proper home: the self-incrimination clause. The self-incrimination clause had finally been made applicable to the states two years before *Miranda*; thus, by the time *Miranda* was decided, the Court no longer needed to rely on its strained due process experiment as it had for the previous three decades.

Second, the Court in *Miranda* seemingly abandoned the voluntariness rubric and recognized that the correct test for confession admissibility in the Bill of Rights is compulsion, as the text of the self-incrimination clause dictates. This important step not only made confession jurisprudence consistent with the Bill of Rights, but it also seemingly overruled the Court's legal error in *Bram* and in which the Court adopted the inapposite common law evidentiary rule of voluntariness as the sine qua non of confession admissibility.

Third, the Court in *Miranda* finally appeared to rid itself of the reliability rationale. This policy rationale had been present in constitutional confession jurisprudence since *Bram* when it was engrafted into confession law as a result of the Court's legal errors. The reliability rationale then flourished during the due process era, as it coincided with the all-encompassing, subjective voluntariness test that the Court constructed during that time period.

Finally, the *Miranda* decision correctly interpreted the self-incrimination clause and the term "compulsion" as requiring an objective test. The definition of "compulsion" in the *Miranda* decision examined only the pressure placed on the suspect from an objective standpoint. The *Miranda* Court specifically refused to consider whether the suspect in question actually felt atmospheric pressure from the custodial interrogation or even whether the suspect was aware of his rights. In other words, *Miranda* stands for the proposition that the government is prohibited from using confessions obtained through compulsion in a general, objective sense, regardless of the state of mind of the specific suspect under interrogation in a given case.

The curative benefits of *Miranda* were fleeting, as a newly constructed Court began turning back the clock to the due process era shortly after *Miranda* was decided. The major flaw with the reasoning in *Miranda*, which perhaps led to its downfall, is that it defined "compulsion" too broadly. *Miranda* essentially held that the atmospheric pressure that exists whenever an officer asks a question—any question—to a suspect in custody is compulsion in violation of the self-incrimination clause (unless the officer dissipates the compulsion by giving the required warnings and obtaining a waiver). Under the *Miranda* paradigm, atmospheric pressure alone equates with compulsion. * * *

[The] Court should develop and implement an objective penalties test to regulate the admissibility of confessions. This test would suppress a confession if the police impose a penalty on a suspect during an interrogation to punish silence or provoke speech because such a penalty would constitute compulsion in violation of the self-incrimination clause if the confession is later admitted into evidence against the suspect. This concept is not entirely without precedent. The 1967 decision of *Garrity v. New Jersey* [, 385 U.S. 493,] is perhaps the one existing bridge that arguably links the objective penalties test from the formal setting cases with the interrogation context. In *Garrity*, several police officers were convicted of participating in a traffic ticket-fixing scheme. At their trials, the government introduced confessions that the officers had previously made at an inquiry held by the Attorney General of New Jersey. The officers had confessed at the inquiry only after being warned that they would lose their jobs if they invoked the right to remain silent. In reversing the convictions and holding the officers' confessions inadmissible, the majority of the Court seemingly relied on two distinct grounds: the due process involuntary confession rule and the objective penalties test from the formal setting cases. Regarding the objective penalties test, the Court stated:

> The choice given petitioners was either to forfeit their jobs or to incriminate themselves. The option to lose their means of livelihood or to pay the penalty of self-incrimination is the antithesis of free choice to speak out or to remain silent. That practice, like the interrogation practices we reviewed in *Miranda v. Arizona*, [is impermissible].

The Court went on to note that the self-incrimination clause provides suspects with a right to remain silent, a right of "constitutional stature whose exercise a State may not condition by the exaction of a price."
* * *

The *Garrity* decision raises the following paramount question: If threatening a suspect with termination violates the self-incrimination clause and renders a confession inadmissible as a matter of law when the threat occurs in a formal inquiry, why would this same sort of threat not render a confession inadmissible as a matter of law when it occurs in the stationhouse interrogation room? For example, an interrogating officer might threaten to make a behind-the-scenes effort to get a suspect fired from his private sector job if the suspect does not confess to a crime. Under existing law, such a threat would render the resulting confession inadmissible only if the court found that the threat overbore the will of the suspect and elicited an involuntary confession. But many courts might hold such a confession voluntary and admissible on the theory that an innocent man would rather lose his job than confess to a crime. Why would such a threat in a police interrogation room not also constitute an impermissible penalty on the exercise of a constitutional right and render the confession inadmissible as a matter of law? There is no satisfactory distinction between the two scenarios. The objective penalties test should be applied in the latter scenario as well. * * *

Conclusion

The involuntary confession rule is perhaps the most criticized doctrine in all of criminal procedure. With a doctrine that is so troubling and problematic, one might rationally assume that the Court has never parted ways with it because it is required by the Bill of Rights, and the Court has no choice but to suffer through it. Or, one might rationally assume that the doctrine has survived through time because no better alternative exists. Neither of these assumptions is accurate.

In adhering to the voluntariness test, the Court has betrayed the text, historical origins, and policies of the self-incrimination clause. These sources demonstrate that a more consistent and theoretically satisfying test for confession admissibility would be an objective analysis of the conduct of the interrogator in question. These sources reveal that the proper test for confession admissibility should be based on the concept of compulsion, found within the text of the self-incrimination clause. These sources, coupled with interpretations of the self-incrimination clause outside of the interrogation context, indicate that the proper test for compulsion is an objective penalties test. * * *

SECTION 7. *MASSIAH* REVISITED; *MASSIAH* AND *MIRANDA* COMPARED AND CONTRASTED

11th ed., p. 742; after the Notes, add new Note (c):

(c) Suppose the police violate a person's Sixth Amendment right to counsel, but a short time later give him the *Miranda* warnings and he waives his rights. Suppose, further, that the police then obtain a new batch of incriminating statements. Would (should) the courts admit them in evidence? Cf. *Patane* (11th ed., p. 703) and *Seibert* (11th ed., p. 707). See the Eighth Circuit opinion in *United States v. Fellers*, this Supplement, p. 68.

Chapter 10
LINEUPS, SHOWUPS AND OTHER PRE-TRIAL IDENTIFICATION PROCEDURES

SECTION 1. *WADE* AND *GILBERT*: CONSTITUTIONAL CONCERN ABOUT THE DANGERS INVOLVED IN EYEWITNESS IDENTIFICATION

11th ed., p. 768; end of Note 7, add:

Consider STEVE BOGIRA, *Courtroom 302* (2005) (the story of one year in one courtroom in Chicago's Cook County Criminal Courthouse) at 266–67:

"This was chiefly an eyewitness case in [defense lawyer Edward] Genson's mind. It boiled down to whether the jury should trust the IDs of Clevan and of William Jaramillo, the Hispanic youth who was also present at the beginning of the attack. Genson hadn't done an eyewitness case in recent years, and so when he'd taken on [defendant Frank] Caruso, he'd boned up on the subject. What he learned, he says, was that misidentifications are commonplace.

"Genson had wanted the jury to hear from Elizabeth Loftus, a psychology professor at the University of California at Irvine and the nation's most prominent expert on eyewitnesses. As Genson outlined in a pretrial filing, Loftus would have testified that eyewitnesses err frequently, particularly when identifying a person of another race. This testimony was especially relevant, Genson had told [Cook County Judge Daniel] Locallo before the trial, because Clevan and Jaramillo had both waffled on their IDs at the police station, first picking Jasas as the initiator of the attack and then switching to Caruso. Loftus would have also informed the jury that suggestions from police to a witness regarding their expectations, even subtle and unintended ones, greatly increase the chance of error. Genson maintained that this was relevant because the second lineup had been so suggestive. Caruso had been in the same position Jasas had been in—on the far left—and he'd been dressed similarly to Jasas.

"Loftus had written five books on eyewitnesses and testified in 225 cases. It may fairly be said that she 'wrote the book' on the subject of eyewitness perception, memory retention and recall, the Arizona Supreme

Court once observed. But like most of his colleagues at 26th Street, Locallo takes a dim view of eyewitness experts. In barring Loftus's testimony, Locallo said he trusted the jury to use its common sense in deciding how much stock to put in Clevan's and Jaramillo's identifications. 'She can write all the books she wants,' Locallo would say later. 'I don't have much faith in these self-styled experts.'

Chapter 11
GRAND JURY INVESTIGATIONS

SECTION 2. FOURTH AMENDMENT CHALLENGES TO THE INVESTIGATION

11th ed., p. 816; following Note 6, add:

7. Spurred on by criticism that all the 9/11 hijackers could have been linked and identified in advance by careful analysis of available data, the federal government has redoubled its efforts to collect and examine enormous quantities of personal information. In addition to the existing databases, numbering almost 2,000, already maintained by federal agencies and departments, the federal government has acquired additional data from the public records of cooperating states and also, sometimes by subpoena (typically administrative, see Note 2, p.799) but often by purchase or other cooperative arrangement, a vast array of data held in the private sector, especially by the travel, telecommunications, financial, service, and relatively new database industries. Using highly sophisticated computer equipment, the federal government has been able to engage in data aggregation, by which an enormous amount of data has been integrated, and data mining, by which otherwise undiscoverable patterns and subtle relationships are uncovered through statistical analysis and modeling. See Christopher Slobogin, *Transaction Surveillance*, ___ Miss.L.Rev. ___ 2005 (reviewing government data-gathering practices, and noting the limited applicability of the various federal statutory provisions governing third party subpoenas, see e.g., Note 3, p.836).

Does the Fourth Amendment have nothing to do with this activity because *Miller* teaches that "when information maintained by third parties is exposed to others, it is not private, and therefore not protected by the Fourth Amendment," and if so, is it thus fair to say that *Miller* and related decisions have become "the new *Olmstead* and *Goldman*," no more protective against the data gathering/mining process than those cases were against wiretapping? Daniel J. Solove, *Digital Dossiers and the Dissipation of Fourth Amendment Privacy*, 75 S.Cal.L.Rev. 1083, 1087, 1137 (2002). What questions should be asked in determining whether *Miller* ought to apply to the data gathering/mining process? Consider: (1) as to aggregation, whether the government's "integration of previously discrete, distributed sources of information—each which it may have the perfect legal right to access individually—"negates the "practical obscurity" the Court in another context, in *Department of Justice v. Reporters Committee for Freedom of the Press*, 489 U.S. 749 (1989) (determining the scope of Freedom of Information Act exemption), concluded was deserving of protection, K.A. Taipale, *Data Mining and Domestic Security: Connecting the Dots to Make Sense of Data,* 5 Colum.Sci. & Tech.L.Rev.2 (2003); and (2) as to mining, which involves acquisition of "new knowledge," whether it is "possible for data that does not in itself deserve legal protection to contain implicit knowledge that does deserve legal protection," Joseph S. Fulda, *Data Mining and Privacy*, 11 Alb.L.J.Sci. & Tech. 105, 106, 109 (2000). Consider also Slobogin supra, arguing that several basic distinctions may play a role in determining the appropriate level of Fourth Amendment governance of data-gathering, including: (1) whether the records sought are "organizational" or "personal," cf. Notes 2–4, p.854; (2) whether the records are privately held records or public records, recognizing, however, that some records held by public entities are just as "personal" as records held by private entities, a distinction commonly acknowledged in FOIA statutes; (3) whether the data sought reveals content or is largely "catalogic", i.e., largely classifying and describing a transaction; and (4) whether the data is accumulated by reference to an individual target or by reference to a type of transaction. Is still another relevant distinct whether the government's data-gathering uses unique technology or governmental authority (e.g., subpoenas) or simply the same technology used by commercial data brokers in their data-gathering?

Chapter 12
THE SCOPE OF THE EXCLUSIONARY RULES

SECTION 2. THE "FRUIT OF THE POISONOUS TREE"

11th ed., p. 922; after the discussion of the *Johnson* case in Note 7, add the following:

Compare *Johnson* with UNITED STATES v. PULLIAM, 405 F.3d 782 (9th Cir. 2005). Los Angeles police followed a car in which suspected gang members Richards and Pulliam were the driver and the passenger, respectively. Upon noticing that the car's left rear brake light was out, the police made a lawful stop of the vehicle. However, the district court ruled that the police had no reasonable basis for going any further and that both the continued detention of Pulliam and the subsequent search of the car were illegal. Since the car search had turned up a gun (which proved to be key evidence in the prosecution of Pulliam for being a felon in possession of a firearm), the district court suppressed the weapon. However, a 2–1 majority of the Ninth Circuit, per WALLACE, J., reversed:

"As a passenger with no possessory interest in the car Richards was driving, Pulliam 'has no reasonable expectation of privacy in a car that would permit [his] Fourth Amendment challenge to a search of the car.' Similarly, the mere fact that Pulliam 'claimed ownership' of the gun does not confer standing upon him to seek its suppression. *Rawlings*. [In] addition, Pulliam does not argue that the detention of the car after the stop constituted a de facto seizure of his person. That is, he does not contend that even if the officers had permitted him to leave, he nonetheless could not reasonably have been expected to do so because the officers continued to detain the car.

"[Pulliam] does have standing to contest the legality of his own detention. [However, he] has failed to demonstrate that the gun is in some sense the product of his detention. The officers conducted no interrogation of him before searching the car and found nothing incriminating during the patdown. Even if they had immediately released him rather than detaining him, the search of the car still would have occurred, and the gun would have been

65

found. The discovery and seizure of the gun was simply in no sense the product of any violation of Pulliam's fourth amendment rights. * * *

"[Pulliam] contends that a passenger should be able to seek suppression of the 'fruits' of all constitutional violations that occur during a traffic stop—including those that do not affect the passenger's own fourth amendment rights—because the officials' actions are closely related in time, place and purpose. [But] when, as here, the initial stop is lawful, the situation is different. The continued detention of the vehicle does not necessarily entail the detention of its occupants; they could simply be permitted to walk away. If a passenger is unlawfully detained after the stop, he can of course seek to suppress evidence that is the product of that invasion of his own rights. But a passenger with no possessory interest in a vehicle usually cannot object to *its* continued detention or suppress the fruits of that detention, because 'Fourth Amendment rights are personal rights [which] may not be vicariously asserted.' *Rakas*. We may not amalgamate the separate police actions of detaining the car, detaining each of its occupants, and searching the car, merely because they occurred in close proximity. * * *

"Pulliam assumes that in reasoning that the gun would have been found as a result of the unlawful *search* of the vehicle even if he had not been unlawfully *detained*, we are essentially holding the gun is admissible because the search provides an alternative, inevitable means of discovery. Accordingly, he argues that because the search was unlawful, we are misapplying this exception. See *United States v. Johnson* (7th Cir. 2004). [If] this case involved any 'exception' to the exclusionary rule at all, it would be the 'independent source' exception, since the gun was actually found in a search of the car. [We] do not, however, have to apply either 'exception' in this case because the indispensable causal connection between his detention and discovery of the gun has not been met. The requisite but-for causation is missing not only because the gun was found as a result of the search, but because his detention simply did not contribute or lead to the gun's discovery."

Dissenting Judge WARDLAW protested:

"Here, the government concedes that the officers lacked authority to detain the car and its occupants. In addition, it is clear that, but for the illegal actions of the police in detaining the car and its passengers, the gun would not have been discovered. Therefore, the district court correctly granted Pulliam's motion to suppress. * * *

"The majority reasons that 'when, as here, the initial stop is lawful, the situation is different' because '[t]he continued detention of the vehicle does not necessarily entail the detention of its occupants; they could simply be permitted to walk away.' But this is too fine a line to draw in our Fourth Amendment jurisprudence. * * * Like illegally stopping an automobile, unlawfully detaining a vehicle after a legal stop 'significantly curtails the "freedom of action" of the driver and the passengers, if any, of the detained vehicle.' This is especially true in this case, where the government admits that once the car stopped, 'the officers got out of their patrol car and, with their guns drawn and aimed low, ordered the driver and Pulliam out of the car' for a pat down search. Even short of the overt threat of force in this case, and the unlawful detention that followed, it is illogical to assume that any passenger would walk away from a vehicle and driver that have been stopped and detained by the police.

"Therefore, there is no principled reason to distinguish between a situation involving an illegal stop, in which case a passenger may suppress evidence found as a result of the illegal stop, and a situation involving a legal stop but illegal detention, in which case, according to the majority's analysis, a passenger may not suppress evidence found as a result of the illegal detention. For purposes of the fruits analysis here, we must focus on the detention of the vehicle and its occupants as the 'primary illegality,' for they all stemmed from the officers' single decision to detain and search the car, Pulliam, and the driver. The detention of the vehicle and the detention of its occupants are part of a single, integrated instance of unconstitutional police conduct. * * *

"[The majority opinion] finds no support in the logic of the Fourth Amendment. The core rationale for extending the exclusionary rule to evidence that is the fruit of unlawful police conduct is that 'this admittedly drastic and socially costly course is needed to deter police from violations of constitutional and statutory protections.'

"[The] majority undermines this rationale. [It tells police officers that] 'there are potential law enforcement benefits to be derived, at least against passengers, in [unlawfully detaining vehicles and their passengers] even when, as [here], such action is flagrantly illegal.' Wayne R. LaFave, *Search and Seizure* § 11.4(d) (4th ed. 2004). [The] majority opinion invites police officers to engage in patently unreasonable detentions, searches, and seizures every time an automobile contains more than one occupant. Should something be found, only the owner of the vehicle will be able to successfully move to suppress the evidence; the evidence will be admissible against the other occupants. After this decision, police officers will have little to lose, but much to gain, by legally stopping but illegally detaining vehicles occupied by more than one person."

Can the *Pulliam* case be squared with *Johnson*? If so, what exactly is the distinction between the two cases? If not, is this because, as the *Pulliam* dissent observes, "we must focus on the detention of the vehicle and its occupants as the 'primary illegality,' for they all stemmed from the officers' single decision to detain and search the car, Pulliam, and the driver"? Is such linking of the detention of the vehicle with the detention of the passenger more appropriate in some circumstances than in others? Consider that the *Pulliam* majority emphasized that Pulliam "did not argue that the detention of the car after the stop constituted a de facto seizure of his person," in the sense that "even if the officers had permitted him to leave, he nonetheless could not reasonably have been expected to do so because the officers continued to detain the car." Does this mean *Pulliam* would have come out differently if the vehicle had been detained on the shoulder of an interstate highway in a desolate rural area rather than, as it was, on the streets of Los Angeles?

11th ed., p. 922; after the references to *Patane* and *Seibert*, add new subsection:

D. Is A "Second Confession" Following A Failure to Comply with the *Massiah* Doctrine Admissible?

In *Nix v. Williams* all the Justices seemed to assume that the "fruit of the poisonous tree" doctrine applied to statements obtained in violation of *Massiah*. (Otherwise, why would there have been any need to establish that the case came within the "inevitable discovery" *exception* to the "poisonous tree" doctrine?) However, in *Fellers v. United States*, 540 U.S. 519 (2004) (discussed briefly in 11th ed. at pp. 739–40), the Court reversed the conviction and remanded the case to the Eighth Circuit to determine whether the defendant's "second confession" should have been suppressed as the fruit of the initial Sixth Amendment violation and whether *Oregon v. Elstad* (11th ed., p. 701) "applies when a suspect makes incriminating statements after a knowing and voluntary waiver of the right to counsel notwithstanding earlier police questioning in violation of Sixth Amendment standards." On remand, the Eighth Circuit upheld the admissibility of the "second confession":

UNITED STATES v. FELLERS
397 F.3d 1090 (8th Cir. 2005).

WOLLMAN, Circuit Judge.

[After defendant Fellers was indicted for conspiracy to distribute methamphetamine, police questioned him in his own home without counsel. Fellers made several incriminating statements. Fifteen minutes later, he was transported to jail, taken to an interview room and given a full *Miranda* warning. After waiving his rights, Fellers repeated the statements he had made earlier and made some additional incriminating remarks. The district court suppressed the statements Fellers had made in his home but admitted the statements he had made at the jailhouse. Fellers was convicted of conspiracy to distribute methamphetamine.]

Fellers argues that *Elstad* does not apply to violations of the Sixth Amendment because the *Elstad* rule was never designed to deal with actual violations of the Constitution. In addition, *Fellers* argues that *Elstad*–which was crafted to serve the Fifth Amendment–is inapplicable because it is ill-suited to serve the distinct concerns raised by the Sixth Amendment and because violations of the *Miranda* rule are fundamentally different from the Sixth Amendment violations at issue in this case. We disagree.

[The] Supreme Court stated in *Elstad* that its rejection of the exclusionary rule in the *Miranda* context was premised on the fact that a violation of *Miranda* was not, by itself, a violation of the Fifth Amendment and on the fact that the protections afforded by the *Miranda* rule sweep more broadly than the Fifth Amendment itself. [This] justification for *Elstad*'s holding, however, was undercut by the Court in *Dickerson*, [holding] that *Elstad*'s rationale rested not only on the fact that *Mi-

randa was not a constitutionally mandated rule, but instead on the fact that unreasonable searches under the Fourth Amendment are different from unwarned interrogation under the Fifth Amendment.

[Although] the exclusionary rule is most often applied in the Fourth Amendment context, its application has not been limited to Fourth Amendment violations. The Supreme Court instead has applied the exclusionary rule to violations of both the Fifth and Sixth Amendment. The Court has repeatedly noted, however, that the core reason for extending the exclusionary rule to these areas is to deter police from violating constitutional and statutory protections. Another relevant consideration in extending the exclusionary rule is whether application of the rule would effectuate the purposes of the constitutional provision at issue. The Fourth Amendment traditionally mandates a "broad application" of the exclusionary rule. The exclusionary rule operates in the Fourth Amendment context to deter unreasonable searches and seizures regardless of the probativeness of their fruits. * * *

[The] Fifth Amendment, in contrast, prohibits the prosecution from using compelled testimony in its case in chief and ensures that any evidence introduced at trial will be voluntary and thus trustworthy. Because confessions or statements taken in violation of *Miranda* give rise to an irrebuttable presumption that they have been compelled, they must be excluded from the prosecution's case in chief. This presumption of compulsion, however, does not bar the use of unwarned statements for impeachment purposes. In addition, as *Elstad* held, the presumption does not preclude the introduction of a subsequent warned statement at trial. Because the *Miranda* warnings give the suspect the information he needs to choose whether to exercise his right to remain silent, the suspect's choice to speak after receiving *Miranda* warnings is normally viewed as an "act of free will." Furthermore, because the introduction of the subsequent warned statement at trial entails no risk that compelled testimony will be used against a suspect, suppression of the subsequent warned statement neither deters violations of the Fifth Amendment nor ensures that the statement was not compelled. Accordingly, the ordinary exclusion rule gives way to the *Elstad* rule, and subsequent warned confessions given after initial *Miranda* violations are admissible. * * *

We conclude that the exclusionary rule is inapplicable in Fellers's case because, as with the Fifth Amendment in *Elstad*, the use of the exclusionary rule in this case would serve neither deterrence nor any other goal of the Sixth Amendment. Both the deterrence of future Sixth Amendment violations and the vindication of the Amendment's right-to-counsel guarantee have been effectuated through the exclusion of Fellers's initial statements. Although the officers acknowledged that they used Fellers's initial jailhouse statements (obtained after securing a *Miranda* waiver) in order to extract further admissions from him, there is no indication that the interrogating officers made any reference to Fellers's prior uncounseled statements in order to prompt him into making new incriminating statements. In addition, because Fellers's initial statements related to persons already named in the indictment and to his own personal use of methamphetamine (the drug he was accused of conspiring to distribute and to possess with intent to distribute), the officers would have had a basis for the questions asked during the jailhouse interrogation even if Fellers had said nothing at all at his home. * * *

[The] similarities between the Sixth Amendment context at issue in Fellers's case and the Fifth Amendment context at issue in *Elstad* support our conclusion that the *Elstad* rule applies when a suspect makes incriminating statements after a knowing and voluntary waiver of his right to counsel, notwithstanding earlier police questioning in violation of the Sixth Amendment. Although the Supreme Court has never explicitly stated that the *Elstad* rationale is applicable to Sixth Amendment violations, it has emphasized the similarity between pre-indictment suspects subjected to custodial interrogation and post-indictment defendants subjected to questioning.

The Court has held that the scope of the right to counsel varies depending upon the usefuless of counsel to the accused at a particular proceeding and the dangers to the accused of proceeding without counsel. *Patterson v. Illinois* [11th ed., p. 740]. Unlike during trial, where the accused truly requires aid in meeting his legal adversary, the full "dangers and disadvantages of self-representation" during post-indictment questioning are more apparent to an accused. Furthermore, because "[t]he State's decision to take an additional step and commence formal adversarial proceedings against the accused does not substantially increase the value of counsel to the accused at questioning or expand the limited purpose that an attorney serves when the accused is questioned by authorities," there is no significant difference between a lawyer's usefulness to a suspect during pre-indictment custodial interrogation and his usefulness at post-indictment questioning. [*Patterson*].

[In] contrast with the statement made at Fellers's home, Fellers's jailhouse statements were given after a proper administration of *Miranda* warnings and a proper oral and written waiver of his *Miranda* rights. The *Miranda* warnings fully informed Fellers of "the sum and substance" of his Sixth Amendment rights. Furthermore, no evidence indicates that either Fellers's initial statements or his subsequent jailhouse statements were coerced, compelled, or otherwise involuntary. As a result, the condition that made his prior statements inadmissible–the inability to have counsel present or to waive the right to counsel–was removed. * * *

Finally, we conclude that the officers' conduct in this case did not vitiate the effectiveness of the *Miranda* warnings given to Fellers. We apply a multi-factor test derived from the Supreme Court's recent plurality opinion in *Missouri v. Seibert*[, 11th ed., p. 707], in order to determine whether *Miranda* warnings delivered between two interrogation sessions are sufficient to fully inform a suspect of his *Miranda* rights. We consider: (1) the extent of the first round of interrogation; (2) the extent to which the first and second rounds of interrogation overlap;

(3) the timing and setting of both questioning sessions, including whether a continuity of police personnel existed; and (4) the extent to which the interrogator's questions treated the second round as continuous with the first.

In Fellers's case, the facts are much closer—if not identical—to the facts at issue in *Elstad* than to the facts at issue in *Seibert*. [As] in *Elstad*, the unwarned conversation at Fellers's home was relatively brief. Although the same officers that deliberately elicited statements from Fellers at his home also conducted Fellers's jailhouse interrogation, that interrogation took place almost one half hour later than the conversation at Fellers's home and in a new and distinct setting. In addition, while Fellers's warned jailhouse statements overlapped to a small degree with his initial unwarned, uncounseled admissions, the jailhouse interrogation went well beyond the scope of Fellers's initial statements by inquiring about different co-conspirators and different allegations. There is also no indication that the officers in this case treated the two rounds of interrogation as continuous, such as by using statements from the unwarned conversation to prompt admissions after receipt of a *Miranda* waiver. * * *

Fellers's case also comports with Justice Kennedy's concurrence in *Seibert*. [Under] Justice Kennedy's framework, the *Elstad* rule applies in the Fifth Amendment context only in the absence of a deliberate law enforcement strategy designed to obtain incriminating statements in violation of *Miranda*. Because there is no evidence that the officers in this case employed such a deliberate strategy, the concerns voiced by Justice Kennedy are satisfied. * * *[a]

[a] The court added that even if Fellers's jailhouse statements were erroneously admitted, any error was harmless beyond a reasonable doubt. For Fellers's statements were either corroborated by other witnesses (whose testimony went largely unchallenged) or were immaterial to the case.

*

Part Three

THE COMMENCEMENT OF FORMAL PROCEEDINGS

Chapter 13

PRETRIAL RELEASE

SECTION 1. THE RIGHT TO BAIL; PRETRIAL RELEASE PROCEDURES

11th ed., p. 958; end of Note 10, add:

10a. Should the crime victim have a right to testify at defendant's bail hearing, as provided in 18 U.S.C.A. § 3771(a)(4), Supp. App. B, and comparable state provisions? About what? Consider Lynne Henderson, *Revisiting Victim's Rights*, 1999 Utah L. Rev. 383, 406, regarding an earlier but similar proposal: "None of these proceedings necessarily invites the telling of the whole story, and it is absolutely unclear how many times in the criminal process it would be necessary for victims to be allowed to tell their stories for therapeutic value. Related to this is the question of the weight that authorities ought to give such statements.

"The provisions * * * are mostly silent on the reasons for victims presenting statements in court—that is, what the relevance and substantive effects of those statements should be—and what procedures ought to be followed in permitting those statements. It seems doubtful—or remains to be proved—that victims would be content to make statements knowing that they would have very little, if any, legal effect."

Chapter 14

THE DECISION WHETHER TO PROSECUTE

SECTION 1. THE OFFICE OF PROSECUTOR AND THE NATURE OF THE DECISION WHETHER TO PROSECUTE

11th ed., p. 981; before LaFave excerpt, add:

BRUCE A. GREEN & FRED C. ZACHARIAS— PROSECUTORIAL NEUTRALITY

2004 Wis.L.Rev. 837, 902–03.

[T]he fact remains that, for better or worse, prosecutors are among the least accountable public officials. As a result, in evaluating prosecutors' work, the public tends to overemphasize the measurable or obvious aspects of what prosecutors do (e.g., the number of convictions they obtain, the length of sentences, and prosecutors' behavior in public trials) and tend to overlook more momentous decisions that occur behind the scenes. Prosecutors' limited public accountability might be acceptable, or at least more acceptable, if there were well-established normative standards governing prosecutors' discretionary decision-making. In that event, the public could elect people of integrity to serve as prosecutors, or higher officials could appoint them, and then trust them faithfully to apply accepted criteria. But our analysis of the concept of "prosecutorial neutrality" demonstrates that there are no settled understandings, except perhaps at the most general and abstract level. All might agree that prosecutors should be "neutral," just as they might agree that prosecutors should be "fair" or that they should "seek justice." But none of these terms has a fixed meaning. They are proxies for a constellation of other, sometimes equally vague, normative expectations about how prosecutors should make decisions.

As we have shown, neutrality has been used in different contexts to denote a range of expectations that can be grouped under three different conceptions: nonbias, nonpartisanship, and principled decision-making. These dimensions of neutrality, though somewhat more concrete than the umbrella term, still have variable content. Nor is it clear how the conceptions fit together. In the end, therefore, these too fall short in providing meaningful guidance for the discretionary decisions that prosecutors routinely must make.

Consequently, there is a need for more robust commentary and analysis. It is neither helpful simply to ask prosecutors to be "neutral" nor fair to criticize prosecutors for alleged failures to act "neutrally." Indeed, the neutrality rhetoric is singularly unpersuasive as criticism, because even the most egregious prosecutorial decisions can ordinarily be defended as "neutral" in some sense of the term.

SECTION 2. SOME VIEWS ON DISCRETION IN THE CRIMINAL PROCESS AND THE PROSECUTOR'S DISCRETION IN PARTICULAR

11th ed., p. 989, end of Note 1, add:

Consider also *Town of Castle Rock v. Gonzales*, Supp. p. 44.

11th ed., p. 990; end of Note 2, add:

Regarding such nullification by a *grand* jury, see United States v. Navarro–Vargas, Supp. p. 76.

Chapter 16
GRAND JURY REVIEW

SECTION 1. THE ROLE OF GRAND JURY REVIEW

11th ed., p. 1067, end of Note 3, add:

As to the court's charge to the jury, consider also *United States v. Navarro–Vargas*, set forth below.

SECTION 4. MISCONDUCT CHALLENGES

11th ed., p. 1096, after Note 3, add:

UNITED STATES v. NAVARRO–VARGAS
408 F.3d 1184 (9th Cir.2005) (en banc).[*]

BYBEE, Circuit Judge.

This is the fourth challenge we have heard in this circuit to consider whether the model grand jury instructions violate the Fifth Amendment by undermining the independence of the grand jury. * * * [In separate prosecutions of defendants Navarro–Vargas and Leon–Jasso], the district court instructed the grand jury using the model charge recommended by the Judicial Conference of the United States. The grand jury charge included the following explanations and instructions (for convenience we have numbered the paragraphs):

[1] The purpose of a Grand Jury is to determine whether there is sufficient evidence to justify a formal accusation against a person. If law enforcement officials were not required to submit to an impartial Grand Jury proof of guilt as to a proposed charge against a person suspected of having committed a crime, they would be free to arrest and bring to trial a suspect no matter how little evidence existed to support the charge.

[2] As members of the Grand Jury, you in a very real sense stand between the government and the accused. It is your duty to see to it

---

[*] Before Schroeder, Chief Judge and Pregerson, Hawkins, Silverman, Wardlaw, W. Fletcher, Berzon, Rawlinson, Clifton, Bybee, and Bea, Circuit Judges.

that indictments are returned only against those whom you find probable cause to believe are guilty and to see to it that the innocent are not compelled to go to trial....

[3] You cannot judge the wisdom of the criminal laws enacted by Congress, that is, whether or not there should or should not be a federal law designating certain activity as criminal. That is to be determined by Congress and not by you. Furthermore, when deciding whether or not to indict, you should not be concerned about punishment in the event of conviction. Judges alone determine punishment.

[4] [Y]our task is to determine whether the government's evidence as presented to you is sufficient to cause you to conclude that there is probable cause to believe that the accused is guilty of the offense charged. To put it another way, you should vote to indict where the evidence presented to you is sufficiently strong to warrant a reasonable person's believing that the accused is probably guilty of the offense with which the accused is charged....

[5] It is extremely important for you to realize that under the United States Constitution, the grand jury is independent of the United States Attorney and is not an arm or agent of the Federal Bureau of Investigation, the Drug Enforcement Administration, the Internal Revenue Service, or any governmental agency charged with prosecuting a crime. There has been some criticism of the institution of the Grand Jury for supposedly acting as a mere rubber stamp, approving prosecutions that are brought before it by governmental representatives. However, as a practical matter, you must work closely with the government attorneys. The United States Attorney and his Assistant United States Attorneys will provide you with important service in helping you to find your way when confronted with complex legal problems. It is entirely proper that you should receive this assistance. If past experience is any indication of what to expect in the future, then you can expect candor, honesty, and good faith in matters presented by the government attorneys. * * *

Navarro–Vargas and Leon–Jasso contend that the grand jury's independence was compromised when it was instructed in paragraphs [3], [4], and [5] that it "should vote to indict" the accused in each case in which it believed probable cause exists, that it could not "judge the wisdom of the criminal laws enacted by Congress," and that government counsel would use "candor, honesty, and good faith." The Appellants argue that this error is structural and requires dismissal of the indictment. * * *

The Grand Jury Clause of the Fifth Amendment provides that "[n]o person shall be held to answer for a capital, or otherwise infamous crime, unless on a presentment or indictment of a Grand Jury, except in cases arising in the land or naval forces, or in the Militia, when in actual service in time of War or public danger." * * * The Clause is remarkably plain in its restrictions. It is also notable for what it does not say. The

Clause presupposes much about grand juries. It does not prescribe the number of jurors. It does not limit the grand jury's function to returning or refusing to return indictments. It does not state whether a person appearing before the grand jury may be accompanied by counsel, whether the rules of evidence apply, or whether its proceedings may be disclosed for any purposes. See, e.g., *United States v. Williams*, [11th ed., p.1085] * * *; *Costello v. United States* [11th ed., p.1077]. The text of the Fifth Amendment simply provides for the right to indictment by a grand jury and does not explain how the grand jury is to fulfill this constitutional role. Either such details were assumed by the framers of the Bill of Rights or they decided to leave such details to Congress, the Executive, and the Judiciary. * * *

The [Supreme] Court has observed that the grand jury is an "English institution, brought to this country by the early colonists and incorporated into the Constitution by the Founders. There is every reason to believe that our constitutional grand jury was intended to operate substantially like its English progenitor." *Costello*. Because the Constitution presumes a role for the grand jury, the Fifth Amendment must be linked to the grand jury's origins. We review briefly the history of the grand jury to understand its function and something of why "[h]istorically, this body has been regarded as a primary security to the innocent against hasty, malicious and oppressive persecution . . . [and] stand[s] between the accuser and the accused." *Wood v. Georgia,* [11th ed., p. 1060]. * * * Whether the model grand jury instructions violate the Grand Jury Clause depends on what the Clause's cryptic reference to "Grand Jury" means and whether independence (in the sense advocated by the Appellants) is an irreducible element of what it means to have a grand jury. And for that inquiry, our starting point must be the grand jury's history, recognizing that any recounting of a near-millennia of history will give us only the broadest contours of an ancient institution.

A. The Historical Role of the Grand Jury

[The Court here discusses, under separate headings, four periods in the historical development of the grand jury: "1. The Early English Grand jury: Quasi–Prosecutor"; "2. The Colonial Grand Jury: Quasi–Legislative, Quasi–Administrative"; "3. The Post–Revolutionary and Nineteenth Century Grand Jury: Screening Function"; and "4. The Modern Grand jury". The grand jury of the first period is characterized as operating as a "sword to be welded on behalf of the Crown", rather than as "a shield to protect the accused." However, in 1681, two London grand juries, in refusing to indict the Earl of Shaftesbury and Stephen College ("political enemies of King Charles II") provided the "first real evidence of the grand jury acting as a shield," and established "grand jury secrecy, which continues to be a crucial element in grand juries serving as an independent screen."

[During the colonial period, the prominent development was the grand jury's assumption of "broad powers to propose legislation and perform various administrative tasks." In this connection, during the period immediately preceding the Revolutionary war, grand juries gained great popularity as a result of their political activism (calling for "boycotts of British goods," etc.) During the colonial period, grand juries also "continued to serve as accusatory bodies," and "they occasionally refused to return indictments in high-profile cases" (the "most celebrated example" being the refusal to indict John Peter Zenger). Grand juries, in this role, also "frustrated prosecutors loyal to the king by refusing to indict those charged under unpopular laws imposed by the Crown, often on the urging of colonial judges."

[During the third period ("post-Revolutionary and 19th century") grand juries continued to act independently, but "judges instructed the jurors to enforce federal laws, even if the jury thought the laws unjust or unconstitutional." Thus, in the administration of the Alien and Sedition Act, federalist judges "impress[ed] upon grand juries the necessity for strict enforcement," although the jurors "often reacted against [such] heated charges and refused to indict." The "political potential in the screening function of the grand jury was also manifest during the Civil War era. Prior to the war, Southern grand juries readily indicted those involved in crimes related to abolition of the slave trade, while Northern grand juries were slow to indict those charged with violations of the fugitive slave laws. Following the Civil War, Southern grand juries frustrated enforcement of Reconstruction-era laws by refusing to indict Ku Klux Klan members and others accused of committing crimes against newly-freed blacks."

[During the fourth period (the 20th century), "confrontations between prosecutors and jurors in grand jury proceedings had become rare." Commentators often claimed "that the modern grand jury has lost its independence," but the "Supreme Court has steadfastly insisted that the grand jury remains as a shield against unfounded prosecutions."]

* * *

[*History of*] *the* * * * *Model Charge*. The first model grand jury charge was issued in 1978 by the Judicial Conference of the United States. * * * The original model charge is very similar to the one used by federal judges today, and includes all of the phrases challenged by Appellants as unconstitutional. In 1986, the Judicial Conference revised and shortened the model grand jury charge. * * * This is the most recent revision of the model charge and contains the phrases to which Appellants have objected here.

At least nine states have addressed issues similar to those before us and have arrived at different conclusions. The majority of the states have adopted instructions similar to the federal model instructions.* * * By contrast, in two states, New York and Minnesota, the model grand jury instructions use language stating that the grand jury "may" indict if the government proves its case rather than "should" indict.* * * The Minnesota instruction [also] goes further to instruct the grand jury that it "is not obliged to return an indictment, even though you find there is probable cause, if you do not feel there is a reasonable prospect of a conviction." * * * In addition, Arkansas' model charge broadly instructs the grand jury that it is to "inquire into all public offenses committed in this county and to indict such persons whom you think guilty."

Finally, we note that a number of courts have considered whether *petit* juries should be informed of their nullification power. The courts have uniformly rejected the idea. *United States v. Trujillo*, [11th ed., p. 1387]; *United States v. Dougherty*, [11th ed., p. 1386]. * * *

* * * Looking over this record, we observe that the weight of U.S. history favors instructing the grand jury to follow the law without judging its wisdom. We candidly admit, however, that the evidence is not overwhelming and the record is not uniform in this regard. We are left to consider the role of federal grand juries on the terms on which the Constitution gave us the right in the first place: by understanding the grand jury's place in the larger structure of our tripartite system.

B. THE STRUCTURAL ROLE OF THE GRAND JURY

The grand jury belongs to no branch of government, but is a "constitutional fixture in its own right." *Williams*. Although no branch may control the grand jury, each branch enjoys some power to direct or check the grand jury's actions. "[T]radition and the dynamics of the constitutional scheme of separation of powers define a limited function for both court and prosecutor in their dealings with the grand jury." *United States v. Chanen* [11th ed., p. 1087] * * *. The grand jury does not belong to the judicial branch, but it is "subject to the supervision of a judge" in some respects. *Branzburg v. Hayes* [11th ed., p. 829]. * * * Grand juries and prosecutors serve as a check on one another. The grand jury, acting on its own information, may return a presentment, may request that the prosecutor prepare an indictment, or may review an indictment submitted by the prosecutor. The prosecutor has no obligation to prosecute the presentment, to sign the return of an indictment, or even to prosecute an indictment properly returned. See *United States v. Batchelder*. [11th ed., p. 1019]. * * * Similarly, the grand jury has no obligation to prepare a presentment or to return an indictment drafted by the prosecutor. The grand jury thus determines not only whether probable cause exists, but also whether to "charge a greater offense or a lesser offense; numerous counts or a single count; and perhaps most significant of all, a capital offense or a noncapital offense—all on the basis of the same facts." *Vasquez v. Hillery*, [11th ed., p. 1075]. And, significantly, the grand jury may refuse to return an indictment even "where a conviction can be obtained." Id.

The grand jury's discretion—its independence—lies in two important characteristics: the absolute secrecy surrounding its deliberations and vote and the unreviewability of its decisions. At least since the seventeenth century, the grand jury has deliberated in secret, and neither the judge nor the prosecutor may question the grand jury's findings, conclusions, or motives. In fact, the 1974 version of the Federal Handbook for Grand Jurors notes that "[t]he secrecy imposed upon grand jurors is a major source of protection for them."

The grand jury's decision to indict or not is unreviewable in any forum; its decision is final. *See Costello,* [11th ed., p. 1077]. * * * It is the fact that its judgments are unreviewable and its deliberations unknowable that gives the grand jury its independence. * * * Indeed, the grand jury is uniquely unaccountable; grand jurors are insulated from public oversight in ways that no other government instrumentality is. Judges must issue their decisions on the public record; prosecutors must inform the accused of the nature of the charges and conduct a public trial. * * * Decisions by judges and prosecutors are subject to review and public criticism; and, in extreme cases, judges and executive officers may be impeached for their decisions and, if convicted, removed from office. * * * Grand juries are not subject to these constraints. * * *

Grand jury independence is a two-edged sword, of course, because the same privilege is due grand jurors who refuse to indict for violations of civil rights laws or who take into account the race or gender of the accused or the victim when deciding to return a no bill. In all of these cases, for better or for worse, it is the *structure* of the grand jury process and its *function* in our system that makes it independent.

C. Appellants' Objections to the Model Instructions

With this in mind, we turn to the Appellants' arguments. They challenge three instructions that in their view "demean" the grand jury's historical responsibility. Appellants do not ask us to rewrite the instructions in any particular way, but they suggest that no instruction would be better than an incorrect instruction. We consider each challenged instruction in turn.

1. *"The Wisdom of the Criminal Laws."* Navarro–Vargas and Leon–Jasso first challenge the passage [in paragraph 3] that states: "You cannot judge the wisdom of the criminal laws enacted by Congress, that is, whether or not there should or should not be a federal law designating certain activity as criminal. That is to be determined by Congress and not by you. Appellants contend that this passage unconstitutionally misinstructs the grand jury as to its role and function." * * *

We first wish to observe that the instruction is not contrary to any long-standing historical practice surrounding the grand jury. We know of no English or American practice to advise grand juries that they may stand in judgment of the wisdom of the laws before them. Indeed, there is strong evidence to support the current instruction. We have previously cited the attestation or oath required of grand jurors in an early and influential colonial constitution which enjoined the jurors to "diligently enquire and true presentment make, of all such matters and things as shall be given thee in charge, or come to thy knowledge." * * * We have also cited evidence of charges given shortly after the adoption of the Bill of Rights in which federal judges charged grand juries with a duty to submit to the law and to strictly enforce it. * * *

The phrase "wisdom of the laws" is not a term of art. We might assume that the phrase means that juries cannot question whether the law represents good policy. If a grand jury can sit in judgment of wisdom of the policy behind a law, then the power to return a no bill in such cases is the clearest form of "jury nullification." The "wisdom of the laws" might also refer to a broader power of substantive constitutional review—the power to determine that the law is unconstitutional and, therefore, void. * * * We doubt that the grand jury is particularly well suited to make either of these judgments, although, as we discuss below, there is no check on the ability of the grand jury to do so. * * *

We recognize and do not discount that some grand jurors might *in fact* vote to return a no bill because they regard the law as unwise at best or even unconstitutional. For all the reasons we have discussed, there is no *post hoc* remedy for that; the grand jury's motives are not open to examination. Moreover, there is no *ex ante* solution either; there is nothing to prevent a grand jury from engaging in nullification or substantive constitutional review, not even the model grand jury instructions. History demonstrates that grand juries do not derive their independence from a judge's instruction. Instead, they derive their independence from an unreviewable power to decide whether to indict or not.

The question before us is whether judging the wisdom of the law is so integral to the role of the grand jury that it is constitutional error for the district court to instruct against it. We cannot say that the instruction is so contrary to the grand jury's role that it violates the Fifth Amendment. Or, put another way, we cannot say that the grand jury's power to judge the wisdom of the laws is so firmly established that the district court must either instruct the jury on its power to nullify the laws or remain silent.

2. *"Should" Indict if Probable Cause Is Found.* Navarro–Vargas and Leon–Jasso also claim that * * * [paragraph 4] misinstructs the grand jury. * * * Appellants claim that this passage is unconstitutional because it instructs grand jurors that they "should" indict if they find probable cause, but does not explain that they can refuse to indict even if they find probable cause. Further, Appellants argue that the instructions use the singular terms "purpose" and "task" in advising the grand jurors that their sole responsibility is to make probable cause determinations. Even though the instructions indicate that the jurors "should" indict if they find probable cause, Appellants believe that the model charge reasonably read, imposes upon the grand jury a *duty* to indict if they find probable cause. Appellants argue that this improper instruction deprives them of the "traditional functioning of the institution that the Fifth Amendment demands."

This instruction does not violate the grand jury's independence. The language of the model charge does not state that the jury "must" or "shall" indict, but merely that it "should" indict if it finds probable cause. As a matter of pure semantics, it does not "eliminate discretion on the part of the grand jurors," leaving room for the grand jury to dismiss even if it finds probable cause. *United States v. Marcucci,* [11th ed., p.1064, fn. c]. * * *

Even assuming that the grand jury should exercise something akin to prosecutorial discretion, the instruction does not infringe upon that discretion. The analogy that the [Supreme] Court [has] recognized between the grand jury and the prosecutor is useful for understanding the source of both the grand jury's and prosecutor's discretion. *See Butz v. Economou,* 438 U.S. 478, 510 (1978). Under Article II, § 3, the president "shall take Care that the Laws be faithfully executed." That duty can be delegated to subordinates, including the attorney general and the U.S. attorneys serving in each judicial district. * * * U.S. attorneys, operating with limited resources, are literally incapable of seeing that each and every federal law is executed.* * * It is also possible that an attorney general might decide not to enforce, or at least to underenforce, politically controversial laws or laws that, in the attorney general's view, are unconstitutional. In effect, a decision not to prosecute someone who would likely be indicted and could be convicted is a form of prosecutorial nullification. *See United States v. Cox,* [11th ed., p. 994]. * * * [But] the president's independence arises not out of any constitutional direction to exercise prosecutorial discretion, prosecutorial nullification, or substantive constitutional review, but out of the lack of any check on the president's ability to do so. * * *

Even though the terms "purpose" and "task" are singular, conveying that the grand jury has one purpose, these instructions do not undermine the grand jury's purpose and function. The instructions remind the grand jury that it has "extensive powers" and in "a very real sense stand[s] between the government and the accused." Admittedly, the instructions do not explain to the grand jury what its "extensive powers" are or have been in the past, including its power to refuse to indict even when a conviction can be obtained. However, the instructions remind the grand jury of its independence from the federal government and leave room for it to refuse to indict. Consequently, we conclude that this instruction is not inconsistent with the Fifth Amendment.

3. *The "Candor, Honesty, and Good Faith" of Government Attorneys.* Finally, Appellants claim that the following passage [in paragraph 5] inappropriately instructs the grand jury: "The United States Attorney and his Assistant United States Attorneys will provide you with important service in helping you to find your way when confronted with complex legal problems. It is entirely proper that you should receive this assistance. If past experience is any indication of what to expect in the future, then you can expect candor, honesty, and good faith in matters presented by the government attorneys."

Appellants claim that this vote of confidence by the judge to the honesty of the government attorneys further undermines the independence of the grand jury. They argue that the grand jury is told to independently evaluate probable cause but that this independence is diluted by this instruction that encourages deference to prosecutors. * * * We also reject this final contention and hold that although this passage may include unnecessary language, it does not violate the Constitution. The "candor, honesty, and good faith" language, when read in the context of the instructions as a whole, does not violate the constitutional relationship between the prosecutor and grand jury. The contested passage may be surplusage, but it is not unprecedented. Apparently, these laudatory comments about the prosecutor have been included in grand jury materials for some time. * * *

Again, the question before us is whether this language is unconstitutional, not whether it is overly deferential or unnecessary. This passage would be problematic if it misinstructed the grand jury that it was an agent of the U.S. attorney and not an independent body acting as a check to the prosecutor's power. However, it does not do this. It reminds the grand jury that it stands between the government and the accused and is independent. The laudatory language is likely unnecessary, but it surely does not threaten the constitutional relationship between the prosecutor and grand jury.

In upholding the model grand jury instructions against Appellants' constitutional challenge, we do not necessarily hold that the current instructions could not or should not be improved. We recognize the commentary pointing to discrete changes [in grand jury practice] that tend to reduce the independence of the modern grand jury and the commentary urging reform in expanding the grand jury's duty and role in the criminal process. We even concede that there may be more done to further increase the shielding power of the modern federal grand jury. However, we are not a drafting committee for the grand jury instructions. We are not faced with the question of how to reform the modern grand jury but whether its model instructions are constitutional. To answer this question, we hold that the provisions of the model grand jury instructions challenged here are constitutional. * * *

HAWKINS, Circuit Judge, with whom Circuit Judges PREGERSON, WARDLAW, W. FLETCHER, and BERZON join, dissenting.

* * * When Congressman James Madison sat down to write out a series of proposed amendments to the freshly-adopted Constitution, he was painfully aware of the ratification process in which the absence of a Bill of Rights had provoked such strident opposition. Fresh in the minds of the former colonists was their treatment at the hands of the British Crown and their reliance on devices that protected them from what they saw as the arrogant exercise of the Crown's authority. Opponents of the proposed constitution wanted assurances that what they viewed as the best of those protections would continue in the new government. On any short list of those protective devices would have been the grand jury. When King George III's colonial appointees sought sedition charges against John Peter Zenger for his editorials critical of the Crown, and when participants in the Boston Tea Party faced criminal charges, what stood between Americans and the dock was a grand jury made up of their fellow citizens, free to refuse a prosecutor's entreaties or a king's demands.

The grand jury requirement now lives in the Fifth Amendment. It says, plainly and simply, that no serious (felony) charge may be brought without the approval of a group of citizens, drawn at large from the community, who are entirely free to charge what the government proposes, to charge differently, or to not charge at all. Operating in secret and answerable to no one for its decisions, the grand jury is a truly unique institution.

Two hundred fifteen years have brought about some considerable changes in the grand jury. Its use as an investigative tool is more common now, as is criticism for its potential for abuse. But regardless of its apparent virtues and vices, the requirement of the grand jury's independent exercise of its discretion is a fixed star in our constitutional universe. For that reason, it is important to consider whether the way in which our courts today instruct grand jurors comports with the constitutional history of the Fifth Amendment and the grand jury institution.
* * *

Critical to an understanding of the serious constitutional issue we face is what the challenged grand jury instructions *do* say and the remedy the appellants *do* seek. As to the first, the grand jurors here were clearly and improperly told that their powers were limited to determining probable cause. They were also told that they could not consider the wisdom of the law or the possible punishment, and that they could expect "candor, honesty, and good faith in matters presented by the government attorneys." As to the second, the appellants do not seek a nullification instruction. Instead, both Leon–Jasso and Navarro–Vargas propose that "the judge not tell the jury that the law requires that the grand jury not consider the wisdom of criminal laws or punishment, since the law is the exact opposite."

Improperly Limiting Grand Jurors to Probable Cause Determination. The instructions begin by telling the grand jurors that what would follow outlines their responsibilities. This prefatory emphasis is significant because the instructions go on to explain that "the purpose of the Grand Jury is to determine whether there is sufficient evidence to justify a formal accusation against a person." A grand juror paying close attention would conclude that the purpose of the grand jury is *singular* and that its discretion is constrained by the instruction.

This impression is confirmed again later in the charge: "Your task is to determine whether the government's evidence as presented to you is sufficient to cause you to conclude that there is probable cause." Once again, the instruction defines the purpose, or "task," singularly, and even the majority concedes that "the terms 'purpose' and 'task' are singular, conveying that the jury has a unique purpose." Once again, the unique purpose conveyed is determining probable cause. The instruction seems to compel the grand jury to indict as long as probable cause exists: "[Y]ou should vote to indict where the evidence presented to you is sufficiently strong to warrant a reasonable person's believing that the accused is probably guilty of the offense with which the accused is charged."

The majority discounts the admonishment "should," arguing that it is distinct from "must" or "shall." Even "[a]s a matter of pure semantics," the majority is incorrect to say that the use of the word "should" preserves the grand jury's discretion. The word "should" is used "to express a duty [or] obligation." *The Oxford American Dictionary and Language Guide* 931 (1999). * * * The "should" and "shall" distinction is a lawyer's distinction, not a difference most lay people sitting as grand jurors would be likely to understand. The instruction's use of the word "should" is most likely to be understood as imposing an inflexible "duty or obligation" on grand jurors, and thus to circumscribe the grand jury's constitutional independence. * * * This "should" admonishment is at odds with the grand jury's broad independent role. As the Supreme Court held in *Vasquez v. Hillery,* [11th ed., p. 1075], "[t]he grand jury does not determine *only* that probable cause exists to believe that a defendant committed a crime, or that it does not." (emphasis added).

Limiting the Grand Jury's Protective Role. The grand jury's independence serves not only in the determination of probable cause, as these grand juries were instructed, but also to protect the accused from the other branches of government by acting as the "conscience of the community." *Gaither v. United States,* 413 F.2d 1061, 1066 n. 6 (D.C.Cir. 1969). * * * The significance of this second—and potentially protective—role should not be understated. Indeed, the strength of this understanding is emphasized in *Vasquez.* There, the Supreme Court said [11th ed., p. 1075]: "In the hands of the grand jury lies the power to charge a greater offense or a lesser offense; numerous counts or a single count; and perhaps most significant of all, a capital offense or a noncapital offense—all on the basis of the same facts. Moreover, '[the] grand jury is not bound to indict in every case where a conviction can be obtained.' *United States v. Ciambrone,* 601 F.2d 616, 629 (C.A.2 1979) (Friendly, J., dissenting)."

* * *Though grand jurors undoubtedly possess these powers, and the majority so acknowledges, * * * the jurors in this case were misled by the instructions given to them, told that their powers were restricted to probable cause. This necessarily compromises their independence. Further eroding the powers described in *Gaither* and *Vasquez,* the instructions admonish grand jurors:

> You cannot judge the wisdom of the criminal laws enacted by Congress, that is, whether or not there should or should not be a federal law designating certain activity as criminal. That is to be determined by Congress and not by you. Furthermore, when deciding whether or not to indict, you should not be concerned about punishment in the event of conviction. Judges alone determine punishment.

This instruction improperly limits the jurors' discretion regarding the proper scope of application of federal criminal law, as well as matters of sentencing. * * *

Questioning the Wisdom of the Law & Prosecutorial Discretion. As to questioning the wisdom of a criminal law, consider the language from the *Gaither* decision: "Since it has the power to refuse to indict even where a clear violation of law is shown, the grand jury can reflect the conscience of the community in providing relief where strict application of the law would prove unduly harsh." *Gaither.* * * * How is it then that the grand jury lacks the power to consider the wisdom of a law applied to a particular case?

The grand jury must have the power to consider the wisdom of a law because it performs what is undeniably a prosecutorial function. * * * [A]n important part of the prosecutorial function is deciding which potential defendants to select for criminal prosecution, and how serious the charges should be. Prosecutors can, and often do, make such decisions based on their judgments as to how wise and important certain laws may be. * * * And herein lies the essential hypocrisy of the government's position. Standing firmly in the defense of its exercise of discretion (amounting at times to nullification), it just as firmly argues that grand jurors are without authority to make similar judgments about which laws deserve vigorous enforcement and which ones do not, in deciding whom to indict, and on what charges. In the government's eye, the grand jury is a mere instrument of prosecutorial will, a probable cause screening device obligated to act at the direction of the prosecutor and then only when the prosecutor has decided whom and how much to charge. * * * But grand jurors have been traditionally viewed as the "conscience of the community," a function that partakes far more of judgment and discretion than of the narrow ministerial role that the challenged instructions assign to them. Because the *petit* jury may not take into account community values to decide whether to convict, it is even more important to foster this traditional function of the grand jury–a body not subject to the prohibition against double jeopardy or other procedural constraints that apply once the case proceeds to trial. * * *

Severity of the Punishment. As to the severity of punishment, the Supreme Court in *Vasquez* stated that the grand jury has "the power to charge a greater offense or a lesser offense; numerous counts or a single count; and perhaps most significant of all, a capital offense or a non-capital offense[,] all on the basis of the same facts." If grand jurors can choose, per *Vasquez,* between capital and non-capital offenses, how could they not be influencing the determination of punishment? They are exerting such influence, and they should be able to continue to do so, not boxed in by jury instructions that seek to eradicate this important function.

Instructions as Structural Protections. After long historical exegesis, the majority apparently agrees that a grand jury has the power to refuse to indict someone even when the prosecutor has established probable cause that this individual has committed a crime. * * * We part company, however, when it comes to how to protect this power of the grand jury. The majority believes that the "structure" and "function" of the grand jury—particularly the secrecy of its proceedings and unreviewability of many of its decisions—sufficiently protects that power. But the majority fails to see that the instructions given a grand jury shape its structure and function. Typical grand juries, including the grand jury in these cases, hear evidence from the prosecutor and receive instructions from the judge. Those instructions do not include a reference to *Vazquez* or a discussion of the full range of the grand jury's powers, and include the language we have discussed, which jurors are likely to understand as *precluding* the authority to refuse to indict if there is probable cause. Conscientious grand jurors, instructed as were the jurors in these cases, will *believe* they lack any authority beyond that on which they are instructed, and will act accordingly.

Instructing a grand jury that it lacks power to do anything beyond making a probable cause determination thus unconstitutionally undermines the very structural protections that the majority believes saves the instruction. The power to deliberate in secret is valuable, but limiting the factors included in that deliberation circumscribes that power. Similarly, the power to make unreviewable decisions is a serious power indeed, but limiting the range of considerations that impact those decisions undermines that power. Given the "almost invariable assumption of the law that jurors follow their instructions," *Richardson v. Marsh,* 481 U.S. 200, 206 (1987), we must assume that grand jurors followed the instructions offered in this case and, therefore, that the instructions undermined the very structural factors on which the majority rests its decision.

Indeed, there is something supremely cynical about saying that it is fine to give jurors erroneous instructions because nothing will happen if they disobey them. Grand jurors come in with no knowledge of the system, but, one would hope, a desire to fulfill their assigned role, not to flout it. Indeed, our legal system assumes that jurors have this desire, an assumption embodied in the *Richardson* presumption that jurors will fulfill their role as instructed by those in authority.

Praising the Government Attorneys. Further invading the independence of the grand jury was the court's instruction that it could expect "candor, honesty, and good faith in matters presented by the government attorneys." In Leon–Jasso's case, the judge also told the grand jurors that the prosecutors were "wonderful public servants." What these instructions do not tell grand jurors is that prosecutors are free to deprive the grand jurors of exculpatory evidence, *Williams,* to provide unconstitutionally seized evidence, *United States v. Calandra,* [11th ed., p. 1082], and to present evidence otherwise inadmissible at trial, *Costello*. How independent can a grand jury be when they are told how wonderful the prosecutors are? The majority concedes that the "candor, honesty, and good faith" instruction is "unnecessary language," but attempts to justify its constitutionality by demonstrating that this language has been included for some time and claiming that the laudatory remarks do not threaten the constitutional relationship between the prosecutor and grand jury. Appellants, however, have the better argument: the grand jury's independence is diluted by this instruction, which encourages deference to prosecutors. By undermining the grand jury's independence, this part of the grand jury instruction is also unconstitutional.

The Petit Jury Analogy. Arguing from a remedy not sought to an institution not involved, the majority relies upon the rejection of nullification instructions in the petit jury context. But this argument ignores an important distinction between the two groups: with petit juries, jeopardy attaches, whereas with grand juries, a new prosecution effort can begin. Because evidence can always be re-presented to a second grand jury, it is far from inevitable that justice will not be done if grand jurors were given a full disclosure instruction.

Because the Framers placed a high value on the kinds of powers articulated by *Vasquez* for grand juries, it would be unjustifiably paternalistic to fail to tell the grand jurors the scope of their constitutional powers over charging decisions specifically entrusted to their judgment. Finally, it is a mistake to conclude that a full disclosure instruction to a grand jury would subvert the rule of law. If our constitutional system permits the grand jury to act on its "conscience," then it hardly makes sense to say that a grand juror who chooses to not indict despite probable cause is acting lawlessly. Rather, that action lies fully within the discretion delegated by the Constitution.

The petit jury analogy not only fails, it also provides a powerful reason for allowing the grand jury the independence to consider, for example, the wisdom of the law under which a suspect is to be prosecuted: we no longer permit petit juries to exercise such discretion, * * * for the perfectly sensible reason that petit jurors decide guilt or innocence in accordance with clearly established legal standards. If grand juries, too, cannot exercise such discretion, then considerations such as the wisdom of the law will be isolated from any citizen's review, subject only to the prosecutor's discretion. * * *

Structural Error. These instructions are unconstitutional because they actively mislead grand jurors into thinking their powers are more constrained than they are. Which raises the next question: if error, is it a structural error, or is it subject to harmless error review?

The answer, based on *Vasquez,* is that it is a structural error. In *Vasquez,* the Supreme Court *presumed* prejudice, concluding that the systematic exclusion of blacks from the grand jury pool amounted to structural error, for which prejudice to the defendant need not be shown. This result issued, despite the argument that "requiring a State to retry a defendant, sometimes years later, imposes on it an unduly harsh penalty for a constitutional defect bearing no relation to the fundamental fairness of the trial." *Vasquez.* The *Vasquez* Court rejected this contention, noting that fundamental flaws, such as racial discrimination in the grand jury, "undermine[ ] the structural integrity of the criminal tribunal itself, and [are] not amenable to harmless-error review."

To determine whether the presumption of prejudice attaches, the Supreme Court demands that we employ a traditional test: to determine whether "the structural protections of the grand jury have been so compromised as to render the proceedings fundamentally unfair." *Bank of Nova Scotia v. United States,* [11th ed., p. 1100]. But the high court also stated that courts should look to whether any inquiry into harmless error would require unguided speculation. Id. * * * And, this is indeed an area of "unguided speculation." Perhaps a grand jury would have exercised its discretion in favor of one or all of the defendants here; among other things, Navarro–Vargas is a young man with no serious criminal record, except one previous drug conviction. The judge exercised discretion in favor of Navarro–Vargas by sentencing him to the "low end of the guidelines." The judge in Leon–Jasso's case noted his military commendation, the impact of a prison term on his family, and his honesty in admitting his conduct, when he granted a two-level downward departure for sentencing, and then sentenced at the bottom of the range. Put differently, it is conceivable that a grand jury made aware of its role as "conscience of the community" would have provided "relief where strict application of the law would prove unduly harsh." *Gaither,* 413 F.2d at 1066 n. 6.

"[A] reviewing court can never know whether or not an unbiased and properly constituted grand jury would have simply declined to indict at all or might have charged a lesser offense." *United States v. Marcucci,* 299 F.3d 1156, 1173 (9th Cir.2002) (Hawkins, J., dissenting). Where structural error occurs, it is no adequate reply that the appellants did not demonstrate that "irregularities" existed such that the presumption of regularity should be disturbed. For it is precisely the "regular" and "traditional" functioning of the grand jury—its potential to exercise either justice-guided discretion or compassion-based mercy even against a finding of probable cause—that was hobbled by these instructions. In short, the appellants were denied the "traditional functioning of the institution that the Fifth Amendment demands." *Williams.* Because the defendants here were convicted after their grand juries were erroneously instructed, and because the erroneous instructions constituted a substantial impediment to the regular functioning of the grand jury as envisioned by the Constitution, I would reverse the convictions, dismiss these indictments, and allow the government to re-present evidence to a grand jury properly instructed as to its independent role.

Chapter 19

THE SCOPE OF THE PROSECUTION: JOINDER AND SEVERANCE OF OFFENSES AND DEFENDANTS

SECTION 2. FAILURE TO JOIN RELATED OFFENSES

11th ed., p. 1186, at end of Note 5, add:

When the *Stumpf* case reached the Supreme Court, *Bradshaw v. Stumpf*, Supp. p. 93, the Court concluded that when the state in the later trial of Stumpf's robbery accomplice Wesley put in evidence that Wesley admitted shooting one Mrs. Stout, this was in any event not inconsistent with Bradshaw's earlier guilty plea to aggravated murder, as the precise identity of the triggerman was immaterial to Stumpf's aggravated murder conviction. As for Stumpf's claim that such evidence at Wesley's trial was inconsistent with the claim at Stumpf's penalty hearing, resulting a sentence of death, that Stumpf had killed Mrs. Stout, the Court found such ambiguity in the court of appeal's view on that distinct issue that it remanded the case to that court.

Part Four

THE ADVERSARY SYSTEM AND THE DETERMINATION OF GUILT OR INNOCENCE

Chapter 22

COERCED, INDUCED AND NEGOTIATED GUILTY PLEAS; PROFESSIONAL RESPONSIBILITY

SECTION 1. SOME VIEWS OF NEGOTIATED PLEAS

C. ACCURATE AND FAIR RESULTS

11th ed., p. 1305; before Note 10, add:

9a. "[W]hy would [Michael] Kwidzinski plead guilty if he was innocent and if the evidence against him was so feeble?

"For the same reason many defendants at 26th Street do. As [defense lawyer Kevin] Bolger explains, once a person is facing felony charges, the issue no longer is whether he did the crime; it's how to limit the damage.

"A wise defendant, with the help of his lawyer, thinks pragmatically, Bolger says. Kwidzinski's choice, when he was offered the plea deal, was a guarantee of no prison, with only a misdemeanor conviction, versus a chance, albeit slim, of conviction and prison if he insisted on trial. Sometimes trials bring surprises—surprises that turn the flimsiest cases into convictions, says Bolger, a former prosecutor. 'Police lie, witnesses lie. It's a fact of life. So you get the best deal you can and you get out of there.'

"[Cook County Judge Daniel] Locallo allows that pleading guilty can sometimes be a 'very attractive scenario,' even for the innocent, and that had he been in Kwidzinski's shoes—considering a possible six to thirty versus misdemeanor probation—he 'probably would have jumped at' the plea offer, innocent or not.

"Prosecutors are apt to make pleading guilty an especially attractive scenario for the innocent. The weaker the case against the defendant, the more likely his acquittal if the case goes to trial—and therefore the better the bargain offered by the state in its attempt to get the conviction. Kwidzinski was offered a better deal than [Victor] Jasas—misdemeanor probation instead of felony probation—because the evidence against him was thinner than it was against Jasas. Never mind that the evidence was thinner because he likely was innocent." STEVE BOGIRA, *Courtroom 302* at 334 (2005).

SECTION 2. REJECTED, KEPT AND BROKEN BARGAINS; UNREALIZED EXPECTATIONS

11th ed., p. 1319; at end of Note 1, add:

As a unanimous Court later put it in *Bradshaw v. Stumpf*, Supp. p. 93, citing *Brady*, "a plea's validity may not be collaterally attacked merely because the defendant made what turned out, in retrospect, to be a poor deal. Rather, the shortcomings of the deal Stumpf obtained cast doubt on the validity of his plea only if they show either that he made the unfavorable plea on the constitutionally defective advice of counsel, or that he could not have understood the terms of the bargain he and Ohio agreed to."

SECTION 3. PROFESSIONAL RESPONSIBILITY; THE ROLE OF PROSECUTOR AND DEFENSE COUNSEL

11th ed., p. 1353; after Note 4, add:

5. An instance of nondisclosure which *does* fall within the *Ruiz* holding might nonetheless be deemed a basis for overturning a guilty plea on other than constitutional grounds, as in *State v. Harris*, 680 N.W.2d 737 (Wis. 2004) (where under state's reciprocal discovery statute prosecutor should have disclosed to defendant before he entered his negotiated plea two weeks before scheduled trial date, in prosecution for sexual assault of child, the material exculpatory impeachment evidence that alleged victim had reported being sexually assaulted by her grandfather on a different occasion, defendant entitled to withdraw negotiated guilty plea, as the evidence could have raised serious questions about credibility of victim).

11th ed., p. 1357; end of Note 2, add:

See 18 U.S.C.A. § 3771(a)(4), Supp. App. B, concerning the right of the victim to be heard at a federal plea hearing.

SECTION 4. RECEIVING THE DEFENDANT'S PLEA; PLEA WITHDRAWAL

C. Determining Guilty Plea is Understandingly Made

11th ed.; p. 1360; before last paragraph in Note 1, add:

In *Bradshaw v. Stumpf*, 125 S.Ct. 2398 (2005), where the court of appeals had held the habeas petitioner's guilty plea was invalid because he had not been informed of the aggravated murder charge's specific intent element, a unanimous Court, per O'Connor, J., disagreed: "In Stumpf's plea hearing, his attorneys represented on the record that they had explained to their client the elements of the aggravated murder charge; Stumpf himself then confirmed that this representation was true. While the court taking a defendant's plea is responsible for ensuring 'a record adequate for any review that may be later sought,' we have never held that the judge must himself explain the elements of each charge to the defendant on the record. Rather, the constitutional prerequisites of a valid plea may be satisfied where the record accurately reflects that the nature of the charge and the elements of the crime were explained to the defendant by his own, competent counsel. Where a defendant is represented by competent counsel, the court usually may rely on that counsel's assurance that the defendant has been properly informed of the nature and elements of the charge to which he is pleading guilty."

11th ed., p. 1365; before Note 5, add:

4a. Regarding the *Kwidzinski* case described in Note 9a, Supp. p. 92, the narration continues: "But in their haste to bag a plea, judges at 26th Street sometimes accept a factual basis that's devoid of facts.

"That's what happened when Kwidzinski and Jasas pled guilty to Locallo. For the factual basis, [prosecutor Ellen] Mandeltort simply said the state and the defense were stipulating that Jasas and Kwidzinski had both been 'legally responsible and accountable' for Caruso's action when Caruso punched Lenard and Clevan at 33rd and Shields. But to be accountable for another offender's actions in Illinois, a person must solicit, aid, or attempt to aid that offender. If there was a witness who could have testified as to how Kwidzinski or Jasas had solicited, aided, or tried to aid Caruso at 33rd and Shields, Mandeltort didn't mention him. She didn't mention any witnesses. While the factual basis doesn't require much specificity, it requires more than a prosecutor asserting, and the defense lawyers agreeing, that the facts would show the defendant was guilty. That would be a meaningless exercise, redundant of the defendant's plea, and providing no protection against guilty pleas from the innocent.

"But Locallo didn't press Mandeltort for more. Instead he perfunctorily asked the lawyers for Kwidzinski and Jasas if they'd stipulate that 'if those witnesses were called that they would testify in the manner as discussed'— an odd question, considering that Mandeltort didn't mention any witnesses testifying. Without hesitation, the defense lawyers stipulated. Locallo asked Jasas and Kwidzinski how they wanted to plead, and they said they wanted to plead guilty. Locallo immediately found their pleas to be 'knowing and voluntary' and that there was a factual basis for them.

"The factual basis 'probably should have been more thorough,' Locallo conceded later, when I read the transcript of the pleas to him." STEVE BOGIRA, *Courtroom 302* at 335 (2005).

Is judge Locallo (and, for that matter, prosecutor Mandeltort and defense attorney Bolger) deserving of sanctions as a result of this occurrence? Would any of them be so deserving if, instead, the factual basis had been found wanting and Kwidzinski was thereafter convicted nonetheless and received something in the predicted 6–30 years imprisonment? Or, is the latter question unfair? Why?

Chapter 23
TRIAL BY JURY

SECTION 1. THE RIGHT TO JURY TRIAL

11th ed., p. 1388; end of Note 6, add:

See also *United States v. Navarro–Vargas*, Supp. p. 76.

11th ed., p. 1389; end of Note 9, add:

Consider also Nancy J. King, David A. Soulé, Sara Steen, & Robert R. Weidner, *When Process Affects Punishment: Differences in Sentences After Guilty Plea, Bench Trial, and Jury Trial in Five Guidelines States*, 105 Colum.L.Rev. 959, 965–66, 979–80 (2005), a statistical study examining if and how a defendant's decision to waive a jury affected his sentence in five states using sentencing guidelines. "The Supreme Court has not yet addressed the constitutionality of *uniform* sentencing credits for waiving the right to a jury, the right to any trial, or the right to appeal. * * * In light of the doubts about the legal and social acceptability of statewide punishment discounts for the waiver of constitutional rights, it is not surprising that no state guidelines system explicitly recommends that defendants who waive a jury trial in favor of either a guilty plea or a bench trial should be punished more leniently than defendants convicted of the very same offense who insist upon jury trial. Yet in many courtrooms these sentencing differences are routine. * * * At least some interviewees in each state suggested that a sentencing discount is expected in exchange for a jury waiver, even if the discount is not explicitly negotiated. And in most of the states examined, there are some offenses that do seem to support the prediction of graduated discounts, with plea cases sentenced most leniently, followed by more severe sentences after bench trials, followed by the most severe sentences following jury trials."

SECTION 2. JURY SELECTION

11th ed., p. 1394; end of first paragraph of Note 2, add:

Consider also *State v. Fulton*, 566 N.E.2d 1195 (Ohio 1991) (Amish comprise distinctive group when they make up about 35% of the population and have a "separate and distinct mode of living"); *State v. Chidester*, 570 N.W.2d 78 (Iowa 1997) (persons whose employers will not compensate them during jury service do not qualify as distinctive group because they do not share an "immutable characteristic" or "similar ideas attitudes, or experiences").

11th ed., p. 1394; before first paragraph of Note 3, add:

Cross-section claims have prompted litigation over the meaning of the "community" to be represented fairly. Sometimes a defendant disputes the geographic boundaries of the area from which jurors are drawn, known as the "vicinage." Just as the choice of boundaries for voting districts can affect the racial and ethnic composition of voters, vicinage determinations can affect the composition of jury pools.

Assuming the appropriate geographic area is settled, a successful cross-section claim requires more than proof that the proportion of the venire made up of group members is small compared to the group's proportion in the total population. Instead, the community that must be represented fairly in the venire is the community of "citizens eligible for jury service," a population sometimes difficult to quantify. See *Sanders v. Woodford*, 373 F.3d 1054 (9th Cir.2004) (prima facie case of underrepresentation of Hispanics not made out when study compared number of Hispanics in the jury wheel with total Hispanic population instead of the population of Hispanics who were jury-eligible citizens), cert. granted on other grounds, 125 S.Ct. 1700 (2005).

11th ed., p. 1395; after Note 3, add:

3a. *What is systematic exclusion?*

Assume that a cognizable group is underrepresented in a given venire in part because members of that group are less likely than members of other groups to stay at one address, register to vote, or respond to juror questionnaires. Is it "systematic exclusion" if the state chooses not to modify its random jury selection procedures to update addresses more frequently, draw potential jurors from drivers' lists as well as voter rolls, or follow-up on questionnaires? See *Le v. State*, ___ So.2d ___, 2005 WL 977007 (Miss.2005) (rejecting cross-section claim, noting that potential jurors were selected by computer and stating, "we fail to see how Asians are excluded from the jury pool, other than the fact that some Asians do not wish to vote and, therefore, willfully exclude themselves from the voter roll"); *People v. Morales*, 770 P.2d 244 (Cal.1989) (disparity attributable to "economic, cultural, social or language considerations * * * must be deemed unavoidable"). See also *State v. Fulton*, 566 N.E.2d 1195 (Ohio 1991) (not systematic exclusion when Amish residents were absent from the venire because they all requested to be excused, and commissioners, sheriff, and clerk routinely granted these requests assuming "that such individuals would not participate in jury duty due to their well-known prohibition" to " '[j]udge not, and ye shall not be judged: condemn not, and ye shall not be condemned: forgive, and ye shall be forgiven' ").

11th ed., p. 1406; in line 2, insert as new footnote "aa" after "black jurors.":

aa. Consider also *Johnson v. California*, 125 S.Ct. 2410 (2005), reversing the conviction of a black defendant for assaulting and murdering a white child. During jury selection, a number of prospective jurors were removed for cause until 43 eligible jurors remained, three of whom were black. The prosecutor used his peremptory challenges to remove the prospective black jurors, resulting in an all-white jury. Responding to the defendant's *Batson* objection, the trial judge did not ask the prosecutor to explain his strikes, but instead simply found that petitioner had failed to establish a prima facie case of purposeful discrimination. The Supreme Court held this was error, reasoning that "we assumed in *Batson* that the trial judge would have the benefit of all relevant circumstances, including the prosecutor's explanation, before deciding whether it was more likely than not that the challenge was improperly motivated. We did not intend the first step to be so onerous that a defendant would have to persuade the judge—on the basis of all the facts, some of which are impossible for the defendant to know with certainty—that the challenge was more likely than not the product of purposeful discrimination. Instead, a defendant satisfies the requirements of *Batson*'s first step by producing evidence sufficient to permit the trial judge to draw an inference that discrimination has occurred.

* * * In this case the inference of discrimination was sufficient to invoke a comment by the trial judge that 'we are very close,' and on review, the [state supreme court] acknowledged that 'it certainly looks suspicious that all three African–American prospective jurors were removed from the jury.' Those inferences that discrimination may have occurred were sufficient to establish a prima facie case under *Batson*."

11th ed., p. 1414; end of Note 6, add:

Consider also MILLER–EL v. DRETKE, 125 S.Ct. 2317 (2005), where the Court rejected the state court's conclusion that the prosecutor did not violate *Batson* when only one of the 20 black members of the 108–person venire served as a juror, and ten were excused by the state's peremptory challenges. Justice SOUTER wrote for the Court: "If a prosecutor's proffered reason for striking a black panelist applies just as well to an otherwise-similar nonblack who is permitted to serve, that is evidence tending to prove purposeful discrimination to be considered at *Batson*'s third step.

"The prosecution used its second peremptory strike to exclude Fields, a black man who expressed unwavering support for the death penalty. * * * [The Prosecutor] represented that Fields said he would not vote for death if rehabilitation was possible * * *. If, indeed, Fields's thoughts on rehabilitation did make the prosecutor uneasy, he should have worried about a number of white panel members he accepted with no evident reservations. * * * [N]onblack jurors whose remarks on rehabilitation could well have signaled a limit on their willingness to impose a death sentence were not questioned further and drew no objection, but the prosecution expressed apprehension about a black juror's belief in the possibility of reformation even though he repeatedly stated his approval of the death penalty and testified that he could impose it according to state legal standards even when the alternative sentence of life imprisonment would give a defendant (like everyone else in the world) the opportunity to reform. * * *

"In sum, when we look for nonblack jurors similarly situated to Fields, we find strong similarities as well as some differences. But the differences[6] seem far from significant, particularly when we read Fields's *voir dire* testimony in its entirety. Upon that reading, Fields should have been an ideal juror in the eyes of a prosecutor seeking a death sentence, and the prosecutors' explanations for the strike cannot reasonably be accepted.

"* * * The case for discrimination goes beyond these comparisons to include broader patterns of practice during the jury selection.* * * The first clue to the prosecutors' intentions, distinct from the peremptory challenges themselves, is their resort during *voir dire* to a procedure known in Texas as

---

6. The dissent contends that * * * " ' "[s]imilarly situated" does not mean matching any one of several reasons the prosecution gave for striking a potential juror—it means matching *all* of them.' " None of our cases announces a rule that no comparison is probative unless the situation of the individuals compared is identical in all respects, and there is no reason to accept one. * * * A *per se* rule that a defendant cannot win a *Batson* claim unless there is an exactly identical white juror would leave *Batson* inoperable; potential jurors are not products of a set of cookie cutters.

the jury shuffle. In the State's criminal practice, either side may literally reshuffle the cards bearing panel members' names, thus rearranging the order in which members of a venire panel are seated and reached for questioning. Once the order is established, the panel members seated at the back are likely to escape *voir dire* altogether, for those not questioned by the end of the week are dismissed. [The] prosecution's decision to seek a jury shuffle when a predominant number of African–Americans were seated in the front of the panel, along with its decision to delay a formal objection to the defense's shuffle until after the new racial composition was revealed, raise a suspicion that the State sought to exclude African–Americans from the jury. Our concerns are amplified by the fact that the state court also had before it, and apparently ignored, testimony demonstrating that the Dallas County District Attorney's Office had, by its own admission, used this process to manipulate the racial composition of the jury in the past. * * *

"The next body of evidence that the State was trying to avoid black jurors is the contrasting *voir dire* questions posed respectively to black and nonblack panel members, on two different subjects. First, there were the prosecutors' statements preceding questions about a potential juror's thoughts on capital punishment. Some of these prefatory statements were cast in general terms, but some followed the so-called graphic script, describing the method of execution in rhetorical and clinical detail.[a] It is intended, Miller–El contends, to prompt some expression of hesitation to consider the death penalty and thus to elicit plausibly neutral grounds for a peremptory strike of a potential juror subjected to it, if not a strike for cause. If the graphic script is given to a higher proportion of blacks than whites, this is evidence that prosecutors more often wanted blacks off the jury, absent some neutral and extenuating explanation. * * * Of the 10 nonblacks whose questionnaires expressed ambivalence or opposition [to the death penalty], only 30% received the graphic treatment. But of the seven blacks who expressed ambivalence or opposition, 86% heard the graphic script. As between the State's ambivalence explanation and Miller–El's racial one, race is much the better, and the reasonable inference is that race was the major consideration when the prosecution chose to follow the graphic script. * * *

"The same is true for another kind of disparate questioning, which might fairly be called trickery. The prosecutors asked members of the panel how low a sentence they would consider imposing for murder. Most potential jurors were first told that Texas law provided for a minimum term of five years, but some members of the panel were not, and if a panel member then insisted on a minimum above five years, the prosecutor would suppress his normal preference for tough jurors and claim cause to strike. * * * The State concedes that the manipulative minimum punishment questioning was used to create cause to strike, but now it offers the extenuation that prosecutors omitted the 5–year information not on the basis of race, but on stated opposition to the death penalty, or ambivalence about it, on the questionnaires and in the *voir dire* testimony. On the State's identification of black panel members opposed or ambivalent, all were asked the trick

---

a. For example, one juror was told, "The man sitting right down there will be taken to Huntsville and will be put on death row and at some point taken to the death house and placed on a gurney and injected with a lethal substance until he is dead as a result of the proceedings that we have in this court on this case."

question. But the State's rationale flatly fails to explain why most white panel members who expressed similar opposition or ambivalence were not subjected to it. * * *

"There is a final body of evidence that confirms [our] conclusion. We know that for decades leading up to the time this case was tried prosecutors in the Dallas County office had followed a specific policy of systematically excluding blacks from juries * * * [A manual distributed to prosecutors contained] an article authored by a former prosecutor (and later a judge) under the direction of his superiors in the District Attorney's Office, outlining the reasoning for excluding minorities from jury service. Although the manual was written in 1968, it remained in circulation until 1976, if not later, and was available at least to one of the prosecutors in Miller–El's trial. * * * The prosecutors took their cues from a 20–year old manual of tips on jury selection, as shown by their notes of the race of each potential juror. * * *"

11th ed., p. 1415; end of note 8, add:

Consider also STEVE BOGIRA, *Courtroom 302* at 261–262 (2005) (the story of one year in one courtroom in Chicago Cook County's Criminal Courthouse by reporter Bogira):

"Since *Batson*, legal scholars and reviewing court judges have chastised prosecutors in particular for the flimsy excuses they often give for striking blacks. In a 1996 ruling, Illinois appellate justice Alan Greiman lamented the 'charade' that jury selection has become. Pointing to the multitude of excuses prosecutors offered for excluding black jurors—too young, too old, unemployed, overeducated, hair unkempt, demeanor bothersome—Justice Greiman wondered facetiously whether new prosecutors were given manuals entitled *Twenty Time–Tested Race–Neutral Explanations* for excusing African American jurors."[a]

"With a white defendant and black victims, the Caruso case has things upside down. Prosecutors Robert Berlin and Ellen Mandeltort don't find any of the black prospects too young or too old or to have unacceptable hair or demeanor. They use all seven of their strikes against whites.

"One of the rejected whites is Ronald Pedelty, a high school physics teacher. He says he'd base his verdict on what's presented by both sides in the courtroom. He says physics has taught him to value 'objective reasoning based on the evidence.' When Berlin and Mandeltort move to strike him, Caruso's lawyers make a *Batson* challenge. [Cook County Judge Daniel] Locallo asks the prosecutes for a race-neutral reason for excluding Pedelty. Mandeltort notes that Pedelty 'indicated that he would use objective reasoning.' Besides that apparently troubling fact, Pedelty's demeanor was 'not satisfactory to the state,' she adds vaguely. Locallo finds these to be valid reasons for the state to strike Pedelty.

"Meanwhile Caruso's lawyer, Ed Genson, uses six of his seven strikes against blacks. When the prosecutors charge Genson with violating *Batson*, Genson insists the strikes aren't due specifically to race. A jury poll he

[a]. See *People v. Randall*, 283 Ill.App.3d 1019.

commissioned advised him against selecting jurors who are mothers or who are elderly, and this explains most of his peremptories, he tells Locallo.

"[After] two days and consideration of sixty-two jurors, the Caruso panel is finalized. Both the state and the defense have reason to feel pleased with their efforts. The prosecutors have held the number of white males to three. There are five minorities on the jury, but the defense has managed to limit the number of blacks to two; the other minority jurors are two Hispanics and one Pakistani American. Both of the black jurors are women. As so often happens here, not a single black male has won a spot."

11th ed., p. 1416; end of Note 9, add:

Consider also Joshua Wilkenfeld, Note, *Newly Compelling: Reexamining Judicial Construction of Juries in the Aftermath of* Grutter v. Bollinger, 104 Colum.L.Rev. 2291 (2004) (arguing that "if the affirmative action program in *Grutter* served a compelling state interest, promoting jury diversity does as well").

10. *Eliminating peremptories?* Concurring in *Miller-El v. Dretke*, Supp., p. 97, Justice Breyer endorsed Justice Marshall's conclusion in *Batson* that the only way to "end the racial discrimination that peremptories inject into the jury-selection process," was to eliminate peremptory challenges. Justice Breyer wrote, "this case illustrates the practical problems of proof that Justice Marshall described. * * * At *Batson*'s first step, litigants remain free to misuse peremptory challenges as long as the strikes fall *below* the prima facie threshold level. At Batson's second step, prosecutors need only tender a neutral reason, not a 'persuasive, or even plausible' one. And most importantly, at step three, *Batson* asks judges to engage in the awkward, sometime hopeless, task of second-guessing a prosecutor's instinctive judgment—the underlying basis for which may be invisible even to the prosecutor exercising the challenge. In such circumstances, it may be impossible for trial courts to discern if a ' "seat-of-the-pants" ' peremptory challenge reflects a ' "seat-of-the-pants" ' racial stereotype.

"Given the inevitably clumsy fit between any objectively measurable standard and the subjective decisionmaking at issue, I am not surprised to find studies and anecdotal reports suggesting that, despite *Batson*, the discriminatory use of peremptory challenges remains a problem. [citing sources reporting that in Philadelphia race-based uses of prosecutorial peremptories declined by only 2% after *Batson*; that in a North Carolina County 71% of excused black jurors were removed by the prosecution and 81% of excused white jurors were removed by the defense.]

"Practical problems of proof to the side, peremptory challenges seem increasingly anomalous in our judicial system. On the one hand, the Court has widened and deepened *Batson*'s basic constitutional rule. It has applied *Batson*'s antidiscrimination test to the use of peremptories by criminal defendants, *McCollum*, by private litigants in civil cases, *Edmonson*, and by prosecutors where the defendant and the excluded juror are of different races, *Powers*. It has recognized that the Constitution protects not just defendants, but the jurors themselves. And it has held that equal protection principles prohibit excusing jurors on account of gender. *J. E. B.* Some lower courts have extended *Batson's* rule to religious affiliation as well. See, *e.g.*, *United States v. Brown*, 352 F.3d 654, 668–669 (CA2 2003).

"On the other hand, the use of race-and gender-based stereotypes in the jury-selection process seems better organized and more systematized than ever before. For example, one jury-selection guide counsels attorneys to perform a 'demographic analysis' that assigns numerical points to characteristics such as age, occupation, and marital status—in addition to race as well as gender. See V. Starr & A. McCormick, Jury Selection 193–200 (3d ed.2001). * * * [M]aterials from a legal convention, [state that] African–Americans 'have always been considered good for the plaintiff,' and '[m]ore politically conservative minorities will be more likely to lean toward defendants.' Blue, Mirroring, Proxemics, Nonverbal Communication and Other Psychological Tools, Advocacy Track—Psychology of Trial, Association of Trial Lawyers of America Annual Convention Reference Materials, 1 Ann. 2001 ATLA–CLE 153, available at WESTLAW, ATLA–CLE database (June 8, 2005). [A] trial consulting firm advertises a new jury-selection technology: 'Whether you are trying a civil case or a criminal case, SmartJURY™ has likely determined the exact demographics (age, race, gender, education, occupation, marital status, number of children, religion, and income) of the type of jurors you should select and the type you should strike.' SmartJURY Product Information, http://www.cts-america.com/smartjury_pi.asp. These examples reflect a professional effort to fulfill the lawyer's obligation to help his or her client. Nevertheless, the outcome in terms of jury selection is the same as it would be were the motive less benign. And as long as that is so, the law's antidiscrimination command and a peremptory jury-selection system that permits or encourages the use of stereotypes work at cross-purposes.

"Finally, a jury system without peremptories is no longer unthinkable. Members of the legal profession have begun serious consideration of that possibility. [citing, e.g., Morris B. Hoffman, *Peremptory Challenges Should be Abolished: A Trial Judge's Perspective*, 64 U.Chi.L.Rev. 809 (1997) (authored by a Colorado judge)]. And England, a common-law jurisdiction that has eliminated peremptory challenges, continues to administer fair trials based largely on random jury selection.

"I recognize that peremptory challenges have a long historical pedigree. They may help to reassure a party of the fairness of the jury. But long ago, Blackstone recognized the peremptory challenge as an 'arbitrary and capricious species of [a] challenge.' 4 W. Blackstone, Commentaries on the Laws of England 346 (1769). If used to express stereotypical judgments about race, gender, religion, or national origin, peremptory challenges betray the jury's democratic origins and undermine its representative function. The 'scientific' use of peremptory challenges may also contribute to public cynicism about the fairness of the jury system and its role in American government. And, of course, the right to a jury free of discriminatory taint is constitutionally protected—the right to use peremptory challenges is not.

"Justice Goldberg, dissenting in *Swain*, wrote, 'Were it necessary to make an absolute choice between the right of a defendant to have a jury chosen in conformity with the requirements of the Fourteenth Amendment and the right to challenge peremptorily, the Constitution compels a choice of the former.' This case suggests the need to confront that choice. In light of the considerations I have mentioned, I believe it necessary to reconsider *Batson*'s test and the peremptory challenge system as a whole. * * *"

11th ed., p. 1416; after Note 4, add:

5. Recusal motions are sometimes filed in response to mid-trial revelations or events. If the alleged bias is a response to the conduct of the defendant or his counsel during the proceedings, courts may be reluctant to grant recusal. See e.g., *Bigby v. Dretke*, 402 F.3d 551 (5th Cir.2005), where the court of appeals declined to find bias per se after Bigby, on trial for murder, attacked the judge during a trial recess and held a gun to the judge's head. The reviewing court reasoned, "Such an automatic rule would invite recusal motions from defendants whose sole purpose in attacking a judge or engaging in unruly behavior is either to manufacture constitutional due process violations or delay trial proceedings." Nor was the requisite bias for recusal demonstrated by the judge's decision to admit testimony about the attack later in Bigby's murder trial, because the judge "provided a basis for admission of the evidence grounded in established law." Compare *In re Nettles*, 394 F.3d 1001 (7th Cir.2005) (where defendant had been charged with plotting to blow up the federal courthouse in Chicago and moved pretrial for recusal of a judge in that building, the court of appeals held proper the recusal of all district and appellate judges in the courthouse because of the appearance of bias when judges are "menaced by an Oklahoma City style attack").

Chapter 25
THE CRIMINAL TRIAL

SECTION 1. PRESENCE OF THE DEFENDANT

11th ed., p. 1452; delete Note 3

11th ed., p. 1453; after Note 4, add:

DECK v. MISSOURI
___ U.S. ___, 125 S.Ct. 2007, 161 L.Ed.2d 953 (2005).

[Deck was convicted and sentenced to death for robbing and murdering an elderly couple. At trial, state authorities required him to wear leg braces that were not visible to the jury. On review, the state courts set aside Deck's sentence. At resentencing, Deck was shackled with leg irons, handcuffs, and a belly chain, and again received a sentence of death.]

Justice BREYER delivered the opinion of the Court.

* * * The law has long forbidden routine use of visible shackles during the guilt phase; it permits a State to shackle a criminal defendant only in the presence of a special need. This rule has deep roots in the common law. In the 18th century, Blackstone wrote that "it is laid down in our ancient books, that, though under an indictment of the highest nature," a defendant "must be brought to the bar without irons, or any manner of shackles or bonds; unless there be evident danger of an escape." Blackstone and other English authorities recognized that the rule did not apply at "the time of arraignment," or like proceedings before the judge. It was meant to protect defendants appearing at trial before a jury.

American courts have traditionally followed Blackstone's "ancient" English rule, while making clear that "in extreme and exceptional cases, where the safe custody of the prisoner and the peace of the tribunal imperatively demand, the manacles may be retained." While these earlier courts disagreed about the degree of discretion to be afforded trial judges, they settled virtually without exception on a basic rule embodying notions of fundamental fairness: trial courts may not shackle defendants routinely, but only if there is a particular reason to do so.

More recently, this Court has suggested that a version of this rule forms part of the Fifth and Fourteenth Amendments' due process guarantee. Thirty-five years ago, when considering the trial of an unusually obstreperous criminal defendant, the Court held that the Constitution sometimes permitted special measures, including physical restraints. *Allen*, 397 U.S., at 343–344. The Court wrote that "binding and gagging might possibly be the fairest and most reasonable way to handle" such a defendant. But the Court immediately added that "even to contemplate such a technique . . . arouses a feeling that no person should be tried while shackled and gagged except as a last resort."

Sixteen years later, the Court considered a special courtroom security arrangement that involved having uniformed security personnel sit in the first row of the courtroom's spectator section. The Court held that the Constitution allowed the arrangement, stating that the deployment of security personnel during trial is not "the sort of inherently prejudicial practice that, like shackling, should be permitted only where justified by an essential state interest specific to each trial." *Holbrook v. Flynn*, 475 U.S. 501, 568–569 (1976).

Lower courts have treated these statements as setting forth a constitutional standard that embodies Blackstone's rule. Courts and commentators share close to a consensus that, during the guilt phase of a trial, a criminal defendant has a right to remain free of physical restraints that are visible to the jury; that the right has a constitutional dimension; but that the right may be overcome in a particular instance by essential state interests such as physical security, escape prevention, or courtroom decorum. * * * In light of this precedent, and of a lower court consensus disapproving routine shackling dating back to the 19th century, it is clear that this Court's prior statements gave voice to a principle deeply embedded in the law. We now conclude that those statements identify a basic element of the "due process of law" protected by the Federal Constitution. Thus, the Fifth and Fourteenth Amendments prohibit the use of physical restraints visible to the jury absent a trial court determination, in the exercise of its discretion, that they are justified by a state interest specific to a particular trial. Such a determination may of course take into account the factors that courts have traditionally relied on in gauging potential security problems and the risk of escape at trial.

We here consider shackling not during the guilt phase of an ordinary criminal trial, but during the punishment phase of a capital case. And we must decide whether that change of circumstance makes a constitutional difference. To do so, we examine the reasons that motivate the guilt-phase constitutional rule and determine whether they apply with similar force in this context.

Judicial hostility to shackling may once primarily have reflected concern for the suffering—the "tortures" and "torments"—that "very painful" chains could cause. More recently, this Court's opinions have not stressed the need to prevent physical suffering (for not all modern physical restraints are painful). Instead they have emphasized the importance of giving effect to three fundamental legal principles.

First, the criminal process presumes that the defendant is innocent until proved guilty. Visible shackling undermines the presumption of innocence and the related fairness of the factfinding process. It suggests to the jury that the justice system itself sees a "need to separate a defendant from the community at large."

Second, the Constitution, in order to help the accused secure a meaningful defense, provides him with a right to counsel. The use of physical restraints diminishes that right. Shackles can interfere with the accused's "ability to communicate" with his lawyer. *Allen,* 397 U.S., at 344. Indeed, they can interfere with a defendant's ability to participate in his own defense, say by freely choosing whether to take the witness stand on his own behalf.

Third, judges must seek to maintain a judicial process that is a dignified process. The courtroom's formal dignity, which includes the respectful treatment of defendants, reflects the importance of the matter at issue, guilt or innocence, and the gravity with which Americans consider any deprivation of an individual's liberty through criminal punishment. And it reflects a seriousness of purpose that helps to explain the judicial system's power to inspire the confidence and to affect the behavior of a general public whose demands for justice our courts seek to serve. The routine use of shackles in the presence of juries would undermine these symbolic yet concrete objectives. As this Court has said, the use of shackles at trial "affront[s]" the "dignity and decorum of judicial proceedings that the judge is seeking to uphold." *Allen,* at 344.

There will be cases, of course, where these perils of shackling are unavoidable. We do not underestimate the need to restrain dangerous defendants to prevent courtroom attacks, or the need to give trial courts latitude in making individualized security determinations. We are mindful of the tragedy that can result if judges are not able to protect themselves and their courtrooms. But given their prejudicial effect, due process does not permit the use of visible restraints if the trial court has not taken account of the circumstances of the particular case.

The considerations that militate against the routine use of visible shackles during the guilt phase of a criminal trial apply with like force to penalty proceedings in capital cases. This is obviously so in respect to the latter two considerations mentioned, securing a meaningful defense and maintaining dignified proceedings. It is less obviously so in respect to the first consideration mentioned, for the defendant's conviction means that the presumption of innocence no longer applies. Hence shackles do not undermine the jury's effort to apply that presumption. Nonetheless, shackles at the penalty phase threaten related concerns. Although the jury is no longer deciding between guilt and innocence, it is deciding between life and death. That decision, given the " 'severity' " and

" 'finality' " of the sanction, is no less important than the decision about guilt.

Neither is accuracy in making that decision any less critical. The Court has stressed the "acute need" for reliable decisionmaking when the death penalty is at issue. The appearance of the offender during the penalty phase in shackles, however, almost inevitably implies to a jury, as a matter of common sense, that court authorities consider the offender a danger to the community—often a statutory aggravator and nearly always a relevant factor in jury decisionmaking, even where the State does not specifically argue the point. It also almost inevitably affects adversely the jury's perception of the character of the defendant. And it thereby inevitably undermines the jury's ability to weigh accurately all relevant considerations—considerations that are often unquantifiable and elusive—when it determines whether a defendant deserves death. In these ways, the use of shackles can be a "thumb [on] death's side of the scale."

Given the presence of similarly weighty considerations, we must conclude that courts cannot routinely place defendants in shackles or other physical restraints visible to the jury during the penalty phase of a capital proceeding. The constitutional requirement, however, is not absolute. It permits a judge, in the exercise of his or her discretion, to take account of special circumstances, including security concerns, that may call for shackling. In so doing, it accommodates the important need to protect the courtroom and its occupants. But any such determination must be case specific; that is to say, it should reflect particular concerns, say special security needs or escape risks, related to the defendant on trial.

* * * [Here,] the record contains no formal or informal findings. The judge did not refer to a risk of escape—a risk the State has raised in this Court—or a threat to courtroom security. Rather, he gave as his reason for imposing the shackles the fact that Deck already "has been convicted." While he also said that the shackles would "take any fear out of" the juror's "minds," he nowhere explained any special reason for fear. Nor did he explain why, if shackles were necessary, he chose not to provide for shackles that the jury could not see—apparently the arrangement used at trial. If there is an exceptional case where the record itself makes clear that there are indisputably good reasons for shackling, it is not this one.

The third argument fails to take account of this Court's statement in *Holbrook* that shackling is "inherently prejudicial." 475 U.S., at 568. That statement is rooted in our belief that the practice will often have negative effects, but—like "the consequences of compelling a defendant to wear prison clothing" or of forcing him to stand trial while medicated—those effects "cannot be shown from a trial transcript." Thus, where a court, without adequate justification, orders the defendant to wear shackles that will be seen by the jury, the defendant need not demonstrate actual prejudice to make out a due process violation. The State must prove "beyond a reasonable doubt that the [shackling] error complained of did not contribute to the verdict obtained." *Chapman v. California*, 386 U.S. 18, 24 (1967).

For these reasons, the judgment of the Missouri Supreme Court is reversed, and the case is remanded for further proceedings not inconsistent with this opinion.

Justice THOMAS, with whom Justice SCALIA joins, dissenting.

* * * English common law in the 17th and 18th centuries recognized a rule against bringing the defendant in irons to the bar for trial. This rule stemmed from none of the concerns to which the Court points,—the presumption of innocence, the right to counsel, concerns about decorum, or accuracy in decisionmaking. Instead, the rule ensured that a defendant was not so distracted by physical pain during his trial that he could not defend himself. This concern was understandable, for the irons of that period were heavy and painful. In fact, leather strips often lined the irons to prevent them from rubbing away a defendant's skin. * * * The concern that felony defendants not be in severe pain at trial was acute because, before the 1730's, defendants were not permitted to have the assistance of counsel at trial, with an early exception made for those charged with treason. Instead, the trial was an " 'accused speaks' " trial, at which the accused defended himself. The accused was compelled to respond to the witnesses, making him the primary source of information at trial. As the Court acknowledges, the rule against shackling did not extend to arraignment. A defendant remained in irons at arraignment because "he [was] only called upon to plead by advice of his counsel"; he was not on trial, where he would play the main role in defending himself.

A modern-day defendant does not spend his pretrial confinement wearing restraints. The belly chain and handcuffs are of modest, if not insignificant, weight. Neither they nor the leg irons cause pain or suffering, let alone pain or suffering that would interfere with a defendant's ability to assist in his defense at trial. And they need not interfere with a defendant's ability to assist his counsel—a defendant remains free to talk with counsel during trial, and restraints can be employed so as to ensure that a defendant can write to his counsel during the trial. Restraints can also easily be removed when a defendant testifies, so that any concerns about testifying can be ameliorated. Modern restraints are therefore unlike those that gave rise to the traditional rule. * * * Yet the Court treats old and modern restraints as similar for constitutional purposes merely because they are both types of physical restraints. This logical leap ignores that modern restraints do not violate the principle animating the common-law rule. In making this leap, the Court's strays from the appropriate legal inquiry of examining common-law traditions to inform our understanding of the Due Process Clause. * * * [I]n the late 19th century States agreed that generally defendants ought to come to trial unfettered, but they disagreed over the breadth of discretion to be afforded trial courts. * * * [T]here was no consensus that supports elevating the rule against shackling to a federal constitutional command.

* * * In recent years, more of a consensus regarding the use of shackling has developed, with many courts concluding that shackling is inherently prejudicial. But rather than being firmly grounded in deeply rooted principles, that consensus stems from a series of ill-considered dicta in [*Allen, Holbrook*, and *Estelle v. Williams*, 425 U.S. 501 (1976).] * * * More important, these decisions represent recent practice, which does not determine whether the Fourteenth Amendment, as properly and traditionally interpreted, i.e., as a statement of law, not policy preferences, embodies a right to be free from visible, painless physical restraints at trial.

* * * Treating shackling at sentencing as inherently prejudicial ignores the commonsense distinction between a defendant who stands accused and a defendant who stands convicted. * * * Deck's jury was surely aware that Deck was jailed; jurors know that convicted capital murderers are not left to roam the streets. It blinks reality to think that seeing a convicted capital murderer in shackles in the courtroom could import any prejudice beyond that inevitable knowledge.

Jurors no doubt also understand that it makes sense for a capital defendant to be restrained at sentencing. By sentencing, a defendant's situation is at its most dire. He no longer may prove himself innocent, and he faces either life without liberty or death. Confronted with this reality, a defendant no longer has much to lose—should he attempt escape and fail, it is still lengthy imprisonment or death that awaits him. For any person in these circumstances, the reasons to attempt escape are at their apex. A defendant's best opportunity to do so is in the courtroom, for he is otherwise in jail or restraints.

In addition, having been convicted, a defendant may be angry. He could turn that ire on his own counsel, who has failed in defending his innocence. Or, for that matter, he could turn on a witness testifying at his hearing or the court reporter. Such thoughts could well enter the mind of any defendant in these circumstances, from the most dangerous to the most docile. That a defendant now convicted of his crimes appears before the jury in shackles thus would be unremarkable to the jury. To presume that such a defendant suffers prejudice by appearing in handcuffs at sentencing does not comport with reality.

* * * Deck does not argue that the shackles caused him pain or impaired his mental faculties. Nor does he argue that the shackles prevented him from communicating with his counsel during trial. * * * The Court further expresses concern that physical restraints might keep a defendant from taking the stand on his own behalf in seeking the jury's mercy. * * * Even assuming this concern is real rather than imagined, it could be ameliorated by removing the restraints if the defendant wishes to take the stand. Instead, the Court says, the concern requires a categorical rule that the use of visible physical restraints

violates the Due Process Clause absent a demanding showing. The Court's solution is overinclusive.

The Court also asserts the rule it adopts is necessary to protect courtroom decorum, which the use of shackles would offend. * * * The power of the courts to maintain order, however, is not a right personal to the defendant, much less one of constitutional proportions. Far from viewing the need for decorum as a right the defendant can invoke, this Court has relied on it to limit the conduct of defendants, even when their constitutional rights are implicated. [*Allen, Faretta v. California*, 422 U.S., at 834–835, n. 46, see 11th ed., p. 121.] * * *

Wholly apart from the unwarranted status the Court accords "courtroom decorum," the Court fails to explain the affront to the dignity of the courts that the sight of physical restraints poses. I cannot understand the indignity in having a convicted double murderer and robber appear before the court in visible physical restraints. Our Nation's judges and juries are exposed to accounts of heinous acts daily, like the brutal murders Deck committed in this case. Even outside the courtroom, prisoners walk through courthouse halls wearing visible restraints. Courthouses are thus places in which members of the judiciary and the public come into frequent contact with defendants in restraints. Yet, the Court says, the appearance of a convicted criminal in a belly chain and handcuffs at a sentencing hearing offends the sensibilities of our courts. The courts of this Nation do not have such delicate constitutions.

Finally, the Court claims that "[t]he appearance of the offender during the penalty phase in shackles ... almost inevitably implies to a jury, as a matter of common sense, that court authorities consider the offender a danger to the community—often a statutory aggravator and nearly always a relevant factor in jury decisionmaking." This argument is flawed. It ignores the fact that only relatively recently have the penalty and guilt phases been conducted separately. That the historical evidence reveals no consensus prohibiting visible modern-day shackles during capital trials suggests that there is similarly no consensus prohibiting shackling during capital sentencing.

* * * Confining the analysis to trial-specific circumstances precludes consideration of limits on the security resources of courts. Under that test, the particulars of a given courthouse (being nonspecific to any particular defendant) are irrelevant, even if the judge himself is the only security, or if a courthouse has few on-duty officers standing guard at any given time, or multiple exits. Forbidding courts from considering such circumstances fails to accommodate the unfortunately dire security situation faced by this Nation's courts. * * * The Court's decision risks the lives of courtroom personnel, with little corresponding benefit to defendants. This is a risk that due process does not require. I respectfully dissent.

Note

1. What about restraints that are not visible? Use of a "stun belt" to restrain a defendant is less obvious to the jury, but lower courts even prior to *Deck* have required the same on-the-record justification that is required for visible restraints. One court explained the reasons: 1) the belt "poses a far more substantial risk of interfering with a defendant's Sixth Amendment right to confer with counsel than do leg shackles," because of "the fear of receiving a painful and humiliating shock for any gesture that could be perceived as threatening"; 2) a defendant wearing a belt is "likely to concentrate on doing everything he can to prevent the belt from being activated and is thus less likely to participate fully in his defense at trial"; and 3) "shackles are a minor threat to the dignity of the courtroom when compared with the discharge of a stun belt, which could cause the defendant to lose control of his limbs, collapse to the floor, and defecate on himself." *United States v. Durham*, 287 F.3d 1297 (11th Cir.2002). Compare *Weaver v. State*, 894 So.2d 178 (Fla.2004) (stun belt use upheld even though murder defendant had no history of violent behavior in a courtroom, because he would be moving about the courtroom, representing himself pro se); *Wrinkles v. State*, 749 N.E.2d 1179 (Ind.2001) (prohibiting use of stun belts in Indiana trials).

SECTION 2. THE DEFENDANT'S RIGHT TO REMAIN SILENT AND TO TESTIFY

11th ed., p. 1460; end of Note 7, add:

For example, a victim-witness may attend a federal trial, unless there is clear and convincing evidence that the victim's testimony "would be materially altered if the victim heard other testimony at that proceeding." A court must "make every effort to permit the fullest attendance possible by the victim," "consider reasonable alternatives to the exclusion of the victim from the criminal proceeding," and clearly state the reasons for exclusion on the record. See 18 U.S.C.A. § 3771 [see Supp., App. B]; FRE 615. What "reasonable alternatives" to sequestration are there for preventing conscious or unconscious tailoring of testimony by a victim witness? Could a judge insist that a victim testify as the very first witness? Require the victim to record a statement prior to testifying in order to allow the defendant to bring to the jury's attention any tailoring that might occur? See Douglas E. Beloof & Paul G. Cassell, *The Crime Victim's Right to Attend the Trial: The Reascendant National Consensus*, 1 Lewis & Clark L. Rev. ___ (forthcoming 2005).

SECTION 4. SUBMITTING THE CASE TO THE JURY

11th ed., p. 1472; following subtitle of Note 2, replace text with:

The common law jury trial included the privilege of the trial judge to comment to the jury on his opinion of the evidence presented, a practice thought to give to the jurors "great light and assistance." *Quercia v. United States*, 289 U.S. 466 (1933) (quoting Hale, History of the Common Law).

Most states have limited the judge's ability to comment on the evidence. The trial judge's duty to retain an atmosphere of impartiality also limits the judge's ability to question witnesses from the bench. See *United States v. Godwin*, 272 F.3d 659 (4th Cir.2001) (reviewing authority); CRIMPROC § 24.6; Principle 13(D), ABA Principles Relating to Juries and Jury Trials, adopted by the ABA February 2005: "Generally, the court should not question a witness about subject matter not raised by any party with that witness, unless the court has provided the parties an opportunity, outside the hearing of the jury, to explain the omission. If the court believes the questioning is necessary, the court should afford the parties an opportunity to develop the subject by further examination prior to its questioning of the witness."

SECTION 5. DELIBERATIONS AND VERDICT

11th ed., p. 1482; end of chapter, add:

Since *Herrera* was decided, "petitioners have presented at least 173 bare-innocence claims squarely before federal courts." Nicholas Berg, Note, *Turning a Blind Eye to Innocence—The Legacy of* Herrera v. Collins, 42 Am.Crim.L.Rev. 121 (2005). According to this author, only a handful of these cases (both capital and noncapital) were resolved in favor of the defendant: two defendants received either an evidentiary hearing or a remand; two others received an order for DNA testing. Five other petitioners received clemency, three of these from Governor Ryan of Illinois who in 2003 granted commutations to all death row defendants in Illinois at the end of his term.

Chapter 27
SENTENCING

SECTION 2. ALLOCATING AND CONTROLLING SENTENCING DISCRETION

11th ed., p. 1533; end of Note 1, add:

Compare Rachel Barkow, *Federalism and the Politics of Sentencing*, 105 Colum.L.Rev. 1276, 1301–08 (2005) (Congress lacks fiscal incentives to moderate punitive sentencing policy because criminal justice makes up tiny proportion of federal spending; even if it paid attention to costs, Congress could simply leave more criminal enforcement to the states rather than amend federal statutes).

11th ed., p. 1537; end of Note 3, add:

Consider also the comments of United States Attorney General Gonzales on June 21, 2005 (available at: http://www.usdoj.gov/ag/speeches), calling for Congress to enact a system of mandatory guidelines with minimum but not maximum sentences to replace the advisory guidelines system that resulted from the Court's decision in *Booker v. United States*, 11th ed., p. 1559:

> "[O]ur U.S. Attorneys consistently report that a critical law enforcement tool has been taken from them. Under the sentencing guidelines [prior to *Booker*], defendants were only eligible to receive reductions in sentences in exchange for cooperation when the government petitioned the court. Under the advisory guidelines system, judges are free to reduce sentences when they believe the defendant has sufficiently cooperated. And since defendants no longer face penalties that are serious and certain, key witnesses are increasingly less inclined to cooperate with prosecutors. We risk a return to the pre-guidelines era, when defendants were encouraged to "play the odds" in our criminal justice system, betting that the luck of the draw—the judge randomly assigned to their case—might result in a lighter sentence. * * *
>
> "One [legislative proposal] I believe would preserve the protections and principles of the Sentencing Reform Act, and is thus deserving of serious consideration, is the construction of a minimum guideline system. Under such a system, the sentencing court would be bound by the guidelines minimum, just as it was before the *Booker* decision. The

guidelines maximum, however, would remain advisory, and the court would be bound to consider it, but not bound to adhere to it, just as it is today under *Booker*. * * * "

11th ed., p. 1538; end of Note 1, add:

No two guidelines systems are identical, even though twenty different jurisdictions have adopted sentencing guidelines. See Richard S. Frase, *State Sentencing Guidelines: Diversity, Consensus, and Unresolved Policy Issues*, 105 Colum.L.Rev. 1190, 1196 (2005) (including useful chart summarizing features of existing guidelines systems).

11th ed., p. 1538; in Note 2, after first paragraph, add:

States have been able to slow incarceration rates by authorizing unelected Commissions to designate mandatory guidelines sentences that are well below the statutory ranges enacted by elected representatives, allowing both elected legislatures and elected judges to avoid the appearance of being "soft on crime." See *Id.*; Rachel Barkow, *Administering Crime*, 52 UCLA L.Rev. 715 (2005). Even with advisory guidelines, a few states have succeeded in using sentencing guidelines to free up prison space. In one state, Virginia, this may have something to do with the unique judicial selection system; trial judges there do not face popular election but are instead reappointed by the state legislature. Instead of the usual assumption that lenient sentencing may cost a judge at the next election, see Sanford Gordon and Gary Hueber, *Accountability and Coercion: Is Justice Blind When it Runs for Office?*, 46 Am.J.Pol.Sci. 247 (2004), some of these judges reportedly believe their chances of retention may suffer if they impose sentences above the guidelines too frequently, threatening the legislature's fiscal goals. Nancy J. King and Rosevelt L. Noble, *Felony Jury Sentencing in Practice: A Three-State Study*, 57 Vand.L.Rev. 885, 916–918 (2004). Delaware's success in controlling sentences is credited in part to the relatively small number of judges in the state, making it easier to coordinate consistent sentencing.

11th ed., p. 1539; in Note 3, add:

Roper v. Simmons, 125 S.Ct. 1183 (2005) (holding 5:4 that the execution of any person who was 17 at the time of the crime violates the Eighth Amendment). On the Court's use of foreign law to interpret the Eighth Amendment in *Roper*, see Supp. p. 1.

11th ed., p. 1539; end of Note 3, add:

4. *Rewarding waivers under guideline systems.* Consider also the study of sentencing in five guidelines states excerpted at Supp., p. 95. At pp. 975–77, 985–86, the authors conclude:

> In these sentencing guidelines states, there are no official discounts for waiving trial, and no specified downward adjustments for 'acceptance of responsibility.' Yet for the very same charge—controlling for criminal history, enhancements, gender, race, multiple counts, and other factors associated with differences in sentence severity—judges and prosecutors are imposing more lenient sentences for defendants who plead guilty.

The mechanisms available to judges and prosecutors to maintain this differential vary from state to state. Alternatives include downward dispositional and durational departures from the presumptive or standard range, dropping sentencing enhancements, sentencing in the mitigated range or at the bottom of the standard range, capping the sentence within the standard range, or making use of discretionary alternative sentences, such as treatment programs, suspended sentences, or stayed sentences. In Pennsylvania, prosecutors also use their option to invoke mandatory minimum sentences to ensure higher sentences for those who do not plead guilty. Interviewees reported very little bargaining over defendants' criminal histories, and little of the fact bargaining described in the federal system. * * *

"Researchers have posited that the more sentencing flexibility a guidelines system allows for any given offense, the more room judges and attorneys have to negotiate discounts using sentencing concessions rather than resorting to charge concessions. We found this difference reflected in interviewees' reports of greater reliance on sentencing bargaining as opposed to charge bargaining in Pennsylvania and Maryland—the two states with voluntary, rather than mandatory, guidelines. * * *

"Washington is a mandatory guidelines state with very narrow ranges. The analysis of several offenses in this state shows no predictable mode-of-conviction disparity at all. * * * [P]rosecutors and defendants reported little sentence bargaining, mostly charge bargaining. Sometimes, in reaching agreements to charges, the parties work backwards from the desired sentence to find the charge that will produce it. Charges are added or increased if the defendant is not going to plead guilty."

11th ed., p. 1547; end of Note 3, add:

Assuming the Constitution does not bar the consideration of some evidence from crime victims in setting a sentence, what is the appropriate role for victims in the sentencing process? Should judges consider a victim's sentence recommendation as well as his description of harm from the offense? Those opposed argue that victims' preferences undermine other sentencing goals, particularly consistency. Victims may be merciful or vindictive, some interested in restitution, others in retribution. Valuing victims' views also creates incentives for others to try to influence the preferences that victims express. Those in favor applaud the greater satisfaction with the process that victims express when they are included, and argue that involving the victim in the process can further traditional punishment goals. Even if victim participation sometimes conflicts with those goals, proponents maintain it is an independent value that is at least as important to pursue. For a collection of commentary, see Douglas E. Beloof, Steve Twist, and Paul G. Cassell, *Victims in Criminal Procedure* (forthcoming North Carolina Academic Press 2d ed.2005).

Apart from victim assessments of harm and preferences for punishment, is information about the victim's character or background relevant to sentencing? Compare Steve Bogira, *Courtroom 302* at 261–262 (2005) ("[Judge] Locallo always factors in the victim's background into his sentencing calculation. * * * 'When a victim is productive and going to school and has potential, that's a greater loss to society than if he's some goof who's involved in gangs,' the judge says later."); Minnesota Sentencing Guidelines, II.D.103. (listing the victim's role as aggressor as mitigating factor that would justify a downward departure, and as an aggravating factor justifying upward departure the victim's vulnerability due to age or infirmity).

11th ed., p. 1581; end of Note 2, add:

Professor Kevin Reitz argues that all of these alternatives, including advisory guidelines, are inferior to mandatory sentencing guidelines, particularly in achieving the goal of slowing the cost of corrections. Kevin R. Reitz, *The New Sentencing Conundrum: Policy and Constitutional Law at Cross Purposes*, 105 Colum.L.Rev. 1082 (2005). So far, a few states affected by *Blakely* have opted for new legislation retaining mandatory guidelines and requiring enhancements to be proven to a jury, but in these states only a small number of cases per year involve contested enhancements. At least one state where enhancing facts are invoked in a large proportion of cases has switched to advisory guidelines. See www.sentencing.typepad.com. Pending in Congress is a bill that would reinstate in the federal courts mandatory minimum sentences for guideline ranges, but remove limits on maximum sentences.

Part Five
APPEALS, POST–CONVICTION REVIEW
Chapter 28
APPEALS

SECTION 1. THE DEFENDANT'S RIGHT TO APPEAL

11th ed., p. 1584; end of Note 2, add:

Relying upon *Douglas*, the Court in *Halbert v. Michigan*, see Supp., p. 19, held that the Due Process and Equal Protection Clauses require the appointment of counsel for indigent defendants who seek discretionary review from the state court of appeals after pleading guilty.

SECTION 3. PROSECUTION APPEALS

11th ed., p. 1607; after Note 4, add:

5. *Victim appeals.* Some jurisdictions have provided victims of crime the right to seek review of trial court rulings denying them procedural rights granted by statute. See, for example, 18 U.S.C.A. § 3771(d) [Supp., App. B], which provides that if the district court denies the relief sought by the victim, the victim may seek a writ of mandamus, which must be decided expeditiously. The act provides, however, "In no case shall a failure to afford a right under this chapter provide grounds for a new trial. A victim may make a motion to re-open a plea or sentence only if—(A) the victim has asserted the right to be heard before or during the proceeding at issue and such right was denied; (B) the victim petitions the court of appeals for a writ of mandamus within 10 days; and (C) in the case of a plea, the accused has not pled to the highest offense charged."

Chapter 29

POST–CONVICTION REVIEW: FEDERAL HABEAS CORPUS

SECTION 2. ISSUES COGNIZABLE

11th ed., p. 1638; before section 3 in Note

The Court has yet to decide whether the habeas statute, which provides for review of claims by state prisoners that they are in custody due to violations of "the Constitution or laws or treatise of the United States," would allow a federal court to review a claim that a state prisoner is held in violation of the Vienna Convention's consular access provision. See *Medellin v. Dretke*, Supp., p. 4.

SECTION 6. LATE OR SUCCESSIVE PETITIONS

11th ed., p. 1675; end of Note 1, add:

The second exception to the one-year limit, see above, suggests that if the Court adopts a new rule of constitutional law that is important enough to be applied retroactively (see 11th ed., p. 1659–61, Note 3), the statute of limitation will not bar a petitioner's claim under that new rule. Realistically, though, this is a false hope for habeas petitioners whose cases are concluded in state court before the Supreme Court recognizes the new rule. Although the statute provides that the one-year clock does not start ticking until the Court initially recognizes the new rule, the statute also requires that the new rule be held retroactively applicable. The clock keeps running while a petitioner waits for such a holding. See *Dodd v. United States*, 125 S. Ct. 2478 (2005) (interpreting nearly identical language in Section 2255, terming this interpretation "strict," but "not absurd," even though it will bar most new-rule petitioners from presenting their claims).

Appendix A

SELECTED PROVISIONS OF THE UNITED STATES CONSTITUTION

Article I

Section 9. * * *

[2] The privilege of the Writ of Habeas Corpus shall not be suspended, unless when in Cases of Rebellion or Invasion the public Safety may require it.

[3] No Bill of Attainder or ex post facto Law shall be passed.

Article III

Section 1. The judicial Power of the United States, shall be vested in one supreme Court, and in such inferior Courts as the Congress may from time to time ordain and establish. The Judges, both of the supreme and inferior Courts, shall hold their Offices during good Behaviour, and shall, at stated Times, receive for their Services a Compensation, which shall not be diminished during their Continuance in Office.

Section 2. [1] The judicial Power shall extend to all Cases, in Law and Equity, arising under this Constitution, the Laws of the United States, and Treaties made, or which shall be made, under their Authority;—to all Cases affecting Ambassadors, other public Ministers and Consuls;—to all Cases of admiralty and maritime Jurisdiction;—to Controversies to which the United States shall be a Party;—to Controversies between two or more States;—between a State and Citizens of another State;—between Citizens of different States;—between Citizens of the same State claiming Lands under the Grants of different States, and between a State, or the Citizens thereof, and foreign States, Citizens or Subjects.

[3] The trial of all Crimes, except in Cases of Impeachment, shall be by Jury; and such Trial shall be held in the State where the said Crimes shall have been committed; but when not committed within any State, the Trial shall be at such Place or Places as the Congress may by Law have directed.

Section 3. [1] Treason against the United States, shall consist only in levying War against them, or, in adhering to their Enemies, giving them Aid and Comfort. No Person shall be convicted of Treason unless on the Testimony of two Witnesses to the same overt Act, or on Confession in open Court.

[2] The Congress shall have Power to declare the Punishment of Treason, but no Attainder of Treason shall work Corruption of Blood, or Forfeiture except during the Life of the Person attainted.

Article IV

Section 2. [1] The Citizens of each State shall be entitled to all Privileges and Immunities of Citizens in the several States.

[2] A Person charged in any State with Treason, Felony, or other Crime, who shall flee from Justice, and be found in another State, shall on demand of the executive Authority of the State from which he fled, be delivered up, to be removed to the State having Jurisdiction of the Crime.

Article VI

[2] This Constitution, and the Laws of the United States which shall be made in Pursuance thereof; and all Treaties made, or which shall be made, under the Authority of the United States, shall be the supreme Law.

Amendment I [1791]

Congress shall make no law respecting an establishment of religion, or prohibiting the free exercise thereof; or abridging the freedom of speech, or of the press; or the right of the people peaceably to assemble, and to petition the Government for a redress of grievances.

Amendment II [1791]

A well regulated Militia, being necessary to the security of a free State, the right of the people to keep and bear Arms, shall not be infringed.

Amendment III [1791]

No Soldier shall, in time of peace be quartered in any house, without the consent of the Owner, nor in time of war, but in a manner to be prescribed by law.

Amendment IV [1791]

The right of the people to be secure in their persons, houses, papers, and effects, against unreasonable searches and seizures, shall not be violated, and no Warrants shall issue, but upon probable cause, supported by Oath or affirmation, and particularly describing the place to be searched, and the persons or things to be seized.

Amendment V [1791]

No person shall be held to answer for a capital, or otherwise infamous crime, unless on a presentment or indictment of a Grand Jury, except in cases arising in the land or naval forces, or in the Militia, when in actual service in time of War or public danger; nor shall any person be subject for the same offence to be twice put in jeopardy of life or limb; nor shall be compelled in any criminal case to be a witness against himself, nor be deprived of life, liberty, or property, without due process of law; nor shall private property be taken for public use, without just compensation.

Amendment VI [1791]

In all criminal prosecutions, the accused shall enjoy the right to a speedy and public trial, by an impartial jury of the State and district wherein the crime shall have been committed, which district shall have been previously ascertained by law, and to be informed of the nature and cause of the accusation; to be confronted with the witnesses against him; to have compulsory process for obtaining witnesses in his favor, and to have the Assistance of Counsel for his defence.

Amendment VII [1791]

In Suits at common law, where the value in controversy shall exceed twenty dollars, the right of trial by jury shall be preserved, and no fact tried by jury, shall be otherwise re-examined in any Court of the United States, than according to the rules of the common law.

Amendment VIII [1791]

Excessive bail shall not be required, nor excessive fines imposed, nor cruel and unusual punishments inflicted.

Amendment IX [1791]

The enumeration in the Constitution, of certain rights, shall not be construed to deny or disparage others retained by the people.

Amendment X [1791]

The powers not delegated to the United States by the Constitution, nor prohibited by it to the States, are reserved to the States respectively, or to the people.

Amendment XIII [1865]

Section 1. Neither slavery nor involuntary servitude, except as a punishment for crime whereof the party shall have been duly convicted, shall exist within the United States, or any place subject to their jurisdiction.

Section 2. Congress shall have power to enforce this article by appropriate legislation.

Amendment XIV [1868]

Section 1. All persons born or naturalized in the United States, and subject to the jurisdiction thereof, are citizens of the United States and of the State wherein they reside. No State shall make or enforce any law which shall abridge the privileges or immunities of citizens of the United States; nor shall any State deprive any person of life, liberty, or property, without due process of law; nor deny to any person within its jurisdiction the equal protection of the laws.

Section 5. The Congress shall have power to enforce, by appropriate legislation, the provisions of the article.

Amendment XV [1870]

Section 1. The right of citizens of the United States to vote shall not be denied or abridged by the United States or by any State on account of race, color, or previous condition of servitude.

Section 2. The Congress shall have power to enforce this article by appropriate legislation.

Appendix B
SELECTED FEDERAL STATUTORY PROVISIONS

Analysis

Wire and Electronic Communications Interception and Interception of Oral Communications (18 U.S.C. §§ 2510–2511, 2515–2518, 2520–2521)
Searches and Seizures (18 U.S.C.A. §§ 3103a, 3105, 3109)
Bail Reform Act of 1984 (18 U.S.C. §§ 3141–3150)
Speedy Trial Act of 1974 (As Amended) (18 U.S.C. §§ 3161–3162, 3164)
Jencks Act (18 U.S.C. § 3500)
Litigation Concerning Sources of Evidence (18 U.S.C. § 3504)
Criminal Appeals Act of 1970 (As Amended) (18 U.S.C. § 3731)
Crime Victims' Rights (18 U.S.C. § 3771)
Jury Selection and Service Act of 1968 (As Amended) (28 U.S.C. §§ 1861–1863, 1865–1867)
Habeas Corpus (28 U.S.C. §§ 2241–2244, 2253–2255, 2261–2266)
Privacy Protection Act of 1980 (42 U.S.C. §§ 2000aa—2000aa–12); Guidelines (28 C.F.R. § 59.4)
Foreign Intelligence Surveillance Act (50 U.S.C.A. § 1861)

WIRE AND ELECTRONIC COMMUNICATIONS INTERCEPTION AND INTERCEPTION OF ORAL COMMUNICATIONS

(18 U.S.C. §§ 2510–2511, 2515–2518, 2520–2521).

§ 2510. Definitions

As used in this chapter

(1) "wire communication means any aural transfer made in whole or in part through the use of facilities for the transmission of communications by the aid of wire, cable, or other like connection between the point of origin and the point of reception (including the use of such connection in a switching station) furnished or operated by any person engaged in providing or operating such facilities for the transmission of interstate or foreign communications or communications affecting interstate or foreign commerce;

(2) "oral communication" means any oral communication uttered by a person exhibiting an expectation that such communication is not subject to interception under circumstances justifying such expectation, but such term does not include any electronic communication;

(3) "State" means any State of the United States, the District of Columbia, the Commonwealth of Puerto Rico, and any territory or possession of the United States;

(4) "intercept" means the aural or other acquisition of the contents of any wire, electronic, or oral communication through the use of any electronic, mechanical, or other device.

(5) "electronic, mechanical, or other device" means any device or apparatus which can be used to intercept a wire, oral, or electronic communication other than—

(a) any telephone or telegraph instrument, equipment or facility, or any component thereof, (i) furnished to the subscriber or user by a provider of wire or electronic communication service in the ordinary course of its business and being used by the subscriber or user in the ordinary course of its business or furnished by such subscriber or user for connection to the facilities of such service and used in the ordinary course of its business; or (ii) being used by a provider of wire or electronic communication service in the ordinary course of its business, or by an investigative or law enforcement officer in the ordinary course of his duties;

(b) a hearing aid or similar device being used to correct subnormal hearing to not better than normal;

(6) "person" means any employee, or agent of the United States or any State or political subdivision thereof, and any individual, partnership, association, joint stock company, trust, or corporation;

(7) "Investigative or law enforcement officer" means any officer of the United States or of a State or political subdivision thereof, who is empowered by law to conduct investigations of or to make arrests for offenses enumerated in this chapter, and any attorney authorized by law to prosecute or participate in the prosecution of such offenses;

(8) "contents", when used with respect to any wire, oral, or electronic communication, includes any information concerning the substance, purport, or meaning of that communication;

(9) "Judge of competent jurisdiction" means—

(a) a judge of a United States district court or a United States court of appeals; and

(b) a judge of any court of general criminal jurisdiction of a State who is authorized by a statute of that State to enter orders authorizing interceptions of wire, oral, or electronic communications;

(10) "communication common carrier" has the meaning given that term in section 3 of the Communications Act of 1934;

(11) "aggrieved person" means a person who was a party to any intercepted wire, oral, or electronic communication or a person against whom the interception was directed;

(12) "electronic communication" means any transfer of signs, signals, writing, images, sounds, data, or intelligence of any nature transmitted in whole or in part by a wire, radio, electromagnetic, photoelectronic or photooptical system that affects interstate or foreign commerce, but does not include—

(A) any wire or oral communication;

(B) any communication made through a tone-only paging device;

(C) any communication from a tracking device (as defined in section 3117 of this title); or

(D) electronic funds transfer information stored by a financial institution in a communications system used for the electronic storage and transfer of funds;

(13) "user" means any person or entity who—

(A) uses an electronic communication service; and

(B) is duly authorized by the provider of such service to engage in such use;

(14) "electronic communications system" means any wire, radio, electromagnetic, photooptical or photoelectronic facilities for the transmission of wire or electronic communications, and any computer facilities or related electronic equipment for the electronic storage of such communications;

(15) "electronic communication service" means any service which provides to users thereof the ability to send or receive wire or electronic communications;

(16) "readily accessible to the general public" means, with respect to a radio communication, that such communication is not—

(A) scrambled or encrypted;

(B) transmitted using modulation techniques whose essential parameters have been withheld from the public with the intention of preserving the privacy of such communication;

(C) carried on a subcarrier or other signal subsidiary to a radio transmission;

(D) transmitted over a communication system provided by a common carrier, unless the communication is a tone only paging system communication; or

(E) transmitted on frequencies allocated under part 25, subpart D, E, or F of part 74, or part 94 of the Rules of the Federal Communications Commission, unless, in the case of a communication transmitted on a frequency allocated under part 74 that is not exclusively allocated to broadcast auxiliary services, the communication is a two-way voice communication by radio;

(17) "electronic storage" means—

(A) any temporary, intermediate storage of a wire or electronic communication incidental to the electronic transmission thereof; and

(B) any storage of such communication by an electronic communication service for purposes of backup protection of such communication;

(18) "aural transfer" means a transfer containing the human voice at any point between and including the point of origin and the point of reception;

(19) "foreign intelligence information", for purposes of section 2517(6) of this title, means—

(A) information, whether or not concerning a United States person, that relates to the ability of the United States to protect against—

(i) actual or potential attack or other grave hostile acts of a foreign power or an agent of a foreign power;

(ii) sabotage or international terrorism by a foreign power or an agent of a foreign power; or

(iii) clandestine intelligence activities by an intelligence service or network of a foreign power or by an agent of a foreign power; or

(B) information, whether or not concerning a United States person, with respect to a foreign power or foreign territory that relates to—

(i) the national defense or the security of the United States; or

(ii) the conduct of the foreign affairs of the United States;

(20) "protected computer" has the meaning set forth in section 1030; and

(21) "computer trespasser"—

(A) means a person who accesses a protected computer without authorization and thus has no reasonable expectation of privacy in any communication transmitted to, through, or from the protected computer; and

(B) does not include a person known by the owner or operator of the protected computer to have an existing contractual relationship with the owner or operator of the protected computer for access to all or part of the protected computer.

§ 2511. Interception and disclosure of wire, oral, or electronic communications prohibited

(1) Except as otherwise specifically provided in this chapter any person who—

(a) intentionally intercepts, endeavors to intercept, or procures any other person to intercept or endeavor to intercept, any wire, oral, or electronic communication;

(b) intentionally uses, endeavors to use, or procures any other person to use or endeavor to use any electronic, mechanical, or other device to intercept any oral communication when—

(i) such device is affixed to, or otherwise transmits a signal through, a wire, cable, or other like connection used in wire communication; or

(ii) such device transmits communications by radio, or interferes with the transmission of such communication; or

(iii) such person knows, or has reason to know, that such device or any component thereof has been sent through the mail or transported in interstate or foreign commerce; or

(iv) such use or endeavor to use (A) takes place on the premises of any business or other commercial establishment the operations of which affect interstate or foreign commerce; or (B) obtains or is for the purpose of obtaining information relating to the operations of any business or other commercial establishment the operations of which affect interstate or foreign commerce; or

(v) such person acts in the District of Columbia, the Commonwealth of Puerto Rico, or any territory or possession of the United States;

(c) intentionally discloses, or endeavors to disclose, to any other person the contents of any wire, oral, or electronic communication, knowing or having reason to know that the information was obtained through the interception of a wire, oral, or electronic communication in violation of this subsection;

(d) intentionally uses, or endeavors to use, the contents of any wire, oral, or electronic communication, knowing or having reason to know that the information was obtained through the interception of a wire, oral, or electronic communication in violation of this subsection; or

(e)(i) intentionally discloses, or endeavors to disclose, to any other person the contents of any wire, oral, or electronic communication, intercepted by means authorized by sections 2511(2)(a)(ii), 2511(2)(b)–(c), 2511(2)(e), 2516, and 2518 of this chapter, (ii) knowing or having reason to know that the information was obtained through the interception of such a communication in connection with a criminal investigation, (iii) having obtained or received the information in connection with a criminal investigation, and (iv) with intent to improperly obstruct, impede, or interfere with a duly authorized criminal investigation,

shall be punished as provided in subsection (4) or shall be subject to suit as provided in subsection (5).

(2)(a)(i) It shall not be unlawful under this chapter for an operator of a switchboard, or an officer, employee, or agent of a provider of wire or electronic communication service, whose facilities are used in the transmission of a wire or electronic communication, to intercept, disclose, or use that communication in the normal course of his employment while engaged in any activity which is a necessary incident to the rendition of his service or to the protection of the rights or property of the provider of that service, except that a provider of wire communication service to the public shall not utilize service observing or random monitoring except for mechanical or service quality control checks.

(ii) Notwithstanding any other law, providers of wire or electronic communication service, their officers, employees, and agents, landlords, custodians, or other persons, are authorized to provide information, facilities, or technical assistance to persons authorized by law to intercept wire, oral, or electronic communications or to conduct electronic surveillance, as defined in section 101 of the Foreign Intelligence Surveillance Act of 1978, if such provider, its officers, employees, or agents, landlord, custodian, or other specified person, has been provided with—

(A) a court order directing such assistance signed by the authorizing judge, or

(B) a certification in writing by a person specified in section 2518(7) of this title or the Attorney General of the United States that no warrant or court order is required by law, that all statutory requirements have been met, and that the specified assistance is required,

setting forth the period of time during which the provision of the information, facilities, or technical assistance is authorized and specifying the information, facilities, or technical assistance required. No provider of wire or electronic communication service, officer, employee, or agent thereof, or landlord, custodian, or other specified person shall disclose the existence of any interception or surveillance or the device used to accomplish the interception or surveillance with respect to which the person has been furnished a court order or certification under this chapter, except as may otherwise be required by legal process and then only after prior notification to the Attorney General or to the principal prosecuting attorney of a State or any political subdivision of a State, as may be appropriate. Any such disclosure, shall render such person liable for the civil damages provided for in section 2520. No cause of action shall lie in any court against any provider of wire or electronic communication service, its officers, employees, or agents, landlord, custodian, or other specified person for providing information, facilities, or assistance in accordance with the terms of a court order, statutory authorization, or certification under this chapter.

(b) It shall not be unlawful under this chapter for an officer, employee, or agent of the Federal Communications Commission, in the normal course of his employment and in discharge of the monitoring responsibilities exercised by the Commission in the enforcement of chapter 5 of title 47 of the United States Code, to intercept a wire or electronic communication, or oral communication transmitted by radio, or to disclose or use the information thereby obtained.

(c) It shall not be unlawful under this chapter for a person acting under color of law to intercept a wire, oral, or electronic communication, where such person is a party to the communication or one of the parties to the communication has given prior consent to such interception.

(d) It shall not be unlawful under this chapter for a person not acting under color of law to intercept a wire, oral, or electronic communication where such person is a party to the communication or where one of the parties to the communication has given prior consent to such interception unless such communication is intercepted for the purpose of committing any criminal or tortious act in violation of the Constitution or laws of the United States or of any State.

(e) Notwithstanding any other provision of this title or section 705 or 706 of the Communications Act of 1934, it shall not be unlawful for an officer, employee, or agent of the United States in the normal course of his official duty to conduct electronic surveillance, as defined in section 101 of the Foreign Intelligence Surveillance Act of 1978, as authorized by that Act.

(f) Nothing contained in this chapter or chapter 121 or 206 of this title, or section 705 of the Communications Act of 1934, shall be deemed to affect the acquisition by the United States Government of foreign intelligence information from international or foreign communications, or foreign intelligence activities conducted in accordance with otherwise applicable Federal law involving a foreign electronic communications system, utilizing a means other than electronic surveillance as defined in section 101 of the Foreign Intelligence Surveillance Act of 1978, and procedures in this chapter or chapter 121 and the Foreign Intelligence Surveillance Act of 1978 shall be the exclusive means by which electronic surveillance, as defined in section 101 of such Act, and the interception of domestic wire, oral, and electronic communications may be conducted.

(g) It shall not be unlawful under this chapter or chapter 121 of this title for any person—

(i) to intercept or access an electronic communication made through an electronic communication system that is configured so that such electronic communication is readily accessible to the general public;

(ii) to intercept any radio communication which is transmitted—

(I) by any station for the use of the general public, or that relates to ships, aircraft, vehicles, or persons in distress;

(II) by any governmental, law enforcement, civil defense, private land mobile, or public safety communications system, including police and fire, readily accessible to the general public;

(III) by a station operating on an authorized frequency within the bands allocated to the amateur, citizens band, or general mobile radio services; or

(IV) by any marine or aeronautical communications system;

(iii) to engage in any conduct which—

(I) is prohibited by section 633 of the Communications Act of 1934; or

(II) is excepted from the application of section 705(a) of the Communications Act of 1934 by section 705(b) of that Act;

(iv) to intercept any wire or electronic communication the transmission of which is causing harmful interference to any lawfully operating station or consumer electronic equipment, to the extent necessary to identify the source of such interference; or

(v) for other users of the same frequency to intercept any radio communication made through a system that utilizes frequencies monitored by individuals engaged in the provision or the use of such system, if such communication is not scrambled or encrypted.

(h) It shall not be unlawful under this chapter—

(i) to use a pen register or a trap and trace device (as those terms are defined for the purposes of chapter 206 (relating to pen registers and trap and trace devices) of this title); or

(ii) for a provider of electronic communication service to record the fact that a wire or electronic communication was initiated or completed in order to protect such provider, another provider furnishing service toward the completion of the wire or electronic communication, or a user of that service, from fraudulent, unlawful or abusive use of such service.

(i) It shall not be unlawful under this chapter for a person acting under color of law to intercept the wire or electronic communications of a computer trespasser transmitted to, through, or from the protected computer, if—

(I) the owner or operator of the protected computer authorizes the interception of the computer trespasser's communications on the protected computer;

(II) the person acting under color of law is lawfully engaged in an investigation;

(III) the person acting under color of law has reasonable grounds to believe that the contents of the computer trespasser's communications will be relevant to the investigation; and

(IV) such interception does not acquire communications other than those transmitted to or from the computer trespasser.

(3)(a) Except as provided in paragraph (b) of this subsection, a person or entity providing an electronic communication service to the public shall not intentionally divulge the contents of any communication (other than one to such person or entity, or an agent thereof) while in transmission on that service to any person or entity other than an addressee or intended recipient of such communication or an agent of such addressee or intended recipient.

(b) A person or entity providing electronic communication service to the public may divulge the contents of any such communication—

(i) as otherwise authorized in section 2511(2)(a) or 2517 of this title;

(ii) with the lawful consent of the originator or any addressee or intended recipient of such communication;

(iii) to a person employed or authorized, or whose facilities are used, to forward such communication to its destination; or

(iv) which were inadvertently obtained by the service provider and which appear to pertain to the commission of a crime, if such divulgence is made to a law enforcement agency.

(4)(a) Except as provided in paragraph (b) of this subsection or in subsection (5), whoever violates subsection (1) of this section shall be fined under this title or imprisoned not more than five years, or both.

(b) Conduct otherwise an offense under this subsection that consists of or relates to the interception of a satellite transmission that is not encrypted or scrambled and that is transmitted—

(i) to a broadcasting station for purposes of retransmission to the general public; or

(ii) as an audio subcarrier intended for redistribution to facilities open to the public, but not including data transmissions or telephone calls,

is not an offense under this subsection unless the conduct is for the purposes of direct or indirect commercial advantage or private financial gain.

[(c) Redesignated (b)]

(5)(a)(i) If the communication is—

(A) a private satellite video communication that is not scrambled or encrypted and the conduct in violation of this chapter is the private viewing of that communication and is not for a tortious or illegal purpose or for purposes of direct or indirect commercial advantage or private commercial gain; or

(B) a radio communication that is transmitted on frequencies allocated under subpart D of part 74 of the rules of the Federal Communications Commission that is not scrambled or encrypted and the conduct in violation of this chapter is not for a tortious or illegal purpose or for purposes of direct or indirect commercial advantage or private commercial gain,

then the person who engages in such conduct shall be subject to suit by the Federal Government in a court of competent jurisdiction.

(ii) In an action under this subsection—

(A) if the violation of this chapter is a first offense for the person under paragraph (a) of subsection (4) and such person has not been found liable in a civil action under section 2520 of this title, the Federal Government shall be entitled to appropriate injunctive relief; and

(B) if the violation of this chapter is a second or subsequent offense under paragraph (a) of subsection (4) or such person has been found liable in any prior civil action under section 2520, the person shall be subject to a mandatory $500 civil fine.

(b) The court may use any means within its authority to enforce an injunction issued under paragraph (ii)(A), and shall impose a civil fine of not less than $500 for each violation of such an injunction.

§ 2515. Prohibition of use as evidence of intercepted wire or oral communications

Whenever any wire or oral communication has been intercepted, no part of the contents of such communication and no evidence derived therefrom may be received in evidence in any trial, hearing, or other proceeding in or before any court, grand jury, department, officer, agency, regulatory body, legislative committee, or other authority of the United States, a State, or a political subdivision thereof if the disclosure of that information would be in violation of this chapter.

§ 2516. Authorization for interception of wire, oral, or electronic communications

(1) The Attorney General, Deputy Attorney General, Associate Attorney General, or any Assistant Attorney General, any acting Assistant Attorney General, or any Deputy Assistant Attorney General or acting Deputy Assistant Attorney General in the Criminal Division specially designated by the Attorney General, may authorize an application to a Federal judge of competent jurisdiction for, and such judge may grant in conformity with section 2518 of this chapter an order authorizing or approving the interception of wire or oral communications by the Federal Bureau of Investigation, or a Federal agency having responsibility for the investigation of the offense as to which the application is made, when such interception may provide or has provided evidence of—

(a) any offense punishable by death or by imprisonment for more than one year under sections 2122 and 2274 through 2277 of title 42 of the United States Code (relating to the enforcement of the Atomic Energy Act of 1954), section 2284 of title 42 of the United States Code (relating to sabotage of nuclear facilities or fuel), or under the following chapters of this title: chapter 37 (relating to espionage), chapter 55 (relating to kidnapping), chapter 90 (relating to protection of trade secrets), chapter 105 (relating to sabotage), chapter 115 (relating to treason), chapter 102 (relating to riots), chapter 65 (relating to malicious mischief), chapter 111 (relating to destruction of vessels), or chapter 81 (relating to piracy);

(b) a violation of section 186 or section 501(c) of title 29, United States Code (dealing with restrictions on payments and loans to labor organizations), or any offense which involves murder, kidnapping, robbery, or extortion, and which is punishable under this title;

(c) any offense which is punishable under the following sections of this title: section 201 (bribery of public officials and witnesses), section 215 (relating to bribery of bank officials), section 224 (bribery in sporting contests), subsection (d), (e), (f), (g), (h), or (i) of section 844 (unlawful use of explosives), section 1032 (relating to concealment of assets), section 1084 (transmission of wagering information), section 751 (relating to escape), section 1014 (relating to loans and credit applications generally; renewals and discounts), sections 1503, 1512, and 1513 (influencing or injuring an officer, juror, or witness generally), section 1510 (obstruction of criminal investigations), section 1511 (obstruction of State or local law enforcement), section 1591 (sex trafficking of children by force, fraud, or coercion), section 1751 (Presidential and Presidential staff assassination, kidnapping, and assault), section 1951 (interference with commerce by threats or violence), section 1952 (interstate and foreign travel or transportation in aid of racketeering enterprises), section 1958 (relating to use of interstate commerce facilities in the commission of murder for hire), section 1959 (relating to violent crimes in aid of racketeering activity), section 1954 (offer, acceptance, or solicitation to influence operations of employee benefit plan), section 1955 (prohibition of business enterprises of gambling), section 1956 (laundering of monetary instruments), section 1957 (relating to engaging in monetary transactions in property derived from specified unlawful activity), section 659 (theft from interstate shipment), section 664 (embezzlement from pension and welfare funds), section 1343 (fraud by wire, radio, or television), section 1344 (relating to bank fraud), sections 2251 and 2252 (sexual exploitation of children), section 2251A (selling or buying of children), section 2252A (relating to material constituting or containing child pornography), section 1466A (relating to child obscenity), section 2260 (production of sexually explicit depictions of a minor for importation into the United States), sections 2421, 2422, 2423, and 2425 (relating to transportation for illegal sexual activity and related crimes), sections 2312, 2313, 2314, and 2315 (interstate transportation of stolen property), section 2321 (relating to trafficking in certain motor vehicles or motor vehicle parts), section 1203 (relating to hostage taking), section 1029 (relating to fraud and related activity in connection with access devices), section 3146 (relating to penalty for failure to appear), section 3521(b)(3) (relating to witness relocation and assistance), section 32 (relating to destruction of aircraft or aircraft facilities), section 38 (relating to aircraft parts fraud), section 1963 (violations with respect to racketeer influenced and corrupt organizations), section 115 (relating to threatening or retaliating against a Federal official), section 1341 (relating to mail fraud), a felony violation of section 1030 (relating to computer fraud and abuse), section 351 (violations with respect to congressional, Cabinet, or Supreme Court assassinations, kidnapping, and assault), section 831 (relating to prohibited transactions involving nuclear materials), section 33 (relating to destruction of motor vehicles or motor vehicle facilities), section 175 (relating to biological weapons), section 175c (relating to variola virus), section 1992 (relating to wrecking trains), a felony violation of section 1028 (relating to production of false identification documentation), section 1425 (relating to the procurement of citizenship or nationalization unlawfully), section 1426 (relating to the reproduction of naturalization or citizenship papers), section 1427 (relating to the sale of naturalization or citizenship papers), section 1541 (relating to passport issuance without authority), section 1542 (relating to false statements in passport applications), section 1543 (relating to forgery or false use of passports), section 1544 (relating to misuse of passports), or section 1546 (relating to fraud and misuse of visas, permits, and other documents);

(d) any offense involving counterfeiting punishable under section 471, 472, or 473 of this title;

(e) any offense involving fraud connected with a case under title 11 or the manufacture, importation, receiving, concealment, buying, selling, or otherwise dealing in narcotic drugs, marihuana, or other dangerous drugs, punishable under any law of the United States;

(f) any offense including extortionate credit transactions under sections 892, 893, or 894 of this title;

(g) a violation of section 5322 of title 31, United States Code (dealing with the reporting of currency transactions);

(h) any felony violation of sections 2511 and 2512 (relating to interception and disclosure of certain communications and to certain intercepting devices) of this title;

(i) any felony violation of chapter 71 (relating to obscenity) of this title;

(j) any violation of section 60123(b) (relating to destruction of a natural gas pipeline) or section 46502 (relating to aircraft piracy) of title 49;

(k) any criminal violation of section 2778 of title 22 (relating to the Arms Export Control Act);

(l) the location of any fugitive from justice from an offense described in this section;

(m) a violation of section 274, 277, or 278 of the Immigration and Nationality Act (8 U.S.C. 1324, 1327, or 1328) (relating to the smuggling of aliens);

(n) any felony violation of sections 922 and 924 of title 18, United States Code (relating to firearms);

(o) any violation of section 5861 of the Internal Revenue Code of 1986 (relating to firearms);

(p) a felony violation of section 1028 (relating to production of false identification documents), section 1542 (relating to false statements in passport applications), section 1546 (relating to fraud and misuse of visas, permits, and other documents) of this title or a violation of section 274, 277, or 278 of the Immigration and Nationality Act (relating to the smuggling of aliens);

(q) any criminal violation of section 229 (relating to chemical weapons); or sections 2332, 2332a, 2332b, 2332d, 2332f, 2332g, 2332h, 2339A, 2339B, or 2339C of this title (relating to terrorism); or

(r) any conspiracy to commit any offense described in any subparagraph of this paragraph.

(2) The principal prosecuting attorney of any State, or the principal prosecuting attorney of any political subdivision thereof, if such attorney is authorized by a statute of that State to make application to a State court judge of competent jurisdiction for an order authorizing or approving the interception of wire, oral, or electronic communications, may apply to such judge for, and such judge may grant in conformity with section 2518 of this chapter and with the applicable State statute an order authorizing, or approving the interception of wire, oral, or electronic communications by investigative or law enforcement officers having responsibility for the investigation of the offense as to which the application is made, when such interception may provide or has provided evidence of the commission of the offense of murder, kidnapping, gambling, robbery, bribery, extortion, or dealing in narcotic drugs, marihuana or other dangerous drugs, or other crime dangerous to life, limb, or property, and punishable by imprisonment for more than one year, designated in any applicable State statute authoriz-

ing such interception, or any conspiracy to commit any of the foregoing offenses.

(3) Any attorney for the Government (as such term is defined for the purposes of the Federal Rules of Criminal Procedure) may authorize an application to a Federal judge of competent jurisdiction for, and such judge may grant, in conformity with section 2518 of this title, an order authorizing or approving the interception of electronic communications by an investigative or law enforcement officer having responsibility for the investigation of the offense as to which the application is made, when such interception may provide or has provided evidence of any Federal felony.

§ 2517. Authorization for disclosure and use of intercepted wire, oral, or electronic communications

(1) Any investigative or law enforcement officer who, by any means authorized by this chapter, has obtained knowledge of the contents of any wire, oral, or electronic communication, or evidence derived therefrom, may disclose such contents to another investigative or law enforcement officer to the extent that such disclosure is appropriate to the proper performance of the official duties of the officer making or receiving the disclosure.

(2) Any investigative or law enforcement officer who, by any means authorized by this chapter, has obtained knowledge of the contents of any wire, oral, or electronic communication or evidence derived therefrom may use such contents to the extent such use is appropriate to the proper performance of his official duties.

(3) Any person who has received, by any means authorized by this chapter, any information concerning a wire, oral, or electronic communication, or evidence derived therefrom intercepted in accordance with the provisions of this chapter may disclose the contents of that communication or such derivative evidence while giving testimony under oath or affirmation in any proceeding held under the authority of the United States or of any State or political subdivision thereof.

(4) No otherwise privileged wire, oral, or electronic communication intercepted in accordance with, or in violation of, the provisions of this chapter shall lose its privileged character.

(5) When an investigative or law enforcement officer, while engaged in intercepting wire, oral, or electronic communications in the manner authorized herein, intercepts wire, oral, or electronic communications relating to offenses other than those specified in the order of authorization or approval, the contents thereof, and evidence derived therefrom, may be disclosed or used as provided in subsections (1) and (2) of this section. Such contents and any evidence derived therefrom may be used under subsection (3) of this section when authorized or approved by a judge of competent jurisdiction where such judge finds on subsequent application that the contents were otherwise intercepted in accordance with the provisions of this chapter. Such application shall be made as soon as practicable.

(6) Any investigative or law enforcement officer, or attorney for the Government, who by any means authorized by this chapter, has obtained knowledge of the contents of any wire, oral, or electronic communication, or

evidence derived therefrom, may disclose such contents to any other Federal law enforcement, intelligence, protective, immigration, national defense, or national security official to the extent that such contents include foreign intelligence or counterintelligence (as defined in section 3 of the National Security Act of 1947 (50 U.S.C. 401a)), or foreign intelligence information (as defined in subsection (19) of section 2510 of this title), to assist the official who is to receive that information in the performance of his official duties. Any Federal official who receives information pursuant to this provision may use that information only as necessary in the conduct of that person's official duties subject to any limitations on the unauthorized disclosure of such information.

(7) Any investigative or law enforcement officer, or other Federal official in carrying out official duties as such Federal official, who by any means authorized by this chapter, has obtained knowledge of the contents of any wire, oral, or electronic communication, or evidence derived therefrom, may disclose such contents or derivative evidence to a foreign investigative or law enforcement officer to the extent that such disclosure is appropriate to the proper performance of the official duties of the officer making or receiving the disclosure, and foreign investigative or law enforcement officers may use or disclose such contents or derivative evidence to the extent such use or disclosure is appropriate to the proper performance of their official duties.

(8) Any investigative or law enforcement officer, or other Federal official in carrying out official duties as such Federal official, who by any means authorized by this chapter, has obtained knowledge of the contents of any wire, oral, or electronic communication, or evidence derived therefrom, may disclose such contents or derivative evidence to any appropriate Federal, State, local, or foreign government official to the extent that such contents or derivative evidence reveals a threat of actual or potential attack or other grave hostile acts of a foreign power or an agent of a foreign power, domestic or international sabotage, domestic or international terrorism, or clandestine intelligence gathering activities by an intelligence service or network of a foreign power or by an agent of a foreign power, within the United States or elsewhere, for the purpose of preventing or responding to such a threat. Any official who receives information pursuant to this provision may use that information only as necessary in the conduct of that person's official duties subject to any limitations on the unauthorized disclosure of such information, and any State, local, or foreign official who receives information pursuant to this provision may use that information only consistent with such guidelines as the Attorney General and Director of Central Intelligence shall jointly issue.

§ 2518. Procedure for interception of wire, oral, or electronic communications

(1) Each application for an order authorizing or approving the interception of a wire, oral, or electronic communication under this chapter shall be made in writing upon oath or affirmation to a judge of competent jurisdiction and shall state the applicant's authority to make such application. Each application shall include the following information:

(a) the identity of the investigative or law enforcement officer making the application, and the officer authorizing the application;

(b) a full and complete statement of the facts and circumstances relied upon by the applicant, to justify his belief that an order should be issued, including (i) details as to the particular offense that has been, is being, or is about to be committed, (ii) except as provided in subsection (11), a particular description of the nature and location of the facilities from which or the place where the communication is to be intercepted, (iii) a particular description of the type of communications sought to be intercepted, (iv) the identity of the person, if known, committing the offense and whose communications are to be intercepted;

(c) a full and complete statement as to whether or not other investigative procedures have been tried and failed or why they reasonably appear to be unlikely to succeed if tried or to be too dangerous;

(d) a statement of the period of time for which the interception is required to be maintained. If the nature of the investigation is such that the authorization for interception should not automatically terminate when the described type of communication has been first obtained, a particular description of facts establishing probable cause to believe that additional communications of the same type will occur thereafter;

(e) a full and complete statement of the facts concerning all previous applications known to the individual authorizing and making the application, made to any judge for authorization to intercept, or for approval of interceptions of, wire, oral, or electronic communications involving any of the same persons, facilities or places specified in the application, and the action taken by the judge on each such application; and

(f) where the application is for the extension of an order, a statement setting forth the results thus far obtained from the interception, or a reasonable explanation of the failure to obtain such results.

(2) The judge may require the applicant to furnish additional testimony or documentary evidence in support of the application.

(3) Upon such application the judge may enter an ex parte order, as requested or as modified, authorizing or approving interception of wire, oral, or electronic communications within the territorial jurisdiction of the court in which the judge is sitting (and outside that jurisdiction but within the United States in the case of a mobile interception device authorized by a Federal court within such jurisdiction), if the judge determines on the basis of the facts submitted by the applicant that—

(a) there is probable cause for belief that an individual is committing, has committed, or is about to commit a particular offense enumerated in section 2516 of this chapter;

(b) there is probable cause for belief that particular communications concerning that offense will be obtained through such interception;

(c) normal investigative procedures have been tried and have failed or reasonably appear to be unlikely to succeed if tried or to be too dangerous;

(d) except as provided in subsection (11), there is probable cause for belief that the facilities from which, or the place where, the wire, oral, or electronic communications are to be intercepted are being used, or are about to be used, in connection with the commission of such offense, or are leased to, listed in the name of, or commonly used by such person.

(4) Each order authorizing or approving the interception of any wire, oral, or electronic communication under this chapter shall specify—

(a) the identity of the person, if known, whose communications are to be intercepted;

(b) the nature and location of the communications facilities as to which, or the place where, authority to intercept is granted;

(c) a particular description of the type of communication sought to be intercepted, and a statement of the particular offense to which it relates;

(d) the identity of the agency authorized to intercept the communications, and of the person authorizing the application; and

(e) the period of time during which such interception is authorized, including a statement as to whether or not the interception shall automatically terminate when the described communication has been first obtained.

An order authorizing the interception of a wire, oral, or electronic communication under this chapter shall, upon request of the applicant, direct that a provider of wire or electronic communication service, landlord, custodian or other person shall furnish the applicant forthwith all information, facilities, and technical assistance necessary to accomplish the interception unobtrusively and with a minimum of interference with the services that such service provider, landlord, custodian, or person is according the person whose communications are to be intercepted. Any provider of wire or electronic communication service, landlord, custodian or other person furnishing such facilities or technical assistance shall be compensated therefor by the applicant for reasonable expenses incurred in providing such facilities or assistance. Pursuant to section 2522 of this chapter, an order may also be issued to enforce the assistance capability and capacity requirements under the Communications Assistance for Law Enforcement Act.

(5) No order entered under this section may authorize or approve the interception of any wire, oral, or electronic communication for any period longer than is necessary to achieve the objective of the authorization, nor in any event longer than thirty days. Such thirty-day period begins on the earlier of the day on which the investigative or law enforcement officer first begins to conduct an interception under the order or ten days after the order is entered. Extensions of an order may be granted, but only upon application for an extension made in accordance with subsection (1) of this section and the court making the findings required by subsection (3) of this section. The period of extension shall be no longer than the authorizing judge deems necessary to achieve the purposes for which it was granted and in no event for longer than thirty days. Every order and extension thereof shall contain a provision that the authorization to intercept shall be executed as soon as practicable, shall be conducted in such a way as to minimize the interception

of communications not otherwise subject to interception under this chapter, and must terminate upon attainment of the authorized objective, or in any event in thirty days. In the event the intercepted communication is in a code or foreign language, and an expert in that foreign language or code is not reasonably available during the interception period, minimization may be accomplished as soon as practicable after such interception. An interception under this chapter may be conducted in whole or in part by Government personnel, or by an individual operating under a contract with the Government, acting under the supervision of an investigative or law enforcement officer authorized to conduct the interception.

(6) Whenever an order authorizing interception is entered pursuant to this chapter, the order may require reports to be made to the judge who issued the order showing what progress has been made toward achievement of the authorized objective and the need for continued interception. Such reports shall be made at such intervals as the judge may require.

(7) Notwithstanding any other provision of this chapter, any investigative or law enforcement officer, specially designated by the Attorney General, the Deputy Attorney General, the Associate Attorney General, or by the principal prosecuting attorney of any State or subdivision thereof acting pursuant to a statute of that State, who reasonably determines that—

> (a) an emergency situation exists that involves—
>
>> (i) immediate danger of death or serious physical injury to any person,
>>
>> (ii) conspiratorial activities threatening the national security interest, or
>>
>> (iii) conspiratorial activities characteristic of organized crime,

that requires a wire, oral, or electronic communication to be intercepted before an order authorizing such interception can, with due diligence, be obtained, and

> (b) there are grounds upon which an order could be entered under this chapter to authorize such interception,

may intercept such wire, oral, or electronic communication if an application for an order approving the interception is made in accordance with this section within forty-eight hours after the interception has occurred, or begins to occur. In the absence of an order, such interception shall immediately terminate when the communication sought is obtained or when the application for the order is denied, whichever is earlier. In the event such application for approval is denied, or in any other case where the interception is terminated without an order having been issued, the contents of any wire, oral, or electronic communication intercepted shall be treated as having been obtained in violation of this chapter, and an inventory shall be served as provided for in subsection (d) of this section on the person named in the application.

(8) (a) The contents of any wire, oral, or electronic communication intercepted by any means authorized by this chapter shall, if possible, be recorded on tape or wire or other comparable device. The recording of the contents of any wire, oral, or electronic communication under this subsection

shall be done in such a way as will protect the recording from editing or other alterations. Immediately upon the expiration of the period of the order, or extensions thereof, such recordings shall be made available to the judge issuing such order and sealed under his directions. Custody of the recordings shall be wherever the judge orders. They shall not be destroyed except upon an order of the issuing or denying judge and in any event shall be kept for ten years. Duplicate recordings may be made for use or disclosure pursuant to the provisions of subsections (1) and (2) of section 2517 of this chapter for investigations. The presence of the seal provided for by this subsection, or a satisfactory explanation for the absence thereof, shall be a prerequisite for the use or disclosure of the contents of any wire, oral, or electronic communication or evidence derived therefrom under subsection (3) of section 2517.

(b) Applications made and orders granted under this chapter shall be sealed by the judge. Custody of the applications and orders shall be wherever the judge directs. Such applications and orders shall be disclosed only upon a showing of good cause before a judge of competent jurisdiction and shall not be destroyed except on order of the issuing or denying judge, and in any event shall be kept for ten years.

(c) Any violation of the provisions of this subsection may be punished as contempt of the issuing or denying judge.

(d) Within a reasonable time but not later than ninety days after the filing of an application for an order of approval under section 2518(7)(b) which is denied or the termination of the period of an order or extensions thereof, the issuing or denying judge shall cause to be served, on the persons named in the order or the application, and such other parties to intercepted communications as the judge may determine in his discretion that is in the interest of justice, an inventory which shall include notice of—

(1) the fact of the entry of the order or the application;

(2) the date of the entry and the period of authorized, approved or disapproved interception, or the denial of the application; and

(3) the fact that during the period wire, oral, or electronic communications were or were not intercepted.

The judge, upon the filing of a motion, may in his discretion make available to such person or his counsel for inspection such portions of the intercepted communications, applications and orders as the judge determines to be in the interest of justice. On an ex parte showing of good cause to a judge of competent jurisdiction the serving of the inventory required by this subsection may be postponed.

(9) The contents of any wire, oral, or electronic communication intercepted pursuant to this chapter or evidence derived therefrom shall not be received in evidence or otherwise disclosed in any trial, hearing, or other proceeding in a Federal or State court unless each party, not less than ten days before the trial, hearing, or proceeding, has been furnished with a copy of the court order, and accompanying application, under which the interception was authorized or approved. This ten-day period may be waived by the judge if he finds that it was not possible to furnish the party with the above

information ten days before the trial, hearing, or proceeding and that the party will not be prejudiced by the delay in receiving such information.

(10)(a) Any aggrieved person in any trial, hearing, or proceeding in or before any court, department, officer, agency, regulatory body, or other authority of the United States, a State, or a political subdivision thereof, may move to suppress the contents of any wire or oral communication intercepted pursuant to this chapter, or evidence derived therefrom, on the grounds that—

> (i) the communication was unlawfully intercepted;
>
> (ii) the order of authorization or approval under which it was intercepted is insufficient on its face; or
>
> (iii) the interception was not made in conformity with the order of authorization or approval.

Such motion shall be made before the trial, hearing, or proceeding unless there was no opportunity to make such motion or the person was not aware of the grounds of the motion. If the motion is granted, the contents of the intercepted wire or oral communication, or evidence derived therefrom, shall be treated as having been obtained in violation of this chapter. The judge, upon the filing of such motion by the aggrieved person, may in his discretion make available to the aggrieved person or his counsel for inspection such portions of the intercepted communication or evidence derived therefrom as the judge determines to be in the interests of justice.

(b) In addition to any other right to appeal, the United States shall have the right to appeal from an order granting a motion to suppress made under paragraph (a) of this subsection, or the denial of an application for an order of approval, if the United States attorney shall certify to the judge or other official granting such motion or denying such application that the appeal is not taken for purposes of delay. Such appeal shall be taken within thirty days after the date the order was entered and shall be diligently prosecuted.

(c) The remedies and sanctions described in this chapter with respect to the interception of electronic communications are the only judicial remedies and sanctions for nonconstitutional violations of this chapter involving such communications.

(11) The requirements of subsections (1)(b)(ii) and (3)(d) of this section relating to the specification of the facilities from which, or the place where, the communication is to be intercepted do not apply if—

> (a) in the case of an application with respect to the interception of an oral communication—
>
>> (i) the application is by a Federal investigative or law enforcement officer and is approved by the Attorney General, the Deputy Attorney General, the Associate Attorney General, an Assistant Attorney General, or an acting Assistant Attorney General;
>>
>> (ii) the application contains a full and complete statement as to why such specification is not practical and identifies the person committing the offense and whose communications are to be intercepted; and
>>
>> (iii) the judge finds that such specification is not practical; and

(b) in the case of an application with respect to a wire or electronic communication—

(i) the application is by a Federal investigative or law enforcement officer and is approved by the Attorney General, the Deputy Attorney General, the Associate Attorney General, an Assistant Attorney General, or an acting Assistant Attorney General;

(ii) the application identifies the person believed to be committing the offense and whose communications are to be intercepted and the applicant makes a showing that there is probable cause to believe that the person's actions could have the effect of thwarting interception from a specified facility;

(iii) the judge finds that such showing has been adequately made; and

(iv) the order authorizing or approving the interception is limited to interception only for such time as it is reasonable to presume that the person identified in the application is or was reasonably proximate to the instrument through which such communication will be or was transmitted.

(12) An interception of a communication under an order with respect to which the requirements of subsections (1)(b)(ii) and (3)(d) of this section do not apply by reason of subsection (11)(a) shall not begin until the place where the communication is to be intercepted is ascertained by the person implementing the interception order. A provider of wire or electronic communications service that has received an order as provided for in subsection (11)(b) may move the court to modify or quash the order on the ground that its assistance with respect to the interception cannot be performed in a timely or reasonable fashion. The court, upon notice to the government, shall decide such a motion expeditiously.

§ 2520. Recovery of civil damages authorized

(a) In general.—Except as provided in section 2511(2)(a)(ii), any person whose wire, oral, or electronic communication is intercepted, disclosed, or intentionally used in violation of this chapter may in a civil action recover from the person or entity, other than the United States, which engaged in that violation such relief as may be appropriate.

(b) Relief.—In an action under this section, appropriate relief includes—

(1) such preliminary and other equitable or declaratory relief as may be appropriate;

(2) damages under subsection (c) and punitive damages in appropriate cases; and

(3) a reasonable attorney's fee and other litigation costs reasonably incurred.

(c) Computation of damages.—(1) In an action under this section, if the conduct in violation of this chapter is the private viewing of a private satellite video communication that is not scrambled or encrypted or if the communication is a radio communication that is transmitted on frequencies allocated under subpart D of part 74 of the rules of the Federal Communications Commission that is not scrambled or encrypted and the conduct is not for a tortious or illegal purpose or for purposes of direct or indirect commercial advantage or private commercial gain, then the court shall assess damages as follows:

(A) If the person who engaged in that conduct has not previously been enjoined under section 2511(5) and has not been found liable in a prior civil action under this section, the court shall assess the greater of the sum of actual damages suffered by the plaintiff, or statutory damages of not less than $50 and not more than $500.

(B) If, on one prior occasion, the person who engaged in that conduct has been enjoined under section 2511(5) or has been found liable in a civil action under this section, the court shall assess the greater of the sum of actual damages suffered by the plaintiff, or statutory damages of not less than $100 and not more than $1000.

(2) In any other action under this section, the court may assess as damages whichever is the greater of—

(A) the sum of the actual damages suffered by the plaintiff and any profits made by the violator as a result of the violation; or

(B) statutory damages of whichever is the greater of $100 a day for each day of violation or $10,000.

(d) Defense.—A good faith reliance on—

(1) a court warrant or order, a grand jury subpoena, a legislative authorization, or a statutory authorization;

(2) a request of an investigative or law enforcement officer under section 2518(7) of this title; or

(3) a good faith determination that section 2511(3) or 2511(2)(i) of this title permitted the conduct complained of;

is a complete defense against any civil or criminal action brought under this chapter or any other law.

(e) Limitation.—A civil action under this section may not be commenced later than two years after the date upon which the claimant first has a reasonable opportunity to discover the violation.

(f) Administrative discipline.—If a court or appropriate department or agency determines that the United States or any of its departments or agencies has violated any provision of this chapter, and the court or appropriate department or agency finds that the circumstances surrounding the violation raise serious questions about whether or not an officer or employee of the United States acted willfully or intentionally with respect to the violation, the department or agency shall, upon receipt of a true and correct copy of the decision and findings of the court or appropriate department or agency promptly initiate a proceeding to determine whether disciplinary action against the officer or employee is warranted. If the head of the department or agency involved determines that disciplinary action is not warranted, he or she shall notify the Inspector General with jurisdiction over the department or agency concerned and shall provide the Inspector General with the reasons for such determination.

(g) Improper disclosure is violation.—Any willful disclosure or use by an investigative or law enforcement officer or governmental entity of information beyond the extent permitted by section 2517 is a violation of this chapter for purposes of section 2520(a).

§ 2521. Injunction against illegal interception

Whenever it shall appear that any person is engaged or is about to engage in any act which constitutes or will constitute a felony violation of this chapter, the Attorney General may initiate a civil action in a district court of the United States to enjoin such violation. The court shall proceed as soon as practicable to the hearing and determination of such an action, and may, at any time before final determination, enter such a restraining order or prohibition, or take such other action, as is warranted to prevent a continuing and substantial injury to the United States or to any person or class of persons for whose protection the action is brought. A proceeding under this section is governed by the Federal Rules of Civil Procedure, except that, if an indictment has been returned against the respondent, discovery is governed by the Federal Rules of Criminal Procedure.

SEARCHES AND SEIZURES

(18 U.S.C.A. §§ 3103a, 3105, 3109).

§ 3103a. Additional grounds for issuing warrant

(a) In general.—In addition to the grounds for issuing a warrant in section 3103 of this title, a warrant may be issued to search for and seize any property that constitutes evidence of a criminal offense in violation of the laws of the United States.

(b) Delay.—With respect to the issuance of any warrant or court order under this section, or any other rule of law, to search for and seize any property or material that constitutes evidence of a criminal offense in violation of the laws of the United States, any notice required, or that may be required, to be given may be delayed if—

    (1) the court finds reasonable cause to believe that providing immediate notification of the execution of the warrant may have an adverse result (as defined in section 2705);

    (2) the warrant prohibits the seizure of any tangible property, any wire or electronic communication (as defined in section 2510), or, except as expressly provided in chapter 121, any stored wire or electronic information, except where the court finds reasonable necessity for the seizure; and

    (3) the warrant provides for the giving of such notice within a reasonable period of its execution, which period may thereafter be extended by the court for good cause shown.

§ 3105. Persons authorized to serve search warrant

A search warrant may in all cases be served by any of the officers mentioned in its direction or by an officer authorized by law to serve such warrant, but by no other person, except in aid of the officer on his requiring it, he being present and acting in its execution.

§ 3109. Breaking doors or windows for entry or exit

The officer may break open any outer or inner door or window of a house, or any part of a house, or anything therein, to execute a search warrant, if, after notice of his authority and purpose, he is refused admittance or when necessary to liberate himself or a person aiding him in the execution of the warrant.

BAIL REFORM ACT OF 1984

(18 U.S.C. §§ 3141–3150).

§ 3141. Release and detention authority generally

(a) Pending trial.—A judicial officer authorized to order the arrest of a person under section 3041 of this title before whom an arrested person is brought shall order that such person be released or detained, pending judicial proceedings, under this chapter.

(b) Pending sentence or appeal.—A judicial officer of a court of original jurisdiction over an offense, or a judicial officer of a Federal appellate court, shall order that, pending imposition or execution of sentence, or pending appeal of conviction or sentence, a person be released or detained under this chapter.

§ 3142. Release or detention of a defendant pending trial

(a) In general.—Upon the appearance before a judicial officer of a person charged with an offense, the judicial officer shall issue an order that, pending trial, the person be—

(1) released on personal recognizance or upon execution of an unsecured appearance bond, under subsection (b) of this section;

(2) released on a condition or combination of conditions under subsection (c) of this section;

(3) temporarily detained to permit revocation of conditional release, deportation, or exclusion under subsection (d) of this section; or

(4) detained under subsection (e) of this section.

(b) Release on personal recognizance or unsecured appearance bond.— The judicial officer shall order the pretrial release of the person on personal recognizance, or upon execution of an unsecured appearance bond in an amount specified by the court, subject to the condition that the person not commit a Federal, State, or local crime during the period of release, unless the judicial officer determines that such release will not reasonably assure the appearance of the person as required or will endanger the safety of any other person or the community.

(c) Release on conditions.—(1) If the judicial officer determines that the release described in subsection (b) of this section will not reasonably assure the appearance of the person as required or will endanger the safety of any other person or the community, such judicial officer shall order the pretrial release of the person—

(A) subject to the condition that the person not commit a Federal, State, or local crime during the period of release; and

(B) subject to the least restrictive further condition, or combination of conditions, that such judicial officer determines will reasonably assure the appearance of the person as required and the safety of any other person and the community, which may include the condition that the person—

(i) remain in the custody of a designated person, who agrees to assume supervision and to report any violation of a release condition to the court, if the designated person is able reasonably to assure the judicial officer that the person will appear as required and will not pose a danger to the safety of any other person or the community;

(ii) maintain employment, or, if unemployed, actively seek employment;

(iii) maintain or commence an educational program;

(iv) abide by specified restrictions on personal associations, place of abode, or travel;

(v) avoid all contact with an alleged victim of the crime and with a potential witness who may testify concerning the offense;

(vi) report on a regular basis to a designated law enforcement agency, pretrial services agency, or other agency;

(vii) comply with a specified curfew;

(viii) refrain from possessing a firearm, destructive device, or other dangerous weapon;

(ix) refrain from excessive use of alcohol, or any use of a narcotic drug or other controlled substance, as defined in section 102 of the Controlled Substances Act (21 U.S.C. 802), without a prescription by a licensed medical practitioner;

(x) undergo available medical, psychological, or psychiatric treatment, including treatment for drug or alcohol dependency, and remain in a specified institution if required for that purpose;

(xi) execute an agreement to forfeit upon failing to appear as required, property of a sufficient unencumbered value, including money, as is reasonably necessary to assure the appearance of the person as required, and shall provide the court with proof of ownership and the value of the property along with information regarding existing encumbrances as the judicial office may require;

(xii) execute a bail bond with solvent sureties; who will execute an agreement to forfeit in such amount as is reasonably necessary to assure appearance of the person as required and shall provide the court with information regarding the value of the assets and liabilities of the surety if other than an approved surety and the nature and extent of encumbrances against the surety's property; such surety shall have a net worth which shall have sufficient unencumbered value to pay the amount of the bail bond;

(xiii) return to custody for specified hours following release for employment, schooling, or other limited purposes; and

(xiv) satisfy any other condition that is reasonably necessary to assure the appearance of the person as required and to assure the safety of any other person and the community.

(2) The judicial officer may not impose a financial condition that results in the pretrial detention of the person.

(3) The judicial officer may at any time amend the order to impose additional or different conditions of release.

(d) Temporary detention to permit revocation of conditional release, deportation, or exclusion.—If the judicial officer determines that—

(1) such person—

(A) is, and was at the time the offense was committed, on—

(i) release pending trial for a felony under Federal, State, or local law;

(ii) release pending imposition or execution of sentence, appeal of sentence or conviction, or completion of sentence, for any offense under Federal, State, or local law; or

(iii) probation or parole for any offense under Federal, State, or local law; or

(B) is not a citizen of the United States or lawfully admitted for permanent residence, as defined in section 101(a)(20) of the Immigration and Nationality Act (8 U.S.C. 1101(a)(20)); and

(2) such person may flee or pose a danger to any other person or the community;

such judicial officer shall order the detention of such person, for a period of not more than ten days, excluding Saturdays, Sundays, and holidays, and direct the attorney for the Government to notify the appropriate court, probation or parole official, or State or local law enforcement official, or the appropriate official of the Immigration and Naturalization Service. If the official fails or declines to take such person into custody during that period, such person shall be treated in accordance with the other provisions of this section, notwithstanding the applicability of other provisions of law governing release pending trial or deportation or exclusion proceedings. If temporary detention is sought under paragraph (1)(B) of this subsection, such person has the burden of proving to the court such person's United States citizenship or lawful admission for permanent residence.

(e) Detention.—If, after a hearing pursuant to the provisions of subsection (f) of this section, the judicial officer finds that no condition or combination of conditions will reasonably assure the appearance of the person as required and the safety of any other person and the community, such judicial officer shall order the detention of the person before trial. In a case described in subsection (f)(1) of this section, a rebuttable presumption arises that no condition or combination of conditions will reasonably assure the safety of any other person and the community if such judicial officer finds that—

(1) the person has been convicted of a Federal offense that is described in subsection (f)(1) of this section, or of a State or local offense that would have been an offense described in subsection (f)(1) of this section if a circumstance giving rise to Federal jurisdiction had existed;

(2) the offense described in paragraph (1) of this subsection was committed while the person was on release pending trial for a Federal, State, or local offense; and

(3) a period of not more than five years has elapsed since the date of conviction, or the release of the person from imprisonment, for the offense described in paragraph (1) of this subsection, whichever is later.

Subject to rebuttal by the person, it shall be presumed that no condition or combination of conditions will reasonably assure the appearance of the person as required and the safety of the community if the judicial officer finds that there is probable cause to believe that the person committed an offense for which a maximum term of imprisonment of ten years or more is prescribed in the Controlled Substances Act (21 U.S.C. 801 et seq.), the Controlled Substances Import and Export Act (21 U.S.C. 951 et seq.), or the Maritime Drug Law Enforcement Act (46 U.S.C. App. 1901 et seq.), an offense under section 924(c), 956(a), or 2332b of this title, or an offense listed in section 2332b(g)(5)(B) of title 18, United States Code, for which a maximum term of imprisonment of 10 years or more is prescribed or an offense involving a minor victim under section 1201, 1591, 2241, 2242, 2244(a)(1), 2245, 2251, 2251A, 2252(a)(1), 2252(a)(2), 2252(a)(3), 2252A(a)(1), 2252A(a)(2), 2252A(a)(3), 2252A(a)(4), 2260, 2421, 2422, 2423, or 2425 of this title.

(f) Detention hearing.—The judicial officer shall hold a hearing to determine whether any condition or combination of conditions set forth in subsection (c) of this section will reasonably assure the appearance of such person as required and the safety of any other person and the community—

(1) upon motion of the attorney for the Government, in a case that involves—

(A) a crime of violence,* or an offense listed in section 2332b(g)(5)(B) for which a maximum term of imprisonment of 10 years or more is prescribed;

(B) an offense for which the maximum sentence is life imprisonment or death;

(C) an offense for which a maximum term of imprisonment of ten years or more is prescribed in the Controlled Substances Act (21 U.S.C. 801 et seq.), the Controlled Substances Import and Export

---

* The phrase "crime of violence" is defined in 18 U.S.C. § 3156(a)(4) as meaning: "(A) an offense that has an element of the offense the use, attempted use, or threatened use of physical force against the person or property of another, or (B) any other offense that is a felony and that, by its nature, involves a substantial risk that physical force against the person or property of another may be used in the course of committing the offense."

Act (21 U.S.C. 951 et seq.), or the Maritime Drug Law Enforcement Act (46 U.S.C. App. 1901 et seq.); or

(D) any felony if such person has been convicted of two or more offenses described in subparagraphs (A) through (C) of this paragraph, or two or more State or local offenses that would have been offenses described in subparagraphs (A) through (C) of this paragraph if a circumstance giving rise to Federal jurisdiction had existed, or a combination of such offenses; or

(2) Upon motion of the attorney for the Government or upon the judicial officer's own motion, in a case that involves—

(A) a serious risk that such person will flee; or

(B) a serious risk that such person will obstruct or attempt to obstruct justice, or threaten, injure, or intimidate, or attempt to threaten, injure, or intimidate, a prospective witness or juror.

The hearing shall be held immediately upon the person's first appearance before the judicial officer unless that person, or the attorney for the Government, seeks a continuance. Except for good cause, a continuance on motion of such person may not exceed five days (not including any intermediate Saturday, Sunday, or legal holiday), and a continuance on motion of the attorney for the Government may not exceed three days (not including any intermediate Saturday, Sunday, or legal holiday). During a continuance, such person shall be detained, and the judicial officer, on motion of the attorney for the Government or sua sponte, may order that, while in custody, a person who appears to be a narcotics addict receive a medical examination to determine whether such person is an addict. At the hearing, such person has the right to be represented by counsel, and, if financially unable to obtain adequate representation, to have counsel appointed. The person shall be afforded an opportunity to testify, to present witnesses, to cross-examine witnesses who appear at the hearing, and to present information by proffer or otherwise. The rules concerning admissibility of evidence in criminal trials do not apply to the presentation and consideration of information at the hearing. The facts the judicial officer uses to support a finding pursuant to subsection (e) that no condition or combination of conditions will reasonably assure the safety of any other person and the community shall be supported by clear and convincing evidence. The person may be detained pending completion of the hearing. The hearing may be reopened, before or after a determination by the judicial officer, at any time before trial if the judicial officer finds that information exists that was not known to the movant at the time of the hearing and that has a material bearing on the issue whether there are conditions of release that will reasonably assure the appearance of such person as required and the safety of any other person and the community.

(g) Factors to be considered.—The judicial officer shall, in determining whether there are conditions of release that will reasonably assure the appearance of the person as required and the safety of any other person and the community, take into account the available information concerning—

(1) The nature and circumstances of the offense charged, including whether the offense is a crime of violence, or an offense listed in section

2332b(g)(5)(B) for which a maximum term of imprisonment of 10 years or more is prescribed or involves a narcotic drug;

(2) the weight of the evidence against the person;

(3) the history and characteristics of the person, including—

(A) the person's character, physical and mental condition, family ties, employment, financial resources, length of residence in the community, community ties, past conduct, history relating to drug or alcohol abuse, criminal history, and record concerning appearance at court proceedings; and

(B) whether, at the time of the current offense or arrest, the person was on probation, on parole, or on other release pending trial, sentencing, appeal, or completion of sentence for an offense under Federal, State, or local law; and

(4) the nature and seriousness of the danger to any person or the community that would be posed by the person's release. In considering the conditions of release described in subsection (c)(1)(B)(xi) or (c)(1)(B)(xii) of this section, the judicial officer may upon his own motion, or shall upon the motion of the Government, conduct an inquiry into the source of the property to be designated for potential forfeiture or offered as collateral to secure a bond, and shall decline to accept the designation, or the use as collateral, of property that, because of its source, will not reasonably assure the appearance of the person as required.

(h) Contents of release order.—In a release order issued under subsection (b) or (c) of this section, the judicial officer shall—

(1) include a written statement that sets forth all the conditions to which the release is subject, in a manner sufficiently clear and specific to serve as a guide for the person's conduct; and

(2) advise the person of—

(A) the penalties for violating a condition of release, including the penalties for committing an offense while on pretrial release;

(B) the consequences of violating a condition of release, including the immediate issuance of a warrant for the person's arrest; and

(C) sections 1503 of this title (relating to intimidation of witnesses, jurors, and officers of the court), 1510 (relating to obstruction of criminal investigations), 1512 (tampering with a witness, victim, or an informant), and 1513 (retaliating against a witness, victim, or an informant).

(i) Contents of detention order.—In a detention order issued under subsection (e) of this section, the judicial officer shall—

(1) include written findings of fact and a written statement of the reasons for the detention;

(2) direct that the person be committed to the custody of the Attorney General for confinement in a corrections facility separate, to

the extent practicable, from persons awaiting or serving sentences or being held in custody pending appeal;

(3) direct that the person be afforded reasonable opportunity for private consultation with counsel; and

(4) direct that, on order of a court of the United States or on request of an attorney for the Government, the person in charge of the corrections facility in which the person is confined deliver the person to a United States marshal for the purpose of an appearance in connection with a court proceeding.

The judicial officer may, by subsequent order, permit the temporary release of the person, in the custody of a United States marshal or another appropriate person, to the extent that the judicial officer determines such release to be necessary for preparation of the person's defense or for another compelling reason.

(j) Presumption of innocence.—Nothing in this section shall be construed as modifying or limiting the presumption of innocence.

§ 3143. Release or detention of a defendant pending sentence or appeal

(a) Release or detention pending sentence.—(1) Except as provided in paragraph (2), the judicial officer shall order that a person who has been found guilty of an offense and who is awaiting imposition or execution of sentence, other than a person for whom the applicable guideline promulgated pursuant to 28 U.S.C. 994 does not recommend a term of imprisonment, be detained, unless the judicial officer finds by clear and convincing evidence that the person is not likely to flee or pose a danger to the safety of any other person or the community if released under section 3142(b) or (c). If the judicial officer makes such a finding, such judicial officer shall order the release of the person in accordance with section 3142(b) or (c).

(2) The judicial officer shall order that a person who has been found guilty of an offense in a case described in subparagraph (A), (B), or (C) of subsection (f)(1) of section 3142 and is awaiting imposition or execution of sentence be detained unless—

(A)(i) the judicial officer finds there is a substantial likelihood that a motion for acquittal or new trial will be granted; or

(ii) an attorney for the Government has recommended that no sentence of imprisonment be imposed on the person; and

(B) the judicial officer finds by clear and convincing evidence that the person is not likely to flee or pose a danger to any other person or the community.

(b) Release or detention pending appeal by the defendant.—(1) Except as provided in paragraph (2), the judicial officer shall order that a person who has been found guilty of an offense and sentenced to a term of imprisonment, and who has filed an appeal or a petition for a writ of certiorari, be detained, unless the judicial officer finds—

(A) by clear and convincing evidence that the person is not likely to flee or pose a danger to the safety of any other person or the community if released under section 3142(b) or (c) of this title; and

(B) that the appeal is not for the purpose of delay and raises a substantial question of law or fact likely to result in—

(i) reversal,

(ii) an order for a new trial,

(iii) a sentence that does not include a term of imprisonment, or

(iv) a reduced sentence to a term of imprisonment less than the total of the time already served plus the expected duration of the appeal process.

If the judicial officer makes such findings, such judicial officer shall order the release of the person in accordance with section 3142(b) or (c) of this title, except that in the circumstance described in subparagraph (B)(iv) of this paragraph, the judicial officer shall order the detention terminated at the expiration of the likely reduced sentence.

(2) The judicial officer shall order that a person who has been found guilty of an offense in a case described in subparagraph (A), (B), or (C) of subsection (f)(1) of section 3142 and sentenced to a term of imprisonment, and who has filed an appeal or a petition for a writ of certiorari, be detained.

(c) Release or detention pending appeal by the government.—The judicial officer shall treat a defendant in a case in which an appeal has been taken by the United States under section 3731 of this title, in accordance with section 3142 of this title, unless the defendant is otherwise subject to a release or detention order.

Except as provided in subsection (b) of this section, the judicial officer, in a case in which an appeal has been taken by the United States under section 3742, shall—

(1) if the person has been sentenced to a term of imprisonment, order that person detained; and

(2) in any other circumstance, release or detain the person under section 3142.

§ 3144. Release or detention of a material witness

If it appears from an affidavit filed by a party that the testimony of a person is material in a criminal proceeding, and if it is shown that it may become impracticable to secure the presence of the person by subpoena, a judicial officer may order the arrest of the person and treat the person in accordance with the provisions of section 3142 of this title. No material witness may be detained because of inability to comply with any condition of release if the testimony of such witness can adequately be secured by deposition, and if further detention is not necessary to prevent a failure of justice. Release of a material witness may be delayed for a reasonable period of time until the deposition of the witness can be taken pursuant to the Federal Rules of Criminal Procedure.

§ 3145. Review and appeal of a release or detention order

(a) Review of a release order.—If a person is ordered released by a magistrate judge, or by a person other than a judge of a court having original jurisdiction over the offense and other than a Federal appellate court—

(1) the attorney for the Government may file, with the court having original jurisdiction over the offense, a motion for revocation of the order or amendment of the conditions of release; and

(2) the person may file, with the court having original jurisdiction over the offense, a motion for amendment of the conditions of release.

The motion shall be determined promptly.

(b) Review of a detention order.—If a person is ordered detained by a magistrate judge, or by a person other than a judge of a court having original jurisdiction over the offense and other than a Federal appellate court, the person may file, with the court having original jurisdiction over the offense, a motion for revocation or amendment of the order. The motion shall be determined promptly.

(c) Appeal from a release or detention order.—An appeal from a release or detention order, or from a decision denying revocation or amendment of such an order, is governed by the provisions of section 1291 of title 28 and section 3731 of this title. The appeal shall be determined promptly. A person subject to detention pursuant to section 3143(a)(2) or (b)(2), and who meets the conditions of release set forth in section 3143(a)(1) or (b)(1), may be ordered released, under appropriate conditions, by the judicial officer, if it is clearly shown that there are exceptional reasons why such person's detention would not be appropriate.

§ 3146. Penalty for failure to appear

(a) Offense.—Whoever, having been released under this chapter knowingly—

(1) fails to appear before a court as required by the conditions of release; or

(2) fails to surrender for service of sentence pursuant to a court order;

shall be punished as provided in subsection (b) of this section.

(b) Punishment.—(1) The punishment for an offense under this section is—

(A) if the person was released in connection with a charge of, or while awaiting sentence, surrender for service of sentence, or appeal or certiorari after conviction for—

(i) an offense punishable by death, life imprisonment, or imprisonment for a term of 15 years or more, a fine under this title or imprisonment for not more than ten years, or both;

(ii) an offense punishable by imprisonment for a term of five years or more, a fine under this title or imprisonment for not more than five years, or both;

(iii) any other felony, a fine under this title or imprisonment for not more than two years, or both; or

(iv) a misdemeanor, a fine under this title or imprisonment for not more than one year, or both; and

(B) if the person was released for appearance as a material witness, a fine under this chapter or imprisonment for not more than one year, or both.

(2) A term of imprisonment imposed under this section shall be consecutive to the sentence of imprisonment for any other offense.

(c) Affirmative defense.—It is an affirmative defense to a prosecution under this section that uncontrollable circumstances prevented the person from appearing or surrendering, and that the person did not contribute to the creation of such circumstances in reckless disregard of the requirement to appear or surrender, and that the person appeared or surrendered as soon as such circumstances ceased to exist.

(d) Declaration of forfeiture.—If a person fails to appear before a court as required, and the person executed an appearance bond pursuant to section 3142(b) of this title or is subject to the release condition set forth in clause (xi) or (xii) of section 3142(c)(1)(B) of this title, the judicial officer may, regardless of whether the person has been charged with an offense under this section, declare any property designated pursuant to that section to be forfeited to the United States.

§ 3147. Penalty for an offense committed while on release

A person convicted of an offense committed while released under this chapter shall be sentenced, in addition to the sentence prescribed for the offense to—

(1) a term of imprisonment of not more than ten years if the offense is a felony; or

(2) a term of imprisonment of not more than one year if the offense is a misdemeanor.

A term of imprisonment imposed under this section shall be consecutive to any other sentence of imprisonment.

§ 3148. Sanctions for violation of a release condition

(a) Available sanctions.—A person who has been released under section 3142 of this title, and who has violated a condition of his release, is subject to a revocation of release, an order of detention, and a prosecution for contempt of court.

(b) Revocation of release.—The attorney for the Government may initiate a proceeding for revocation of an order of release by filing a motion with the district court. A judicial officer may issue a warrant for the arrest of a person charged with violating a condition of release, and the person shall be brought before a judicial officer in the district in which such person's arrest was ordered for a proceeding in accordance with this section. To the extent practicable, a person charged with violating the condition of release that such person not commit a Federal, State, or local crime during the period of release, shall be brought before the judicial officer who ordered the release and whose order is alleged to have been violated. The judicial officer shall enter an order of revocation and detention if, after a hearing, the judicial officer—

 (1) finds that there is—

  (A) probable cause to believe that the person has committed a Federal, State, or local crime while on release; or

  (B) clear and convincing evidence that the person has violated any other condition of release; and

 (2) finds that—

  (A) based on the factors set forth in section 3142(g) of this title, there is no condition or combination of conditions of release that will assure that the person will not flee or pose a danger to the safety of any other person or the community; or

  (B) the person is unlikely to abide by any condition or combination of conditions of release.

If there is probable cause to believe that, while on release, the person committed a Federal, State, or local felony, a rebuttable presumption arises that no condition or combination of conditions will assure that the person will not pose a danger to the safety of any other person or the community. If the judicial officer finds that there are conditions of release that will assure that the person will not flee or pose a danger to the safety of any other person or the community, and that the person will abide by such conditions, the judicial officer shall treat the person in accordance with the provisions of section 3142 of this title and may amend the conditions of release accordingly.

 (c) Prosecution for contempt.—The judicial officer may commence a prosecution for contempt, under section 401 of this title, if the person has violated a condition of release.

§ 3149. Surrender of an offender by a surety

 A person charged with an offense, who is released upon the execution of an appearance bond with a surety, may be arrested by the surety, and if so arrested, shall be delivered promptly to a United States marshal and brought before a judicial officer. The judicial officer shall determine in accordance with the provisions of section 3148(b) whether to revoke the release of the person, and may absolve the surety of responsibility to pay all or part of the bond in accordance with the provisions of Rule 46 of the Federal Rules of Criminal Procedure. The person so committed shall be held in official detention until released pursuant to this chapter or another provision of law.

§ 3150. Applicability to a case removed from a State court

 The provisions of this chapter apply to a criminal case removed to a Federal court from a State court.

SPEEDY TRIAL ACT OF 1974 (AS AMENDED)

(18 U.S.C. §§ 3161–3162, 3164).

§ 3161. Time limits and exclusions

(a) In any case involving a defendant charged with an offense, the appropriate judicial officer, at the earliest practicable time, shall, after consultation with the counsel for the defendant and the attorney for the Government, set the case for trial on a day certain, or list it for trial on a weekly or other short-term trial calendar at a place within the judicial district, so as to assure a speedy trial.

(b) Any information or indictment charging an individual with the commission of an offense shall be filed within thirty days from the date on which such individual was arrested or served with a summons in connection with such charges. If an individual has been charged with a felony in a district in which no grand jury has been in session during such thirty-day period, the period of time for filing of the indictment shall be extended an additional thirty days.

(c)(1) In any case in which a plea of not guilty is entered, the trial of a defendant charged in an information or indictment with the commission of an offense shall commence within seventy days from the filing date (and making public) of the information or indictment, or from the date the defendant has appeared before a judicial officer of the court in which such charge is pending, whichever date last occurs. If a defendant consents in writing to be tried before a magistrate judge on a complaint, the trial shall commence within seventy days from the date of such consent.

(2) Unless the defendant consents in writing to the contrary, the trial shall not commence less than thirty days from the date on which the defendant first appears through counsel or expressly waives counsel and elects to proceed pro se.

(d)(1) If any indictment or information is dismissed upon motion of the defendant, or any charge contained in a complaint filed against an individual is dismissed or otherwise dropped, and thereafter a complaint is filed against such defendant or individual charging him with the same offense or an offense based on the same conduct or arising from the same criminal episode, or an information or indictment is filed charging such defendant with the same offense or an offense based on the same conduct or arising from the same criminal episode, the provisions of subsections (b) and (c) of this section shall be applicable with respect to such subsequent complaint, indictment, or information, as the case may be.

(2) If the defendant is to be tried upon an indictment or information dismissed by a trial court and reinstated following an appeal, the trial shall commence within seventy days from the date the action occasioning the trial becomes final, except that the court retrying the case may extend the period for trial not to exceed one hundred and eighty days from the date the action occasioning the trial becomes final if the unavailability of witnesses or other factors resulting from the passage of time shall make trial within seventy

days impractical. The periods of delay enumerated in section 3161(h) are excluded in computing the time limitations specified in this section. The sanctions of section 3162 apply to this subsection.

(e) If the defendant is to be tried again following a declaration by the trial judge of a mistrial or following an order of such judge for a new trial, the trial shall commence within seventy days from the date the action occasioning the retrial becomes final. If the defendant is to be tried again following an appeal or a collateral attack, the trial shall commence within seventy days from the date the action occasioning the retrial becomes final, except that the court retrying the case may extend the period for retrial not to exceed one hundred and eighty days from the date the action occasioning the retrial becomes final if unavailability of witnesses or other factors resulting from passage of time shall make trial within seventy days impractical. The periods of delay enumerated in section 3161(h) are excluded in computing the time limitations specified in this section. The sanctions of section 3162 apply to this subsection.

(f) Notwithstanding the provisions of subsection (b) of this section, for the first twelve-calendar-month period following the effective date of this section as set forth in section 3163(a) of this chapter the time limit imposed with respect to the period between arrest and indictment by subsection (b) of this section shall be sixty days, for the second such twelve-month period such time limit shall be forty-five days and for the third such period such time limit shall be thirty-five days.

(g) Notwithstanding the provisions of subsection (c) of this section, for the first twelve-calendar-month period following the effective date of this section as set forth in section 3163(b) of this chapter, the time limit with respect to the period between arraignment and trial imposed by subsection (c) of this section shall be one hundred and eighty days, for the second such twelve-month period such time limit shall be one hundred and twenty days, and for the third such period such time limit with respect to the period between arraignment and trial shall be eighty days.

(h) The following periods of delay shall be excluded in computing the time within which an information or an indictment must be filed, or in computing the time within which the trial of any such offense must commence:

(1) Any period of delay resulting from other proceedings concerning the defendant, including but not limited to—

(A) delay resulting from any proceeding, including any examinations, to determine the mental competency or physical capacity of the defendant;

(B) delay resulting from any proceeding, including any examination of the defendant, pursuant to section 2902 of title 28, United States Code;

(C) delay resulting from deferral of prosecution pursuant to section 2902 of title 28, United States Code;

(D) delay resulting from trial with respect to other charges against the defendant;

(E) delay resulting from any interlocutory appeal;

(F) delay resulting from any pretrial motion, from the filing of the motion through the conclusion of the hearing on, or other prompt disposition of, such motion;

(G) delay resulting from any proceeding relating to the transfer of a case or the removal of any defendant from another district under the Federal Rules of Criminal Procedure;

(H) delay resulting from transportation of any defendant from another district, or to and from places of examination or hospitalization, except that any time consumed in excess of ten days from the date an order of removal or an order directing such transportation, and the defendant's arrival at the destination shall be presumed to be unreasonable;

(I) delay resulting from consideration by the court of a proposed plea agreement to be entered into by the defendant and the attorney for the Government; and

(J) delay reasonably attributable to any period, not to exceed thirty days, during which any proceeding concerning the defendant is actually under advisement by the court.

(2) Any period of delay during which prosecution is deferred by the attorney for the Government pursuant to written agreement with the defendant, with the approval of the court, for the purpose of allowing the defendant to demonstrate his good conduct.

(3)(A) Any period of delay resulting from the absence or unavailability of the defendant or an essential witness.

(B) For purposes of subparagraph (A) of this paragraph, a defendant or an essential witness shall be considered absent when his whereabouts are unknown and, in addition, he is attempting to avoid apprehension or prosecution or his whereabouts cannot be determined by due diligence. For purposes of such subparagraph, a defendant or an essential witness shall be considered unavailable whenever his whereabouts are known but his presence for trial cannot be obtained by due diligence or he resists appearing at or being returned for trial.

(4) Any period of delay resulting from the fact that the defendant is mentally incompetent or physically unable to stand trial.

(5) Any period of delay resulting from the treatment of the defendant pursuant to section 2902 of title 28, United States Code.

(6) If the information or indictment is dismissed upon motion of the attorney for the Government and thereafter a charge is filed against the defendant for the same offense, or any offense required to be joined with that offense, any period of delay from the date the charge was dismissed to the date the time limitation would commence to run as to the subsequent charge had there been no previous charge.

(7) A reasonable period of delay when the defendant is joined for trial with a codefendant as to whom the time for trial has not run and no motion for severance has been granted.

(8)(A) Any period of delay resulting from a continuance granted by any judge on his own motion or at the request of the defendant or his counsel or at the request of the attorney for the Government, if the judge granted such continuance on the basis of his findings that the ends of justice served by taking such action outweigh the best interest of the public and the defendant in a speedy trial. No such period of delay resulting from a continuance granted by the court in accordance with this paragraph shall be excludable under this subsection unless the court sets forth, in the record of the case, either orally or in writing, its reasons for finding that the ends of justice served by the granting of such continuance outweigh the best interests of the public and the defendant in a speedy trial.

(B) The factors, among others, which a judge shall consider in determining whether to grant a continuance under subparagraph (A) of this paragraph in any case are as follows:

(i) Whether the failure to grant such a continuance in the proceeding would be likely to make a continuation of such proceeding impossible, or result in a miscarriage of justice.

(ii) Whether the case is so unusual or so complex, due to the number of defendants, the nature of the prosecution, or the existence of novel questions of fact or law, that it is unreasonable to expect adequate preparation for pretrial proceedings or for the trial itself within the time limits established by this section.

(iii) Whether, in a case in which arrest precedes indictment, delay in the filing of the indictment is caused because the arrest occurs at a time such that it is unreasonable to expect return and filing of the indictment within the period specified in section 3161(b), or because the facts upon which the grand jury must base its determination are unusual or complex.

(iv) Whether the failure to grant such a continuance in a case which, taken as a whole, is not so unusual or so complex as to fall within clause (ii), would deny the defendant reasonable time to obtain counsel, would unreasonably deny the defendant or the Government continuity of counsel, or would deny counsel for the defendant or the attorney for the Government the reasonable time necessary for effective preparation, taking into account the exercise of due diligence.

(C) No continuance under subparagraph (A) of this paragraph shall be granted because of general congestion of the court's calendar, or lack of diligent preparation or failure to obtain available witnesses on the part of the attorney for the Government.

(9) Any period of delay, not to exceed one year, ordered by a district court upon an application of a party and a finding by a preponderance of the evidence that an official request, as defined in section 3292 of this title, has been made for evidence of any such offense and that it reasonably appears, or reasonably appeared at the time the request was made, that such evidence is, or was, in such foreign country.

(i) If trial did not commence within the time limitation specified in section 3161 because the defendant had entered a plea of guilty or nolo contendere subsequently withdrawn to any or all charges in an indictment or information, the defendant shall be deemed indicted with respect to all charges therein contained within the meaning of section 3161, on the day the order permitting withdrawal of the plea becomes final.

(j)(1) If the attorney for the Government knows that a person charged with an offense is serving a term of imprisonment in any penal institution, he shall promptly—

(A) undertake to obtain the presence of the prisoner for trial; or

(B) cause a detainer to be filed with the person having custody of the prisoner and request him to so advise the prisoner and to advise the prisoner of his right to demand trial.

(2) If the person having custody of such prisoner receives a detainer, he shall promptly advise the prisoner of the charge and of the prisoner's right to demand trial. If at any time thereafter the prisoner informs the person having custody that he does demand trial, such person shall cause notice to that effect to be sent promptly to the attorney for the Government who caused the detainer to be filed.

(3) Upon receipt of such notice, the attorney for the Government shall promptly seek to obtain the presence of the prisoner for trial.

(4) When the person having custody of the prisoner receives from the attorney for the Government a properly supported request for temporary custody of such prisoner for trial, the prisoner shall be made available to that attorney for the Government (subject, in cases of interjurisdictional transfer, to any right of the prisoner to contest the legality of his delivery).

(k)(1) If the defendant is absent (as defined by subsection (h)(3)) on the day set for trial, and the defendant's subsequent appearance before the court on a bench warrant or other process or surrender to the court occurs more than 21 days after the day set for trial, the defendant shall be deemed to have first appeared before a judicial officer of the court in which the information or indictment is pending within the meaning of subsection (c) on the date of the defendant's subsequent appearance before the court.

(2) If the defendant is absent (as defined by subsection (h)(3)) on the day set for trial, and the defendant's subsequent appearance before the court on a bench warrant or other process or surrender to the court occurs not more than 21 days after the day set for trial, the time limit required by subsection (c), as extended by subsection (h), shall be further extended by 21 days.

§ 3162. Sanctions

(a)(1) If, in the case of any individual against whom a complaint is filed charging such individual with an offense, no indictment or information is filed within the time limit required by section 3161(b) as extended by section 3161(h) of this chapter, such charge against that individual contained in such complaint shall be dismissed or otherwise dropped. In determining whether to dismiss the case with or without prejudice, the court shall consider, among others, each of the following factors: the seriousness of the offense; the facts and circumstances of the case which led to the dismissal; and the impact of a reprosecution on the administration of this chapter and on the administration of justice.

(2) If a defendant is not brought to trial within the time limit required by section 3161(c) as extended by section 3161(h), the information or indictment shall be dismissed on motion of the defendant. The defendant shall have the burden of proof of supporting such motion but the Government shall have the burden of going forward with the evidence in connection with any exclusion of time under subparagraph 3161(h) (3). In determining whether to dismiss the case with or without prejudice, the court shall consider, among others, each of the following factors: the seriousness of the offense; the facts and circumstances of the case which led to the dismissal; and the impact of a reprosecution on the administration of this chapter and on the administration of justice. Failure of the defendant to move for dismissal prior to trial or entry of a plea of guilty or nolo contendere shall constitute a waiver of the right to dismissal under this section.

(b) In any case in which counsel for the defendant or the attorney for the Government (1) knowingly allows the case to be set for trial without disclosing the fact that a necessary witness would be unavailable for trial; (2) files a motion solely for the purpose of delay which he knows is totally frivolous and without merit; (3) makes a statement for the purpose of obtaining a continuance which he knows to be false and which is material to the granting of a continuance; or (4) otherwise willfully fails to proceed to trial without justification consistent with section 3161 of this chapter, the court may punish any such counsel or attorney, as follows:

(A) in the case of an appointed defense counsel, by reducing the amount of compensation that otherwise would have been paid to such counsel pursuant to section 3006A of this title in an amount not to exceed 25 per centum thereof;

(B) in the case of a counsel retained in connection with the defense of a defendant, by imposing on such counsel a fine of not to exceed 25 per centum of the compensation to which he is entitled in connection with his defense of such defendant;

(C) by imposing on any attorney for the Government a fine of not to exceed $250;

(D) by denying any such counsel or attorney for the Government the right to practice before the court considering such case for a period of not to exceed ninety days; or

(E) by filing a report with an appropriate disciplinary committee.

The authority to punish provided for by this subsection shall be in addition to any other authority or power available to such court.

(c) The court shall follow procedures established in the Federal Rules of Criminal Procedure in punishing any counsel or attorney for the Government pursuant to this section.

§ 3164. Persons detained or designated as being of high risk

(a) The trial or other disposition of cases involving—

(1) a detained person who is being held in detention solely because he is awaiting trial, and

(2) a released person who is awaiting trial and has been designated by the attorney for the Government as being of high risk,

shall be accorded priority.

(b) The trial of any person described in subsection (a) (1) or (a) (2) of this section shall commence not later than ninety days following the beginning of such continuous detention or designation of high risk by the attorney for the Government. The periods of delay enumerated in section 3161(h) are excluded in computing the time limitation specified in this section.

(c) Failure to commence trial of a detainee as specified in subsection (b), through no fault of the accused or his counsel, or failure to commence trial of a designated releasee as specified in subsection (b), through no fault of the attorney for the Government, shall result in the automatic review by the court of the conditions of release. No detainee, as defined in subsection (a), shall be held in custody pending trial after the expiration of such ninety-day period required for the commencement of his trial. A designated releasee, as defined in subsection (a), who is found by the court to have intentionally delayed the trial of his case shall be subject to an order of the court modifying his nonfinancial conditions of release under this title to insure that he shall appear at trial as required.

JENCKS' ACT

(18 U.S.C. § 3500).

§ 3500. Demands for production of statements and reports of witnesses

(a) In any criminal prosecution brought by the United States, no statement or report in the possession of the United States which was made by a Government witness or prospective Government witness (other than the defendant) shall be the subject of subpena, discovery, or inspection until said witness has testified on direct examination in the trial of the case.

(b) After a witness called by the United States has testified on direct examination, the court shall, on motion of the defendant, order the United States to produce any statement (as hereinafter defined) of the witness in the possession of the United States which relates to the subject matter as to which the witness has testified. If the entire contents of any such statement relate to the subject matter of the testimony of the witness, the court shall order it to be delivered directly to the defendant for his examination and use.

(c) If the United States claims that any statement ordered to be produced under this section contains matter which does not relate to the subject matter of the testimony of the witness, the court shall order the United States to deliver such statement for the inspection of the court in camera. Upon such delivery the court shall excise the portions of such statement which do not relate to the subject matter of the testimony of the witness. With such material excised, the court shall then direct delivery of such statement to the defendant for his use. If, pursuant to such procedure, any portion of such statement is withheld from the defendant and the defendant objects to such withholding, and the trial is continued to an adjudication of the guilt of the defendant, the entire text of such statement shall be preserved by the United States and, in the event the defendant appeals, shall be made available to the appellate court for the purpose of determining the correctness of the ruling of the trial judge. Whenever any statement is delivered to a defendant pursuant to this section, the court in its discretion, upon application of said defendant, may recess proceedings in the trial for such time as it may determine to be reasonably required for the examination of such statement by said defendant and his preparation for its use in the trial.

(d) If the United States elects not to comply with an order of the court under subsection (b) or (c) hereof to deliver to the defendant any such statement, or such portion thereof as the court may direct, the court shall strike from the record the testimony of the witness, and the trial shall proceed unless the court in its discretion shall determine that the interests of justice require that a mistrial be declared.

(e) The term "statement", as used in subsections (b), (c), and (d) of this section in relation to any witness called by the United States, means—

> (1) a written statement made by said witness and signed or otherwise adopted or approved by him;

> (2) a stenographic, mechanical, electrical, or other recording, or a transcription thereof, which is a substantially verbatim recital of an oral statement made by said witness and recorded contemporaneously with the making of such oral statement; or

> (3) a statement, however taken or recorded, or a transcription thereof, if any, made by said witness to a grand jury.

LITIGATION CONCERNING SOURCES OF EVIDENCE

(18 U.S.C. § 3504).

§ 3504. Litigation concerning sources of evidence

(a) In any trial, hearing, or other proceeding in or before any court, grand jury, department, officer, agency, regulatory body, or other authority of the United States—

> (1) upon a claim by a party aggrieved that evidence is inadmissible because it is the primary product of an unlawful act or because it was obtained by the exploitation of an unlawful act, the opponent of the claim shall affirm or deny the occurrence of the alleged unlawful act;

> (2) disclosure of information for a determination if evidence is inadmissible because it is the primary product of an unlawful act occurring prior to June 19, 1968, or because it was obtained by the exploitation of an unlawful act occurring prior to June 19, 1968, shall not be required unless such information may be relevant to a pending claim of such inadmissibility; and

(3) no claim shall be considered that evidence of an event is inadmissible on the ground that such evidence was obtained by the exploitation of an unlawful act occurring prior to June 19, 1968, if such event occurred more than five years after such allegedly unlawful act.

(b) As used in this section "unlawful act" means any act the use of any electronic, mechanical, or other device (as defined in section 2510(5) of this title) in violation of the Constitution or laws of the United States or any regulation or standard promulgated pursuant thereto.

CRIMINAL APPEALS ACT OF 1970 (AS AMENDED)

(18 U.S.C. § 3731).

§ 3731. Appeal by United States

In a criminal case an appeal by the United States shall lie to a court of appeals from a decision, judgment, or order of a district court dismissing an indictment or information or granting a new trial after verdict or judgment, as to any one or more counts, or any part thereof, except that no appeal shall lie where the double jeopardy clause of the United States Constitution prohibits further prosecution.

An appeal by the United States shall lie to a court of appeals from a decision or order of a district court suppressing or excluding evidence or requiring the return of seized property in a criminal proceeding, not made after the defendant has been put in jeopardy and before the verdict or finding on an indictment or information, if the United States attorney certifies to the district court that the appeal is not taken for purpose of delay and that the evidence is a substantial proof of a fact material in the proceeding.

An appeal by the United States shall lie to a court of appeals from a decision or order, entered by a district court of the United States, granting the release of a person charged with or convicted of an offense, or denying a motion for revocation of, or modification of the conditions of, a decision or order granting release.

The appeal in all such cases shall be taken within thirty days after the decision, judgment or order has been rendered and shall be diligently prosecuted.

The provisions of this section shall be liberally construed to effectuate its purposes.

CRIME VICTIMS' RIGHTS

(18 U.S.C. § 3771).

§ 3771. Crime victims' rights

(a) Rights of crime victims.—A crime victim has the following rights:

(1) The right to be reasonably protected from the accused.

(2) The right to reasonable, accurate, and timely notice of any public court proceeding, or any parole proceeding, involving the crime or of any release or escape of the accused.

(3) The right not to be excluded from any such public court proceeding, unless the court, after receiving clear and convincing evidence, determines that testimony by the victim would be materially altered if the victim heard other testimony at that proceeding.

(4) The right to be reasonably heard at any public proceeding in the district court involving release, plea, sentencing, or any parole proceeding.

(5) The reasonable right to confer with the attorney for the Government in the case.

(6) The right to full and timely restitution as provided in law.

(7) The right to proceedings free from unreasonable delay.

(8) The right to be treated with fairness and with respect for the victim's dignity and privacy.

(b) Rights afforded.—In any court proceeding involving an offense against a crime victim, the court shall ensure that the crime victim is afforded the rights described in subsection (a). Before making a determination described in subsection (a)(3), the court shall make every effort to permit the fullest attendance possible by the victim and shall consider reasonable alternatives to the exclusion of the victim from the criminal proceeding. The reasons for any decision denying relief under this chapter shall be clearly stated on the record.

(c) Best efforts to accord rights.—

(1) Government.—Officers and employees of the Department of Justice and other departments and agencies of the United States engaged in the detection, investigation, or prosecution of crime shall make their best efforts to see that crime victims are notified of, and accorded, the rights described in subsection (a).

(2) Advice of attorney.—The prosecutor shall advise the crime victim that the crime victim can seek the advice of an attorney with respect to the rights described in subsection (a).

(3) Notice.—Notice of release otherwise required pursuant to this chapter shall not be given if such notice may endanger the safety of any person.

(d) Enforcement and limitations.—

(1) Rights.—The crime victim or the crime victim's lawful representative, and the attorney for the Government may assert the rights described in subsection (a). A person accused of the crime may not obtain any form of relief under this chapter.

(2) Multiple crime victims.—In a case where the court finds that the number of crime victims makes it impracticable to accord all of the crime victims the rights described in subsection (a), the court shall fashion a reasonable procedure to give effect to this chapter that does not unduly complicate or prolong the proceedings.

(3) Motion for relief and writ of mandamus.—The rights described in subsection (a) shall be asserted in the district court in which a defendant is being prosecuted for the crime or, if no prosecution is underway, in the district court in the district in which the crime occurred. The district court shall take up and decide any motion asserting a victim's right forthwith. If the district court denies the relief sought, the movant may petition the court of appeals for a writ of mandamus. The court of appeals may issue the writ on the order of a single judge pursuant to circuit rule or the Federal Rules of Appellate Procedure. The court of appeals shall take up and decide such application forthwith within 72 hours after the petition has been filed. In no event shall proceedings be stayed or subject to a continuance of more than five days for purposes of enforcing this chapter. If the court of appeals denies the relief sought, the reasons for the denial shall be clearly stated on the record in a written opinion.

(4) Error.—In any appeal in a criminal case, the Government may assert as error the district court's denial of any crime victim's right in the proceeding to which the appeal relates.

(5) Limitation on relief.—In no case shall a failure to afford a right under this chapter provide grounds for a new trial. A victim may make a motion to re-open a plea or sentence only if—

(A) the victim has asserted the right to be heard before or during the proceeding at issue and such right was denied;

(B) the victim petitions the court of appeals for a writ of mandamus within 10 days; and

(C) in the case of a plea, the accused has not pled to the highest offense charged.

This paragraph does not affect the victim's right to restitution as provided in title 18, United States Code.

(6) No cause of action.—Nothing in this chapter shall be construed to authorize a cause of action for damages or to create, to enlarge, or to imply any duty or obligation to any victim or other person for the breach of which the United States or any of its officers or employees could be held liable in damages. Nothing in this chapter shall be construed to impair the prosecutorial discretion of the Attorney General or any officer under his direction.

(e) Definitions.—For the purposes of this chapter, the term "crime victim" means a person directly and proximately harmed as a result of the commission of a Federal offense or an offense in the District of Columbia. In the case of a crime victim who is under 18 years of age, incompetent, incapacitated, or deceased, the legal guardians of the crime victim or the representatives of the crime victim's estate, family members, or any other persons appointed as suitable by the court, may assume the crime victim's rights under this chapter, but in no event shall the defendant be named as such guardian or representative.

(f) Procedures to promote compliance.—

(1) Regulations.—Not later than 1 year after the date of enactment of this chapter, the Attorney General of the United States shall promulgate regulations to enforce the rights of crime victims and to ensure compliance by responsible officials with the obligations described in law respecting crime victims.

(2) Contents.—The regulations promulgated under paragraph (1) shall—

(A) designate an administrative authority within the Department of Justice to receive and investigate complaints relating to the provision or violation of the rights of a crime victim;

(B) require a course of training for employees and offices of the Department of Justice that fail to comply with provisions of Federal law pertaining to the treatment of crime victims, and otherwise assist such employees and offices in responding more effectively to the needs of crime victims;

(C) contain disciplinary sanctions, including suspension or termination from employment, for employees of the Department of Justice who willfully or wantonly fail to comply with provisions of Federal law pertaining to the treatment of crime victims; and

(D) provide that the Attorney General, or the designee of the Attorney General, shall be the final arbiter of the complaint, and that there shall be no judicial review of the final decision of the Attorney General by a complainant.

JURY SELECTION AND SERVICE ACT OF 1968 (AS AMENDED)

(28 U.S.C. §§ 1861–1863, 1865–1867).

§ 1861. Declaration of policy

It is the policy of the United States that all litigants in Federal courts entitled to trial by jury shall have the right to grand and petit juries selected at random from a fair cross section of the community in the district or division wherein the court convenes. It is further the policy of the United States that all citizens shall have the opportunity to be considered for service on grand and petit juries in the district courts of the United States, and shall have an obligation to serve as jurors when summoned for that purpose.

§ 1862. Discrimination prohibited

No citizen shall be excluded from service as a grand or petit juror in the district courts of the United States or in the Court of International Trade on account of race, color, religion, sex, national origin, or economic status.

§ 1863. Plan for random jury selection

(a) Each United States district court shall devise and place into operation a written plan for random selection of grand and petit jurors that shall be designed to achieve the objectives of sections 1861 and 1862 of this title, and that shall otherwise comply with the provisions of this title. The plan shall be placed into operation after approval by a reviewing panel consisting of the members of the judicial council of the circuit and either the chief judge of the district whose plan is being reviewed or such other active district judge of that district as the chief judge of the district may designate. The panel shall examine the plan to ascertain that it complies with the provisions of this title. If the reviewing panel finds that the plan does not comply, the panel shall state the particulars in which the plan fails to comply and direct the district court to present within a reasonable time an alternative plan remedying the defect or defects. Separate plans may be adopted for each division or combination of divisions within a judicial district. The district court may modify a plan at any time and it shall modify the plan when so directed by the reviewing panel. The district court shall promptly notify the panel, the Administrative Office of the United States Courts, and the Attorney General of the United States, of the initial adoption and future modifications of the plan by filing copies therewith. Modifications of the plan made at the instance of the district court shall become effective after approval by the panel. Each district court shall submit a report on the jury selection process within its jurisdiction to the Administrative Office of the United States Courts in such form and at such times as the Judicial Conference of the United States may specify. The Judicial Conference of the United States may, from time to time, adopt rules and regulations governing the provisions and the operation of the plans formulated under this title.

(b) Among other things, such plan shall—

(1) either establish a jury commission, or authorize the clerk of the court, to manage the jury selection process. If the plan establishes a jury commission, the district court shall appoint one citizen to serve with the clerk of the court as the jury commission: *Provided, however*, That the plan for the District of Columbia may establish a jury commission consisting of three citizens. The citizen jury commissioner shall not belong to the same political party as the clerk serving with him. The clerk or the jury commission, as the case may be, shall act under the supervision and control of the chief judge of the district court or such other judge of the district court as the plan may provide. Each jury commissioner shall, during his tenure in office, reside in the judicial district or division for which he is appointed. Each citizen jury commissioner shall receive compensation to be fixed by the district court plan at a rate not to exceed $50 per day for each day necessarily employed in the performance of his duties, plus reimbursement for travel, subsistence, and other necessary expenses incurred by him in the performance of such duties. The Judicial Conference of the United States may establish standards for allowance of travel, subsistence, and other necessary expenses incurred by jury commissioners.

(2) specify whether the names of prospective jurors shall be selected from the voter registration lists or the lists of actual voters of the political subdivisions within the district or division. The plan shall prescribe some other source or sources of names in addition to voter lists where necessary to foster the policy and protect the rights secured by sections 1861 and 1862 of this title. The plan for the District of Columbia may require the names of prospective jurors to be selected from the city directory rather than from voter lists. The plans for the

districts of Puerto Rico and the Canal Zone may prescribe some other source or sources of names of prospective jurors in lieu of voter lists, the use of which shall be consistent with the policies declared and rights secured by sections 1861 and 1862 of this title. The plan for the district of Massachusetts may require the names of prospective jurors to be selected from the resident list provided for in chapter 234A, Massachusetts General Laws, or comparable authority, rather than from voter lists.

(3) specify detailed procedures to be followed by the jury commission or clerk in selecting names from the sources specified in paragraph (2) of this subsection. These procedures shall be designed to ensure the random selection of a fair cross section of the persons residing in the community in the district or division wherein the court convenes. They shall ensure that names of persons residing in each of the counties, parishes, or similar political subdivisions within the judicial district or division are placed in a master jury wheel; and shall ensure that each county, parish, or similar political subdivision within the district or division is substantially proportionally represented in the master jury wheel for that judicial district, division, or combination of divisions. For the purposes of determining proportional representation in the master jury wheel, either the number of actual voters at the last general election in each county, parish, or similar political subdivision, or the number of registered voters if registration of voters is uniformly required throughout the district or division, may be used.

(4) provide for a master jury wheel (or a device similar in purpose and function) into which the names of those randomly selected shall be placed. The plan shall fix a minimum number of names to be placed initially in the master jury wheel, which shall be at least one-half of 1 per centum of the total number of persons on the lists used as a source of names for the district or division; but if this number of names is believed to be cumbersome and unnecessary, the plan may fix a smaller number of names to be placed in the master wheel, but in no event less than one thousand. The chief judge of the district court, or such other district court judge as the plan may provide, may order additional names to be placed in the master jury wheel from time to time as necessary. The plan shall provide for periodic emptying and refilling of the master jury wheel at specified times, the interval for which shall not exceed four years.

(5)(A) except as provided in subparagraph (B), specify those groups of persons or occupational classes whose members shall, on individual request therefor, be excused from jury service. Such groups or classes shall be excused only if the district court finds, and the plan states, that jury service by such class or group would entail undue hardship or extreme inconvenience to the members thereof, and excuse of members thereof would not be inconsistent with sections 1861 and 1862 of this title.

(B) specify that volunteer safety personnel, upon individual request, shall be excused from jury service. For purposes of this subparagraph, the term "volunteer safety personnel" means individuals serving a public agency (as defined in section 1203(6) of title I of the Omnibus Crime Control and Safe Streets Act of 1968) in an official capacity, without compensation, as firefighters or members of a rescue squad or ambulance crew.

(6) specify that the following persons are barred from jury service on the ground that they are exempt: (A) members in active service in the Armed Forces of the United States; (B) members of the fire or police departments of any State, the District of Columbia, any territory or possession of the United States, or any subdivision of a State, the District of Columbia, or such territory or possession; (C) public officers in the executive, legislative, or judicial branches of the Government of the United States, or of any State, the District of Columbia, any territory or possession of the United States, or any subdivision of a State, the District of Columbia, or such territory or possession, who are actively engaged in the performance of official duties.

(7) fix the time when the names drawn from the qualified jury wheel shall be disclosed to parties and to the public. If the plan permits these names to be made public, it may nevertheless permit the chief judge of the district court, or such other district court judge as the plan may provide, to keep these names confidential in any case where the interests of justice so require.

(8) specify the procedures to be followed by the clerk or jury commission in assigning persons whose names have been drawn from the qualified jury wheel to grand and petit jury panels.

(c) The initial plan shall be devised by each district court and transmitted to the reviewing panel specified in subsection (a) of this section within one hundred and twenty days of the date of enactment of the Jury Selection and Service Act of 1968. The panel shall approve or direct the modification of each plan so submitted within sixty days thereafter. Each plan or modification made at the direction of the panel shall become effective after approval at such time thereafter as the panel directs, in no event to exceed ninety days from the date of approval. Modifications made at the instance of the district court under subsection (a) of this section shall be effective at such time thereafter as the panel directs, in no event to exceed ninety days from the date of modification.

(d) State, local, and Federal officials having custody, possession, or control of voter registration lists, lists of actual voters, or other appropriate records shall make such lists and records available to the jury commission or clerks for inspection, reproduction, and copying at all reasonable times as the commission or clerk may deem necessary and proper for the performance of duties under this title. The district courts shall have jurisdiction upon application by the Attorney General of the United States to compel compliance with this subsection by appropriate process.

§ 1865. Qualifications for jury service

(a) The chief judge of the district court, or such other district court judge as the plan may provide, on his initiative or upon recommendation of the clerk or jury commission, or the clerk under supervision of the court if the court's jury selection plan so authorizes, shall determine solely on the basis of information provided on the juror qualification form and other competent evidence whether a person is unqualified for, or exempt, or to be excused from jury service. The clerk shall enter such determination in the space provided on the juror qualification form and in any alphabetical list of names drawn from the master jury wheel. If a person did not appear in response to a summons, such fact shall be noted on said list.

(b) In making such determination the chief judge of the district court, or such other district court judge as the plan may provide, or the clerk if the court's jury selection plan so provides, shall deem any person qualified to serve on grand and petit juries in the district court unless he—

(1) is not a citizen of the United States eighteen years old who has resided for a period of one year within the judicial district;

(2) is unable to read, write, and understand the English language with a degree of proficiency sufficient to fill out satisfactorily the juror qualification form;

(3) is unable to speak the English language;

(4) is incapable, by reason of mental or physical infirmity, to render satisfactory jury service; or

(5) has a charge pending against him for the commission of, or has been convicted in a State or Federal court of record of, a crime punishable by imprisonment for more than one year and his civil rights have not been restored.

§ 1866. Selection and summoning of jury panels

(a) The jury commission, or in the absence thereof the clerk, shall maintain a qualified jury wheel and shall place in such wheel names of all persons drawn from the master jury wheel who are determined to be qualified as jurors and not exempt or excused pursuant to the district court plan. From time to time, the jury commission or the clerk shall publicly draw at random from the qualified jury wheel such number of names of persons as may be required for assignment to grand and petit jury panels. The jury commission or the clerk shall prepare a separate list of names of persons assigned to each grand and petit jury panel.

(b) When the court orders a grand or petit jury to be drawn, the clerk or jury commission or their duly designated deputies shall issue summonses for the required number of jurors.

Each person drawn for jury service may be served personally, or by registered, certified, or first-class mail addressed to such person at his usual residence or business address.

If such service is made personally, the summons shall be delivered by the clerk or the jury commission or their duly designated deputies to the marshal who shall make such service.

If such service is made by mail, the summons may be served by the marshal or by the clerk, the jury commission or their duly designated deputies, who shall make affidavit of service and shall attach thereto any receipt from the addressee for a registered or certified summons.

(c) Except as provided in section 1865 of this title or in any jury selection plan provision adopted pursuant to paragraph (5) or (6) of section 1863(b) of this title, no person or class of persons shall be disqualified, excluded, excused, or exempt from service as jurors: *Provided*, That any person summoned for jury service may be (1) excused by the court, or by the clerk under supervision of the court if the court's jury selection plan so authorizes, upon a showing of undue hardship or extreme inconvenience, for such period as the court deems necessary, at the conclusion of which such person either shall be summoned again for jury service under subsections (b) and (c) of this section or, if the court's jury selection plan so provides, the name of such person shall be reinserted into the qualified jury wheel for selection pursuant to subsection (a) of this section, or (2) excluded by the court on the ground that such person may be unable to render impartial jury service or that his service as a juror would be likely to disrupt the proceedings, or (3) excluded upon peremptory challenge as provided by law, or (4) excluded pursuant to the procedure specified by law upon a challenge by any party for good cause shown, or (5) excluded upon determination by the court that his service as a juror would be likely to threaten the secrecy of the proceedings, or otherwise adversely affect the integrity of jury deliberations. No person shall be excluded under clause (5) of this subsection unless the judge, in open court, determines that such is warranted and that exclusion of the person will not be inconsistent with sections 1861 and 1862 of this title. The number of persons excluded under clause (5) of this subsection shall not exceed one per centum of the number of persons who return executed jury qualification forms during the period, specified in the plan, between two consecutive fillings of the master jury wheel. The names of persons excluded under clause (5) of this subsection, together with detailed explanations for the exclusions, shall be forwarded immediately to the judicial council of the circuit, which shall have the power to make any appropriate order, prospective or retroactive, to redress any misapplication of clause (5) of this subsection, but otherwise exclusions effectuated under such clause shall not be subject to challenge under the provisions of this title. Any person excluded from a particular jury under clause (2), (3), or (4) of this subsection shall be eligible to sit on another jury if the basis for his initial exclusion would not be relevant to his ability to serve on such other jury.

(d) Whenever a person is disqualified, excused, exempt, or excluded from jury service, the jury commission or clerk shall note in the space provided on his juror qualification form or on the juror's card drawn from the qualified jury wheel the specific reason therefor.

(e) In any two-year period, no person shall be required to (1) serve or attend court for prospective service as a petit juror for a total of more than thirty days, except when necessary to complete service in a particular case, or (2) serve on more than one grand jury, or (3) serve as both a grand and petit juror.

(f) When there is an unanticipated shortage of available petit jurors drawn from the qualified jury wheel, the court may require the marshal to summon a sufficient number of petit jurors selected at random from the voter registration lists, lists of actual voters, or other lists specified in the plan, in a manner ordered by the court consistent with sections 1861 and 1862 of this title.

(g) Any person summoned for jury service who fails to appear as directed shall be ordered by the district court to appear forthwith and show cause for his failure to comply with the summons. Any person who fails to show good cause for noncompliance with a summons may be fined not more than $100 or imprisoned not more than three days, or both.

§ 1867. Challenging compliance with selection procedures

(a) In criminal cases, before the voir dire examination begins, or within seven days after the defendant discovered or could have discovered, by the exercise of diligence, the grounds therefor, whichever is earlier, the defendant may move to dismiss the indictment or stay the proceedings against him on the ground of substantial failure to comply with the provisions of this title in selecting the grand or petit jury.

(b) In criminal cases, before the voir dire examination begins, or within seven days after the Attorney General of the United States discovered or could have discovered, by the exercise of diligence, the grounds therefor, whichever is earlier, the Attorney General may move to dismiss the indictment or stay the proceedings on the ground of substantial failure to comply with the provisions of this title in selecting the grand or petit jury.

(c) In civil cases, before the voir dire examination begins, or within seven days after the party discovered or could have discovered, by the exercise of diligence, the grounds therefor, whichever is earlier, any party may move to stay the proceedings on the ground of substantial failure to comply with the provisions of this title in selecting the petit jury.

(d) Upon motion filed under subsection (a), (b), or (c) of this section, containing a sworn statement of facts which, if true, would constitute a substantial failure to comply with the provisions of this title, the moving party shall be entitled to present in support of such motion the testimony of the jury commission or clerk, if available, any relevant records and papers not public or otherwise available used by the jury commissioner or clerk, and any other relevant evidence. If the court determines that there has been a substantial failure to comply with the provisions of this title in selecting the grand jury, the court shall stay the proceedings pending the selection of a grand jury in conformity with this title or dismiss the indictment, whichever is appropriate. If the court determines that there has been a substantial failure to comply with the provisions of this title in selecting the petit jury, the court shall stay the proceedings pending the selection of a petit jury in conformity with this title.

(e) The procedures prescribed by this section shall be the exclusive means by which a person accused of a Federal crime, the Attorney General of the United States or a party in a civil case may challenge any jury on the ground that such jury was not selected in conformity with the provisions of this title. Nothing in this section shall preclude any person or the United States from pursuing any other remedy, civil or criminal, which may be available for the vindication or enforcement of any law prohibiting discrimination on account of race, color, religion, sex, national origin or economic status in the selection of persons for service on grand or petit juries.

(f) The contents of records or papers used by the jury commission or clerk in connection with the jury selection process shall not be disclosed, except pursuant to the district court plan or as may be necessary in the preparation or presentation of a motion under subsection (a), (b), or (c) of this section, until after the master jury wheel has been emptied and refilled pursuant to section 1863(b)(4) of this title and all persons selected to serve as jurors before the master wheel was emptied have completed such service. The parties in a case shall be allowed to inspect, reproduce, and copy such records or papers at all reasonable times during the preparation and pendency of such a motion. Any person who discloses the contents of any record or paper in violation of this subsection may be fined not more than $1,000 or imprisoned not more than one year, or both.

HABEAS CORPUS

(28 U.S.C. §§ 2241–2244, 2253–2255, 2261–2266).

§ 2241. Power to grant writ

(a) Writs of habeas corpus may be granted by the Supreme Court, any justice thereof, the district courts and any circuit judge within their respective jurisdictions. The order of a circuit judge shall be entered in the records of the district court of the district wherein the restraint complained of is had.

(b) The Supreme Court, any justice thereof, and any circuit judge may decline to entertain an application for a writ of habeas corpus and may transfer the application for hearing and determination to the district court having jurisdiction to entertain it.

(c) The writ of habeas corpus shall not extend to a prisoner unless—

(1) He is in custody under or by color of the authority of the United States or is committed for trial before some court thereof; or

(2) He is in custody for an act done or omitted in pursuance of an Act of Congress, or an order, process, judgment or decree of a court or judge of the United States; or

(3) He is in custody in violation of the Constitution or laws or treaties of the United States; or

(4) He, being a citizen of a foreign state and domiciled therein is in custody for an act done or omitted under any alleged right, title, authority, privilege, protection, or exemption claimed under the commission, order or sanction of any foreign state, or under color thereof, the validity and effect of which depend upon the law of nations; or

(5) It is necessary to bring him into court to testify or for trial.

(d) Where an application for a writ of habeas corpus is made by a person in custody under the judgment and sentence of a State court of a State which contains two or more Federal judicial districts, the application may be filed in the district court for the district wherein such person is in custody or in the district court for the district within which the State court was held which convicted and sentenced him and each of such district courts shall have concurrent jurisdiction to entertain the application. The district court for the district wherein such an application is filed in the exercise of its discretion and in furtherance of justice may transfer the application to the other district court for hearing and determination.

§ 2242. Application

Application for a writ of habeas corpus shall be in writing signed and verified by the person for whose relief it is intended or by someone acting in his behalf.

It shall allege the facts concerning the applicant's commitment or detention, the name of the person who has custody over him and by virtue of what claim or authority, if known.

It may be amended or supplemented as provided in the rules of procedure applicable to civil actions.

If addressed to the Supreme Court, a justice thereof or a circuit judge it shall state the reasons for not making application to the district court of the district in which the applicant is held.

§ 2243. Issuance of writ; return; hearing; decision

A court, justice or judge entertaining an application for a writ of habeas corpus shall forthwith award the writ or issue an order directing the respondent to show cause why the writ should not be granted, unless it appears from the application that the applicant or person detained is not entitled thereto.

The writ, or order to show cause shall be directed to the person having custody of the person detained. It shall be returned within three days unless for good cause additional time, not exceeding twenty days, is allowed.

The person to whom the writ or order is directed shall make a return certifying the true cause of the detention.

When the writ or order is returned a day shall be set for hearing, not more than five days after the return unless for good cause additional time is allowed.

Unless the application for the writ and the return present only issues of law the person to whom the writ is directed shall be required to produce at the hearing the body of the person detained.

The applicant or the person detained may, under oath, deny any of the facts set forth in the return or allege any other material facts.

The return and all suggestions made against it may be amended, by leave of court, before or after being filed.

The court shall summarily hear and determine the facts, and dispose of the matter as law and justice require.

§ 2244. Finality of determination

(a) No circuit or district judge shall be required to entertain an application for a writ of habeas corpus to inquire into the detention of a person pursuant to a judgment of a court of the United States if it appears that the legality of such detention has been determined by a judge or court of the United States on a prior application for a writ of habeas corpus, except as provided in section 2255.

(b)(1) A claim presented in a second or successive habeas corpus application under section 2254 that was presented in a prior application shall be dismissed.

(2) A claim presented in a second or successive habeas corpus application under section 2254 that was not presented in a prior application shall be dismissed unless—

(A) the applicant shows that the claim relies on a new rule of constitutional law, made retroactive to cases on collateral review by the Supreme Court, that was previously unavailable; or

(B)(i) the factual predicate for the claim could not have been discovered previously through the exercise of due diligence; and

(ii) the facts underlying the claim, if proven and viewed in light of the evidence as a whole, would be sufficient to establish by clear and convincing evidence that, but for constitutional error, no reasonable factfinder would have found the applicant guilty of the underlying offense.

(3)(A) Before a second or successive application permitted by this section is filed in the district court, the applicant shall move in the appropriate court of appeals for an order authorizing the district court to consider the application.

(B) A motion in the court of appeals for an order authorizing the district court to consider a second or successive application shall be determined by a three-judge panel of the court of appeals.

(C) The court of appeals may authorize the filing of a second or successive application only if it determines that the application makes a prima facie showing that the application satisfies the requirements of this subsection.

(D) The court of appeals shall grant or deny the authorization to file a second or successive application not later than 30 days after the filing of the motion.

(E) The grant or denial of an authorization by a court of appeals to file a second or successive application shall not be appealable and shall not be the subject of a petition for rehearing or for a writ of certiorari.

(4) A district court shall dismiss any claim presented in a second or successive application that the court of appeals has authorized to be filed unless the applicant shows that the claim satisfies the requirements of this section.

(c) In a habeas corpus proceeding brought in behalf of a person in custody pursuant to the judgment of a State court, a prior judgment of the Supreme Court of the United States on an appeal or review by a writ of certiorari at the instance of the prisoner of the decision of such State court, shall be conclusive as to all issues of fact or law with respect to an asserted denial of a Federal right which constitutes ground for discharge in a habeas corpus proceeding, actually adjudicated by the Supreme Court therein, unless the applicant for the writ of habeas corpus shall plead and the court shall find the existence of a material and controlling fact which did not appear in the record of the proceeding in the Supreme Court and the court shall further find that the applicant for the writ of habeas corpus could not have caused such fact to appear in such record by the exercise of reasonable diligence.

(d)(1) A 1-year period of limitation shall apply to an application for a writ of habeas corpus by a person in custody pursuant to the judgment of a State court. The limitation period shall run from the latest of—

(A) the date on which the judgment became final by the conclusion of direct review or the expiration of the time for seeking such review;

(B) the date on which the impediment to filing an application created by State action in violation of the Constitution or laws of the United States is removed, if the applicant was prevented from filing by such State action;

(C) the date on which the constitutional right asserted was initially recognized by the Supreme Court, if the right has been newly recognized by the Supreme Court and made retroactively applicable to cases on collateral review; or

(D) the date on which the factual predicate of the claim or claims presented could have been discovered through the exercise of due diligence.

(2) The time during which a properly filed application for State post-conviction or other collateral review with respect to the pertinent judgment or claim is pending shall not be counted toward any period of limitation under this subsection.

§ 2253. Appeal

(a) In a habeas corpus proceeding or a proceeding under section 2255 before a district judge, the final order shall be subject to review, on appeal, by the court of appeals for the circuit in which the proceeding is held.

(b) There shall be no right of appeal from a final order in a proceeding to test the validity of a warrant to remove to another district or place for commitment or trial a person charged with a criminal offense against the United States, or to test the validity of such person's detention pending removal proceedings.

(c)(1) Unless a circuit justice or judge issues a certificate of appealability, an appeal may not be taken to the court of appeals from—

(A) the final order in a habeas corpus proceeding in which the detention complained of arises out of process issued by a State court; or

(B) the final order in a proceeding under section 2255.

(2) A certificate of appealability may issue under paragraph (1) only if the applicant has made a substantial showing of the denial of a constitutional right.

(3) The certificate of appealability under paragraph (1) shall indicate which specific issue or issues satisfy the showing required by paragraph (2).

§ 2254. State custody; remedies in Federal courts

(a) The Supreme Court, a Justice thereof, a circuit judge, or a district court shall entertain an application for a writ of habeas corpus in behalf of a person in custody pursuant to the judgment of a State court only on the ground that he is in custody in violation of the Constitution or laws or treaties of the United States.

(b)(1) An application for a writ of habeas corpus on behalf of a person in custody pursuant to the judgment of a State court shall not be granted unless it appears that—

(A) the applicant has exhausted the remedies available in the courts of the State; or

(B)(i) there is an absence of available State corrective process; or

(ii) circumstances exist that render such process ineffective to protect the rights of the applicant.

(2) An application for a writ of habeas corpus may be denied on the merits, notwithstanding the failure of the applicant to exhaust the remedies available in the courts of the State.

(3) A State shall not be deemed to have waived the exhaustion requirement or be estopped from reliance upon the requirement unless the State, through counsel, expressly waives the requirement.

(c) An applicant shall not be deemed to have exhausted the remedies available in the courts of the State, within the meaning of this section, if he has the right under the law of the State to raise, by any available procedure, the question presented.

(d) An application for a writ of habeas corpus on behalf of a person in custody pursuant to the judgment of a State court shall not be granted with respect to any claim that was adjudicated on the merits in State court proceedings unless the adjudication of the claim—

(1) resulted in a decision that was contrary to, or involved an unreasonable application of, clearly established Federal law, as determined by the Supreme Court of the United States; or

(2) resulted in a decision that was based on an unreasonable determination of the facts in light of the evidence presented in the State court proceeding.

(e)(1) In a proceeding instituted by an application for a writ of habeas corpus by a person in custody pursuant to the judgment of a State court, a determination of a factual issue made by a State court shall be presumed to be correct. The applicant shall have the burden of rebutting the presumption of correctness by clear and convincing evidence.

(2) If the applicant has failed to develop the factual basis of a claim in State court proceedings, the court shall not hold an evidentiary hearing on the claim unless the applicant shows that—

(A) the claim relies on—

(i) a new rule of constitutional law, made retroactive to cases on collateral review by the Supreme Court, that was previously unavailable; or

(ii) a factual predicate that could not have been previously discovered through the exercise of due diligence; and

(B) the facts underlying the claim would be sufficient to establish by clear and convincing evidence that but for constitutional error, no reasonable factfinder would have found the applicant guilty of the underlying offense.

(f) If the applicant challenges the sufficiency of the evidence adduced in such State court proceeding to support the State court's determination of a factual issue made therein, the applicant, if able, shall produce that part of the record pertinent to a determination of the sufficiency of the evidence to support such determination. If the applicant, because of indigency or other reason is unable to produce such part of the record, then the State shall produce such part of the record and the Federal court shall direct the State to do so by order directed to an appropriate State official. If the State cannot provide such pertinent part of the record, then the court shall determine under the existing facts and circumstances what weight shall be given to the State court's factual determination.

(g) A copy of the official records of the State court, duly certified by the clerk of such court to be a true and correct copy of a finding, judicial opinion, or other reliable written indicia showing such a factual determination by the State court shall be admissible in the Federal court proceeding.

(h) Except as provided in section 408 of the Controlled Substances Act, in all proceedings brought under this section, and any subsequent proceedings on review, the court may appoint counsel for an applicant who is or becomes financially unable to afford counsel, except as provided by a rule promulgated by the Supreme Court pursuant to statutory authority. Appointment of counsel under this section shall be governed by section 3006A of title 18.

(i) The ineffectiveness or incompetence of counsel during Federal or State collateral post-conviction proceedings shall not be a ground for relief in a proceeding arising under section 2254.

§ 2255. Federal custody; remedies on motion attacking sentence

A prisoner in custody under sentence of a court established by Act of Congress claiming the right to be released upon the ground that the sentence was imposed in violation of the Constitution or laws of the United States, or that the court was without jurisdiction to impose such sentence, or that the sentence was in excess of the maximum authorized by law, or is otherwise subject to collateral attack, may move the court which imposed the sentence to vacate, set aside or correct the sentence.

Unless the motion and the files and records of the case conclusively show that the prisoner is entitled to no relief, the court shall cause notice thereof to be served upon the United States attorney, grant a prompt hearing thereon, determine the issues and make findings of fact and conclusions of law with respect thereto. If the court finds that the judgment was rendered without jurisdiction, or that the sentence imposed was not authorized by law or otherwise open to collateral attack, or that there has been such a denial or infringement of the constitutional rights of the prisoner as to render the judgment vulnerable to collateral attack, the court shall vacate and set the judgment aside and shall discharge the prisoner or resentence him or grant a new trial or correct the sentence as may appear appropriate.

A court may entertain and determine such motion without requiring the production of the prisoner at the hearing.

An appeal may be taken to the court of appeals from the order entered on the motion as from a final judgment on application for a writ of habeas corpus.

An application for a writ of habeas corpus in behalf of a prisoner who is authorized to apply for relief by motion pursuant to this section, shall not be entertained if it appears that the applicant has failed to apply for relief, by motion, to the court which sentenced him, or that such court has denied him relief, unless it also appears that the remedy by motion is inadequate or ineffective to test the legality of his detention.

A 1-year period of limitation shall apply to a motion under this section. The limitation period shall run from the latest of—

> (1) the date on which the judgment of conviction becomes final;

> (2) the date on which the impediment to making a motion created by governmental action in violation of the Constitution or laws of the United States is removed, if the movant was prevented from making a motion by such governmental action;

> (3) the date on which the right asserted was initially recognized by the Supreme Court, if that right has been newly recognized by the Supreme Court and made retroactively applicable to cases on collateral review; or

> (4) the date on which the facts supporting the claim or claims presented could have been discovered through the exercise of due diligence.

Except as provided in section 408 of the Controlled Substances Act, in all proceedings brought under this section, and any subsequent proceedings on review, the court may appoint counsel, except as provided by a rule promulgated by the Supreme Court pursuant to statutory authority. Appointment of counsel under this section shall be governed by section 3006A of title 18.

A second or successive motion must be certified as provided in section 2244 by a panel of the appropriate court of appeals to contain—

> (1) newly discovered evidence that, if proven and viewed in light of the evidence as a whole, would be sufficient to establish by clear and convincing evidence that no reasonable factfinder would have found the movant guilty of the offense; or

> (2) a new rule of constitutional law, made retroactive to cases on collateral review by the Supreme Court, that was previously unavailable.

§ 2261. Prisoners in State custody subject to capital sentence; appointment of counsel; requirement of rule of court or statute; procedures for appointment

(a) This chapter shall apply to cases arising under section 2254 brought by prisoners in State custody who are subject to a capital sentence. It shall apply only if the provisions of subsections (b) and (c) are satisfied.

(b) This chapter is applicable if a State establishes by statute, rule of its court of last resort, or by another agency authorized by State law, a mechanism for the appointment, compensation, and payment of reasonable litigation expenses of competent counsel in State post-conviction proceedings brought by indigent prisoners whose capital convictions and sentences have been upheld on direct appeal to the court of last resort in the State or have otherwise become final for State law purposes. The rule of court or statute must provide standards of competency for the appointment of such counsel.

(c) Any mechanism for the appointment, compensation, and reimbursement of counsel as provided in subsection (b) must offer counsel to all State prisoners under capital sentence and must provide for the entry of an order by a court of record—

(1) appointing one or more counsels to represent the prisoner upon a finding that the prisoner is indigent and accepted the offer or is unable competently to decide whether to accept or reject the offer;

(2) finding, after a hearing if necessary, that the prisoner rejected the offer of counsel and made the decision with an understanding of its legal consequences; or

(3) denying the appointment of counsel upon a finding that the prisoner is not indigent.

(d) No counsel appointed pursuant to subsections (b) and (c) to represent a State prisoner under capital sentence shall have previously represented the prisoner at trial or on direct appeal in the case for which the appointment is made unless the prisoner and counsel expressly request continued representation.

(e) The ineffectiveness or incompetence of counsel during State or Federal post-conviction proceedings in a capital case shall not be a ground for relief in a proceeding arising under section 2254. This limitation shall not preclude the appointment of different counsel, on the court's own motion or at the request of the prisoner, at any phase of State or Federal post-conviction proceedings on the basis of the ineffectiveness or incompetence of counsel in such proceedings.

§ 2262. Mandatory stay of execution; duration; limits on stays of execution; successive petitions

(a) Upon the entry in the appropriate State court of record of an order under section 2261(c), a warrant or order setting an execution date for a State prisoner shall be stayed upon application to any court that would have jurisdiction over any proceedings filed under section 2254. The application shall recite that the State has invoked the post-conviction review procedures of this chapter and that the scheduled execution is subject to stay.

(b) A stay of execution granted pursuant to subsection (a) shall expire if—

(1) a State prisoner fails to file a habeas corpus application under section 2254 within the time required in section 2263;

(2) before a court of competent jurisdiction, in the presence of counsel, unless the prisoner has competently and knowingly waived such

counsel, and after having been advised of the consequences, a State prisoner under capital sentence waives the right to pursue habeas corpus review under section 2254; or

(3) a State prisoner files a habeas corpus petition under section 2254 within the time required by section 2263 and fails to make a substantial showing of the denial of a Federal right or is denied relief in the district court or at any subsequent stage of review.

(c) If one of the conditions in subsection (b) has occurred, no Federal court thereafter shall have the authority to enter a stay of execution in the case, unless the court of appeals approves the filing of a second or successive application under section 2244(b).

§ 2263. Filing of habeas corpus application; time requirements; tolling rules

(a) Any application under this chapter for habeas corpus relief under section 2254 must be filed in the appropriate district court not later than 180 days after final State court affirmance of the conviction and sentence on direct review or the expiration of the time for seeking such review.

(b) The time requirements established by subsection (a) shall be tolled—

(1) from the date that a petition for certiorari is filed in the Supreme Court until the date of final disposition of the petition if a State prisoner files the petition to secure review by the Supreme Court of the affirmance of a capital sentence on direct review by the court of last resort of the State or other final State court decision on direct review;

(2) from the date on which the first petition for post-conviction review or other collateral relief is filed until the final State court disposition of such petition; and

(3) during an additional period not to exceed 30 days, if—

(A) a motion for an extension of time is filed in the Federal district court that would have jurisdiction over the case upon the filing of a habeas corpus application under section 2254; and

(B) a showing of good cause is made for the failure to file the habeas corpus application within the time period established by this section.

§ 2264. Scope of Federal review; district court adjudications

(a) Whenever a State prisoner under capital sentence files a petition for habeas corpus relief to which this chapter applies, the district court shall only consider a claim or claims that have been raised and decided on the merits in the State courts, unless the failure to raise the claim properly is—

(1) the result of State action in violation of the Constitution or laws of the United States;

(2) the result of the Supreme Court's recognition of a new Federal right that is made retroactively applicable; or

(3) based on a factual predicate that could not have been discovered through the exercise of due diligence in time to present the claim for State or Federal post-conviction review.

(b) Following review subject to subsections (a), (d), and (e) of section 2254, the court shall rule on the claims properly before it.

§ 2265. Application to State unitary review procedure

(a) For purposes of this section, a "unitary review" procedure means a State procedure that authorizes a person under sentence of death to raise, in the course of direct review of the judgment, such claims as could be raised on collateral attack. This chapter shall apply, as provided in this section, in relation to a State unitary review procedure if the State establishes by rule of its court of last resort or by statute a mechanism for the appointment, compensation, and payment of reasonable litigation expenses of competent counsel in the unitary review proceedings, including expenses relating to the litigation of collateral claims in the proceedings. The rule of court or statute must provide standards of competency for the appointment of such counsel.

(b) To qualify under this section, a unitary review procedure must include an offer of counsel following trial for the purpose of representation on unitary review, and entry of an order, as provided in section 2261(c), concerning appointment of counsel or waiver or denial of appointment of counsel for that purpose. No counsel appointed to represent the prisoner in the unitary review proceedings shall have previously represented the prisoner at trial in the case for which the appointment is made unless the prisoner and counsel expressly request continued representation.

(c) Sections 2262, 2263, 2264, and 2266 shall apply in relation to cases involving a sentence of death from any State having a unitary review procedure that qualifies under this section. References to State "post-conviction review" and "direct review" in such sections shall be understood as referring to unitary review under the State procedure. The reference in section 2262(a) to "an order under section 2261(c)" shall be understood as referring to the post-trial order under subsection (b) concerning representation in the unitary review proceedings, but if a transcript of the trial proceedings is unavailable at the time of the filing of such an order in the appropriate State court, then the start of the 180-day limitation period under section 2263 shall be deferred until a transcript is made available to the prisoner or counsel of the prisoner.

§ 2266. Limitation periods for determining applications and motions

(a) The adjudication of any application under section 2254 that is subject to this chapter, and the adjudication of any motion under section 2255 by a person under sentence of death, shall be given priority by the district court and by the court of appeals over all noncapital matters.

(b)(1)(A) A district court shall render a final determination and enter a final judgment on any application for a writ of habeas corpus brought under this chapter in a capital case not later than 180 days after the date on which the application is filed.

(B) A district court shall afford the parties at least 120 days in which to complete all actions, including the preparation of all pleadings and briefs, and if necessary, a hearing, prior to the submission of the case for decision.

(C)(i) A district court may delay for not more than one additional 30-day period beyond the period specified in subparagraph (A), the rendering of a determination of an application for a writ of habeas corpus if the court issues a written order making a finding, and stating the reasons for the finding, that the ends of justice that would be served by allowing the delay outweigh the best interests of the public and the applicant in a speedy disposition of the application.

(ii) The factors, among others, that a court shall consider in determining whether a delay in the disposition of an application is warranted are as follows:

(I) Whether the failure to allow the delay would be likely to result in a miscarriage of justice.

(II) Whether the case is so unusual or so complex, due to the number of defendants, the nature of the prosecution, or the existence of novel questions of fact or law, that it is unreasonable to expect adequate briefing within the time limitations established by subparagraph (A).

(III) Whether the failure to allow a delay in a case that, taken as a whole, is not so unusual or so complex as described in subclause (II), but would otherwise deny the applicant reasonable time to obtain counsel, would unreasonably deny the applicant or the government continuity of counsel, or would deny counsel for the applicant or the government the reasonable time necessary for effective preparation, taking into account the exercise of due diligence.

(iii) No delay in disposition shall be permissible because of general congestion of the court's calendar.

(iv) The court shall transmit a copy of any order issued under clause (i) to the Director of the Administrative Office of the United States Courts for inclusion in the report under paragraph (5).

(2) The time limitations under paragraph (1) shall apply to—

(A) an initial application for a writ of habeas corpus;

(B) any second or successive application for a writ of habeas corpus; and

(C) any redetermination of an application for a writ of habeas corpus following a remand by the court of appeals or the Supreme Court for further proceedings, in which case the limitation period shall run from the date the remand is ordered.

(3)(A) The time limitations under this section shall not be construed to entitle an applicant to a stay of execution, to which the applicant would otherwise not be entitled, for the purpose of litigating any application or appeal.

(B) No amendment to an application for a writ of habeas corpus under this chapter shall be permitted after the filing of the answer to the application, except on the grounds specified in section 2244(b).

(4)(A) The failure of a court to meet or comply with a time limitation under this section shall not be a ground for granting relief from a judgment of conviction or sentence.

(B) The State may enforce a time limitation under this section by petitioning for a writ of mandamus to the court of appeals. The court of appeals shall act on the petition for a writ of mandamus not later than 30 days after the filing of the petition.

(5)(A) The Administrative Office of the United States Courts shall submit to Congress an annual report on the compliance by the district courts with the time limitations under this section.*

(B) The report described in subparagraph (A) shall include copies of the orders submitted by the district courts under paragraph (1)(B)(iv).

(c)(1)(A) A court of appeals shall hear and render a final determination of any appeal of an order granting or denying, in whole or in part, an application brought under this chapter in a capital case not later than 120 days after the date on which the reply brief is filed, or if no reply brief is filed, not later than 120 days after the date on which the answering brief is filed.

(B)(i) A court of appeals shall decide whether to grant a petition for rehearing or other request for rehearing en banc not later than 30 days after the date on which the petition for rehearing is filed unless a responsive pleading is required, in which case the court shall decide whether to grant the petition not later than 30 days after the date on which the responsive pleading is filed.

(ii) If a petition for rehearing or rehearing en banc is granted, the court of appeals shall hear and render a final determination of the appeal not later than 120 days after the date on which the order granting rehearing or rehearing en banc is entered.

(2) The time limitations under paragraph (1) shall apply to—

(A) an initial application for a writ of habeas corpus;

(B) any second or successive application for a writ of habeas corpus; and

(C) any redetermination of an application for a writ of habeas corpus or related appeal following a remand by the court of appeals en banc or the Supreme Court for further proceedings, in which case the limitation period shall run from the date the remand is ordered.

(3) The time limitations under this section shall not be construed to entitle an applicant to a stay of execution, to which the applicant would otherwise not be entitled, for the purpose of litigating any application or appeal.

(4)(A) The failure of a court to meet or comply with a time limitation under this section shall not be a ground for granting relief from a judgment of conviction or sentence.

(B) The State may enforce a time limitation under this section by applying for a writ of mandamus to the Supreme Court.

(5) The Administrative Office of the United States Courts shall submit to Congress an annual report on the compliance by the courts of appeals with the time limitations under this section.*

PRIVACY PROTECTION ACT OF 1980

(42 U.S.C. §§ 2000aa–2000aa–12); Guidelines (28 C.F.R. § 59.4).

§ 2000aa. Searches and seizures by government officers and employees in connection with investigation or prosecution of criminal offenses

(a) Work product materials

Notwithstanding any other law, it shall be unlawful for a government officer or employee, in connection with the investigation or prosecution of a criminal offense, to search for or seize any work product materials possessed by a person reasonably believed to have a purpose to disseminate to the public a newspaper, book, broadcast, or other similar form of public communication, in or affecting interstate or foreign commerce; but this provision shall not impair or affect the ability of any government officer or employee, pursuant to otherwise applicable law, to search for or seize such materials, if—

(1) there is probable cause to believe that the person possessing such materials has committed or is committing the criminal offense to which the materials relate: *Provided, however,* That a government officer or employee may not search for or seize such materials under the provisions of this paragraph if the offense to which the materials relate consists of the receipt, possession, communication, or withholding of such materials or the information contained therein (but such a search or seizure may be conducted under the provisions of this paragraph if the offense consists of the receipt, possession, or communication of information relating to the national defense, classified information, or restricted data under the provisions of section 793, 794, 797, or 798 of Title 18, or section 2274, 2275 or 2277 of this title, or section 783 of Title 50, or if the offense involves the production, possession, receipt, mailing, sale, distribution, shipment, or transportation of child pornography, the sexual exploitation of children, or the sale or purchase of children under section 2251, 2251A, 2252, or 2252A of Title 18); or

(2) there is reason to believe that the immediate seizure of such materials is necessary to prevent the death of, or serious bodily injury to, a human being.

(b) Other documents

Notwithstanding any other law, it shall be unlawful for a government officer or employee, in connection with the investigation or prosecution of a criminal offense, to search for or seize documentary materials, other than work product materials, possessed by a person in connection with a purpose to disseminate to the public a newspaper, book, broadcast, or other similar

---

* The enacting legislation states that new sections 2261–2266 "shall apply to cases pending on or after the date of enactment of this Act."

form of public communication, in or affecting interstate or foreign commerce; but this provision shall not impair or affect the ability of any government officer or employee, pursuant to otherwise applicable law, to search for or seize such materials, if—

(1) there is probable cause to believe that the person possessing such materials has committed or is committing the criminal offense to which the materials relate: *Provided, however*, That a government officer or employee may not search for or seize such materials under the provisions of this paragraph if the offense to which the materials relate consists of the receipt, possession, communication, or withholding of such materials or the information contained therein (but such a search or seizure may be conducted under the provisions of this paragraph if the offense consists of the receipt, possession, or communication of information relating to the national defense, classified information, or restricted data under the provisions of section 793, 794, 797, or 798 of Title 18, or section 2274, 2275, or 2277 of this title, or section 783 of Title 50, or if the offense involves the production, possession, receipt, mailing, sale, distribution, shipment, or transportation of child pornography, the sexual exploitation of children, or the sale or purchase of children under section 2251, 2251A, 2252, or 2252A of Title 18);

(2) there is reason to believe that the immediate seizure of such materials is necessary to prevent the death of, or serious bodily injury to, a human being;

(3) there is reason to believe that the giving of notice pursuant to a subpena duces tecum would result in the destruction, alteration, or concealment of such materials; or

(4) such materials have not been produced in response to a court order directing compliance with a subpena duces tecum, and—

(A) all appellate remedies have been exhausted; or

(B) there is reason to believe that the delay in an investigation or trial occasioned by further proceedings relating to the subpena would threaten the interests of justice.

(c) Objections to court ordered subpoenas; affidavits

In the event a search warrant is sought pursuant to paragraph (4)(B) of subsection (b) of this section, the person possessing the materials shall be afforded adequate opportunity to submit an affidavit setting forth the basis for any contention that the materials sought are not subject to seizure.

§ 2000aa–5. Border and customs searches

This chapter shall not impair or affect the ability of a government officer or employee, pursuant to otherwise applicable law, to conduct searches and seizures at the borders of, or at international points of, entry into the United States in order to enforce the customs laws of the United States.

§ 2000aa–6. Civil actions by aggrieved persons

(a) Right of action

A person aggrieved by a search for or seizure of materials in violation of this chapter shall have a civil cause of action for damages for such search or seizure—

(1) against the United States, against a State which has waived its sovereign immunity under the Constitution to a claim for damages resulting from a violation of this chapter, or against any other governmental unit, all of which shall be liable for violations of this chapter by their officers or employees while acting within the scope or under color of their office or employment; and

(2) against an officer or employee of a State who has violated this chapter while acting within the scope or under color of his office or employment, if such State has not waived its sovereign immunity as provided in paragraph (1).

(b) Good faith defense

It shall be a complete defense to a civil action brought under paragraph (2) of subsection (a) of this section that the officer or employee had a reasonable good faith belief in the lawfulness of his conduct.

(c) Official immunity

The United States, a State, or any other governmental unit liable for violations of this chapter under subsection (a)(1) of this section, may not assert as a defense to a claim arising under this chapter the immunity of the officer or employee whose violation is complained of or his reasonable good faith belief in the lawfulness of his conduct, except that such a defense may be asserted if the violation complained of is that of a judicial officer.

(d) Exclusive nature of remedy

The remedy provided by subsection (a)(1) of this section against the United States, a State, or any other governmental unit is exclusive of any other civil action or proceeding for conduct constituting a violation of this chapter, against the officer or employee whose violation gave rise to the claim, or against the estate of such officer or employee.

(e) Admissibility of evidence

Evidence otherwise admissible in a proceeding shall not be excluded on the basis of a violation of this chapter.

(f) Damages; costs and attorneys' fees

A person having a cause of action under this section shall be entitled to recover actual damages but not less than liquidated damages of $1,000, and such reasonable attorneys' fees and other litigation costs reasonably incurred as the court, in its discretion, may award: *Provided, however*, That the United States, a State, or any other governmental unit shall not be liable for interest prior to judgment.

(g) Attorney General; claims settlement; regulations

The Attorney General may settle a claim for damages brought against the United States under this section, and shall promulgate regulations to provide for the commencement of an administrative inquiry following a determination of a violation of this chapter by an officer or employee of the

United States and for the imposition of administrative sanctions against such officer or employee, if warranted.

(h) Jurisdiction

The district courts shall have original jurisdiction of all civil actions arising under this section.

§ 2000aa–7. Definitions

(a) "Documentary materials", as used in this chapter, means materials upon which information is recorded, and includes, but is not limited to, written or printed materials, photographs, motion picture films, negatives, video tapes, audio tapes, and other mechanically, magentically or electronically recorded cards, tapes, or discs, but does not include contraband or the fruits of a crime or things otherwise criminally possessed, or property designed or intended for use, or which is or has been used as, the means of committing a criminal offense.

(b) "Work product materials", as used in this chapter, means materials, other than contraband or the fruits of a crime or things otherwise criminally possessed, or property designed or intended for use, or which is or has been used, as the means of committing a criminal offense, and—

(1) in anticipation of communicating such materials to the public, are prepared, produced, authored, or created, whether by the person in possession of the materials or by any other person;

(2) are possessed for the purposes of communicating such materials to the public; and

(3) include mental impressions, conclusions, opinions, or theories of the person who prepared, produced, authored, or created such material.

(c) "Any other governmental unit", as used in this chapter, includes the District of Columbia, the Commonwealth of Puerto Rico, any territory or possession of the United States, and any local government, unit of local government, or any unit of State government.

§ 2000aa–11. Guidelines for Federal officers and employees

(a) Procedures to obtain documentary evidence; protection of certain privacy interests

The Attorney General shall, within six months of October 13, 1980, issue guidelines for the procedures to be employed by any Federal officer or employee, in connection with the investigation or prosecution of an offense, to obtain documentary materials in the private possession of a person when the person is not reasonably believed to be a suspect in such offense or related by blood or marriage to such a suspect, and when the materials sought are not contraband or the fruits or instrumentalities of an offense. The Attorney General shall incorporate in such guidelines—

(1) a recognition of the personal privacy interests of the person in possession of such documentary materials;

(2) a requirement that the least intrusive method or means of obtaining such materials be used which do not substantially jeopardize the availability or usefulness of the materials sought to be obtained;

(3) a recognition of special concern for privacy interests in cases in which a search or seizure for such documents would intrude upon a known confidential relationship such as that which may exist between clergyman and parishioner; lawyer and client; or doctor and patient; and

(4) a requirement that an application for a warrant to conduct a search governed by this subchapter be approved by an attorney for the government, except that in an emergency situation the application may be approved by another appropriate supervisory official if within 24 hours of such emergency the appropriate United States Attorney is notified.

(b) Use of search warrants; reports to Congress

The Attorney General shall collect and compile information on, and report annually to the Committees on the Judiciary of the Senate and the House of Representatives on the use of search warrants by Federal officers and employees for documentary materials described in subsection (a)(3) of this section.

§ 2000aa–12. Binding nature of guidelines; disciplinary actions for violations; legal proceedings for non-compliance prohibited

Guidelines issued by the Attorney General under this subchapter shall have the full force and effect of Department of Justice regulations and any violation of these guidelines shall make the employee or officer involved subject to appropriate administrative disciplinary action. However, an issue relating to the compliance, or the failure to comply, with guidelines issued pursuant to this subchapter may not be litigated, and a court may not entertain such an issue as the basis for the suppression or exclusion of evidence.

[EDITOR'S NOTE: These guidelines appear in 28 C.F.R. Pt. 59. The procedural provisions are set out below.]

GUIDELINES

(28 C.F.R. § 59.4).

§ 59.4 Procedures.[1]

(a) Provisions governing the use of search warrants generally.

(1) A search warrant should not be used to obtain documentary materials believed to be in the private possession of a disinterested third party unless it appears that the use of a subpoena, summons, request, or other less intrusive alternative means of obtaining the materials would substantially jeopardize the availability or usefulness of the materials sought, and the application for the warrant has been authorized as provided in paragraph (a)(2) of this section.

---

[1] Notwithstanding the provisions of this section, any application for a warrant to search for evidence of a criminal tax offense under the jurisdiction of the Tax Division must be specifically approved in advance by the Tax Division pursuant to section 6–2.330 of the U.S. Attorneys' Manual.

(2) No federal officer or employee shall apply for a warrant to search for and seize documentary materials believed to be in the private possession of a disinterested third party unless the application for the warrant has been authorized by an attorney for the government. Provided, however, that in an emergency situation in which the immediacy of the need to seize the materials does not permit an opportunity to secure the authorization of an attorney for the government, the application may be authorized by a supervisory law enforcement officer in the applicant's department or agency, if the appropriate U.S. Attorney (or where the case is not being handled by a U.S. Attorney's Office, the appropriate supervisory official of the Department of Justice) is notified of the authorization and the basis for justifying such authorization under this part within 24 hours of the authorization.

(b) Provisions governing the use of search warrants which may intrude upon professional, confidential relationships.

(1) A search warrant should not be used to obtain documentary materials believed to be in the private possession of a disinterested third party physician,[2] lawyer, or clergyman, under circumstances in which the materials sought, or other materials likely to be reviewed during the execution of the warrant, contain confidential information on patients, clients, or parishioners which was furnished or developed for the purposes of professional counseling or treatment, unless—

(i) It appears that the use of a subpoena, summons, request or other less intrusive alternative means of obtaining the materials would substantially jeopardize the availability or usefulness of the materials sought;

(ii) Access to the documentary materials appears to be of substantial importance to the investigation or prosecution for which they are sought; and

(iii) The application for the warrant has been approved as provided in paragraph (b)(2) of this section.

(2) No federal officer or employee shall apply for a warrant to search for and seize documentary materials believed to be in the private possession of a disinterested third party physician, lawyer, or clergyman under the circumstances described in paragraph (b)(1) of this section, unless, upon the recommendation of the U.S. Attorney (or where a case is not being handled by a U.S. Attorney's Office, upon the recommendation of the appropriate supervisory official of the Department of Justice), an appropriate Deputy Assistant Attorney General has authorized the application for the warrant. Provided, however, that in an emergency situation in which the immediacy of the need to seize the materials does not permit an opportunity to secure the authorization of a Deputy Assistant Attorney General, the application may be authorized by the U.S. Attorney (or where the case is not being handled by a U.S. Attorney's Office, by the appropriate supervisory official of the Department of Justice) if an appropriate Deputy Assistant Attorney General is notified of the authorization and the basis for justifying such authorization under this part within 72 hours of the authorization.

---

2. Documentary materials created or compiled by a physician, but retained by the physician as a matter of practice at a hospital or clinic shall be deemed to be in the private possession of the physician, unless the clinic or hospital is a suspect in the offense.

(3) Whenever possible, a request for authorization by an appropriate Deputy Assistant Attorney General of a search warrant application pursuant to paragraph (b)(2) of this section shall be made in writing and shall include:

(i) The application for the warrant; and

(ii) A brief description of the facts and circumstances advanced as the basis for recommending authorization of the application under this part.

If a request for authorization of the application is made orally or if, in an emergency situation, the application is authorized by the U.S. Attorney or a supervisory official of the Department of Justice as provided in paragraph (b)(2) of this section, a written record of the request including the materials specified in paragraphs (b)(3)(i) and (ii) of this section shall be transmitted to an appropriate Deputy Assistant Attorney General within 7 days. The Deputy Assistant Attorneys General shall keep a record of the disposition of all requests for authorizations of search warrant applications made under paragraph (b) of this section.

(4) A search warrant authorized under paragraph (b)(2) of this section shall be executed in such a manner as to minimize, to the greatest extent practicable, scrutiny of confidential materials.

(5) Although it is impossible to define the full range of additional doctor-like therapeutic relationships which involve the furnishing or development of private information, the U.S. Attorney (or where a case is not being handled by a U.S. Attorney's Office, the appropriate supervisory official of the Department of Justice) should determine whether a search for documentary materials held by other disinterested third party professionals involved in such relationships (e.g. psychologists or psychiatric social workers or nurses) would implicate the special privacy concerns which are addressed in paragraph (b) of this section. If the U.S. Attorney (or other supervisory official of the Department of Justice) determines that such a search would require review of extremely confidential information furnished or developed for the purposes of professional counseling or treatment, the provisions of this subsection should be applied. Otherwise, at a minimum, the requirements of paragraph (a) of this section must be met.

(c) *Considerations bearing on choice of methods.* In determining whether, as an alternative to the use of a search warrant, the use of a subpoena or other less intrusive means of obtaining documentary materials would substantially jeopardize the availability or usefulness of the materials sought, the following factors, among others, should be considered:

(1) Whether it appears that the use of a subpoena or other alternative which gives advance notice of the government's interest in obtaining the materials would be likely to result in the destruction, alteration, concealment, or transfer of the materials sought; considerations, among others, bearing on this issue may include:

(i) Whether a suspect has access to the materials sought;

(ii) Whether there is a close relationship of friendship, loyalty, or sympathy between the possessor of the materials and a suspect;

(iii) Whether the possessor of the materials is under the domination or control of a suspect;

(iv) Whether the possessor of the materials has an interest in preventing the disclosure of the materials to the government;

(v) Whether the possessor's willingness to comply with a subpoena or request by the government would be likely to subject him to intimidation or threats of reprisal;

(vi) Whether the possessor of the materials has previously acted to obstruct a criminal investigation or judicial proceeding or refused to comply with or acted in defiance of court orders; or

(vii) Whether the possessor has expressed an intent to destroy, conceal, alter, or transfer the materials;

(2) The immediacy of the government's need to obtain the materials; considerations, among others, bearing on this issue may include:

(i) Whether the immediate seizure of the materials is necessary to prevent injury to persons or property;

(ii) Whether the prompt seizure of the materials is necessary to preserve their evidentiary value;

(iii) Whether delay in obtaining the materials would significantly jeopardize an ongoing investigation or prosecution; or

(iv) Whether a legally enforceable form of process, other than a search warrant, is reasonably available as a means of obtaining the materials.

The fact that the disinterested third party possessing the materials may have grounds to challenge a subpoena or other legal process is not in itself a legitimate basis for the use of a search warrant.

FOREIGN INTELLIGENCE SURVEILLANCE ACT

(50 U.S.C.A. § 1861).

§ 1861. Access to certain business records for foreign intelligence and international terrorism investigations

(a)(1) The Director of the Federal Bureau of Investigation or a designee of the Director (whose rank shall be no lower than Assistant Special Agent in Charge) may make an application for an order requiring the production of any tangible things (including books, records, papers, documents, and other items) for an investigation to obtain foreign intelligence information not concerning a United States person or to protect against international terrorism or clandestine intelligence activities, provided that such investigation of a United States person is not conducted solely upon the basis of activities protected by the first amendment to the Constitution.

(2) An investigation conducted under this section shall

(A) be conducted under guidelines approved by the Attorney General under Executive Order 12333 (or a successor order); and

(B) not be conducted of a United States person solely upon the basis of activities protected by the first amendment to the Constitution of the United States.

(b) Each application under this section

(1) shall be made to—

(A) a judge of the court established by section 1803(a) of this title; or

(B) a United States Magistrate Judge under chapter 43 of Title 28, who is publicly designated by the Chief Justice of the United States to have the power to hear applications and grant orders for the production of tangible things under this section on behalf of a judge of that court; and

(2) shall specify that the records concerned are sought for an authorized investigation conducted in accordance with subsection (a)(2) of this section to obtain foreign intelligence information not concerning a United States person or to protect against international terrorism or clandestine intelligence activities.

(c)(1) Upon an application made pursuant to this section, the judge shall enter an ex parte order as requested, or as modified, approving the release of records if the judge finds that the application meets the requirements of this section.

(2) An order under this subsection shall not disclose that it is issued for purposes of an investigation described in subsection (a).

(d) No person shall disclose to any other person (other than those persons necessary to produce the tangible things under this section) that the Federal Bureau of Investigation has sought or obtained tangible things under this section.

(e) A person who, in good faith, produces tangible things under an order pursuant to this section shall not be liable to any other person for such production. Such production shall not be deemed to constitute a waiver of any privilege in any other proceeding or context.

Appendix C

FEDERAL RULES OF CRIMINAL PROCEDURE FOR THE UNITED STATES DISTRICT COURTS

I. SCOPE, PURPOSE AND CONSTRUCTION

Rule 1. Scope; Definitions

(a) Scope.

(1) In General. These rules govern the procedure in all criminal proceedings in the United States district courts, the United States courts of appeals, and the Supreme Court of the United States.

(2) State or Local Judicial Officer. When a rule so states, it applies to a proceeding before a state or local judicial officer.

(3) Territorial Courts. These rules also govern the procedure in all criminal proceedings in the following courts:

(A) the district court of Guam;

(B) the district court for the Northern Mariana Islands, except as otherwise provided by law; and

(C) the district court of the Virgin Islands, except that the prosecution of offenses in that court must be by indictment or information as otherwise provided by law.

(4) Removed Proceedings. Although these rules govern all proceedings after removal from a state court, state law governs a dismissal by the prosecution.

(5) Excluded Proceedings. Proceedings not governed by these rules include:

(A) the extradition and rendition of a fugitive;

(B) a civil property forfeiture for violating a federal statute;

(C) the collection of a fine or penalty;

(D) a proceeding under a statute governing juvenile delinquency to the extent the procedure is inconsistent with the statute, unless Rule 20(d) provides otherwise;

(E) a dispute between seamen under 22 U.S.C. §§ 256–258; and

(F) a proceeding against a witness in a foreign country under 28 U.S.C. § 1784.

(b) Definitions. The following definitions apply to these rules:

(1) "Attorney for the government" means:

(A) the Attorney General or an authorized assistant;

(B) a United States attorney or an authorized assistant;

(C) when applicable to cases arising under Guam law, the Guam Attorney General or other person whom Guam law authorizes to act in the matter; and

(D) any other attorney authorized by law to conduct proceedings under these rules as a prosecutor.

(2) "Court" means a federal judge performing functions authorized by law.

(3) "Federal judge" means:

(A) a justice or judge of the United States as these terms are defined in 28 U.S.C. § 451;

(B) a magistrate judge; and

(C) a judge confirmed by the United States Senate and empowered by statute in any commonwealth, territory, or possession to perform a function to which a particular rule relates.

(4) "Judge" means a federal judge or a state or local judicial officer.

(5) "Magistrate judge" means a United States magistrate judge as defined in 28 U.S.C. §§ 631–639.

(6) "Oath" includes an affirmation.

(7) "Organization" is defined in 18 U.S.C. § 18.

(8) "Petty offense" is defined in 18 U.S.C. § 19.

(9) "State" includes the District of Columbia, and any commonwealth, territory, or possession of the United States.

(10) "State or local judicial officer" means:

(A) a state or local officer authorized to act under 18 U.S.C. § 3041; and

(B) a judicial officer empowered by statute in the District of Columbia or in any commonwealth, territory, or possession to perform a function to which a particular rule relates.

(c) **Authority of a Justice or Judge of the United States.** When these rules authorize a magistrate judge to act, any other federal judge may also act.

Rule 2. Interpretation

These rules are to be interpreted to provide for the just determination of every criminal proceeding, to secure simplicity in procedure and fairness in administration, and to eliminate unjustifiable expense and delay.

Rule 3. The Complaint

The complaint is a written statement of the essential facts constituting the offense charged. It must be made under oath before a magistrate judge or, if none is reasonably available, before a state or local judicial officer.

Rule 4. Arrest Warrant or Summons on a Complaint

(a) Issuance. If the complaint or one or more affidavits filed with the complaint establish probable cause to believe that an offense has been committed and that the defendant committed it, the judge must issue an arrest warrant to an officer authorized to execute it. At the request of an attorney for the government, the judge must issue a summons, instead of a warrant, to a person authorized to serve it. A judge may issue more than one warrant or summons on the same complaint. If a defendant fails to appear in response to a summons, a judge may, and upon request of an attorney for the government must, issue a warrant.

(b) Form.

    (1) Warrant. A warrant must:

        (A) contain the defendant's name or, if it is unknown, a name or description by which the defendant can be identified with reasonable certainty;

        (B) describe the offense charged in the complaint;

        (C) command that the defendant be arrested and brought without unnecessary delay before a magistrate judge or, if none is reasonably available, before a state or local judicial officer; and

        (D) be signed by a judge.

    (2) Summons. A summons must be in the same form as a warrant except that it must require the defendant to appear before a magistrate judge at a stated time and place.

(c) Execution or Service, and Return.

    (1) By Whom. Only a marshal or other authorized officer may execute a warrant. Any person authorized to serve a summons in a federal civil action may serve a summons.

    (2) Location. A warrant may be executed, or a summons served, within the jurisdiction of the United States or anywhere else a federal statute authorizes an arrest.

    (3) Manner.

        (A) A warrant is executed by arresting the defendant. Upon arrest, an officer possessing the warrant must show it to the defendant. If the officer does not possess the warrant, the officer must inform the defendant of the warrant's existence and of the offense charged and, at the defendant's request, must show the warrant to the defendant as soon as possible.

        (B) A summons is served on an individual defendant:

            (i) by delivering a copy to the defendant personally; or

            (ii) by leaving a copy at the defendant's residence or usual place of abode with a person of suitable age and discretion residing at that location and by mailing a copy to the defendant's last known address.

        (C) A summons is served on an organization by delivering a copy to an officer, to a managing or general agent, or to another agent appointed or legally authorized to receive service of process. A copy must also be mailed to the organization's last known address within the district or to its principal place of business elsewhere in the United States.

(4) Return.

(A) After executing a warrant, the officer must return it to the judge before whom the defendant is brought in accordance with Rule 5. At the request of an attorney for the government, an unexecuted warrant must be brought back to and canceled by a magistrate judge or, if none is reasonably available, by a state or local judicial officer.

(B) The person to whom a summons was delivered for service must return it on or before the return day.

(C) At the request of an attorney for the government, a judge may deliver an unexecuted warrant, an unserved summons, or a copy of the warrant or summons to the marshal or other authorized person for execution or service.

Rule 5. Initial Appearance

(a) In General.

(1) Appearance Upon an Arrest.

(A) A person making an arrest within the United States must take the defendant without unnecessary delay before a magistrate judge, or before a state or local judicial officer as Rule 5(c) provides, unless a statute provides otherwise.

(B) A person making an arrest outside the United States must take the defendant without unnecessary delay before a magistrate judge, unless a statute provides otherwise.

(2) Exceptions.

(A) An officer making an arrest under a warrant issued upon a complaint charging solely a violation of 18 U.S.C. § 1073 need not comply with this rule if:

(i) the person arrested is transferred without unnecessary delay to the custody of appropriate state or local authorities in the district of arrest; and

(ii) an attorney for the government moves promptly, in the district where the warrant was issued, to dismiss the complaint.

(B) If a defendant is arrested for violating probation or supervised release, Rule 32.1 applies.

(C) If a defendant is arrested for failing to appear in another district, Rule 40 applies.

(3) Appearance Upon a Summons. When a defendant appears in response to a summons under Rule 4, a magistrate judge must proceed under Rule 5(d) or (e), as applicable.

(b) Arrest Without a Warrant. If a defendant is arrested without a warrant, a complaint meeting Rule 4(a)'s requirement of probable cause must be promptly filed in the district where the offense was allegedly committed.

(c) Place of Initial Appearance; Transfer to Another District.

(1) Arrest in the District Where the Offense Was Allegedly Committed. If the defendant is arrested in the district where the offense was allegedly committed:

(A) the initial appearance must be in that district; and

(B) if a magistrate judge is not reasonably available, the initial appearance may be before a state or local judicial officer.

(2) Arrest in a District Other Than Where the Offense Was Allegedly Committed. If the defendant was arrested in a district other than where the offense was allegedly committed, the initial appearance must be:

(A) in the district of arrest; or

(B) in an adjacent district if:

(i) the appearance can occur more promptly there; or

(ii) the offense was allegedly committed there and the initial appearance will occur on the day of arrest.

(3) Procedures in a District Other Than Where the Offense Was Allegedly Committed. If the initial appearance occurs in a district other than where the offense was allegedly committed, the following procedures apply:

(A) the magistrate judge must inform the defendant about the provisions of Rule 20;

(B) if the defendant was arrested without a warrant, the district court where the offense was allegedly committed must first issue a warrant before the magistrate judge transfers the defendant to that district;

(C) the magistrate judge must conduct a preliminary hearing if required by Rule 5.1 or Rule 58(b)(2)(G);

(D) the magistrate judge must transfer the defendant to the district where the offense was allegedly committed if:

(i) the government produces the warrant, a certified copy of the warrant, a facsimile of either, or other appropriate form of either; and

(ii) the judge finds that the defendant is the same person named in the indictment, information, or warrant; and

(E) when a defendant is transferred and discharged, the clerk must promptly transmit the papers and any bail to the clerk in the district where the offense was allegedly committed.

(d) Procedure in a Felony Case.

(1) Advice. If the defendant is charged with a felony, the judge must inform the defendant of the following:

(A) the complaint against the defendant, and any affidavit filed with it;

(B) the defendant's right to retain counsel or to request that counsel be appointed if the defendant cannot obtain counsel;

(C) the circumstances, if any, under which the defendant may secure pretrial release;

(D) any right to a preliminary hearing; and

(E) the defendant's right not to make a statement, and that any statement made may be used against the defendant.

(2) Consulting with Counsel. The judge must allow the defendant reasonable opportunity to consult with counsel.

(3) Detention or Release. The judge must detain or release the defendant as provided by statute or these rules.

(4) Plea. A defendant may be asked to plead only under Rule 10.

(e) Procedure in a Misdemeanor Case. If the defendant is charged with a misdemeanor only, the judge must inform the defendant in accordance with Rule 58(b)(2).

(f) Video Teleconferencing. Video teleconferencing may be used to conduct an appearance under this rule if the defendant consents.

Rule 5.1. Preliminary Hearing

(A) In General. If a defendant is charged with an offense other than a petty offense, a magistrate judge must conduct a preliminary hearing unless:

(1) the defendant waives the hearing;

(2) the defendant is indicted;

(3) the government files an information under Rule 7(b) charging the defendant with a felony;

(4) the government files an information charging the defendant with a misdemeanor; or

(5) the defendant is charged with a misdemeanor and consents to trial before a magistrate judge.

(b) Selecting a District. A defendant arrested in a district other than where the offense was allegedly committed may elect to have the preliminary hearing conducted in the district where the prosecution is pending.

(c) Scheduling. The magistrate judge must hold the preliminary hearing within a reasonable time, but no later than 10 days after the initial appearance if the defendant is in custody and no later than 20 days if not in custody.

(d) Extending the Time. With the defendant's consent and upon a showing of good cause—taking into account the public interest in the prompt disposition of criminal cases—a magistrate judge may extend the time limits in Rule 5.1(c) one or more times. If the defendant does not consent, the magistrate judge may extend the time limits only on a showing that extraordinary circumstances exist and justice requires the delay.

(e) Hearing and Finding. At the preliminary hearing, the defendant may cross-examine adverse witnesses and may introduce evidence but may not object to evidence on the ground that it was unlawfully acquired. If the magistrate judge finds probable cause to believe an offense has been committed and the defendant committed it, the magistrate judge must promptly require the defendant to appear for further proceedings.

(f) Discharging the Defendant. If the magistrate judge finds no probable cause to believe an offense has been committed or the defendant committed it, the magistrate judge must dismiss the complaint and discharge the defendant. A discharge does not preclude the government from later prosecuting the defendant for the same offense.

(g) Recording the Proceedings. The preliminary hearing must be recorded by a court reporter or by a suitable recording device. A recording of the proceeding may be made available to any party upon request. A copy of the recording and a transcript may be provided to any party upon request and upon any payment required by applicable Judicial Conference regulations.

(h) Producing a Statement.

(1) In General. Rule 26.2(a)–(d) and (f) applies at any hearing under this rule, unless the magistrate judge for good cause rules otherwise in a particular case.

(2) Sanctions for Not Producing a Statement. If a party disobeys a Rule 26.2 order to deliver a statement to the moving party, the magistrate judge must not consider the testimony of a witness whose statement is withheld.

Rule 6. The Grand Jury

(a) Summoning a Grand Jury.

(1) In General. When the public interest so requires, the court must order that one or more grand juries be summoned. A grand jury must have 16 to 23 members, and the court must order that enough legally qualified persons be summoned to meet this requirement.

(2) Alternate Jurors. When a grand jury is selected, the court may also select alternate jurors. Alternate jurors must have the same qualifications and be selected in the same manner as any other juror. Alternate jurors replace jurors in the same sequence in which the alternates were selected. An alternate juror who replaces a juror is subject to the same challenges, takes the same oath, and has the same authority as the other jurors.

(b) Objection to the Grand Jury or to a Grand Juror.

(1) Challenges. Either the government or a defendant may challenge the grand jury on the ground that it was not lawfully drawn, summoned, or selected, and may challenge an individual juror on the ground that the juror is not legally qualified.

(2) Motion to Dismiss an Indictment. A party may move to dismiss the indictment based on an objection to the grand jury or on an individual juror's lack of legal qualification, unless the court has previously ruled on the same objection under Rule 6(b)(1). The motion to dismiss is governed by 28 U.S.C. § 1867(e). The court must not dismiss the indictment on the ground that a grand juror was not legally qualified if the record shows that at least 12 qualified jurors concurred in the indictment.

(c) Foreperson and Deputy Foreperson. The court will appoint one juror as the foreperson and another as the deputy foreperson. In the foreperson's absence, the deputy foreperson will act as the foreperson. The foreperson may administer oaths and affirmations and will sign all indictments. The foreperson—or another juror designated by the foreperson—will record the number of jurors concurring in every indictment and will file the record with the clerk, but the record may not be made public unless the court so orders.

(d) Who May Be Present.

(1) While the Grand Jury Is in Session. The following persons may be present while the grand jury is in session: attorneys for the government, the witness being questioned, interpreters when needed, and a court reporter or an operator of a recording device.

(2) During Deliberations and Voting. No person other than the jurors, and any interpreter needed to assist a hearing-impaired or speech-impaired juror, may be present while the grand jury is deliberating or voting.

(e) Recording and Disclosing the Proceedings.

(1) Recording the Proceedings. Except while the grand jury is deliberating or voting, all proceedings must be recorded by a court reporter or by a suitable recording device. But the validity of a prosecution is not affected by the unintentional failure to make a recording. Unless the court orders otherwise, an attorney for the government will retain control of the recording, the reporter's notes, and any transcript prepared from those notes.

(2) Secrecy.

(A) No obligation of secrecy may be imposed on any person except in accordance with Rule 6(e)(2)(B).

(B) Unless these rules provide otherwise, the following persons must not disclose a matter occurring before the grand jury:

(i) a grand juror;

(ii) an interpreter;

(iii) a court reporter;

(iv) an operator of a recording device;

(v) a person who transcribes recorded testimony;

(vi) an attorney for the government; or

(vii) a person to whom disclosure is made under Rule 6(e)(3)(A)(ii) or (iii).

(3) Exceptions.

(A) Disclosure of a grand-jury matter—other than the grand jury's deliberations or any grand juror's vote—may be made to:

(i) an attorney for the government for use in performing that attorney's duty;

(ii) any government personnel—including those of a state, state subdivision, Indian tribe, or foreign government—that an attorney for the government considers necessary to assist in performing that attorney's duty to enforce federal criminal law; or

(iii) a person authorized by 18 U.S.C. § 3322.

(B) A person to whom information is disclosed under Rule 6(e)(3)(A)(ii) may use that information only to assist an attorney for the government in performing that attorney's duty to enforce federal criminal law. An attorney for the government must promptly provide the court that impaneled the grand jury with the names of all persons to whom a disclosure has been made, and must certify that the attorney has advised those persons of their obligation of secrecy under this rule.

(C) An attorney for the government may disclose any grand-jury matter to another federal grand jury.

(D) An attorney for the government may disclose any grand-jury matter involving foreign intelligence, counterintelligence (as defined in 50 U.S.C. § 401a), or foreign intelligence information (as defined in Rule 6(e)(3)(D)(iii)) to any federal law enforcement, intelligence, protective, immigration, national defense, or national security official to assist the official receiving the information in the performance of that official's duties. An attorney for the government may also disclose any grand jury matter involving, within the United States or elsewhere, a threat of attack or other grave hostile acts of a foreign power or its agent, a threat of domestic or international sabotage or terrorism, or clandestine intelligence gathering activities by an intelligence service or network of a foreign power or by its agent, to any appropriate Federal, State, State subdivision, Indian tribal, or foreign government official, for the purpose of preventing or responding to such threat or activities.

(i) Any official who receives information under Rule 6(e)(3)(D) may use the information only as necessary in the conduct of that person's official duties subject to any limitations on the unauthorized disclosure of such information. Any State, State subdivision, Indian tribal, or foreign government official who receives information under Rule 6(e)(3)(D) may use the information only consistent with such guidelines as the Attorney General and the Director of National Intelligence shall jointly issue.

(ii) Within a reasonable time after disclosure is made under Rule 6(e)(3)(D), an attorney for the government must file, under seal, a notice with the court in the district where the grand jury convened stating that such information was disclosed and the departments, agencies, or entities to which the disclosure was made.

(iii) As used in Rule 6(e)(3)(D), the term "foreign intelligence information" means:

(a) information, whether or not it concerns a United States person, that relates to the ability of the United States to protect against—

- actual or potential attack or other grave hostile acts of a foreign power or its agent;

- sabotage or international terrorism by a foreign power or its agent; or

- clandestine intelligence activities by an intelligence service or network of a foreign power or by its agent; or

(b) information, whether or not it concerns a United States person, with respect to a foreign power or foreign territory that relates to—

- the national defense or the security of the United States; or

- the conduct of the foreign affairs of the United States.

(E) The court may authorize disclosure—at a time, in a manner, and subject to any other conditions that it directs—of a grand-jury matter:

(i) preliminarily to or in connection with a judicial proceeding;

(ii) at the request of a defendant who shows that a ground may exist to dismiss the indictment because of a matter that occurred before the grand jury;

(iii) at the request of the government, when sought by a foreign court or prosecutor for use in an official criminal investigation;

(iv) at the request of the government if it shows that the matter may disclose a violation of State, Indian tribal, or foreign criminal law, as long as the disclosure is to an appropriate state, state-subdivision, Indian tribal, or foreign government official for the purpose of enforcing that law; or

(v) at the request of the government if it shows that the matter may disclose a violation of military criminal law under the Uniform Code of Military Justice, as long as the disclosure is to an appropriate military official for the purpose of enforcing that law.

(F) A petition to disclose a grand-jury matter under Rule 6(e)(3)(E)(i) must be filed in the district where the grand jury convened. Unless the hearing is ex parte—as it may be when the government is the petitioner—the petitioner must serve the petition on, and the court must afford a reasonable opportunity to appear and be heard to:

    (i) an attorney for the government;

    (ii) the parties to the judicial proceeding; and

    (iii) any other person whom the court may designate.

(G) If the petition to disclose arises out of a judicial proceeding in another district, the petitioned court must transfer the petition to the other court unless the petitioned court can reasonably determine whether disclosure is proper. If the petitioned court decides to transfer, it must send to the transferee court the material sought to be disclosed, if feasible, and a written evaluation of the need for continued grand-jury secrecy. The transferee court must afford those persons identified in Rule 6(e)(3)(F) a reasonable opportunity to appear and be heard.

(4) Sealed Indictment. The magistrate judge to whom an indictment is returned may direct that the indictment be kept secret until the defendant is in custody or has been released pending trial. The clerk must then seal the indictment, and no person may disclose the indictment's existence except as necessary to issue or execute a warrant or summons.

(5) Closed Hearing. Subject to any right to an open hearing in a contempt proceeding, the court must close any hearing to the extent necessary to prevent disclosure of a matter occurring before a grand jury.

(6) Sealed Records. Records, orders, and subpoenas relating to grand-jury proceedings must be kept under seal to the extent and as long as necessary to prevent the unauthorized disclosure of a matter occurring before a grand jury.

(7) Contempt. A knowing violation of Rule 6, or of guidelines jointly issued by the Attorney General and the Director of National Intelligence pursuant to Rule 6, may be punished as a contempt of court.

(f) Indictment and Return. A grand jury may indict only if at least 12 jurors concur. The grand jury—or its foreperson or deputy foreperson—must return the indictment to a magistrate judge in open court. If a complaint or information is pending against the defendant and 12 jurors do not concur in the indictment, the foreperson must promptly and in writing report the lack of concurrence to the magistrate judge.

(g) Discharging the Grand Jury. A grand jury must serve until the court discharges it, but it may serve more than 18 months only if the court, having determined that an extension is in the public interest, extends the grand jury's service. An extension may be granted for no more than 6 months, except as otherwise provided by statute.

(h) Excusing a Juror. At any time, for good cause, the court may excuse a juror either temporarily or permanently, and if permanently, the court may impanel an alternate juror in place of the excused juror.

(i) "Indian Tribe" Defined. "Indian tribe" means an Indian tribe recognized by the Secretary of the Interior on a list published in the Federal Register under 25 U.S.C. § 479a–1.

Rule 7. The Indictment and the Information

(a) When Used.

(1) **Felony.** An offense (other than criminal contempt) must be prosecuted by an indictment if it is punishable:

(A) by death; or

(B) by imprisonment for more than one year.

(2) **Misdemeanor.** An offense punishable by imprisonment for one year or less may be prosecuted in accordance with Rule 58(b)(1).

(b) Waiving Indictment. An offense punishable by imprisonment for more than one year may be prosecuted by information if the defendant—in open court and after being advised of the nature of the charge and of the defendant's rights—waives prosecution by indictment.

(c) Nature and Contents.

(1) **In General.** The indictment or information must be a plain, concise, and definite written statement of the essential facts constituting the offense charged and must be signed by an attorney for the government. It need not contain a formal introduction or conclusion. A count may incorporate by reference an allegation made in another count. A count may allege that the means by which the defendant committed the offense are unknown or that the defendant committed it by one or more specified means. For each count, the indictment or information must give the official or customary citation of the statute, rule, regulation, or other provision of law that the defendant is alleged to have violated. For purposes of an indictment referred to in section 3282 of title 18, United States Code, for which the identity of the defendant is unknown, it shall be sufficient for the indictment to describe the defendant as an individual whose name is unknown, but who has a particular DNA profile, as that term is defined in that section 3282.

(2) **Criminal Forfeiture.** No judgment of forfeiture may be entered in a criminal proceeding unless the indictment or the information provides notice that the defendant has an interest in property that is subject to forfeiture in accordance with the applicable statute.

(3) **Citation Error.** Unless the defendant was misled and thereby prejudiced, neither an error in a citation nor a citation's omission is a ground to dismiss the indictment or information or to reverse a conviction.

(d) Surplusage. Upon the defendant's motion, the court may strike surplusage from the indictment or information.

(e) Amending an Information. Unless an additional or different offense is charged or a substantial right of the defendant is prejudiced, the court may permit an information to be amended at any time before the verdict or finding.

(f) Bill of Particulars. The court may direct the government to file a bill of particulars. The defendant may move for a bill of particulars before or within 10 days after arraignment or at a later time if the court permits. The government may amend a bill of particulars subject to such conditions as justice requires.

Rule 8. Joinder of Offenses or Defendants

(a) Joinder of Offenses. The indictment or information may charge a defendant in separate counts with 2 or more offenses if the offenses charged—whether felonies or misdemeanors or both—are of the same or similar character, or are based on the same act or transaction, or are connected with or constitute parts of a common scheme or plan.

(b) Joinder of Defendants. The indictment or information may charge 2 or more defendants if they are alleged to have participated in the same act or transaction, or in the same series of acts or transactions, constituting an offense or offenses. The defendants may be charged in one or more counts together or separately. All defendants need not be charged in each count.

Rule 9. Arrest Warrant or Summons on an Indictment or Information

(a) Issuance. The court must issue a warrant—or at the government's request, a summons—for each defendant named in an indictment or named in an information if one or more affidavits accompanying the information establish probable cause to believe that an offense has been committed and that the defendant committed it. The court may issue more than one warrant or summons for the same defendant. If a defendant fails to appear in response to a summons, the court may, and upon request of an attorney for the government must, issue a warrant. The court must issue the arrest warrant to an officer authorized to execute it or the summons to a person authorized to serve it.

(b) Form.

(1) Warrant. The warrant must conform to Rule 4(b)(1) except that it must be signed by the clerk and must describe the offense charged in the indictment or information.

(2) Summons. The summons must be in the same form as a warrant except that it must require the defendant to appear before the court at a stated time and place.

(c) Execution or Service; Return; Initial Appearance.

(1) Execution or Service.

(A) The warrant must be executed or the summons served as provided in Rule 4(c)(1), (2), and (3).

(B) The officer executing the warrant must proceed in accordance with Rule 5(a)(1).

(2) Return. A warrant or summons must be returned in accordance with Rule 4(c)(4).

(3) Initial Appearance. When an arrested or summoned defendant first appears before the court, the judge must proceed under Rule 5.

Rule 10. Arraignment

(a) In General. An arraignment must be conducted in open court and must consist of:

(1) ensuring that the defendant has a copy of the indictment or information;

(2) reading the indictment or information to the defendant or stating to the defendant the substance of the charge; and then

(3) asking the defendant to plead to the indictment or information.

(b) Waiving Appearance. A defendant need not be present for the arraignment if:

(1) the defendant has been charged by indictment or misdemeanor information;

(2) the defendant, in a written waiver signed by both the defendant and defense counsel, has waived appearance and has affirmed that the defendant received a copy of the indictment or information and that the plea is not guilty; and

(3) the court accepts the waiver.

(c) Video Teleconferencing. Video teleconferencing may be used to arraign a defendant if the defendant consents.

Rule 11. Pleas

(a) Entering a Plea.

(1) In General. A defendant may plead not guilty, guilty, or (with the court's consent) nolo contendere.

(2) Conditional Plea. With the consent of the court and the government, a defendant may enter a conditional plea of guilty or nolo contendere, reserving in writing the right to have an appellate court review an adverse determination of a specified pretrial motion. A defendant who prevails on appeal may then withdraw the plea.

(3) Nolo Contendere Plea. Before accepting a plea of nolo contendere, the court must consider the parties' views and the public interest in the effective administration of justice.

(4) Failure to Enter a Plea. If a defendant refuses to enter a plea or if a defendant organization fails to appear, the court must enter a plea of not guilty.

(b) Considering and Accepting a Guilty or Nolo Contendere Plea.

(1) Advising and Questioning the Defendant. Before the court accepts a plea of guilty or nolo contendere, the defendant may be placed under oath, and the court must address the defendant personally in open court. During this address, the court must inform the defendant of, and determine that the defendant understands, the following:

(A) the government's right, in a prosecution for perjury or false statement, to use against the defendant any statement that the defendant gives under oath;

(B) the right to plead not guilty, or having already so pleaded, to persist in that plea;

(C) the right to a jury trial;

(D) the right to be represented by counsel—and if necessary have the court appoint counsel—at trial and at every other stage of the proceeding;

(E) the right at trial to confront and cross-examine adverse witnesses, to be protected from compelled self-incrimination, to testify and present evidence, and to compel the attendance of witnesses;

(F) the defendant's waiver of these trial rights if the court accepts a plea of guilty or nolo contendere;

(G) the nature of each charge to which the defendant is pleading;

(H) any maximum possible penalty, including imprisonment, fine, and term of supervised release;

(I) any mandatory minimum penalty;

(J) any applicable forfeiture;

(K) the court's authority to order restitution;

(L) the court's obligation to impose a special assessment;

(M) the court's obligation to apply the Sentencing Guidelines, and the court's discretion to depart from those guidelines under some circumstances; and

(N) the terms of any plea-agreement provision waiving the right to appeal or to collaterally attack the sentence.

(2) Ensuring That a Plea Is Voluntary. Before accepting a plea of guilty or nolo contendere, the court must address the defendant personally in open court and determine that the plea is voluntary and did not result from force, threats, or promises (other than promises in a plea agreement).

(3) Determining the Factual Basis for a Plea. Before entering judgment on a guilty plea, the court must determine that there is a factual basis for the plea.

(c) Plea Agreement Procedure.

(1) In General. An attorney for the government and the defendant's attorney, or the defendant when proceeding pro se, may discuss and reach a plea agreement. The court must not participate in these discussions. If the defendant pleads guilty or nolo contendere to either a charged offense or a lesser or related offense, the plea agreement may specify that an attorney for the government will:

(A) not bring, or will move to dismiss, other charges;

(B) recommend, or agree not to oppose the defendant's request, that a particular sentence or sentencing range is appropriate or that a particular provision of the Sentencing Guidelines, or policy statement, or sentencing factor does or does not apply (such a recommendation or request does not bind the court); or

(C) agree that a specific sentence or sentencing range is the appropriate disposition of the case, or that a particular provision of the Sentencing Guidelines, or policy statement, or sentencing factor does or does not apply (such a recommendation or request binds the court once the court accepts the plea agreement).

(2) Disclosing a Plea Agreement. The parties must disclose the plea agreement in open court when the plea is offered, unless the court for good cause allows the parties to disclose the plea agreement in camera.

(3) Judicial Consideration of a Plea Agreement.

(A) To the extent the plea agreement is of the type specified in Rule 11(c)(1)(A) or (C), the court may accept the agreement, reject it, or defer a decision until the court has reviewed the presentence report.

(B) To the extent the plea agreement is of the type specified in Rule 11(c)(1)(B), the court must advise the defendant that the defendant has no right to withdraw the plea if the court does not follow the recommendation or request.

(4) Accepting a Plea Agreement. If the court accepts the plea agreement, it must inform the defendant that to the extent the plea agreement is of the type specified in Rule 11(c)(1)(A) or (C), the agreed disposition will be included in the judgment.

(5) Rejecting a Plea Agreement. If the court rejects a plea agreement containing provisions of the type specified in Rule 11(c)(1)(A) or (C), the court must do the following on the record and in open court (or, for good cause, in camera):

(A) inform the parties that the court rejects the plea agreement;

(B) advise the defendant personally that the court is not required to follow the plea agreement and give the defendant an opportunity to withdraw the plea; and

(C) advise the defendant personally that if the plea is not withdrawn, the court may dispose of the case less favorably toward the defendant than the plea agreement contemplated.

(d) Withdrawing a Guilty or Nolo Contendere Plea. A defendant may withdraw a plea of guilty or nolo contendere:

(1) before the court accepts the plea, for any reason or no reason; or

(2) after the court accepts the plea, but before it imposes sentence if:

(A) the court rejects a plea agreement under Rule 11(c)(5); or

(B) the defendant can show a fair and just reason for requesting the withdrawal.

(e) Finality of a Guilty or Nolo Contendere Plea. After the court imposes sentence, the defendant may not withdraw a plea of guilty or nolo contendere, and the plea may be set aside only on direct appeal or collateral attack.

(f) Admissibility or Inadmissibility of a Plea, Plea Discussions, and Related Statements. The admissibility or inadmissibility of a plea, a plea discussion, and any related statement is governed by Federal Rule of Evidence 410.

(g) Recording the Proceedings. The proceedings during which the defendant enters a plea must be recorded by a court reporter or by a suitable recording device. If there is a guilty plea or a nolo contendere plea, the record must include the inquiries and advice to the defendant required under Rule 11(b) and (c).

(h) Harmless Error. A variance from the requirements of this rule is harmless error if it does not affect substantial rights.

Rule 12. Pleadings and Pretrial Motions

(A) Pleadings. The pleadings in a criminal proceeding are the indictment, the information, and the pleas of not guilty, guilty, and nolo contendere.

(b) Pretrial Motions.

(1) **In General.** Rule 47 applies to a pretrial motion.

(2) **Motions That May Be Made Before Trial.** A party may raise by pretrial motion any defense, objection, or request that the court can determine without a trial of the general issue.

(3) **Motions That Must Be Made Before Trial.** The following must be raised before trial:

(A) a motion alleging a defect in instituting the prosecution;

(B) a motion alleging a defect in the indictment or information—but at any time while the case is pending, the court may hear a claim that the indictment or information fails to invoke the court's jurisdiction or to state an offense;

(C) a motion to suppress evidence;

(D) a Rule 14 motion to sever charges or defendants; and

(E) a Rule 16 motion for discovery.

(4) Notice of the Government's Intent to Use Evidence.

(A) At the Government's Discretion. At the arraignment or as soon afterward as practicable, the government may notify the defendant of its intent to use specified evidence at trial in order to afford the defendant an opportunity to object before trial under Rule 12(b)(3)(C).

(B) At the Defendant's Request. At the arraignment or as soon afterward as practicable, the defendant may, in order to have an opportunity to move to suppress evidence under Rule 12(b)(3)(C), request notice of the government's intent to use (in its evidence-in-chief at trial) any evidence that the defendant may be entitled to discover under Rule 16.

(c) Motion Deadline. The court may, at the arraignment or as soon afterward as practicable, set a deadline for the parties to make pretrial motions and may also schedule a motion hearing.

(d) Ruling on a Motion. The court must decide every pretrial motion before trial unless it finds good cause to defer a ruling. The court must not defer ruling on a pretrial motion if the deferral will adversely affect a party's right to appeal. When factual issues are involved in deciding a motion, the court must state its essential findings on the record.

(e) Waiver of a Defense, Objection, or Request. A party waives any Rule 12(b)(3) defense, objection, or request not raised by the deadline the court sets under Rule 12(c) or by any extension the court provides. For good cause, the court may grant relief from the waiver.

(f) Recording the Proceedings. All proceedings at a motion hearing, including any findings of fact and conclusions of law made orally by the court, must be recorded by a court reporter or a suitable recording device.

(g) Defendant's Continued Custody or Release Status. If the court grants a motion to dismiss based on a defect in instituting the prosecution, in the indictment, or in the information, it may order the defendant to be released or detained under 18 U.S.C. § 3142 for a specified time until a new indictment or information is filed. This rule does not affect any federal statutory period of limitations.

(h) Producing Statements at a Suppression Hearing. Rule 26.2 applies at a suppression hearing under Rule 12(b)(3)(C). At a suppression hearing, a law enforcement officer is considered a government witness.

Rule 12.1. Notice of an Alibi Defense

(a) Government's Request for Notice and Defendant's Response.

(1) Government's Request. An attorney for the government may request in writing that the defendant notify an attorney for the government of any intended alibi defense. The request must state the time, date, and place of the alleged offense.

(2) Defendant's Response. Within 10 days after the request, or at some other time the court sets, the defendant must serve written notice on an attorney for the government of any intended alibi defense. The defendant's notice must state:

(A) each specific place where the defendant claims to have been at the time of the alleged offense; and

(B) the name, address, and telephone number of each alibi witness on whom the defendant intends to rely.

(b) Disclosing Government Witnesses.

(1) Disclosure. If the defendant serves a Rule 12.1(a)(2) notice, an attorney for the government must disclose in writing to the defendant or the defendant's attorney:

(A) the name, address, and telephone number of each witness the government intends to rely on to establish the defendant's presence at the scene of the alleged offense; and

(B) each government rebuttal witness to the defendant's alibi defense.

(2) Time to Disclose. Unless the court directs otherwise, an attorney for the government must give its Rule 12.1(b)(1) disclosure within 10 days after the defendant serves notice of an intended alibi defense under Rule 12.1(a)(2), but no later than 10 days before trial.

(c) Continuing Duty to Disclose. Both an attorney for the government and the defendant must promptly disclose in writing to the other party the name, address, and telephone number of each additional witness if:

(1) the disclosing party learns of the witness before or during trial; and

(2) the witness should have been disclosed under Rule 12.1(a) or (b) if the disclosing party had known of the witness earlier.

(d) Exceptions. For good cause, the court may grant an exception to any requirement of Rule 12.1(a)–(c).

(e) Failure to Comply. If a party fails to comply with this rule, the court may exclude the testimony of any undisclosed witness regarding the defendant's alibi. This rule does not limit the defendant's right to testify.

(f) Inadmissibility of Withdrawn Intention. Evidence of an intention to rely on an alibi defense, later withdrawn, or of a statement made in connection with that intention, is not, in any civil or criminal proceeding, admissible against the person who gave notice of the intention.

Rule 12.2. Notice of an Insanity Defense; Mental Examination

(a) Notice of an Insanity Defense. A defendant who intends to assert a defense of insanity at the time of the alleged offense must so notify an attorney for the government in writing within the time provided for filing a pretrial motion, or at any later time the court sets, and file a copy of the notice with the clerk. A defendant who fails to do so cannot rely on an insanity defense. The court may, for good cause, allow the defendant to file the notice late, grant additional trial-preparation time, or make other appropriate orders.

(b) Notice of Expert Evidence of a Mental Condition. If a defendant intends to introduce expert evidence relating to a mental disease or defect or any other mental condition of the defendant bearing on either (1) the issue of guilt or **(2)** the issue of punishment in a capital case, the defendant must—within the time provided for filing a pretrial motion or at any later time the court sets—notify an attorney for the government in writing of this intention and file a copy of the notice with the clerk. The court may, for good cause, allow the defendant to file the notice late, grant the parties additional trial-preparation time, or make other appropriate orders.

(c) Mental Examination.

(1) Authority to Order an Examination; Procedures.

(A) The court may order the defendant to submit to a competency examination under 18 U.S.C. § 4241.

(B) If the defendant provides notice under Rule 12.2(a), the court must, upon the government's motion, order the defendant to be examined under 18 U.S.C. § 4242. If the defendant provides notice under Rule 12.2(b) the court may, upon the government's motion, order the defendant to be examined under procedures ordered by the court.

(2) Disclosing Results and Reports of Capital Sentencing Examination. The results and reports of any examination conducted solely under Rule 12.2(c)(1) after notice under Rule 12.2(b)(2) must be sealed and must not be disclosed to any attorney for the government or the defendant unless the defendant is found guilty of one or more capital crimes and the defendant confirms an intent to offer during sentencing proceedings expert evidence on mental condition.

(3) Disclosing Results and Reports of the Defendant's Expert Examination. After disclosure under Rule 12.2(c)(2) of the results and reports of the government's examination, the defendant must disclose to the government the results and reports of any examination on mental condition conducted by the defendant's expert about which the defendant intends to introduce expert evidence.

(4) Inadmissibility of a Defendant's Statements. No statement made by a defendant in the course of any examination conducted under this rule (whether conducted with or without the defendant's consent), no testimony by the expert based on the statement, and no other fruits of the statement may be admitted into evidence against the defendant in any criminal proceeding except on an issue regarding mental condition on which the defendant:

(A) has introduced evidence of incompetency or evidence requiring notice under Rule 12.2(a) or (b)(1), or

(B) has introduced expert evidence in a capital sentencing proceeding requiring notice under Rule 12.2(b)(2).

(d) Failure to Comply. If the defendant fails to give notice under Rule 12.2(b) or does not submit to an examination when ordered under Rule 12.2(c), the court may exclude any expert evidence from the defendant on the issue of the defendant's mental disease, mental defect, or any other mental condition bearing on the defendant's guilt or the issue of punishment in a capital case.

(e) Inadmissibility of Withdrawn Intention. Evidence of an intention as to which notice was given under Rule 12.2(a) or (b), later withdrawn, is not, in any civil or criminal proceeding, admissible against the person who gave notice of the intention.

Rule 12.3. Notice of a Public–Authority Defense

(a) Notice of the Defense and Disclosure of Witnesses.

(1) Notice in General. If a defendant intends to assert a defense of actual or believed exercise of public authority on behalf of a law enforcement agency or federal intelligence agency at the time of the alleged offense, the defendant must so notify an attorney for the government in writing and must file a copy of the notice with the clerk within the time provided for filing a pretrial motion, or at any later time the court sets. The notice filed with the clerk must be under seal if the notice identifies a federal intelligence agency as the source of public authority.

(2) Contents of Notice. The notice must contain the following information:

(A) the law enforcement agency or federal intelligence agency involved;

(B) the agency member on whose behalf the defendant claims to have acted; and

(C) the time during which the defendant claims to have acted with public authority.

(3) Response to the Notice. An attorney for the government must serve a written response on the defendant or the defendant's attorney within 10 days after receiving the defendant's notice, but no later than 20 days before trial. The response must admit or deny that the defendant exercised the public authority identified in the defendant's notice.

(4) Disclosing Witnesses.

(A) Government's Request. An attorney for the government may request in writing that the defendant disclose the name, address, and telephone number of each witness the defendant intends to rely on to establish a public-authority defense. An attorney for the government may serve the request when the government serves its response to the defendant's notice under Rule 12.3(a)(3), or later, but must serve the request no later than 20 days before trial.

(B) Defendant's Response. Within 7 days after receiving the government's request, the defendant must serve on an attorney for the government a written statement of the name, address, and telephone number of each witness.

(C) Government's Reply. Within 7 days after receiving the defendant's statement, an attorney for the government must serve on the defendant or the defendant's attorney a written statement of the name, address, and telephone number of each witness the government intends to rely on to oppose the defendant's public-authority defense.

(5) Additional Time. The court may, for good cause, allow a party additional time to comply with this rule.

(b) Continuing Duty to Disclose. Both an attorney for the government and the defendant must promptly disclose in writing to the other party the name, address, and telephone number of any additional witness if:

(1) the disclosing party learns of the witness before or during trial; and

(2) the witness should have been disclosed under Rule 12.3(a)(4) if the disclosing party had known of the witness earlier.

(c) Failure to Comply. If a party fails to comply with this rule, the court may exclude the testimony of any undisclosed witness regarding the public-authority defense. This rule does not limit the defendant's right to testify.

(d) Protective Procedures Unaffected. This rule does not limit the court's authority to issue appropriate protective orders or to order that any filings be under seal.

(e) Inadmissibility of Withdrawn Intention. Evidence of an intention as to which notice was given under Rule 12.3(a), later withdrawn, is not, in any civil or criminal proceeding, admissible against the person who gave notice of the intention.

Rule 15. Depositions

(a) When Taken.

(1) In General. A party may move that a prospective witness be deposed in order to preserve testimony for trial. The court may grant the motion because of exceptional circumstances and in the interest of justice. If the court orders the deposition to be taken, it may also require the deponent to produce at the deposition any designated material that is not privileged, including any book, paper, document, record, recording, or data.

(2) Detained Material Witness. witness who is detained under 18 U.S.C. § 3144 may request to be deposed by filing a written motion and giving notice to the parties. The court may then order that the deposition be taken and may discharge the witness after the witness has signed under oath the deposition transcript.

(b) Notice.

(1) In General. A party seeking to take a deposition must give every other party reasonable written notice of the deposition's date and location. The notice must state the name and address of each deponent. If requested by a party receiving the notice, the court may, for good cause, change the deposition's date or location.

(2) To the Custodial Officer. party seeking to take the deposition must also notify the officer who has custody of the defendant of the scheduled date and location.

(c) Defendant's Presence.

(1) Defendant in Custody. The officer who has custody of the defendant must produce the defendant at the deposition and keep the defendant in the witness's presence during the examination, unless the defendant:

(A) waives in writing the right to be present; or

(B) persists in disruptive conduct justifying exclusion after being warned by the court that disruptive conduct will result in the defendant's exclusion.

(2) Defendant Not in Custody. A defendant who is not in custody has the right upon request to be present at the deposition, subject to any conditions imposed by the court. If the government tenders the defendant's expenses as provided in Rule 15(d) but the defendant still fails to appear, the defendant—absent good cause—waives both the right to appear and any objection to the taking and use of the deposition based on that right.

(d) Expenses. If the deposition was requested by the government, the court may—or if the defendant is unable to bear the deposition expenses, the court must—order the government to pay:

(1) any reasonable travel and subsistence expenses of the defendant and the defendant's attorney to attend the deposition; and

(2) the costs of the deposition transcript.

(e) Manner of Taking. Unless these rules or a court order provides otherwise, a deposition must be taken and filed in the same manner as a deposition in a civil action, except that:

(1) A defendant may not be deposed without that defendant's consent.

(2) The scope and manner of the deposition examination and cross-examination must be the same as would be allowed during trial.

(3) The government must provide to the defendant or the defendant's attorney, for use at the deposition, any statement of the deponent in the government's possession to which the defendant would be entitled at trial.

(f) Use as Evidence. A party may use all or part of a deposition as provided by the Federal Rules of Evidence.

(g) Objections. A party objecting to deposition testimony or evidence must state the grounds for the objection during the deposition.

(h) Depositions by Agreement Permitted. The parties may by agreement take and use a deposition with the court's consent.

Rule 16. Discovery and Inspection

(a) Government's Disclosure.

(1) Information Subject to Disclosure.

(A) Defendant's Oral Statement. Upon a defendant's request, the government must disclose to the defendant the substance of any relevant oral statement made by the defendant, before or after arrest, in response to interrogation by a person the defendant knew was a government agent if the government intends to use the statement at trial.

(B) Defendant's Written or Recorded Statement. Upon a defendant's request, the government must disclose to the defendant, and make available for inspection, copying, or photographing, all of the following:

(i) any relevant written or recorded statement by the defendant if:

• the statement is within the government's possession, custody, or control; and

• the attorney for the government knows—or through due diligence could know—that the statement exists;

(ii) the portion of any written record containing the substance of any relevant oral statement made before or after arrest if the defendant made the statement in response to interrogation by a person the defendant knew was a government agent; and

(iii) the defendant's recorded testimony before a grand jury relating to the charged offense.

(C) Organizational Defendant. Upon a defendant's request, if the defendant is an organization, the government must disclose to the defendant any statement described in Rule 16(a)(1)(A) and (B) if the government contends that the person making the statement:

(i) was legally able to bind the defendant regarding the subject of the statement because of that person's position as the defendant's director, officer, employee, or agent; or

(ii) was personally involved in the alleged conduct constituting the offense and was legally able to bind the defendant regarding that conduct because of that person's position as the defendant's director, officer, employee, or agent.

(D) Defendant's Prior Record. Upon a defendant's request, the government must furnish the defendant with a copy of the defendant's prior criminal record that is within the government's possession, custody, or control if the attorney for the government knows—or through due diligence could know—that the record exists.

(E) Documents and Objects. Upon a defendant's request, the government must permit the defendant to inspect and to copy or photograph books, papers, documents, data, photographs, tangible objects, buildings or places, or copies or portions of any of these items, if the item is within the government's possession, custody, or control and:

(i) the item is material to preparing the defense;

(ii) the government intends to use the item in its case-in-chief at trial; or

(iii) the item was obtained from or belongs to the defendant.

(F) Reports of Examinations and Tests. Upon a defendant's request, the government must permit a defendant to inspect and to copy or photograph the results or reports of any physical or mental examination and of any scientific test or experiment if:

(i) the item is within the government's possession, custody, or control;

(ii) the attorney for the government knows—or through due diligence could know—that the item exists; and

(iii) the item is material to preparing the defense or the government intends to use the item in its case-in-chief at trial.

(G) Expert witnesses.—At the defendant's request, the government must give to the defendant a written summary of any testimony that the government intends to use under Rules 702, 703, or 705 of the Federal Rules of Evidence during its case-in-chief at trial. If the government requests discovery under subdivision (b)(1)(C)(ii) and the defendant complies, the government must, at the defendant's request, give to the defendant a written summary of testimony that the government intends to use under Rules 702, 703, or 705 of the Federal Rules of Evidence as evidence at trial on the issue of the defendant's mental condition. The summary provided under this subparagraph must describe the witness's opinions, the bases and reasons for those opinions, and the witness's qualifications.

(2) Information Not Subject to Disclosure. Except as Rule 16(a)(1) provides otherwise, this rule does not authorize the discovery or inspection of reports, memoranda, or other internal government documents made by an attorney for the government or other government agent in connection with investigating or prosecuting the case. Nor does this rule authorize the discovery or inspection of statements made by prospective government witnesses except as provided in 18 U.S.C. § 3500.*

(3) Grand Jury Transcripts. This rule does not apply to the discovery or inspection of a grand jury's recorded proceedings, except as provided in Rules 6, 12(h), 16(a)(1), and 26.2.

(b) Defendant's Disclosure.

(1) Information Subject to Disclosure.

(A) Documents and Objects. If a defendant requests disclosure under Rule 16(a)(1)(E) and the government complies, then the defendant must permit the government, upon request, to inspect and to copy or photograph books, papers, documents, data, photographs, tangible objects, buildings or places, or copies or portions of any of these items if:

(i) the item is within the defendant's possession, custody, or control; and

---

* This provision is set out in Appendix B.

(ii) the defendant intends to use the item in the defendant's case-in-chief at trial.

(B) Reports of Examinations and Tests. If a defendant requests disclosure under Rule 16(a)(1)(F) and the government complies, the defendant must permit the government, upon request, to inspect and to copy or photograph the results or reports of any physical or mental examination and of any scientific test or experiment if:

(i) the item is within the defendant's possession, custody, or control; and

(ii) the defendant intends to use the item in the defendant's case-in-chief at trial, or intends to call the witness who prepared the report and the report relates to the witness's testimony.

(C) Expert witnesses.—The defendant must, at the government's request, give to the government a written summary of any testimony that the defendant intends to use under Rules 702, 703, or 705 of the Federal Rules of Evidence as evidence at trial, if—

(i) the defendant requests disclosure under subdivision (a)(1)(G) and the government complies; or

(ii) the defendant has given notice under Rule 12.2(b) of an intent to present expert testimony on the defendant's mental condition.

This summary must describe the witness's opinions, the bases and reasons for those opinions, and the witness's qualifications.

(2) Information Not Subject to Disclosure. Except for scientific or medical reports, Rule 16(b)(1) does not authorize discovery or inspection of:

(A) reports, memoranda, or other documents made by the defendant, or the defendant's attorney or agent, during the case's investigation or defense; or

(B) a statement made to the defendant, or the defendant's attorney or agent, by:

(i) the defendant;

(ii) a government or defense witness; or

(iii) a prospective government or defense witness.

(c) Continuing Duty to Disclose. A party who discovers additional evidence or material before or during trial must promptly disclose its existence to the other party or the court if:

(1) the evidence or material is subject to discovery or inspection under this rule; and

(2) the other party previously requested, or the court ordered, its production.

(d) Regulating Discovery.

(1) Protective and Modifying Orders. At any time the court may, for good cause, deny, restrict, or defer discovery or inspection, or grant other appropriate relief. The court may permit a party to show good cause by a written statement that the court will inspect ex parte. If relief is granted, the court must preserve the entire text of the party's statement under seal.

(2) Failure to Comply. If a party fails to comply with this rule, the court may:

(A) order that party to permit the discovery or inspection; specify its time, place, and manner; and prescribe other just terms and conditions;

(B) grant a continuance;

(C) prohibit that party from introducing the undisclosed evidence; or

(D) enter any other order that is just under the circumstances.

Rule 17. Subpoena

(a) Content. A subpoena must state the court's name and the title of the proceeding, include the seal of the court, and command the witness to attend and testify at the time and place the subpoena specifies. The clerk must issue a blank subpoena—signed and sealed—to the party requesting it, and that party must fill in the blanks before the subpoena is served.

(b) Defendant Unable to Pay. Upon a defendant's ex parte application, the court must order that a subpoena be issued for a named witness if the defendant shows an inability to pay the witness's fees and the necessity of the witness's presence for an adequate defense. If the court orders a subpoena to be issued, the process costs and witness fees will be paid in the same manner as those paid for witnesses the government subpoenas.

(c) Producing Documents and Objects.

(1) In General. A subpoena may order the witness to produce any books, papers, documents, data, or other objects the subpoena designates. The court may direct the witness to produce the designated items in court before trial or before they are to be offered in evidence. When the items arrive, the court may permit the parties and their attorneys to inspect all or part of them.

(2) Quashing or Modifying the Subpoena. On motion made promptly, the court may quash or modify the subpoena if compliance would be unreasonable or oppressive.

(d) Service. A marshal, a deputy marshal, or any nonparty who is at least 18 years old may serve a subpoena. The server must deliver a copy of the subpoena to the witness and must tender to the witness one day's witness-attendance fee and the legal mileage allowance. The server need not tender the attendance fee or mileage allowance when the United States, a federal officer, or a federal agency has requested the subpoena.

(e) Place of Service.

(1) In the United States. A subpoena requiring a witness to attend a hearing or trial may be served at any place within the United States.

(2) In a Foreign Country. If the witness is in a foreign country, 28 U.S.C. § 1783 governs the subpoena's service.

(f) Issuing a Deposition Subpoena.

(1) Issuance. A court order to take a deposition authorizes the clerk in the district where the deposition is to be taken to issue a subpoena for any witness named or described in the order.

(2) Place. After considering the convenience of the witness and the parties, the court may order—and the subpoena may require—the witness to appear anywhere the court designates.

(g) Contempt. The court (other than a magistrate judge) may hold in contempt a witness who, without adequate excuse, disobeys a subpoena issued by a federal court in that district. A magistrate judge may hold in contempt a witness who, without adequate excuse, disobeys a subpoena issued by that magistrate judge as provided in 28 U.S.C. § 636(e).

(h) Information Not Subject to a Subpoena. No party may subpoena a statement of a witness or of a prospective witness under this rule. Rule 26.2 governs the production of the statement.

Rule 18. Place of Prosecution and Trial

Unless a statute or these rules permit otherwise, the government must prosecute an offense in a district where the offense was committed. The court must set the place of trial within the district with due regard for the convenience of the defendant and the witnesses, and the prompt administration of justice.

Rule 19. [Reserved]

Rule 20. Transfer for Plea and Sentence

(a) Consent to Transfer. A prosecution may be transferred from the district where the indictment or information is pending, or from which a warrant on a complaint has been issued, to the district where the defendant is arrested, held, or present if:

(1) the defendant states in writing a wish to plead guilty or nolo contendere and to waive trial in the district where the indictment, information, or complaint is pending, consents in writing to the court's disposing of the case in the transferee district, and files the statement in the transferee district; and

(2) the United States attorneys in both districts approve the transfer in writing.

(b) Clerk's Duties. After receiving the defendant's statement and the required approvals, the clerk where the indictment, information, or complaint is pending must send the file, or a certified copy, to the clerk in the transferee district.

(c) Effect of a Not Guilty Plea. If the defendant pleads not guilty after the case has been transferred under Rule 20(a), the clerk must return the papers to the court where the prosecution began, and that court must restore the proceeding to its docket. The defendant's statement that the defendant wished to plead guilty or nolo contendere is not, in any civil or criminal proceeding, admissible against the defendant.

(d) Juveniles.

(1) Consent to Transfer. A juvenile, as defined in 18 U.S.C. § 5031, may be proceeded against as a juvenile delinquent in the district where the juvenile is arrested, held, or present if:

(A) the alleged offense that occurred in the other district is not punishable by death or life imprisonment;

(B) an attorney has advised the juvenile;

(C) the court has informed the juvenile of the juvenile's rights—including the right to be returned to the district where the offense allegedly occurred—and the consequences of waiving those rights;

(D) the juvenile, after receiving the court's information about rights, consents in writing to be proceeded against in the transferee district, and files the consent in the transferee district;

(E) the United States attorneys for both districts approve the transfer in writing; and

(F) the transferee court approves the transfer.

(2) Clerk's Duties. After receiving the juvenile's written consent and the required approvals, the clerk where the indictment, information, or complaint is pending or where the alleged offense occurred must send the file, or a certified copy, to the clerk in the transferee district.

Rule 21. Transfer for Trial

(a) For Prejudice. Upon the defendant's motion, the court must transfer the proceeding against that defendant to another district if the court is satisfied that so great a prejudice against the defendant exists in the transferring district that the defendant cannot obtain a fair and impartial trial there.

(b) For Convenience. Upon the defendant's motion, the court may transfer the proceeding, or one or more counts, against that defendant to another district for the convenience of the parties and witnesses and in the interest of justice.

(c) Proceedings on Transfer. When the court orders a transfer, the clerk must send to the transferee district the file, or a certified copy, and any bail taken. The prosecution will then continue in the transferee district.

(d) Time to File a Motion to Transfer. A motion to transfer may be made at or before arraignment or at any other time the court or these rules prescribe.

Rule 22. [Transferred]

Rule 23. Jury or Nonjury Trial

(a) Jury Trial. If the defendant is entitled to a jury trial, the trial must be by jury unless:

(1) the defendant waives a jury trial in writing;

(2) the government consents; and

(3) the court approves.

(b) Jury Size.

(1) In General. A jury consists of 12 persons unless this rule provides otherwise.

(2) Stipulation for a Smaller Jury. At any time before the verdict, the parties may, with the court's approval, stipulate in writing that:

(A) the jury may consist of fewer than 12 persons; or

(B) a jury of fewer than 12 persons may return a verdict if the court finds it necessary to excuse a juror for good cause after the trial begins.

(3) Court Order for a Jury of 11. After the jury has retired to deliberate, the court may permit a jury of 11 persons to return a verdict, even without a stipulation by the parties, if the court finds good cause to excuse a juror.

(c) Nonjury Trial. In a case tried without a jury, the court must find the defendant guilty or not guilty. If a party requests before the finding of guilty or not guilty, the court must state its specific findings of fact in open court or in a written decision or opinion.

Rule 24. Trial Jurors

(a) Examination.

(1) In General. The court may examine prospective jurors or may permit the attorneys for the parties to do so.

(2) Court Examination. If the court examines the jurors, it must permit the attorneys for the parties to:

(A) ask further questions that the court considers proper; or

(B) submit further questions that the court may ask if it considers them proper.

(b) Peremptory Challenges. Each side is entitled to the number of peremptory challenges to prospective jurors specified below. The court may allow additional peremptory challenges to multiple defendants, and may allow the defendants to exercise those challenges separately or jointly.

(1) Capital Case. Each side has 20 peremptory challenges when the government seeks the death penalty.

(2) Other Felony Case. The government has 6 peremptory challenges and the defendant or defendants jointly have 10 peremptory challenges when the defendant is charged with a crime punishable by imprisonment of more than one year.

(3) Misdemeanor Case. Each side has 3 peremptory challenges when the defendant is charged with a crime punishable by fine, imprisonment of one year or less, or both.

(c) Alternate Jurors.

(1) In General. The court may impanel up to 6 alternate jurors to replace any jurors who are unable to perform or who are disqualified from performing their duties.

(2) Procedure.

(A) Alternate jurors must have the same qualifications and be selected and sworn in the same manner as any other juror.

(B) Alternate jurors replace jurors in the same sequence in which the alternates were selected. An alternate juror who replaces a juror has the same authority as the other jurors.

(3) Retaining Alternate Jurors. The court may retain alternate jurors after the jury retires to deliberate. The court must ensure that a retained alternate does not discuss the case with anyone until that alternate replaces a juror or is discharged. If an alternate replaces a juror after deliberations have begun, the court must instruct the jury to begin its deliberations anew.

(4) Peremptory Challenges. Each side is entitled to the number of additional peremptory challenges to prospective alternate jurors specified below. These additional challenges may be used only to remove alternate jurors.

(A) One or Two Alternates. One additional peremptory challenge is permitted when one or two alternates are impaneled.

(B) Three or Four Alternates. Two additional peremptory challenges are permitted when three or four alternates are impaneled.

(C) Five or Six Alternates. Three additional peremptory challenges are permitted when five or six alternates are impaneled.

Rule 25. Judge's Disability

(a) During Trial. Any judge regularly sitting in or assigned to the court may complete a jury trial if:

(1) the judge before whom the trial began cannot proceed because of death, sickness, or other disability; and

(2) the judge completing the trial certifies familiarity with the trial record.

(b) After a Verdict or Finding of Guilty.

(1) **In General.** After a verdict or finding of guilty, any judge regularly sitting in or assigned to a court may complete the court's duties if the judge who presided at trial cannot perform those duties because of absence, death, sickness, or other disability.

(2) Granting a New Trial. The successor judge may grant a new trial if satisfied that:

(A) a judge other than the one who presided at the trial cannot perform the post-trial duties; or

(B) a new trial is necessary for some other reason.

Rule 26. Taking Testimony

In every trial the testimony of witnesses must be taken in open court, unless otherwise provided by a statute or by rules adopted under 28 U.S.C. §§ 2072–2077.

Rule 26.1. Foreign Law Determination

A party intending to raise an issue of foreign law must provide the court and all parties with reasonable written notice. Issues of foreign law are questions of law, but in deciding such issues a court may consider any relevant material or source—including testimony—without regard to the Federal Rules of Evidence.

Rule 26.2. Producing a Witness's Statement

(a) Motion to Produce. After a witness other than the defendant has testified on direct examination, the court, on motion of a party who did not call the witness, must order an attorney for the government or the defendant and the defendant's attorney to produce, for the examination and use of the moving party, any statement of the witness that is in their possession and that relates to the subject matter of the witness's testimony.

(b) Producing the Entire Statement. If the entire statement relates to the subject matter of the witness's testimony, the court must order that the statement be delivered to the moving party.

(c) Producing a Redacted Statement. If the party who called the witness claims that the statement contains information that is privileged or does not relate to the subject matter of the witness's testimony, the court must inspect the statement in camera. After excising any privileged or unrelated portions, the court must order delivery of the redacted statement to the moving party. If the defendant objects to an excision, the court must preserve the entire statement with the excised portion indicated, under seal, as part of the record.

(d) Recess to Examine a Statement. The court may recess the proceedings to allow time for a party to examine the statement and prepare for its use.

(e) Sanction for Failure to Produce or Deliver a Statement. If the party who called the witness disobeys an order to produce or deliver a statement, the court must strike the witness's testimony from the record. If an attorney for the government disobeys the order, the court must declare a mistrial if justice so requires.

(f) "Statement" Defined. As used in this rule, a witness's "statement" means:

(1) a written statement that the witness makes and signs, or otherwise adopts or approves;

(2) a substantially verbatim, contemporaneously recorded recital of the witness's oral statement that is contained in any recording or any transcription of a recording; or

(3) the witness's statement to a grand jury, however taken or recorded, or a transcription of such a statement.

(g) Scope. This rule applies at trial, at a suppression hearing under Rule 12, and to the extent specified in the following rules:

(1) Rule 5.1(h) (preliminary hearing);

(2) Rule 32(i)(2) (sentencing);

(3) Rule 32.1(e) (hearing to revoke or modify probation or supervised release);

(4) Rule 46(j) (detention hearing); and

(5) Rule 8 of the Rules Governing Proceedings under 28 U.S.C. § 2255.

Rule 26.3. Mistrial

Before ordering a mistrial, the court must give each defendant and the government an opportunity to comment on the propriety of the order, to state whether that party consents or objects, and to suggest alternatives.

Rule 27. Proving an Official Record

A party may prove an official record, an entry in such a record, or the lack of a record or entry in the same manner as in a civil action.

Rule 28. Interpreters

The court may select, appoint, and set the reasonable compensation for an interpreter. The compensation must be paid from funds provided by law or by the government, as the court may direct.

Rule 29. Motion for a Judgment of Acquittal

(a) Before Submission to the Jury. After the government closes its evidence or after the close of all the evidence, the court on the defendant's motion must enter a judgment of acquittal of any offense for which the evidence is insufficient to sustain a conviction. The court may on its own consider whether the evidence is insufficient to sustain a conviction. If the court denies a motion for a judgment of acquittal at the close of the government's evidence, the defendant may offer evidence without having reserved the right to do so.

(b) Reserving Decision. The court may reserve decision on the motion, proceed with the trial (where the motion is made before the close of all the evidence), submit the case to the jury, and decide the motion either before the jury returns a verdict or after it returns a verdict of guilty or is discharged without having returned a verdict. If the court reserves decision, it must decide the motion on the basis of the evidence at the time the ruling was reserved.

(c) After Jury Verdict or Discharge.

(1) Time for a Motion. A defendant may move for a judgment of acquittal, or renew such a motion, within 7 days after a guilty verdict or after the court discharges the jury, whichever is later, or within any other time the court sets during the 7–day period.

(2) Ruling on the Motion. If the jury has returned a guilty verdict, the court may set aside the verdict and enter an acquittal. If the jury has failed to return a verdict, the court may enter a judgment of acquittal.

(3) No Prior Motion Required. A defendant is not required to move for a judgment of acquittal before the court submits the case to the jury as a prerequisite for making such a motion after jury discharge.

(d) Conditional Ruling on a Motion for a New Trial.

(1) Motion for a New Trial. If the court enters a judgment of acquittal after a guilty verdict, the court must also conditionally determine whether any motion for a new trial should be granted if the judgment of acquittal is later vacated or reversed. The court must specify the reasons for that determination.

(2) Finality. The court's order conditionally granting a motion for a new trial does not affect the finality of the judgment of acquittal.

(3) Appeal.

(A) Grant of a Motion for a New Trial. If the court conditionally grants a motion for a new trial and an appellate court later reverses the judgment of acquittal, the trial court must proceed with the new trial unless the appellate court orders otherwise.

(B) Denial of a Motion for a New Trial. If the court conditionally denies a motion for a new trial, an appellee may assert that the denial was erroneous. If the appellate court later reverses the judgment of acquittal, the trial court must proceed as the appellate court directs.

Rule 29.1. Closing Argument

Closing arguments proceed in the following order:

(a) the government argues;

(b) the defense argues; and

(c) the government rebuts.

Rule 30. Jury Instructions

(a) In General. Any party may request in writing that the court instruct the jury on the law as specified in the request. The request must be made at the close of the evidence or at any earlier time that the court reasonably sets. When the request is made, the requesting party must furnish a copy to every other party.

(b) Ruling on a Request. The court must inform the parties before closing arguments how it intends to rule on the requested instructions.

(c) Time for Giving Instructions. The court may instruct the jury before or after the arguments are completed, or at both times.

(d) Objections to Instructions. A party who objects to any portion of the instructions or to a failure to give a requested instruction must inform the court of the specific objection and the grounds for the objection before the jury retires to deliberate. An opportunity must be given to object out of the jury's hearing and, on request, out of the jury's presence. Failure to object in accordance with this rule precludes appellate review, except as permitted under Rule 52(b).

Rule 31. Jury Verdict

(a) Return. The jury must return its verdict to a judge in open court. The verdict must be unanimous.

(b) Partial Verdicts, Mistrial, and Retrial.

    (1) Multiple Defendants. If there are multiple defendants, the jury may return a verdict at any time during its deliberations as to any defendant about whom it has agreed.

    (2) Multiple Counts. If the jury cannot agree on all counts as to any defendant, the jury may return a verdict on those counts on which it has agreed.

    (3) Mistrial and Retrial. If the jury cannot agree on a verdict on one or more counts, the court may declare a mistrial on those counts. The government may retry any defendant on any count on which the jury could not agree.

(c) Lesser Offense or Attempt. A defendant may be found guilty of any of the following:

    (1) an offense necessarily included in the offense charged;

    (2) an attempt to commit the offense charged; or

    (3) an attempt to commit an offense necessarily included in the offense charged, if the attempt is an offense in its own right.

(d) Jury Poll. After a verdict is returned but before the jury is discharged, the court must on a party's request, or may on its own, poll the jurors individually. If the poll reveals a lack of unanimity, the court may direct the jury to deliberate further or may declare a mistrial and discharge the jury.

Rule 32. Sentencing and Judgment

(a) Definitions. The following definitions apply under this rule:

    (1) "Crime of violence or sexual abuse" means:

        (A) a crime that involves the use, attempted use, or threatened use of physical force against another's person or property; or

        (B) a crime under 18 U.S.C. §§ 2241–2248 or §§ 2251–2257.

    (2) "Victim" means an individual against whom the defendant committed an offense for which the court will impose sentence.

(b) Time of Sentencing.

(1) In General. The court must impose sentence without unnecessary delay.

(2) Changing Time Limits. The court may, for good cause, change any time limits prescribed in this rule.

(c) Presentence Investigation.

(1) Required Investigation.

(A) In General. The probation officer must conduct a presentence investigation and submit a report to the court before it imposes sentence unless:

(i) 18 U.S.C. § 3593(c) or another statute requires otherwise; or

(ii) the court finds that the information in the record enables it to meaningfully exercise its sentencing authority under 18 U.S.C. § 3553, and the court explains its finding on the record.

(B) Restitution. If the law requires restitution, the probation officer must conduct an investigation and submit a report that contains sufficient information for the court to order restitution.

(2) Interviewing the Defendant. The probation officer who interviews a defendant as part of a presentence investigation must, on request, give the defendant's attorney notice and a reasonable opportunity to attend the interview.

(d) Presentence Report.

(1) Applying the Sentencing Guidelines. The presentence report must:

(A) identify all applicable guidelines and policy statements of the Sentencing Commission;

(B) calculate the defendant's offense level and criminal history category;

(C) state the resulting sentencing range and kinds of sentences available;

(D) identify any factor relevant to:

(i) the appropriate kind of sentence, or

(ii) the appropriate sentence within the applicable sentencing range; and

(E) identify any basis for departing from the applicable sentencing range.

(2) Additional Information. The presentence report must also contain the following information:

(A) the defendant's history and characteristics, including:

(i) any prior criminal record;

(ii) the defendant's financial condition; and

(iii) any circumstances affecting the defendant's behavior that may be helpful in imposing sentence or in correctional treatment;

(B) verified information, stated in a nonargumentative style, that assesses the financial, social, psychological, and medical impact on any individual against whom the offense has been committed;

(C) when appropriate, the nature and extent of nonprison programs and resources available to the defendant;

(D) when the law provides for restitution, information sufficient for a restitution order;

(E) if the court orders a study under 18 U.S.C. § 3552(b), any resulting report and recommendation; and

(F) any other information that the court requires.

(3) Exclusions. The presentence report must exclude the following:

(A) any diagnoses that, if disclosed, might seriously disrupt a rehabilitation program;

(B) any sources of information obtained upon a promise of confidentiality; and

(C) any other information that, if disclosed, might result in physical or other harm to the defendant or others.

(e) Disclosing the Report and Recommendation.

(1) Time to Disclose. Unless the defendant has consented in writing, the probation officer must not submit a presentence report to the court or disclose its contents to anyone until the defendant has pleaded guilty or nolo contendere, or has been found guilty.

(2) Minimum Required Notice. The probation officer must give the presentence report to the defendant, the defendant's attorney, and an attorney for the government at least 35 days before sentencing unless the defendant waives this minimum period.

(3) Sentence Recommendation. By local rule or by order in a case, the court may direct the probation officer not to disclose to anyone other than the court the officer's recommendation on the sentence.

(f) Objecting to the Report.

(1) Time to Object. Within 14 days after receiving the presentence report, the parties must state in writing any objections, including objections to material information, sentencing guideline ranges, and policy statements contained in or omitted from the report.

(2) Serving Objections. An objecting party must provide a copy of its objections to the opposing party and to the probation officer.

(3) Action on Objections. After receiving objections, the probation officer may meet with the parties to discuss the objections. The probation officer may then investigate further and revise the presentence report as appropriate.

(g) Submitting the Report. At least 7 days before sentencing, the probation officer must submit to the court and to the parties the presentence report and an addendum containing any unresolved objections, the grounds for those objections, and the probation officer's comments on them.

(h) Notice of Possible Departure from Sentencing Guidelines. Before the court may depart from the applicable sentencing range on a ground not identified for departure either in the presentence report or in a party's prehearing submission, the court must give the parties reasonable notice that it is contemplating such a departure. The notice must specify any ground on which the court is contemplating a departure.

(i) Sentencing.

    (1) In General. At sentencing, the court:

        (A) must verify that the defendant and the defendant's attorney have read and discussed the presentence report and any addendum to the report;

        (B) must give to the defendant and an attorney for the government a written summary of—or summarize in camera—any information excluded from the presentence report under Rule 32(d)(3) on which the court will rely in sentencing, and give them a reasonable opportunity to comment on that information;

        (C) must allow the parties' attorneys to comment on the probation officer's determinations and other matters relating to an appropriate sentence; and

        (D) may, for good cause, allow a party to make a new objection at any time before sentence is imposed.

    (2) Introducing Evidence; Producing a Statement. The court may permit the parties to introduce evidence on the objections. If a witness testifies at sentencing, Rule 26.2(a)–(d) and (f) applies. If a party fails to comply with a Rule 26.2 order to produce a witness's statement, the court must not consider that witness's testimony.

    (3) Court Determinations. At sentencing, the court:

        (A) may accept any undisputed portion of the presentence report as a finding of fact;

        (B) must—for any disputed portion of the presentence report or other controverted matter—rule on the dispute or determine that a ruling is unnecessary either because the matter will not affect sentencing, or because the court will not consider the matter in sentencing; and

        (C) must append a copy of the court's determinations under this rule to any copy of the presentence report made available to the Bureau of Prisons.

    (4) Opportunity to Speak.

        (A) By a Party. Before imposing sentence, the court must:

            (i) provide the defendant's attorney an opportunity to speak on the defendant's behalf;

(ii) address the defendant personally in order to permit the defendant to speak or present any information to mitigate the sentence; and

(iii) provide an attorney for the government an opportunity to speak equivalent to that of the defendant's attorney.

(B) By a Victim. Before imposing sentence, the court must address any victim of a crime of violence or sexual abuse who is present at sentencing and must permit the victim to speak or submit any information about the sentence. Whether or not the victim is present, a victim's right to address the court may be exercised by the following persons if present:

(i) a parent or legal guardian, if the victim is younger than 18 years or is incompetent; or

(ii) one or more family members or relatives the court designates, if the victim is deceased or incapacitated.

(C) In Camera Proceedings. Upon a party's motion and for good cause, the court may hear in camera any statement made under Rule 32(i)(4).

(j) Defendant's Right to Appeal.

(1) Advice of a Right to Appeal.

(A) Appealing a Conviction. If the defendant pleaded not guilty and was convicted, after sentencing the court must advise the defendant of the right to appeal the conviction.

(B) Appealing a Sentence. After sentencing—regardless of the defendant's plea—the court must advise the defendant of any right to appeal the sentence.

(C) Appeal Costs. The court must advise a defendant who is unable to pay appeal costs of the right to ask for permission to appeal in forma pauperis.

(2) Clerk's Filing of Notice. If the defendant so requests, the clerk must immediately prepare and file a notice of appeal on the defendant's behalf.

(k) Judgment.

(1) In General. In the judgment of conviction, the court must set forth the plea, the jury verdict or the court's findings, the adjudication, and the sentence. If the defendant is found not guilty or is otherwise entitled to be discharged, the court must so order. The judge must sign the judgment, and the clerk must enter it.

(2) Criminal Forfeiture. Forfeiture procedures are governed by Rule 32.2.

Rule 32.1. Revoking or Modifying Probation or Supervised Release

(a) Initial Appearance.

(1) Person In Custody. A person held in custody for violating probation or supervised release must be taken without unnecessary delay before a magistrate judge.

(A) If the person is held in custody in the district where an alleged violation occurred, the initial appearance must be in that district.

(B) If the person is held in custody in a district other than where an alleged violation occurred, the initial appearance must be in that district, or in an adjacent district if the appearance can occur more promptly there.

(2) **Upon a Summons.** When a person appears in response to a summons for violating probation or supervised release, a magistrate judge must proceed under this rule.

(3) **Advice.** The judge must inform the person of the following:

(A) the alleged violation of probation or supervised release;

(B) the person's right to retain counsel or to request that counsel be appointed if the person cannot obtain counsel; and

(C) the person's right, if held in custody, to a preliminary hearing under Rule 32.1(b)(1).

(4) **Appearance in the District With Jurisdiction.** If the person is arrested or appears in the district that has jurisdiction to conduct a revocation hearing—either originally or by transfer of jurisdiction—the court must proceed under Rule 32.1(b)–(e).

(5) **Appearance in a District Lacking Jurisdiction.** If the person is arrested or appears in a district that does not have jurisdiction to conduct a revocation hearing, the magistrate judge must:

(A) if the alleged violation occurred in the district of arrest, conduct a preliminary hearing under Rule 32.1(b) and either:

(i) transfer the person to the district that has jurisdiction, if the judge finds probable cause to believe that a violation occurred; or

(ii) dismiss the proceedings and so notify the court that has jurisdiction, if the judge finds no probable cause to believe that a violation occurred; or

(B) if the alleged violation did not occur in the district of arrest, transfer the person to the district that has jurisdiction if:

(i) the government produces certified copies of the judgment, warrant, and warrant application; and

(ii) the judge finds that the person is the same person named in the warrant.

(6) **Release or Detention.** The magistrate judge may release or detain the person under 18 U.S.C. § 3143(a) pending further proceedings. The burden of establishing that the person will not flee or pose a danger to any other person or to the community rests with the person.

(b) Revocation.

(1) **Preliminary Hearing.**

(A) **In General.** If a person is in custody for violating a condition of probation or supervised release, a magistrate judge must promptly conduct a hearing to determine whether there is probable cause to believe that a violation occurred. The person may waive the hearing.

(B) Requirements. The hearing must be recorded by a court reporter or by a suitable recording device. The judge must give the person:

(i) notice of the hearing and its purpose, the alleged violation, and the person's right to retain counsel or to request that counsel be appointed if the person cannot obtain counsel;

(ii) an opportunity to appear at the hearing and present evidence; and

(iii) upon request, an opportunity to question any adverse witness, unless the judge determines that the interest of justice does not require the witness to appear.

(C) Referral. If the judge finds probable cause, the judge must conduct a revocation hearing. If the judge does not find probable cause, the judge must dismiss the proceeding.

(2) Revocation Hearing. Unless waived by the person, the court must hold the revocation hearing within a reasonable time in the district having jurisdiction. The person is entitled to:

(A) written notice of the alleged violation;

(B) disclosure of the evidence against the person;

(C) an opportunity to appear, present evidence, and question any adverse witness unless the court determines that the interest of justice does not require the witness to appear; and

(D) notice of the person's right to retain counsel or to request that counsel be appointed if the person cannot obtain counsel.

(c) Modification.

(1) In General. Before modifying the conditions of probation or supervised release, the court must hold a hearing, at which the person has the right to counsel.

(2) Exceptions. A hearing is not required if:

(A) the person waives the hearing; or

(B) the relief sought is favorable to the person and does not extend the term of probation or of supervised release; and

(C) an attorney for the government has received notice of the relief sought, has had a reasonable opportunity to object, and has not done so.

(d) Disposition of the Case. The court's disposition of the case is governed by 18 U.S.C. § 3563 and § 3565 (probation) and § 3583 (supervised release).

(e) Producing a Statement. Rule 26.2(a)–(d) and (f) applies at a hearing under this rule. If a party fails to comply with a Rule 26.2 order to produce a witness's statement, the court must not consider that witness's testimony.

Rule 32.2. Criminal Forfeiture

(a) Notice to the Defendant. A court must not enter a judgment of forfeiture in a criminal proceeding unless the indictment or information contains notice to the defendant that the government will seek the forfeiture of property as part of any sentence in accordance with the applicable statute.

(b) Entering a Preliminary Order of Forfeiture.

(1) In General. As soon as practicable after a verdict or finding of guilty, or after a plea of guilty or nolo contendere is accepted, on any count in an indictment or information regarding which criminal forfeiture is sought, the court must determine what property is subject to forfeiture under the applicable statute. If the government seeks forfeiture of specific property, the court must determine whether the government has established the requisite nexus between the property and the offense. If the government seeks a personal money judgment, the court must determine the amount of money that the defendant will be ordered to pay. The court's determination may be based on evidence already in the record, including any written plea agreement or, if the forfeiture is contested, on evidence or information presented by the parties at a hearing after the verdict or finding of guilt.

(2) Preliminary Order. If the court finds that property is subject to forfeiture, it must promptly enter a preliminary order of forfeiture setting forth the amount of any money judgment or directing the forfeiture of specific property without regard to any third party's interest in all or part of it. Determining whether a third party has such an interest must be deferred until any third party files a claim in an ancillary proceeding under Rule 32.2(c).

(3) Seizing Property. The entry of a preliminary order of forfeiture authorizes the Attorney General (or a designee) to seize the specific property subject to forfeiture; to conduct any discovery the court considers proper in identifying, locating, or disposing of the property; and to commence proceedings that comply with any statutes governing third-party rights. At sentencing—or at any time before sentencing if the defendant consents—the order of forfeiture becomes final as to the defendant and must be made a part of the sentence and be included in the judgment. The court may include in the order of forfeiture conditions reasonably necessary to preserve the property's value pending any appeal.

(4) Jury Determination. Upon a party's request in a case in which a jury returns a verdict of guilty, the jury must determine whether the government has established the requisite nexus between the property and the offense committed by the defendant.

(c) Ancillary Proceeding; Entering a Final Order of Forfeiture.

(1) In General. If, as prescribed by statute, a third party files a petition asserting an interest in the property to be forfeited, the court must conduct an ancillary proceeding, but no ancillary proceeding is required to the extent that the forfeiture consists of a money judgment.

(A) In the ancillary proceeding, the court may, on motion, dismiss the petition for lack of standing, for failure to state a claim, or for any other lawful reason. For purposes of the motion, the facts set forth in the petition are assumed to be true.

(B) After disposing of any motion filed under Rule 32.2(c)(1)(A) and before conducting a hearing on the petition, the court may permit the parties to conduct discovery in accordance with the Federal Rules of Civil Procedure if the court determines that discovery is necessary or desirable to resolve factual issues. When discovery ends, a party may move for summary judgment under Federal Rule of Civil Procedure 56.

(2) Entering a Final Order. When the ancillary proceeding ends, the court must enter a final order of forfeiture by amending the preliminary order as necessary to account for any third-party rights. If no third party files a timely petition, the preliminary order becomes the final order of forfeiture if the court finds that the defendant (or any combination of defendants convicted in the case) had an interest in the property that is forfeitable under the applicable statute. The defendant may not object to the entry of the final order on the ground that the property belongs, in whole or in part, to a codefendant or third party; nor may a third party object to the final order on the ground that the third party had an interest in the property.

(3) Multiple Petitions. If multiple third-party petitions are filed in the same case, an order dismissing or granting one petition is not appealable until rulings are made on all the petitions, unless the court determines that there is no just reason for delay.

(4) Ancillary Proceeding Not Part of Sentencing. An ancillary proceeding is not part of sentencing.

(d) Stay Pending Appeal. If a defendant appeals from a conviction or an order of forfeiture, the court may stay the order of forfeiture on terms appropriate to ensure that the property remains available pending appellate review. A stay does not delay the ancillary proceeding or the determination of a third party's rights or interests. If the court rules in favor of any third party while an appeal is pending, the court may amend the order of forfeiture but must not transfer any property interest to a third party until the decision on appeal becomes final, unless the defendant consents in writing or on the record.

(e) Subsequently Located Property; Substitute Property.

(1) In General. On the government's motion, the court may at any time enter an order of forfeiture or amend an existing order of forfeiture to include property that:

(A) is subject to forfeiture under an existing order of forfeiture but was located and identified after that order was entered; or

(B) is substitute property that qualifies for forfeiture under an applicable statute.

(2) Procedure. If the government shows that the property is subject to forfeiture under Rule 32.2(e)(1), the court must:

(A) enter an order forfeiting that property, or amend an existing preliminary or final order to include it; and

(B) if a third party files a petition claiming an interest in the property, conduct an ancillary proceeding under Rule 32.2(c).

(3) Jury Trial Limited. There is no right to a jury trial under Rule 32.2(e).

Rule 33. New Trial

(a) Defendant's Motion. Upon the defendant's motion, the court may vacate any judgment and grant a new trial if the interest of justice so requires. If the case was tried without a jury, the court may take additional testimony and enter a new judgment.

(b) Time to File.

(1) Newly Discovered Evidence. Any motion for a new trial grounded on newly discovered evidence must be filed within 3 years after the verdict or finding of guilty. If an appeal is pending, the court may not grant a motion for a new trial until the appellate court remands the case.

(2) Other Grounds. Any motion for a new trial grounded on any reason other than newly discovered evidence must be filed within 7 days after the verdict or finding of guilty, or within such further time as the court sets during the 7–day period.

Rule 34. Arresting Judgment

(a) In General. Upon the defendant's motion or on its own, the court must arrest judgment if:

(1) the indictment or information does not charge an offense; or

(2) the court does not have jurisdiction of the charged offense.

(b) Time to File. The defendant must move to arrest judgment within 7 days after the court accepts a verdict or finding of guilty, or after a plea of guilty or nolo contendere, or within such further time as the court sets during the 7–day period.

Rule 35. Correcting or Reducing a Sentence

(a) Correcting Clear Error. Within 7 days after sentencing, the court may correct a sentence that resulted from arithmetical, technical, or other clear error.

(b) Reducing a Sentence for Substantial Assistance.

(1) In General. Upon the government's motion made within one year of sentencing, the court may reduce a sentence if:

(A) the defendant, after sentencing, provided substantial assistance in investigating or prosecuting another person; and

(B) reducing the sentence accords with the Sentencing Commission's guidelines and policy statements.

(2) Later Motion. Upon the government's motion made more than one year after sentencing, the court may reduce a sentence if the defendant's substantial assistance involved:

(A) information not known to the defendant until one year or more after sentencing;

(B) information provided by the defendant to the government within one year of sentencing, but which did not become useful to the government until more than one year after sentencing; or

(C) information the usefulness of which could not reasonably have been anticipated by the defendant until more than one year after sentencing and which was promptly provided to the government after its usefulness was reasonably apparent to the defendant.

(3) Evaluating Substantial Assistance. In evaluating whether the defendant has provided substantial assistance, the court may consider the defendant's presentence assistance.

(4) Below Statutory Minimum. When acting under Rule 35(b), the court may reduce the sentence to a level below the minimum sentence established by statute.

(c) "Sentencing" Defined. As used in this rule, "sentencing" means the oral announcement of the sentence.

Rule 36. Clerical Error

After giving any notice it considers appropriate, the court may at any time correct a clerical error in a judgment, order, or other part of the record, or correct an error in the record arising from oversight or omission.

Rule 37. [Reserved]

Rule 38. Staying a Sentence or a Disability

(a) Death Sentence. The court must stay a death sentence if the defendant appeals the conviction or sentence.

(b) Imprisonment.

(1) Stay Granted. If the defendant is released pending appeal, the court must stay a sentence of imprisonment.

(2) Stay Denied; Place of Confinement. If the defendant is not released pending appeal, the court may recommend to the Attorney General that the defendant be confined near the place of the trial or appeal for a period reasonably necessary to permit the defendant to assist in preparing the appeal.

(c) Fine. If the defendant appeals, the district court, or the court of appeals under Federal Rule of Appellate Procedure 8, may stay a sentence to pay a fine or a fine and costs. The court may stay the sentence on any terms considered appropriate and may require the defendant to:

(1) deposit all or part of the fine and costs into the district court's registry pending appeal;

(2) post a bond to pay the fine and costs; or

(3) submit to an examination concerning the defendant's assets and, if appropriate, order the defendant to refrain from dissipating assets.

(d) Probation. If the defendant appeals, the court may stay a sentence of probation. The court must set the terms of any stay.

(e) Restitution and Notice to Victims.

(1) **In General.** If the defendant appeals, the district court, or the court of appeals under Federal Rule of Appellate Procedure 8, may stay—on any terms considered appropriate—any sentence providing for restitution under 18 U.S.C. § 3556 or notice under 18 U.S.C. § 3555.

(2) **Ensuring Compliance.** The court may issue any order reasonably necessary to ensure compliance with a restitution order or a notice order after disposition of an appeal, including:

(A) a restraining order;

(B) an injunction;

(C) an order requiring the defendant to deposit all or part of any monetary restitution into the district court's registry; or

(D) an order requiring the defendant to post a bond.

(f) Forfeiture. A stay of a forfeiture order is governed by Rule 32.2(d).

(g) Disability. If the defendant's conviction or sentence creates a civil or employment disability under federal law, the district court, or the court of appeals under Federal Rule of Appellate Procedure 8, may stay the disability pending appeal on any terms considered appropriate. The court may issue any order reasonably necessary to protect the interest represented by the disability pending appeal, including a restraining order or an injunction.

Rule 39. [Reserved]

Rule 40. Arrest for Failing to Appear in Another District

(a) In General. If a person is arrested under a warrant issued in another district for failing to appear—as required by the terms of that person's release under 18 U.S.C. §§ 3141–3156 or by a subpoena—the person must be taken without unnecessary delay before a magistrate judge in the district of the arrest.

(b) Proceedings. The judge must proceed under Rule 5(c)(3) as applicable.

(c) Release or Detention Order. The judge may modify any previous release or detention order issued in another district, but must state in writing the reasons for doing so.

Rule 41. Search and Seizure

(a) Scope and Definitions.

(1) **Scope.** This rule does not modify any statute regulating search or seizure, or the issuance and execution of a search warrant in special circumstances.

(2) **Definitions.** The following definitions apply under this rule:

(A) "Property" includes documents, books, papers, any other tangible objects, and information.

(B) "Daytime" means the hours between 6:00 a.m. and 10:00 p.m. according to local time.

(C) "Federal law enforcement officer" means a government agent (other than an attorney for the government) who is engaged in enforcing the criminal laws and is within any category of officers authorized by the Attorney General to request a search warrant.

(b) **Authority to Issue a Warrant.** At the request of a federal law enforcement officer or an attorney for the government:

(1) a magistrate judge with authority in the district—or if none is reasonably available, a judge of a state court of record in the district—has authority to issue a warrant to search for and seize a person or property located within the district;

(2) a magistrate judge with authority in the district has authority to issue a warrant for a person or property outside the district if the person or property is located within the district when the warrant is issued but might move or be moved outside the district before the warrant is executed; and

(3) a magistrate judge—in an investigation of domestic terrorism or international terrorism (as defined in 18 U.S.C. § 2331)—having authority in any district in which activities related to the terrorism may have occurred, may issue a warrant for a person or property within or outside that district.

(c) **Persons or Property Subject to Search or Seizure.** A warrant may be issued for any of the following:

(1) evidence of a crime;

(2) contraband, fruits of crime, or other items illegally possessed;

(3) property designed for use, intended for use, or used in committing a crime; or

(4) a person to be arrested or a person who is unlawfully restrained.

(d) **Obtaining a Warrant.**

(1) **Probable Cause.** After receiving an affidavit or other information, a magistrate judge or a judge of a state court of record must issue the warrant if there is probable cause to search for and seize a person or property under Rule 41(c).

(2) **Requesting a Warrant in the Presence of a Judge.**

(A) **Warrant on an Affidavit.** When a federal law enforcement officer or an attorney for the government presents an affidavit in support of a warrant, the judge may require the affiant to appear personally and may examine under oath the affiant and any witness the affiant produces.

(B) Warrant on Sworn Testimony. The judge may wholly or partially dispense with a written affidavit and base a warrant on sworn testimony if doing so is reasonable under the circumstances.

(C) Recording Testimony. Testimony taken in support of a warrant must be recorded by a court reporter or by a suitable recording device, and the judge must file the transcript or recording with the clerk, along with any affidavit.

(3) Requesting a Warrant by Telephonic or Other Means.

(A) In General. A magistrate judge may issue a warrant based on information communicated by telephone or other appropriate means, including facsimile transmission.

(B) Recording Testimony. Upon learning that an applicant is requesting a warrant, a magistrate judge must:

(i) place under oath the applicant and any person on whose testimony the application is based; and

(ii) make a verbatim record of the conversation with a suitable recording device, if available, or by a court reporter, or in writing.

(C) Certifying Testimony. The magistrate judge must have any recording or court reporter's notes transcribed, certify the transcription's accuracy, and file a copy of the record and the transcription with the clerk. Any written verbatim record must be signed by the magistrate judge and filed with the clerk.

(D) Suppression Limited. Absent a finding of bad faith, evidence obtained from a warrant issued under Rule 41(d)(3)(A) is not subject to suppression on the ground that issuing the warrant in that manner was unreasonable under the circumstances.

(e) Issuing the Warrant.

(1) In General. The magistrate judge or a judge of a state court of record must issue the warrant to an officer authorized to execute it.

(2) Contents of the Warrant. The warrant must identify the person or property to be searched, identify any person or property to be seized, and designate the magistrate judge to whom it must be returned. The warrant must command the officer to:

(A) execute the warrant within a specified time no longer than 10 days;

(B) execute the warrant during the daytime, unless the judge for good cause expressly authorizes execution at another time; and

(C) return the warrant to the magistrate judge designated in the warrant.

(3) Warrant by Telephonic or Other Means. If a magistrate judge decides to proceed under Rule 41(d)(3)**(A)**, the following additional procedures apply:

(A) Preparing a Proposed Duplicate Original Warrant. The applicant must prepare a "proposed duplicate original warrant" and must read or otherwise transmit the contents of that document verbatim to the magistrate judge.

(B) Preparing an Original Warrant. The magistrate judge must enter the contents of the proposed duplicate original warrant into an original warrant.

(C) Modifications. The magistrate judge may direct the applicant to modify the proposed duplicate original warrant. In that case, the judge must also modify the original warrant.

(D) Signing the Original Warrant and the Duplicate Original Warrant. Upon determining to issue the warrant, the magistrate judge must immediately sign the original warrant, enter on its face the exact time it is issued, and direct the applicant to sign the judge's name on the duplicate original warrant.

(f) Executing and Returning the Warrant.

(1) Noting the Time. The officer executing the warrant must enter on its face the exact date and time it is executed.

(2) Inventory. An officer present during the execution of the warrant must prepare and verify an inventory of any property seized. The officer must do so in the presence of another officer and the person from whom, or from whose premises, the property was taken. If either one is not present, the officer must prepare and verify the inventory in the presence of at least one other credible person.

(3) Receipt. The officer executing the warrant must:

(A) give a copy of the warrant and a receipt for the property taken to the person from whom, or from whose premises, the property was taken; or

(B) leave a copy of the warrant and receipt at the place where the officer took the property.

(4) Return. The officer executing the warrant must promptly return it—together with a copy of the inventory—to the magistrate judge designated on the warrant. The judge must, on request, give a copy of the inventory to the person from whom, or from whose premises, the property was taken and to the applicant for the warrant.

(g) Motion to Return Property. A person aggrieved by an unlawful search and seizure of property or by the deprivation of property may move for the property's return. The motion must be filed in the district where the property was seized. The court must receive evidence on any factual issue necessary to decide the motion. If it grants the motion, the court must return the property to the movant, but may impose reasonable conditions to protect access to the property and its use in later proceedings.

(h) Motion to Suppress. A defendant may move to suppress evidence in the court where the trial will occur, as Rule 12 provides.

(i) Forwarding Papers to the Clerk. The magistrate judge to whom the warrant is returned must attach to the warrant a copy of the return, of the inventory, and of all other related papers and must deliver them to the clerk in the district where the property was seized.

Rule 42. Criminal Contempt

(a) Disposition After Notice. Any person who commits criminal contempt may be punished for that contempt after prosecution on notice.

(1) **Notice.** The court must give the person notice in open court, in an order to show cause, or in an arrest order. The notice must:

(A) state the time and place of the trial;

(B) allow the defendant a reasonable time to prepare a defense; and

(C) state the essential facts constituting the charged criminal contempt and describe it as such.

(2) **Appointing a Prosecutor.** The court must request that the contempt be prosecuted by an attorney for the government, unless the interest of justice requires the appointment of another attorney. If the government declines the request, the court must appoint another attorney to prosecute the contempt.

(3) **Trial and Disposition.** A person being prosecuted for criminal contempt is entitled to a jury trial in any case in which federal law so provides and must be released or detained as Rule 46 provides. If the criminal contempt involves disrespect toward or criticism of a judge, that judge is disqualified from presiding at the contempt trial or hearing unless the defendant consents. Upon a finding or verdict of guilty, the court must impose the punishment.

(b) Summary Disposition. Notwithstanding any other provision of these rules, the court (other than a magistrate judge) may summarily punish a person who commits criminal contempt in its presence if the judge saw or heard the contemptuous conduct and so certifies; a magistrate judge may summarily punish a person as provided in 28 U.S.C. § 636(e). The contempt order must recite the facts, be signed by the judge, and be filed with the clerk.

Rule 43. Defendant's Presence

(a) When Required. Unless this rule, Rule 5, or Rule 10 provides otherwise, the defendant must be present at:

(1) the initial appearance, the initial arraignment, and the plea;

(2) every trial stage, including jury impanelment and the return of the verdict; and

(3) sentencing.

(b) When Not Required. A defendant need not be present under any of the following circumstances:

(1) **Organizational Defendant.** The defendant is an organization represented by counsel who is present.

(2) **Misdemeanor Offense.** The offense is punishable by fine or by imprisonment for not more than one year, or both, and with the

defendant's written consent, the court permits arraignment, plea, trial, and sentencing to occur in the defendant's absence.

(3) Conference or Hearing on a Legal Question. The proceeding involves only a conference or hearing on a question of law.

(4) Sentence Correction. The proceeding involves the correction or reduction of sentence under Rule 35 or 18 U.S.C. § 3582(c).

(c) Waiving Continued Presence.

(1) In General. A defendant who was initially present at trial, or who had pleaded guilty or nolo contendere, waives the right to be present under the following circumstances:

(A) when the defendant is voluntarily absent after the trial has begun, regardless of whether the court informed the defendant of an obligation to remain during trial;

(B) in a noncapital case, when the defendant is voluntarily absent during sentencing; or

(C) when the court warns the defendant that it will remove the defendant from the courtroom for disruptive behavior, but the defendant persists in conduct that justifies removal from the courtroom.

(2) Waiver's Effect. If the defendant waives the right to be present, the trial may proceed to completion, including the verdict's return and sentencing, during the defendant's absence.

Rule 44. Right to and Appointment of Counsel

(a) Right to Appointed Counsel. A defendant who is unable to obtain counsel is entitled to have counsel appointed to represent the defendant at every stage of the proceeding from initial appearance through appeal, unless the defendant waives this right.

(b) Appointment Procedure. Federal law and local court rules govern the procedure for implementing the right to counsel.

(c) Inquiry Into Joint Representation.

(1) Joint Representation. Joint representation occurs when:

(A) two or more defendants have been charged jointly under Rule 8(b) or have been joined for trial under Rule 13; and

(B) the defendants are represented by the same counsel, or counsel who are associated in law practice.

(2) Court's Responsibilities in Cases of Joint Representation. The court must promptly inquire about the propriety of joint representation and must personally advise each defendant of the right to the effective assistance of counsel, including separate representation. Unless there is good cause to believe that no conflict of interest is likely to arise, the court must take appropriate measures to protect each defendant's right to counsel.

Rule 45. Computing and Extending Time

(a) Computing Time. The following rules apply in computing any period of time specified in these rules, any local rule, or any court order:

(1) Day of the Event Excluded. Exclude the day of the act, event, or default that begins the period.

(2) Exclusion from Brief Periods. Exclude intermediate Saturdays, Sundays, and legal holidays when the period is less than 11 days.

(3) Last Day. Include the last day of the period unless it is a Saturday, Sunday, legal holiday, or day on which weather or other conditions make the clerk's office inaccessible. When the last day is excluded, the period runs until the end of the next day that is not a Saturday, Sunday, legal holiday, or day when the clerk's office is inaccessible.

(4) "Legal Holiday" Defined. As used in this rule, "legal holiday" means:

(A) the day set aside by statute for observing:

(i) New Year's Day;

(ii) Martin Luther King, Jr.'s Birthday;

(iii) Washington's Birthday;

(iv) Memorial Day;

(v) Independence Day;

(vi) Labor Day;

(vii) Columbus Day;

(viii) Veterans' Day;

(ix) Thanksgiving Day;

(x) Christmas Day; and

(B) any other day declared a holiday by the President, the Congress, or the state where the district court is held.

(b) Extending Time.

(1) In General. When an act must or may be done within a specified period, the court on its own may extend the time, or for good cause may do so on a party's motion made:

(A) before the originally prescribed or previously extended time expires; or

(B) after the time expires if the party failed to act because of excusable neglect.

(2) Exceptions. The court may not extend the time to take any action under Rules 29, 33, 34, and 35, except as stated in those rules.

(c) Additional Time After Service. When these rules permit or require a party to act within a specified period after a notice or a paper has been served on that party, 3 days are added to the period if service occurs in the manner provided under Federal Rule of Civil Procedure 5(b)(2)(B), (C), or (D).

Rule 46. Release from Custody; Supervising Detention

(a) Before Trial. The provisions of 18 U.S.C. §§ 3142 and 3144 govern pretrial release.

(b) During Trial. A person released before trial continues on release during trial under the same terms and conditions. But the court may order different terms and conditions or terminate the release if necessary to ensure that the person will be present during trial or that the person's conduct will not obstruct the orderly and expeditious progress of the trial.

(c) Pending Sentencing or Appeal. The provisions of 18 U.S.C. § 3143 govern release pending sentencing or appeal. The burden of establishing that the defendant will not flee or pose a danger to any other person or to the community rests with the defendant.

(d) Pending Hearing on a Violation of Probation or Supervised Release. Rule 32.1(a)(6) governs release pending a hearing on a violation of probation or supervised release.

(e) Surety. The court must not approve a bond unless any surety appears to be qualified. Every surety, except a legally approved corporate surety, must demonstrate by affidavit that its assets are adequate. The court may require the affidavit to describe the following:

(1) the property that the surety proposes to use as security;

(2) any encumbrance on that property;

(3) the number and amount of any other undischarged bonds and bail undertakings the surety has issued; and

(4) any other liability of the surety.

(f) Bail Forfeiture.

(1) **Declaration.** The court must declare the bail forfeited if a condition of the bond is breached.

(2) **Setting Aside.** The court may set aside in whole or in part a bail forfeiture upon any condition the court may impose if:

(A) the surety later surrenders into custody the person released on the surety's appearance bond; or

(B) it appears that justice does not require bail forfeiture.

(3) **Enforcement.**

(A) **Default Judgment and Execution.** If it does not set aside a bail forfeiture, the court must, upon the government's motion, enter a default judgment.

(B) **Jurisdiction and Service.** By entering into a bond, each surety submits to the district court's jurisdiction and irrevocably appoints the district clerk as its agent to receive service of any filings affecting its liability.

(C) **Motion to Enforce.** The court may, upon the government's motion, enforce the surety's liability without an independent action. The government must serve any motion, and notice as the court prescribes, on the district clerk. If so served, the clerk must promptly mail a copy to the surety at its last known address.

(4) Remission. After entering a judgment under Rule 46(f)(3), the court may remit in whole or in part the judgment under the same conditions specified in Rule 46(f)(2).

(g) Exoneration. The court must exonerate the surety and release any bail when a bond condition has been satisfied or when the court has set aside or remitted the forfeiture. The court must exonerate a surety who deposits cash in the amount of the bond or timely surrenders the defendant into custody.

(h) Supervising Detention Pending Trial.

(1) In General. To eliminate unnecessary detention, the court must supervise the detention within the district of any defendants awaiting trial and of any persons held as material witnesses.

(2) Reports. An attorney for the government must report biweekly to the court, listing each material witness held in custody for more than 10 days pending indictment, arraignment, or trial. For each material witness listed in the report, an attorney for the government must state why the witness should not be released with or without a deposition being taken under Rule 15(a).

(i) Forfeiture of Property. The court may dispose of a charged offense by ordering the forfeiture of 18 U.S.C. § 3142(c)(1)(B)(xi) property under 18 U.S.C. § 3146(d), if a fine in the amount of the property's value would be an appropriate sentence for the charged offense.

(j) Producing a Statement.

(1) In General. Rule 26.2(a)–(d) and (f) applies at a detention hearing under 18 U.S.C. § 3142, unless the court for good cause rules otherwise.

(2) Sanctions for Not Producing a Statement. If a party disobeys a Rule 26.2 order to produce a witness's statement, the court must not consider that witness's testimony at the detention hearing.

Rule 47. Motions and Supporting Affidavits

(a) In General. A party applying to the court for an order must do so by motion.

(b) Form and Content of a Motion. A motion—except when made during a trial or hearing—must be in writing, unless the court permits the party to make the motion by other means. A motion must state the grounds on which it is based and the relief or order sought. A motion may be supported by affidavit.

(c) Timing of a Motion. A party must serve a written motion—other than one that the court may hear ex parte—and any hearing notice at least 5 days before the hearing date, unless a rule or court order sets a different period. For good cause, the court may set a different period upon ex parte application.

(d) Affidavit Supporting a Motion. The moving party must serve any supporting affidavit with the motion. A responding party must serve any opposing affidavit at least one day before the hearing, unless the court permits later service.

Rule 48. Dismissal

(a) By the Government. The government may, with leave of court, dismiss an indictment, information, or complaint. The government may not dismiss the prosecution during trial without the defendant's consent.

(b) By the Court. The court may dismiss an indictment, information, or complaint if unnecessary delay occurs in:

(1) presenting a charge to a grand jury;

(2) filing an information against a defendant; or

(3) bringing a defendant to trial.

Rule 49. Serving and Filing Papers

(a) When Required. A party must serve on every other party any written motion (other than one to be heard ex parte), written notice, designation of the record on appeal, or similar paper.

(b) How Made. Service must be made in the manner provided for a civil action. When these rules or a court order requires or permits service on a party represented by an attorney, service must be made on the attorney instead of the party, unless the court orders otherwise.

(c) Notice of a Court Order. When the court issues an order on any post-arraignment motion, the clerk must provide notice in a manner provided for in a civil action. Except as Federal Rule of Appellate Procedure 4(b) provides otherwise, the clerk's failure to give notice does not affect the time to appeal, or relieve—or authorize the court to relieve—a party's failure to appeal within the allowed time.

(d) Filing. A party must file with the court a copy of any paper the party is required to serve. A paper must be filed in a manner provided for in a civil action.

Rule 50. Prompt Disposition

Scheduling preference must be given to criminal proceedings as far as practicable.

Rule 51. Preserving Claimed Error

(a) Exceptions Unnecessary. Exceptions to rulings or orders of the court are unnecessary.

(b) Preserving a Claim of Error. A party may preserve a claim of error by informing the court—when the court ruling or order is made or sought—of the action the party wishes the court to take, or the party's objection to the court's action and the grounds for that objection. If a party does not have an opportunity to object to a ruling or order, the absence of an objection does not later prejudice that party. A ruling or order that admits or excludes evidence is governed by Federal Rule of Evidence 103.

Rule 52. Harmless and Plain Error

(a) Harmless Error. Any error, defect, irregularity, or variance that does not affect substantial rights must be disregarded.

(b) Plain Error. A plain error that affects substantial rights may be considered even though it was not brought to the court's attention.

Rule 53. Courtroom Photographing and Broadcasting Prohibited

Except as otherwise provided by a statute or these rules, the court must not permit the taking of photographs in the courtroom during judicial proceedings or the broadcasting of judicial proceedings from the courtroom.

Rule 54. [Transferred [1]]

Rule 55. Records

The clerk of the district court must keep records of criminal proceedings in the form prescribed by the Director of the Administrative Office of the United States courts. The clerk must enter in the records every court order or judgment and the date of entry.

Rule 56. When Court is Open

(a) In General. A district court is considered always open for any filing, and for issuing and returning process, making a motion, or entering an order.

(b) Office Hours. The clerk's office—with the clerk or a deputy in attendance—must be open during business hours on all days except Saturdays, Sundays, and legal holidays.

(c) Special Hours. A court may provide by local rule or order that its clerk's office will be open for specified hours on Saturdays or legal holidays other than those set aside by statute for observing New Year's Day, Martin Luther King, Jr.'s Birthday, Washington's Birthday, Memorial Day, Independence Day, Labor Day, Columbus Day, Veterans' Day, Thanksgiving Day, and Christmas Day.

Rule 57. District Court Rules

(a) In General.

(1) Adopting Local Rules. Each district court acting by a majority of its district judges may, after giving appropriate public notice and an opportunity to comment, make and amend rules governing its practice. A local rule must be consistent with—but not duplicative of—federal statutes and rules adopted under 28 U.S.C. § 2072 and must conform to any uniform numbering system prescribed by the Judicial Conference of the United States.

(2) Limiting Enforcement. A local rule imposing a requirement of form must not be enforced in a manner that causes a party to lose

---

1. All of Rule 54 was moved to Rule 1.

rights because of an unintentional failure to comply with the requirement.

(b) Procedure When There Is No Controlling Law. A judge may regulate practice in any manner consistent with federal law, these rules, and the local rules of the district. No sanction or other disadvantage may be imposed for noncompliance with any requirement not in federal law, federal rules, or the local district rules unless the alleged violator was furnished with actual notice of the requirement before the noncompliance.

(c) Effective Date and Notice. A local rule adopted under this rule takes effect on the date specified by the district court and remains in effect unless amended by the district court or abrogated by the judicial council of the circuit in which the district is located. Copies of local rules and their amendments, when promulgated, must be furnished to the judicial council and the Administrative Office of the United States Courts and must be made available to the public.

Rule 58. Petty Offenses and Other Misdemeanors

(a) Scope.

(1) In General. These rules apply in petty offense and other misdemeanor cases and on appeal to a district judge in a case tried by a magistrate judge, unless this rule provides otherwise.

(2) Petty Offense Case Without Imprisonment. In a case involving a petty offense for which no sentence of imprisonment will be imposed, the court may follow any provision of these rules that is not inconsistent with this rule and that the court considers appropriate.

(3) Definition. As used in this rule, the term "petty offense for which no sentence of imprisonment will be imposed" means a petty offense for which the court determines that, in the event of conviction, no sentence of imprisonment will be imposed.

(b) Pretrial Procedure.

(1) Charging Document The trial of a misdemeanor may proceed on an indictment, information, or complaint. The trial of a petty offense may also proceed on a citation or violation notice.

(2) Initial Appearance. At the defendant's initial appearance on a petty offense or other misdemeanor charge, the magistrate judge must inform the defendant of the following:

(A) the charge, and the minimum and maximum penalties, including imprisonment, fines, any special assessment under 18 U.S.C. § 3013, and restitution under 18 U.S.C. § 3556;

(B) the right to retain counsel;

(C) the right to request the appointment of counsel if the defendant is unable to retain counsel—unless the charge is a petty offense for which the appointment of counsel is not required;

(D) the defendant's right not to make a statement, and that any statement made may be used against the defendant;

(E) the right to trial, judgment, and sentencing before a district judge—unless:

(i) the charge is a petty offense; or

(ii) the defendant consents to trial, judgment, and sentencing before a magistrate judge;

(F) the right to a jury trial before either a magistrate judge or a district judge—unless the charge is a petty offense; and

(G) if the defendant is held in custody and charged with a misdemeanor other than a petty offense, the right to a preliminary hearing under Rule 5.1, and the general circumstances, if any, under which the defendant may secure pretrial release.

(3) **Arraignment.**

(A) **Plea Before a Magistrate Judge.** A magistrate judge may take the defendant's plea in a petty offense case. In every other misdemeanor case, a magistrate judge may take the plea only if the defendant consents either in writing or on the record to be tried before a magistrate judge and specifically waives trial before a district judge. The defendant may plead not guilty, guilty, or (with the consent of the magistrate judge) nolo contendere.

(B) **Failure to Consent.** Except in a petty offense case, the magistrate judge must order a defendant who does not consent to trial before a magistrate judge to appear before a district judge for further proceedings.

(c) Additional Procedures in Certain Petty Offense Cases. The following procedures also apply in a case involving a petty offense for which no sentence of imprisonment will be imposed:

(1) **Guilty or Nolo Contendere Plea.** The court must not accept a guilty or nolo contendere plea unless satisfied that the defendant understands the nature of the charge and the maximum possible penalty.

(2) **Waiving Venue.**

(A) **Conditions of Waiving Venue.** If a defendant is arrested, held, or present in a district different from the one where the indictment, information, complaint, citation, or violation notice is pending, the defendant may state in writing a desire to plead guilty or nolo contendere; to waive venue and trial in the district where the proceeding is pending; and to consent to the court's disposing of the case in the district where the defendant was arrested, is held, or is present.

(B) **Effect of Waiving Venue.** Unless the defendant later pleads not guilty, the prosecution will proceed in the district where the defendant was arrested, is held, or is present. The district clerk must notify the clerk in the original district of the defendant's waiver of venue. The defendant's statement of a desire to plead guilty or nolo contendere is not admissible against the defendant.

(3) **Sentencing.** The court must give the defendant an opportunity to be heard in mitigation and then proceed immediately to sentencing. The court may, however, postpone sentencing to allow the probation service to investigate or to permit either party to submit additional information.

(4) **Notice of a Right to Appeal.** After imposing sentence in a case tried on a not-guilty plea, the court must advise the defendant of a right to appeal the conviction and of any right to appeal the sentence. If

the defendant was convicted on a plea of guilty or nolo contendere, the court must advise the defendant of any right to appeal the sentence.

(d) Paying a Fixed Sum in Lieu of Appearance.

(1) In General. If the court has a local rule governing forfeiture of collateral, the court may accept a fixed-sum payment in lieu of the defendant's appearance and end the case, but the fixed sum may not exceed the maximum fine allowed by law.

(2) Notice to Appear. If the defendant fails to pay a fixed sum, request a hearing, or appear in response to a citation or violation notice, the district clerk or a magistrate judge may issue a notice for the defendant to appear before the court on a date certain. The notice may give the defendant an additional opportunity to pay a fixed sum in lieu of appearance. The district clerk must serve the notice on the defendant by mailing a copy to the defendant's last known address.

(3) Summons or Warrant. Upon an indictment, or upon a showing by one of the other charging documents specified in Rule 58(b)(1) of probable cause to believe that an offense has been committed and that the defendant has committed it, the court may issue an arrest warrant or, if no warrant is requested by an attorney for the government, a summons. The showing of probable cause must be made under oath or under penalty of perjury, but the affiant need not appear before the court. If the defendant fails to appear before the court in response to a summons, the court may summarily issue a warrant for the defendant's arrest.

(e) Recording the Proceedings. The court must record any proceedings under this rule by using a court reporter or a suitable recording device.

(f) New Trial. Rule 33 applies to a motion for a new trial.

(g) Appeal.

(1) From a District Judge's Order or Judgment. The Federal Rules of Appellate Procedure govern an appeal from a district judge's order or a judgment of conviction or sentence.

(2) From a Magistrate Judge's Order or Judgment.

(A) Interlocutory Appeal. Either party may appeal an order of a magistrate judge to a district judge within 10 days of its entry if a district judge's order could similarly be appealed. The party appealing must file a notice with the clerk specifying the order being appealed and must serve a copy on the adverse party.

(B) Appeal from a Conviction or Sentence. A defendant may appeal a magistrate judge's judgment of conviction or sentence to a district judge within 10 days of its entry. To appeal, the defendant must file a notice with the clerk specifying the judgment being appealed and must serve a copy on an attorney for the government.

(C) Record. The record consists of the original papers and exhibits in the case; any transcript, tape, or other recording of the proceedings; and a certified copy of the docket entries. For purposes of the appeal, a copy of the record of the proceedings must be made available to a defendant who establishes by affidavit an inability to pay or give security for the record. The Director of the Administrative Office of the United States Courts must pay for those copies.

(D) Scope of Appeal. The defendant is not entitled to a trial de novo by a district judge. The scope of the appeal is the same as in an appeal to the court of appeals from a judgment entered by a district judge.

(3) Stay of Execution and Release Pending Appeal. Rule 38 applies to a stay of a judgment of conviction or sentence. The court may release the defendant pending appeal under the law relating to release pending appeal from a district court to a court of appeals.

Rule 59. [Deleted]
Rule 60. Title

These rules may be known and cited as the Federal Rules of Criminal Procedure.

Appendix D

PENDING AMENDMENTS TO FEDERAL RULES OF CRIMINAL PROCEDURE

[These amendments to Rules 12.2, 29, 32.1, 33, 34 and 45, and new Rule 59 were approved by the Supreme Court on April 25, 2005, and were forwarded to Congress. They will take effect on December 1, 2005 unless Congress enacts legislation to reject, modify or defer the amendments. New material is underlined; matter to be omitted is lined through.]

Rule 12.2. Notice of an Insanity Defense; Mental Examination

* * *

(d) Failure to Comply.

(1) Failure to Give Notice or to Submit to Examination. ~~If the defendant fails to give notice under Rule 12.2(b) or does not submit to an examination when ordered under Rule 12.2(c), the~~ <u>The</u> court may exclude any expert evidence from the defendant on the issue of the defendant's mental disease, mental defect, or any other mental condition bearing on the defendant's guilt or the issue of punishment in a capital case~~.~~ <u>if the defendant fails to:</u>

<u>**(A)** give notice under Rule I 2.2(b); or</u>

<u>**(B)** submit to an examination when ordered under Rule 12.2(c).</u>

<u>**(2) Failure to Disclose.** The court may exclude any expert evidence for which the defendant has failed to comply with the disclosure requirement of Rule 12.2(c)(3).</u>

* * *

Rule 29. Motion for a Judgment of Acquittal

* * *

(c) After Jury Verdict or Discharge.

(1) Time for a Motion. A defendant may move for a judgment of acquittal, or renew such a motion, within 7 days after a guilty verdict or after the court discharges the jury, whichever is later<u>,</u> ~~or within any other time the court sets during the 7 day period~~.

* * *

Rule 32.1. Revoking or Modifying Probation or Supervised Release

* * *

(b) Revocation.

* * *

(2) Revocation Hearing. Unless waived by the person, the court must hold the revocation hearing within a reasonable time in the district having jurisdiction. The person is entitled to:

(A) written notice of the alleged violation;

(B) disclosure of the evidence against the person;

(C) an opportunity to appear, present evidence, and question any adverse witness unless the court determines that the interest of justice does not require the witness to appear; ~~and~~

(D) notice of the person's right to retain counsel or to request that counsel be appointed if the person cannot obtain counsel~~.~~ ; and

(E) an opportunity to make a statement and present any information in mitigation.

(c) Modification.

(1) In General. Before modifying the conditions of probation or supervised release, the court must hold a hearing, at which the person has the right to counsel~~.~~ and an opportunity to make a statement and present any information in mitigation.

* * *

Rule 33. New Trial

* * *

(b) Time to File.

* * *

(2) Other Grounds. Any motion for a new trial grounded on any reason other than newly discovered evidence must be filed within 7 days after the verdict or finding of guilty~~, or within such further time as the court sets during the 7-day period~~.

Rule 34. Arresting Judgment

* * *

(b) Time to File. The defendant must move to arrest judgment within 7 days after the court accepts a verdict or finding of guilty, or after a plea of guilty or nolo contendere~~, or within such further time as the court sets during the 7-day period~~.

Rule 45. Computing and Extending Time

* * *

(b) Extending Time.

(1) In General. When an act must or may be done within a specified period, the court on its own may extend the time, or for good cause may do so on a party's motion made:

(A) before the originally prescribed or previously extended time expires; or

(B) after the time expires if the party failed to act because of excusable neglect.

(2) ~~Exceptions~~ Exception. The court may not extend the time to take any action under <u>Rule</u> ~~Rules 29, 33, 34 and~~ 35, except as stated in ~~those rules~~ <u>that rule</u>.

* * *

Rule 59. Matters Before a Magistrate Judge

<u>(a) **Nondispositive Matters.** A district judge may refer to a magistrate judge for determination any matter that does not dispose of a charge or defense. The magistrate judge must promptly conduct the required proceedings and, when appropriate, enter on the record an oral or written order stating the determination. A party may serve and file objections to the order within 10 days after being served with a copy of a written order or after the oral order is stated on the record, or at some other time the court sets. The district judge must consider timely objections and modify or set aside any part of the order that is contrary to law or clearly erroneous. Failure to object in accordance with this rule waives a party's right to review.</u>

<u>**(b) Dispositive Matters.**</u>

<u>**(1) Referral to Magistrate Judge.** A district judge may refer to a magistrate judge for recommendation a defendant's motion to dismiss or quash an indictment or information, a motion to suppress evidence, or any matter that may dispose of a charge or defense. The magistrate judge must promptly conduct the required proceedings. A record must be made of any evidentiary proceeding and of any other proceeding if the magistrate judge considers it necessary. The magistrate judge must enter on the record a recommendation for disposing of the matter, including any proposed findings of fact. The clerk must immediately serve copies on all parties.</u>

<u>**(2) Objections to Findings and Recommendations.** Within 10 days after being served with a copy of the recommended disposition, or at some other time the court sets, a party may serve and file specific written objections to the proposed findings and recommendations. Unless the district judge directs otherwise. the objecting party must promptly arrange for transcribing the record, or whatever portions of it the parties agree to or the magistrate judge considers sufficient. Failure to object in accordance with this rule waives a party's right to review.</u>

<u>**(3) De Novo Review of Recommendations.** The district judge must consider de novo any objection to the magistrate judge's recommendation. The district judge may accept, reject, or modify the recommendation, receive further evidence, or resubmit the matter to the magistrate judge with instructions.</u>

Appendix E

PROPOSED AMENDMENTS TO FEDERAL RULES OF CRIMINAL PROCEDURE

[These proposed amendments to Rules 5, 32.1, 40, 41 and 58 have been circulated to bench and bar for comment, but have not yet been finally adopted by the Judicial Conference. New material is underlined; matter to be omitted is lined through.]

Rule 5. Initial Appearance

* * *

(c) Place of Initial Appearance; Transfer to Another District.

(3) Procedures in a District Other Than Where the Offense Was Allegedly Committed. If the initial appearance occurs in a district other than where the offense was allegedly committed, the following procedures apply:

* * *

(C) the magistrate judge must conduct a preliminary hearing if required by Rule 5.1 ~~or Rule 58(b)(2)(G)~~;

(D) the magistrate judge must transfer the defendant to the district where the offense was allegedly committed if:

(i) the government produces the warrant, a certified copy of the warrant, ~~a facsimile of either~~, or ~~other appropriate~~ <u>a reliable electronic</u> form of either; and

* * *

Rule 32.1. Revoking or Modifying Probation or Supervised Release

(A) **Initial Appearance.**

* * *

(5) Appearance in a District Lacking Jurisdiction. If the person is arrested or appears in a district that does not have jurisdiction to conduct a revocation hearing, the magistrate judge must:

* * *

(B) if the alleged violation did not occur in the district of arrest, transfer the person to the district that has jurisdiction if:

(i) the government produces certified copies of the judgment, warrant, and warrant application, or copies of those certified documents by reliable electronic means; and

ii) the judge finds that the person is the same person named in the warrant.

* * *

Rule 40. Arrest for Failing to Appear in Another District or for Violating Conditions of Release Set in Another District

~~(a) **In General.** If a person is arrested under a warrant issued in another district for failing to appear—as required by the terms of that person's release under 18 U.S.C. §§ 3141, 3156 or by a subpoena—the person must be taken without unnecessary delay before a magistrate judge in the district of arrest.~~

(a) **In General.** A person must be taken without unnecessary delay before a magistrate judge in the district of arrest if the person has been arrested under a warrant issued in another district for:

(i) failing to appear, as required by the terms of that person's release under 18 U.S.C. §§ 3141–3156 or by subpoena; or

(ii) violating conditions of release set in another district.

* * *

Rule 41. Search and Seizure

* * *

(d) Obtaining a Warrant.

* * *

(3) Requesting a Warrant by Telephonic or Other Means.

(A) In General. A magistrate judge may issue a warrant based on information communicated by telephone or other reliable electronic means. ~~appropriate means, including facsimile transmission.~~

(B) Recording Testimony. Upon learning that an applicant is requesting a warrant under Rule 41(d)(3)(A), a magistrate judge must:

(i) place under oath the applicant and any person on whose testimony the application is based; and

(ii) make a verbatim record of the conversation with a suitable recording device, if available, or by a court reporter, or in writing.

* * *

(e) Issuing the Warrant.

* * *

(3) Warrant by Telephonic or Other Means. If a magistrate judge decides to proceed under Rule 41(d)(3)(A), the following additional procedures apply:

(A) Preparing a Proposed Duplicate Original Warrant. The applicant must prepare a "proposed duplicate original warrant" and must read or otherwise transmit the contents of that document verbatim to the magistrate judge.

(B) Preparing an Original Warrant. If the applicant reads the contents of the proposed duplicate original warrant, the ~~The~~ magistrate judge must enter ~~the~~ those contents ~~of the proposed duplicate original warrant~~ into an original warrant. If the applicant transmits the contents by reliable electronic means, that transmission may serve as the original warrant.

(C) Modifications. The magistrate judge may modify the original warrant. The judge must transmit any modified warrant to the applicant by reliable electronic means under Rule 41(e)(3)(D) or direct the applicant to modify the proposed duplicate original warrant accordingly. ~~In that case, the judge must also modify the original warrant.~~

(D) Signing the ~~Original Warrant and the Duplicate Original~~ Warrant. Upon determining to issue the warrant, the magistrate judge must immediately sign the original warrant, enter on its face the exact date and time it is issued, and transmit it by reliable electronic means to the applicant or direct the applicant to sign the judge's name on the duplicate original warrant.

* * *

Rule 58. Petty Offenses and Other Misdemeanors

* * *

(b) Pretrial Procedure.

* * *

(2) Initial Appearance. At the defendant's initial appearance on a petty offense or other misdemeanor charge, the magistrate judge must inform the defendant of the following:

* * *

(G) ~~if the defendant is held in custody and charged with a misdemeanor other than a petty offense, the~~ any right to a preliminary hearing under Rule 5.1, and the general circumstances, if any, under which the defendant may secure pretrial release.

* * *

†